The Nobleman's Guide to Scandal and Shipwrecks

Also by Mackenzi Lee

The Gentleman's Guide to Vice and Virtue
The Lady's Guide to Petticoats and Piracy
The Gentleman's Guide to Getting Lucky
This Monstrous Thing

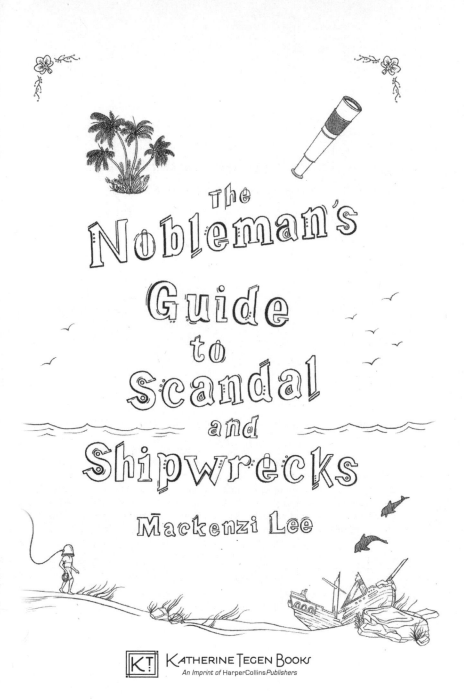

The Nobleman's Guide to Scandal and Shipwrecks

Mackenzi Lee

KATHERINE TEGEN BOOKS
An Imprint of HarperCollins Publishers

Katherine Tegen Books is an imprint of HarperCollins Publishers.

ISBN 978-0-06-291601-3

Typography by Carla Weise
Map by David Curtis
21 22 23 24 25   PC/LSCH   10 9 8 7 6 5 4 3 2 1
❖
First Edition

For anyone who needs reminding—
No one is mad at you.

Things I have
learned about Mum:

- In hospital for health nerves??
- Grew up in Barbados
- Had another son and daughter???

Iceland

Questions to ask
Henry Monty:

- What's your middle name?
- How long have you lived in London?
- Why does everyone call you Monty?
- Do you know what a stupid nickname that is?
- WHY DIDN'T I KNOW
YOU EXISTED??

Adrian
+
Louisa

The Persephone

Porto

Azores
Are there
snakes here?

Sa
(Pira

Felicity??

Rabat
(No pirates)

His mind resembled the vast amphitheater, the Coliseum at Rome. In the center stood his judgment, which, like a mighty gladiator, combated those apprehensions that, like the wild beasts of the arena, were all around in cells, ready to be let out upon him. After a conflict, he drives them back into their dens; but not killing them, they were still assailing him.

—James Boswell, *The Life of Samuel Johnson*

There must be Ghosts all the country over, as thick as the sand of the sea. And then we are, one and all, so pitifully afraid of the light.

—Henrik Ibsen, *Ghosts*

London

17—

1

In my defense, I did not intend to punch Richard Peele in the face.

I cannot imagine any scenario in which I would intentionally swing at a fellow member of the peerage, face or otherwise. I am not my soon-to-be brother-in-law Edward Davies, who just last month was expelled from the Kit-Kat Club for boxing Lord Dennyson in the nose when he suggested that whores should be publicly flogged more often as punishment for solicitation.

I would have *wanted* to do the same, but because I am Adrian Montague, not Edward Davies, notorious affable radical, I would have sat on my hands and kept my mouth shut as I composed a reply in my head that I could later put in a pamphlet. I would then write and rewrite and edit and rewrite and edit more and scrutinize the language until it no longer sounded like English and I had convinced myself I was illiterate and no one had ever had the heart to tell me.

Copies of the most recent of my certainly unreadable pamphlets are currently being foisted by Louisa Davies upon every pedestrian crossing the Hyde Park mall with the confidence usually only carried off by white rich men. Meanwhile I—said white rich man—lurk on the edges of the lawn, smudging the ink on my own stack with how much my palms are sweating. Even though I've now written four printed treatises on reform, I still don't like seeing my words in print. It makes me want to reach for a pen and start striking things out. Anyone who says they enjoy my writing is clearly either lying or has terrible taste.

"We're going to be arrested," I say for at least the sixth time as Louisa returns to me, her stack noticeably thinner while mine remains robust.

And for the sixth time—perhaps the seventh, for she has a knack for speaking to my fears before I can voice them—Louisa replies, "We are not going to be arrested. There is nothing illegal about offering gratis literature in a public park."

I tug down my knit cap, though I'm sweating so much it seems likely to slip from my head like I've been greased. "It's going to rain."

"It's not going to rain," Louisa replies, though with less conviction and a glance upward. The sky is gray, and the thin clouds leach all color from the world. The

4

park around us looks like a charcoal drawing, the skeletal tree branches smudgy from the London fog. We could have picked a fairer day, one with more ramblers out along these trails, feeding the ducks or playing lawn games, so that every approach didn't feel like such an event. Though were the park more crowded, my anxiety would easily rearrange itself into a fear of being recognized. Even though my father is currently at our home in Cheshire, all gossip, like the proverbial roads to Rome, finds its way back to him. The news that his only son was handing out a radical leaflet calling for the closure of his primary charitable cause, the Saint James Workhouse, will reach him before the week's end.

A tall man with a greatcoat pulled tight around him passes us. He's walking quickly, head down, but Louisa still thrusts a pamphlet at him. "Support the closure of the Saint James Workhouse, sir!"

He spits at her. She manages to dodge, and it lands on the path at her feet, foamy and yellow like an uncooked egg.

"Arsehole!" Louisa shouts at the man's back.

"Bitch," he returns, throwing a lewd gesture over his shoulder without turning.

"Very creative!" She shoves a strand of hair from her eyes, then, like nothing happened, steps into the path of the next pedestrian. "Support the closure of the Saint James Workhouse? I have a pamphlet."

This man pauses. "You want money for it?"

"No, sir," she replies. "It's yours to take, free of charge. A plea for reform from a new and exciting writer who goes by the name John Everyman."

He takes it, and as he starts again on his way, Louisa whirls on me with a triumphant smile. "See, it's not so bad!"

"You were just spit at."

"Spit is easy to wash out. And he missed!" She gestures victoriously at her still-clean skirt. She's dressed much plainer than I'm accustomed to seeing her—her usual silk day dress has been swapped for a neckerchief and a rough-cloth short gown pinned over a gray wool skirt. Her cardinal cloak feels almost violently red. It puts the ruby stone on the ring I gave her for our engagement to shame.

My own attire is driving me mad. After months of wearing nothing but mourning clothes in black and gray, any sort of color—even the unobtrusive browns and olive green I'm currently sporting—feels garish. The collar of my shirt is so tight I can't breathe right. Or maybe it's the buttons on the waistcoat. Or maybe it's the fact that I'm wearing clothes at all. It all feels too small on me, and every spot on my body where the cloth touches my skin itches. The day is chilly and damp in the way London is always damp, even when it's not raining, but I can't stop sweating. How does sweat actually work?

Does it leak out of every pore simultaneously? Because that feels like what's happening to me. Is there a point at which I will have expelled all the sweat from my body and start dripping blood instead? I try to resist checking the front of my shirt, but if I don't, it will be all I can think of, and maybe I *am* bleeding, in which case I really need to know—

"Adrian."

I look up, and Louisa is watching me. I expect she'll scold me for not doing my part—though I don't know why I think that, for Louisa has never scolded me for anything. But I've been scolding myself the entire time we've been here for my limp participation, so I assume she's thinking the same.

"Are you cold?" she asks, then arches a skeptical eyebrow when I shake my head. "Really?"

I'm always cold. I'm cold in the middle of summer. I'm cold even though I've sweated through my shirt. Since I was young, my father has told me I'm too thin, my appetite overly affected by my moods. After my mother died, I almost stopped entirely, gripped with a fear that whatever I ate would make me sick and I too would meet a sudden end like she had. That fear would quickly tumble into its most refined form, panic, and that panic would have me gagging up anything I tried to swallow, terrified of death by pheasant or porridge or lukewarm tea. It made no matter that her stepping off a cliff into the sea was entirely unrelated to my own hypothetical demise. It was the unanticipated nature, death as a sudden impact without even a warning fall to precede it.

While before it has only ever been my father who commented on my weight, in the eight months since Mum died, I have crossed whatever threshold makes strangers feel entitled to comment upon my body and its failings. And though Lou has been heaping sugar into my tea and slicking everything she makes for me in so much butter even toast feels slippery, I still haven't taken the stitching out of the waistband of my breeches, and I can feel the jut of my hipbones in a way that makes me too aware of my own frame.

Lou thumbs the edges of her stack like a card dealer in a casino, and I catch sight of the title and attribution. Even the fake name under which I write Whig literature, John Everyman, makes me queasy. It's such a stupid name; why did I ever think it was funny or clever? I can't even come up with a decent nom de plume; what made me think I was smart enough to write an entire pamphlet on workhouse reform?

"We can go," Louisa says. "We needn't stay if you're struggling."

I resist the urge to pull my collar up over my face and retreat into my clothes like a miserable turtle. "Is it that obvious?"

She fans herself with her stack of leaflets, and the

fine hairs that have come loose from her plait flutter against her forehead. "Well, you have yet to make eye contact with any passersby, and you're making a face like someone's pulling out your fingernails. So call it an educated guess."

"Sorry." I shake out my coat—borrowed from one of Edward's clerks and too short in the cuffs by inches— and try to stand up straight. I can almost feel my father poking me in the back, hissing "Don't slouch!" like he does at every society party, but I am so much taller than almost everyone I know, the urge to make myself as small as possible often overtakes me before I've realized it.

"I can do this," I tell her.

"I know you *can*," she says.

"I want to."

"But you don't *have* to. I know Edward and I like to shout from the turnpikes and throw rocks at Newgate, but you know I'll still marry you whether or not you join in on those particular family outings." She grins at me, though it fades when I don't offer her one back. "It also doesn't mean that you're not helping the cause. For God's sake, you wrote this." She holds the pamphlet up, and I almost resist the urge to shush her, like my father might suddenly pop up from the bushes, hidden all this time in the guise of a judgmental gardener. "If you keep writing treatises like this, I'm happy to do the handing out in the park."

And the copying out of my drafts because I'm terrified someone might recognize my handwriting, and the checking of my spelling, and the handling of the printers, and the distribution to salons and bookshops and at rallies across London, and how much longer before she grows weary of my inability to take ownership of my political beliefs?

What good is a desire to stand up for the poor if you never actually do the standing? Where will you hide once you take your seat in Parliament and have to start publicly voting on these subjects? What sort of coward hides behind a false name and a satirical style?

I squeeze my eyes shut for a moment, then say to Lou, "I should do more."

She waves that away with a casual sincerity I covet like filigreed gold. "So you aren't as shameless as I am and find it stressful to walk up to strangers and shove your politics down their throat? So what? There are other ways to advocate for reform."

My posture starts to slope again. She likely didn't mean it as a reminder of the fact that I had the chance to take up exactly that advocacy in Parliament—my father sought approval for a writ of acceleration, advancing me to the House of Lords before his seat officially passed to me on the back of his subsidiary title as Viscount of Disley. His hope was I'd add another critical vote against Edward Davies's bill on workhouse reform that would soon be coming up from the Commons. Edward, in contrast, hoped I might be a vote in favor of it, my radical politics hidden from my father until after the ink of the king's signature had already dried and my premature summons to the Lords was official.

Instead, I panicked and refused the acceleration entirely. My father had tried fruitlessly to bully me into changing my mind, though my mother's death stopped him shouting at me about it daily. Or at least distracted him for a time—I suspect that, when he joins me in London at the end of the summer for the vote, grief will no longer be a sufficient excuse for the delay.

Lou stands on her tiptoes and presses her lips to mine, then smiles. It feels like the first bloom of spring opening in the middle of that gray walk. I want to be the sun it turns its face toward to drink in the light. I want to be everything someone as fierce and bright as Lou deserves in a partner and lover and friend and husband. My chest tightens.

"Let's go home," she urges, but I shake my head.

"I can do this. I want to do this," I say, though the conviction behind the words is weak as milky tea.

"You can and you do!" Louisa repeats with sincere enthusiasm, then wiggles her hands in front of her in a little cheer.

"I can. Right." I resist the urge to pull on the front of my shirt, afraid of the suctioning sound it may make because of all the sweat—maybe blood?—adhering it to my chest, and straighten. My hands are shaking, which somehow seems both an embarrassing overreaction and an insufficient expression of my fear.

There's a man coming down the path toward us, dark skinned and tall, with an instrument case tucked under one arm. He looks kind. He's probably kind. Most people are kind, aren't they?

He's going to laugh at me. *So what if he does?* He's going to think I look strange or sound strange or that I am just plain strange. *So what? He won't say that to my face.* But he'll go home to his wife and tell her about this odd maypole of a man in a too-small coat who tried to give him a piece of poorly written propaganda on his way to the office, and they'll have a good laugh at me.

So. What?

It doesn't matter what this stranger thinks of me. It does. It doesn't. I wish it didn't. Why does it? It doesn't. It shouldn't. It does.

All you have to do, I tell myself, *is walk up to that most likely kind gentleman and ask him if he wants a leaflet. You don't have to look him in the eye or say anything more than that. He won't know you wrote it. He won't tell your father. Most likely he'll simply say no and you'll say all right, thank you, carry on, and you'll both move on with your days.*

He's getting closer. Louisa gives me an encouraging thump on the shoulder.

He's not going to laugh at you. He's not going to think you're strange-looking. He's not going to demand to know the authorship of the pamphlet. He's not going to tell you you're too thin. He's not going to think you so odd he'll pull his hypothetical monetary support from the Whig party because of the oddness of its members. He's not going to remember this interaction for more than five minutes, but you will be dissecting it for the rest of your goddamn life.

I have forgotten every word I know. I have lost any command of the English language I may have once possessed. I could not muster a three-word sentence were I standing on the gallows with a noose around my neck and asked to choose between a single utterance and death.

The man passes by us without glancing our way, and I don't say a word.

Louisa looks from me to the man's retreating back, and I can tell she is debating whether to run after him and offer what I failed to. "I'll . . . ," she starts, then holds up a finger to me. "I'll be right back." I watch her jog after the man until she's near enough to touch his shoulder, watch him turn and take the offered pamphlet with a word of thanks, and oh my God it would have been so easy. What is the matter with me? I stare down at my hands, white-knuckled around my stack of pamphlets. My head is spinning and I'm breathing too fast.

Grow a goddamn backbone, Adrian. Jesus Christ, you're pathetic.

When Louisa returns, she pries my fingers from around my pamphlets and adds mine to her own waning pile, then takes my hand. She rolls my wrists gently, and I try—I really try—to release the tension I've been bottling up in my joints, but God, my palms are so sweaty, that must be all she's thinking of. And then wondering why she has agreed to marry such a sweaty lunatic.

"Let me find a hack," Lou says gently. "We can go home."

"But you had all those pamphlets printed," I say, though it's a watery protest. I feel rotten—this whole day, this whole great plan, ruined because I yet again could not pull myself together. But good God, it's such a relief to think I could be at home, in bed, undressed and under the covers with the curtains closed, within the hour. I'll likely be awake all night reliving every embarrassing thing I said or did today, and over the past weeks, months, years, maybe my whole life. But at least I'll be home and out of this too-small coat.

"I'm sure I'll find a use for them." Louisa shuffles the stack against her leg so the edges sit evenly. "Or Edward will."

My throat goes dry. "Has he read it?"

"Not this one, no. Do you want me to ask him to?"

"Maybe. I don't know. He'll probably think it's amateur." Aside from Louisa, there is no one on God's green earth whose opinion I value as highly as Edward Davies's, rabble-rouser in the House of Commons and one of London's most notorious social reformers. I know Lou gave him the first of my John Everyman pamphlets, and though she didn't tell him who the author was, I still broke out in hives at the thought of him reading it. And though this new one is leagues better than that first attempt over a year ago, it's also the least satirical and most pointed I've yet penned, and the chance that Edward may read my sincere attempts at political writing and find them wanting is mortifying.

Louisa does a quick tally of her remaining pamphlets, minus the stack she took from me. "I've only got six left. Let me give these out, then we'll get a carriage and take you home. Stay here. I'll be quick."

As she starts down the path, scarlet cloak flapping behind her, I collapse onto a nearby bench and try to breathe and not obsess about how *take you home* makes me feel like a child she's minding. My muscles are shaking. My hands are shaking. What is wrong with me that my body has registered the prospect of offering a single piece of political writing to a stranger as something close to a near-death experience? In spite of how passionate I find my own heart on the subject of reform, and in spite of the privileged position I will one way or another find myself in someday as a member of the House of Lords, I suspect I'm a man better suited to living in a folly on a nobleman's grounds.

Adrian Montague, professional hermit. It's not an uappealing idea.

A wind whips down the park path, strong enough to shake ice from the branches above me. I feel the crystals melt against my neck and drip down my back. I must be steaming. If my mother were here, she would tell me to breathe. That's always the first thing—breath. She was the only other person I knew who understood how literally I meant it when I said I couldn't breathe. The only time I tried the line on my father, he bellowed back at me, "Well, obviously you're breathing or else you'd be dead!" And I thought, *That would probably be better for all of us, really.*

But my mother would sit quietly with me, sometimes breathing slowly and encouraging me to match her speed, sometimes taking my hand and rubbing her thumbs into my palms. Louisa saw her do it once, and has taken up the same practice, whenever she can feel the walls beginning to close in around me. I want her here, now, warm at my side as she huddles into my shoulder and tucks her face against the wind. Suddenly I'm certain she's gotten her own carriage to take her home without me and is so embarrassed by my failure that she'll never speak to me again. I look up, trying not to feel frantic as I scan the park, searching the trees for that bright wing of scarlet, trying to get my breath back, trying not to panic, trying not to think of ways this day could get worse.

Until one sits down next to me.

"Adrian Montague!"

Richard Peele, Viscount of Parkgate, nearly lands in my lap as he collapses onto the bench at my side, sitting unbearably close and reeking of boozy sweat. His valet—a man far too blond and handsome for a life in service—stands over his shoulder, smirking at me in the way that men who have no personality beyond being too blond and handsome do. Peele swings an arm over my shoulder like we're school chums, and my muscles tense. I think of the crabs Lou and I caught one summer in Penzance—when we picked them up, their whole bodies would flinch before they tucked themselves inside their shell and out of sight. I wish I could hide that easily. I wish I had a shell. I wish I were a crab on a Penzance beach who didn't know what a Richard Peele was.

"How are you? And what the hell are you wearing?" He slaps my chest with a flat palm that knocks what little breath I have straight out of me. "You look like a beggar." I open my mouth to respond but he keeps talking, and I'm reminded that the only good thing about a conversation with Richard Peele is that one is not required to contribute anything. Every time he has cornered me at a ball or party or dinner—his unrequited affection toward me as baffling as it is unwanted—that has been my only comfort. "Are you walking alone? Poor thing, you just can't make any friends, can you? It would be easier to like you if you weren't so shy and odd, you know."

Then he looks at me like he expects me to thank him for the advice. Either that or he's trying to give me some sort of visual cue that he's granting me permission to speak.

"I'm . . . waiting." It is a Herculean effort to get those two words out of my constricted throat. I do not like how close he is sitting. I do not like him touching me. I do not like the way that every smell clinging to him feels like an assault on my senses. His presence is aggressive: from the light glinting off the greasy spot on his nose to the slick of his hair to the too-many-colors of his suit. "Waiting for someone," I finally manage to finish.

"Well then, I'll wait with you!" Somehow, Peele scoots even closer to me, his arm a lead weight on my shoulders. His valet is still staring at me, still smirking at me in a way that makes me check my shirtfront for sweat stains. "I've been meaning to call on you since you arrived. How's your father? Will he be coming for the next vote, or is he sending you to the House to face the wolves?" He clamps his hands on my shoulders and shakes me in a way that is likely meant to be conspiratorial but instead makes my teeth feel loose. "Don't worry,

I won't let them bully you any more than you deserve. What have you got there, Mortimer?"

Peele's valet has chased a crumpled piece of paper caught in the wind, and as he retrieves it off the ground, I realize with horror he's holding one of my pamphlets. Louisa must have dropped one. Or I did. Probably it was me. My vision spots with panic as he smooths it out across his knee and squints at it.

Peele holds out a hand. "Give it here."

There is, of course, no conceivable way Richard Peele would know it's my writing—or even any reason he should guess at such—but the idea of that suddenly becomes a load-bearing anxiety in the already precarious architecture of my mind. I stop breathing as I watch him read the title.

He's going to know I wrote it. Somehow. Maybe I left my name on it or he saw me drop it or maybe he'll just know. He's going to know I'm a radical trying to get my father's workhouse shut down. He's going to tell my father, who will then bar me from taking over his seat in Parliament and I'll be disgraced and Louisa will be disgraced and any children we may have will be disgraced and I will die a disgraced death having not done a goddamn thing except worry for all my odd, friendless days.

Peele snorts, then holds the pamphlet out for my inspection. "They're coming for your father's workhouse,

Montague. Bloody radicals—what sort of idiots make a charity the subject of their ire? And look there, they haven't even spelled *impoverished* correctly—it's got two *p*'s."

I'm almost sure it hasn't, but hearing him say it makes me doubt my own mind. If I spelled it wrong, surely the printer would have caught that error. For God's sake, Louisa would have. She's a tyrant about spelling. Also, how is it that I could not possibly think less of this man, and yet his opinion of me immediately weighs heavier in my mind than my own sense of self?

Peele makes a show of skimming the pamphlet, though I'm sure he's not reading a word. "Falsehoods, slander, lies, more slander, more lies, that's all it is." He runs a dramatic finger under each line, tracing them in mimicry of reading, then taps the final line and declares, "All a pile of Whig shite. Your poor father puts up with so much nonsense from these dunces who don't have a notion what they're talking of."

In actuality, my father puts up with very little. He has an army of secretaries and clerks who do it for him. And the Saint James Workhouse is the furthest thing from a charity.

I should say that. I should say that to him. Or at least defend my spelling of *impoverished,* which I'm sure is correct. Almost sure. I should not be this completely paralyzed. My heart should not be beating so hard it feels about to explode.

"Adrian," someone calls, and Peele and I both look up. Louisa is crossing the path toward us at a quick trot.

"Ah." Peele folds the pamphlet in half and flicks it in her direction. "Speaking of Whig shite."

"Good morning, Lord Parkgate." Louisa stops in front of us, smoothing the front of her work skirt like it's brocade. "You're looking pickled. How's your wife?"

"How's your brother?" Peele counters. "I haven't seen him since he brutalized poor Lord Dennyson."

"Yes, well, we all try our best to avoid you." Lou's eyes dart to the pamphlet on the ground, like she's trying to calculate the likelihood that I offered it to him. Low. The likelihood is very, very low. Subterraneanly so. She must realize that, based only on the fact that I'm breathing as though I'm trying to climb a mountain and my lungs are full of porridge. Is that an actual medical condition? Porridge lungs? It's not even real and suddenly I'm sure that's what I'm afflicted with. I might be dying. There seems about a fifty percent chance I'm dying.

"Were you enjoying your reading?" Louisa asks Peele.

"Oh yes." Peele snickers, obscenely proud of the joke he hasn't yet made. "I love a good piece of fiction."

Louisa purses her lips, thin as a thread.

"You do know, Miss Davies," Peele continues, and his grip tightens on my shoulders. My flesh feels raw and tender, like an overripe fruit, and for a moment I'm concerned he's grasping me so tight he broke through it. The sweat pooling along my back starts to feel like blood again. "That your dear fiancé's father is one of the patrons of the Saint James Workhouse."

Louisa folds her arms. "I don't believe a personal relationship to someone who supports the exploitation of the poor is reason enough not to speak up against it."

Peele laughs with his mouth so wide I can see bits of his lunch stuck in his back teeth as he turns to me. "It's admirable to try and tame a bitch, Montague," he says, like Louisa isn't here. "But no one would blame you if you tossed this one out in a sack."

"Those workhouses," Louisa pushes on, unmoved as ever by the names men call her, "exploit their occupants for free labor without providing the sanitary, safe living conditions promised in return."

"Are you going to let her tell stories like that when you're married?" Parkgate asks me, still ignoring her. "Were she my wife, I'd buy her a Bible and an education in manners before I permit her out in public."

"Good job I'm not your wife, then," Louisa says. Mortimer is staring at Louisa like she's an animal in a zoo, his hungry gaze dipping from her face to the neckline of her dress.

Louisa's eyes meet mine, a silent plea to say something to the effect that not only will I never try to control her movements, but woe be to those upon whom she unleashes her brilliant self? Or at the very least, tell Parkgate's lackey that it's polite to look a lady in the face when speaking to her, and if he continues to make eye contact with her breasts instead, perhaps he and I should take a walk so that I can give him a basic anatomy lesson. I'd *like* to be the kind of man who says any of that—what sort of selfish, cowardly fool am I that I can't advocate for the woman I love, to say nothing of the fact that I am putting my own bodily comfort above the actual human souls trapped in workhouses across the country? I have the audacity to keep my mouth shut when asked to step to the defense of those who cannot defend themselves? I am pinned by the anvils on the end of Peele's arms, swallowing and gasping like he's holding me underwater.

Louisa's mouth turns down with what I assume is disappointment and I want to say, *Yes! I know! I am also deeply disappointed with who I am! We are in agreement on that subject!* But then she tips her chin back toward the entrance to the park. "Let's go, Adrian," she says.

"I would suggest you try a less demanding tone with your soon-to-be husband," Peele says. I swear to God, he's pushing me into the earth.

"I'm not demanding," Louisa says evenly.

"Just because you want to walk away from an argument you know you can't win, doesn't mean Adrian has to come with you," Peele says.

Louisa cocks her head, eyes narrowing. "I am not walking away because I am wrong, I am walking away because this is a conversation that will be entirely unproductive and I'd rather waste my time elsewhere."

"Well then." At last—at last!—Peele releases me. I swear I hear my ribs crack as they slot back into place. "Please, don't let me *waste* any more of your time, Miss Davies." He bends down to retrieve the pamphlet from the dirt, and Louisa extends her hand to me.

"Adrian."

And then a series of things happens all at once.

As Louisa reaches out, Peele straightens and thrusts the discarded pamphlet into my chest, knocking her hand out of the way. At the same time, his valet steps forward for God knows what purpose, but his shadow falls over me. And suddenly I feel trapped. I feel surrounded. Peele has batted Louisa from me and I am about to be squashed between these two vile men and their terrible breath and their conservatism. Peele is going to grab my shoulders again, and this time my arms will break off in his hands. He's going to look at the pamphlet and realize I wrote it and find more spelling errors and I'm never going to take a proper breath again in my whole goddamn life and I have nowhere to run.

And, like any animal cornered, my instinct takes over.

So when Peele thrusts the pamphlet at me, I punch him in the face.

He screams. Actually *screams*, a sound whose closest kin is the wails the foxes make when they smell the dogs closing in. That noise used to make my mother cover her ears, and I almost do the same thing now.

Peele tumbles off the bench and curls into a ball on the ground, his fingers pressed to his face as blood seeps between them.

"Good Lord!" Mortimer drops to his knees at Peele's side and cradles him in his arms, like this is a valiant death upon the battlefield. "What the hell is the matter with you?" he shouts at me.

I don't know! I want to shout in return. Peele is keening in Mortimer's arms and I have just broken his nose without meaning to and can't even protest it was an accident because all three of them saw there was nothing accidental about it. The handful of passersby likely saw it as well—I hear a woman on the next path over gasp, and her companion says, "Good gracious, is he all right?"

"Adrian, we need to go." Louisa pulls me to my feet, trying to drag me down the trail and away from the carnage, but I stumble, unable to find my footing. My head spins. I'm breathing too fast. Panic over nothing and also everything is clawing at my chest, filling it up like a boat sinking slowly into the ocean, and am I dying? I may, truly, be dying this time. Now I'm once again panicked that I'm dying—I'm at least seventy-five percent sure I am. I cannot get a breath to eke its way through my porridgy lungs and my heart feels as though it's about to burst and I can still feel Richard Peele shaking me by the shoulders like a dog with a pigeon in its mouth.

"Get back here!" Mortimer shouts after us, but Louisa keeps pulling me toward the gate leading out to the street.

"Ignore them," she says, though her pace is quicker than I feel it should be if I were entirely without fault. She clasps my hand suddenly in both of hers and presses it to her chest. "That was the greatest thing I've ever seen." She kisses my knuckles, breathless for an entirely different reason than I am. "Is your hand all right?"

"Yes—yes," I manage to stammer. I may have been as surprised as anyone by my attack, but I wasn't stupid enough to tuck my thumb into my fist or some other amateur mistake like that. I doubt my knuckles will even bruise. "I didn't hit him *that* hard."

"I know. Try to get some more momentum before you swing next time."

"How are you joking about this?" I ask, my voice coming out in a squeak.

"You've killed him!" I hear Mortimer wail behind us, and I start to turn back.

"Oh God, have I?"

Louisa nearly wrenches my shoulder trying to keep me from going back.

"You absolutely haven't. He just wants attention."

"I think I'd better—" I glance backward, and catch a glimpse of the small crowd forming. Mortimer is still holding Peele like they're Achilles and Patroclus at Hector's feet. There seems to be some debate among the congregation of what to do next, and whether or not this is a rehearsal for a new tragedy playing in Covent Garden.

"He's fine," Louisa says again, stepping on my untied bootlace and nearly tripping us both.

"Then why are we making a run for it?"

"We are not running!"

"An overly fast walk for it."

"Because in spite of being blameless, no one is going to side with the young radicals punching noblemen of a certain age. Hurry up!"

We are nearly to the park entrance when a man on horseback veers suddenly from the street, blocking our path. Louisa and I both skid to a stop to avoid being trampled, as he pulls on the reins to avoid doing any trampling.

"What's going on here?" he calls, and I recognize his blue coat, marking him a member of the Bow Street Runners.

Louisa glances over her shoulder, like she hadn't noticed the commotion until he pointed it out. "Oh, I think a gentleman took a fall."

"That man attacked us!" Mortimer screams, and when Louisa and I turn, he has forsaken his pietà to stand and point an accusatory finger at me. "They were trying to force their Whig puffery upon us, and when we politely declined, he attacked Lord Parkgate!"

And though only the barest foundations of that story are anything near to true, I feel so truly and deeply that I have done something wrong, I almost start to cry.

"We did no such thing!" Louisa protests, and the constable looks from Peele and his valet to us and *Dear Lord, don't let me start crying, please, let me stop thinking about crying for that will only hasten it.*

"*We?*" he repeats. "Who are you, precisely?"

And there's really no good answer to that, for we are two raggedy-looking political agitators whose identity would not be believed if we said it, and heaven help us if it were.

"Did anyone witness this attack?" the constable asks, swinging himself down off his mare. The crowd shifts, but no one comes forward. He turns back to us. "I think it's best," he says, "if you come with me."

As the Bow Street Runner takes the reins of his horse, I feel Louisa's hand slide from its death grip on my wrist and into mine. "So I was wrong," she says with a huff. "We *may* get arrested."

Just then, it begins to rain.

2

The constable sees a bleeding Lord Parkgate and a howling Mortimer installed in a carriage and takes their names in case a further investigation is required, then escorts Louisa and me to Bow Street, where the Runners have their offices in the first story of the home of their founder, Henry Fielding, who is, coincidentally, my favorite writer. And who I pray to God is not at home, for if I'm made to meet Henry Fielding under the circumstances of my arrest by his constabulary, I think I shall have to excuse myself to dig my own grave and then lie facedown in it. In fact, I hope to never meet Henry Fielding, in detention or otherwise, as I suspect I will be even worse at meeting people whose novels I have obsessively read over and over than I am at meeting ordinary people, which I'm quite rubbish at.

Thank God, the office is empty, except for another

blue-coated constable Louisa begs to run to Edward's and ask him to come fetch us. He agrees, only after her offer comes with a guinea, though he departs not at the promised run but rather what might be generously termed a saunter.

"Edward will come," Lou assures me as we sit on a long bench pushed up against the hallway wall opposite the open office door, through which we can see the man who collared us making careful documentation of the incident, no doubt in hopes we are some sort of criminal gang and he can collect a government bounty upon us.

When I don't say anything, Louisa adds, "He's been arrested loads of times." Then, "He won't be bothered. And he won't say anything. To anyone. And he'll pay the constables." Then, lower, "Are you all right?"

I am impossibly far from all right. I can still feel Richard Peele's hands on my shoulders like a ghost standing behind me, and I can't let my mind circle too close to the memory of feeling trapped between him and his valet, that final grain of anxiety that tipped the scales into panic. My head is spinning and my heart still feels as though it's trying to break free of my rib cage. My throat is raw, like I've been screaming.

I double over, elbows on my knees and head between them.

"May I touch you?" Louisa says gently, and when I nod, she takes my hand, pressing her thumbs into my

31

palms. She may have hoped it would be soothing, but instead, it somehow feels like more evidence that she hates me and my nerves and my sweat and my inability to speak for myself and the way I sat there while Richard Peele harassed her and his valet undressed her with his eyes. No matter how much I tell myself that that is an irrational conclusion to vault to so quickly and with so little information, my brain refuses rationality.

Neither of us says anything after that. It's over an hour that we're made to sit—I hear a clock several rooms over strike twice. Finally, the blue-coated constable comes into the hallway and says we're free to go, but when we both stand, he holds up a hand to Louisa.

"Just Mr. Montague."

"My brother—" she starts, but he interrupts her.

"Constable Derrick has gone to fetch your brother, Miss Davies. For now, I'm only authorized to release Mr. Montague." I suspect there was no formal authorization involved, only coins changing hands.

Louisa frowns. "Are you sure you've understood—"

"I've understood everything fine, Miss Davies, but thank you for your concern," the constable replies before she can finish. "You'll be released when your brother comes for you." He steps back, gesturing toward the door. "Mr. Montague."

I don't want to go if Louisa can't as well. And I certainly don't want to go with anyone who isn't Edward.

He is the only man on earth I'd trust to bail me out of the Bow Street office without succumbing to the temptation to pass the story down the table at his next club dinner. Maybe it's Peele, paying for my freedom in exchange for something he can lord over me for years. Or perhaps so he can walk me home and give me a stern and not-at-all-informed talking-to about respect and charity and how to spell other words that don't contain double letters. Maybe it's Mortimer come to challenge me to a duel for Peele's honor. Or the news reached one of our house servants and they've taken pity on me, or they're hoping for compensation for a favor I didn't ask for.

Then, from the front office, someone calls, "Adrian. Quickly, please. You've wasted enough of my time already."

And this day could not be worse. How did I wake this morning, thinking myself an anxious but bold warrior for reformation in my country, and now I'm a cowering puppy called to the feet of its master with its tail tucked? I am not strong or brave in the way I hoped I'd be. I'm no one near who I hoped I'd be.

I duck my head and step into the office. I don't have to look up to know who's come to fetch me from prison.

It's my father.

In his study at the townhouse, my father settles into his chair, an act that requires more production than it used to, as his knees are gout-riddled. He sucks his teeth as he surveys me across the desk, a habit he's developed since having them all pulled and replaced with ivory dentures. I look down at my lap without thinking. "Meet my eyes, Adrian," he snaps.

I force myself to obey. My father hates nothing so much as men who do not look others in the eyes, whereas I find eye contact excruciating. It makes me feel examined, pinned down and spread out like an anatomical drawing.

My father has aged a century since my mother died. I had begun to think time couldn't touch him, but now suddenly his eyebrows are white, what hair he has left likely the same, though he never wears it unwigged. He's soft around the edges like a half-melted candle, his skin dripping down his face and flabbing along his neck. His eyelids droop, and the bones of his age-spotted hands jut sharply at the knuckles.

His mind is still sharper than those of most men his age, though he forgets things with increasing frequency. Names, mostly, though that had already begun before my mother died. She was always leaning over to prompt him as to what lord and lady were crossing a concert hall toward them the moment before they opened their mouths in greeting. I had not often had reason to think of my parents as a single entity, but suddenly, seeing him now without her after several months apart, my father seems only a fraction of himself, a man standing half in shadow.

"Adrian," he starts, and I have no clue what he's going to say, so I preemptively blurt, "I'm sorry."

He pauses. I sit on my hands and resist the urge to apologize again, this time for apologizing before he'd had a chance to speak. Some men can cut another down with their words, but my father has a particular way of making me feel like an idiot with nothing but silence.

"For what," he prompts after a protracted moment, "are you apologizing?"

"I didn't know you were coming to London," I say, then immediately regret it, for the unspoken conclusion to that thought blossoms between us like dust motes from a shaken rug—*or I wouldn't have been sneaking around.*

"It was not my intention to leave Cheshire for several months," he replies. "But a rather pressing matter arose, and I needed to speak with you."

"Me?" I repeat, but he continues to speechify.

"So imagine my surprise upon arriving last night to find my son absent from my home without explanation—"

Why had I stayed the night at Louisa's? Edward isn't bothered, but the fear that someone who was would notice and report back to my father has always dogged me.

"—where I have graciously allowed him to stay unchaperoned in hopes it will broaden his mind after a lifetime in his countryside cell."

It's such a struggle not to look down that the muscles in my neck shudder. This has always been a source of hefty contention between us—he wanted me to go to Eton. He wanted me to go abroad. He wanted me to go a mile down the road to a Christmas ball at the Brammers'. I had, again and again, declined in favor of staying home, where I had a schedule and the house had a routine and I knew what lay behind every door and where every hallway led. Like a fragile tropical flower kept in a hothouse, I thrive only in extremely specific conditions. He finally prodded me to London after my mother died— his success in part because she was no longer there to come to my defense—and I went because, as a general rule, I would rather give in to anyone's wants rather than argue with them, and also because Edward finally allowed Louisa to stay with him in London, her private education that they both felt so passionately about put on temporary hold so she could join his political cause. And wherever Louisa was was where I wanted to be.

"I was told," my father continues, "that his absence is not unusual. He has been spending a great deal of time with his fiancée lately. And I thought to myself, as little as I think of her brother and guardian, Edward Davies must have the good sense not to allow them to be alone together. Whether or not they are to be married, a young lady and a gentleman unaccompanied and given free rein of all of London is unthinkable. Little did I know that not only were you unsupervised, but you and Miss Davies have been gallivanting around the city together, assaulting members of the peerage."

Gallivanting hardly seems the word. Louisa and I spend most of our time together reading in the side-by-side armchairs in Edward's library, our fingers chastely linked between us. We make tea and play cards and talk and sit quietly, and I listen to her play the piano and she reads my essays, and yes, we've shagged, but that started long before leaving Cheshire. The only difference is that French letters are so much easier to come by in London, and even if they weren't, fornicating responsibly hardly counts as gallivanting.

Neither does my accidentally boxing Richard Peele in the nose seem to count as assault, though protest shrivels in my throat as my father pulls a sheaf of paper from his pocket. I realize what it is as he places it on the table between us.

It's my pamphlet—John Everyman's pamphlet—speckled with a few errant drops of blood.

Breathe, Adrian.

I want to run. I want to throw myself out the window. I want to grip the arms of the chair like I'm riding the imperial on a runaway carriage. I want my heart to stop beating so fast and hard it fills my whole body. I want the feeling back in my fingers. I want to not care so goddamn much what my father thinks of my politics.

"Where . . . did you get that?" I ask, taking each word at a measured pace and praying none of my rising panic bleeds into my voice.

"Lord Parkgate's valet brought it," Father replies, "when he came to tell me you and Miss Davies had been picked up by the Bow Street Runners and were awaiting bail in their office." He glances down at the pamphlet without moving his head, like it's a grotesque corpse he is trying hard not to look at but he cannot resist his own morbid curiosity. "I can only assume you have no knowledge of this slander or its contents."

I don't answer. I'm not sure if it's a question, but I am certain he'll keep talking if I don't give him a reason to stop.

"When I agreed to your marriage with Miss Davies, her parents were still alive and her brother had not yet gained his particular"—he makes a show of selecting his next word, like a man perusing proffered cigars—"*reputation*. Had I known what he would become, I would never have permitted the two of you to be matched. However, I am a man of my word, and I hope that when you take over the management of this estate, you will follow in that example." He pauses, and when I still don't say anything, again continues, "And I hope you will uphold the political foundations I have worked for my entire career to establish." He taps a finger against the pamphlet. "The Saint James Workhouse is one of my proudest accomplishments, and I hope you will defend it in Parliament as I have. Any behavior otherwise would effectively sever the majority of our relationships within the peerage, and make you and any family you might have social exiles. The scandal of a son turning against his father would be"—another pause and perusal—"considerable."

I bite the inside of my cheek. If Louisa were here, she would say something like, *It says quite a lot about the character of a man that his proudest achievement is an exploitive money-grubbing death camp disguised as charity.*

When I don't immediately offer an affirmation that of course I'm not going to torch his legacy as soon as he hands me the flint, Father sighs, pressing his fingers to the bridge of his nose for a moment, then turns in his chair. "Now. The reason I've come." He retrieves a box from the windowsill and sets it on the desk between us. My heart rate spikes for no reason. It looks like a box for a hat—he could be about to pull out a hat. Or a pistol.

What is wrong with me? Who thinks like that?

Father fumbles with the ribbon, struggling to undo the knot. The ever-present quaver in his fingers seems more pronounced, and his brittle nails can't find purchase on the satin.

"May I—" I start, but he snaps, "I don't require your assistance."

The ribbon snaps, and he yanks it roughly away, like

he's shucking an ear of corn. The edges of the box are soft and collapsed under the press of the ribbon, not quite reshaping themselves entirely once free. I can't imagine what's in this box that he's taken such pains to bring to me but is now mauling like it's rubbish meant for the fire.

He tosses the ribbon onto the desk, and I wait for him to open the box. Instead, he lets out another one of his through-the-nose sighs and presses the tips of his fingers together. "This was sent to me by the Woolman Hostel, in Aberdeen, where your mother was staying while she took the waters at Well O'Spa. Where she—"

"I know," I interrupt, like I need a reminder of where it was my mother died.

"Apparently she left this behind."

I stare at the box, all the noise suddenly snuffed out by a far more terrifying silence. I'm not ready for this. I haven't had time to shore up the particular bastions of my heart needed to talk about my mother, though I'm not sure any warning would have been sufficient. It feels like there will never be a day I can look her memory in the eye without blinking first.

"Why wasn't it sent before?" I ask. Her trunk was sent with her body. I assumed that was everything she left.

"The hostel is being renovated, and the staff found this box when they were cleaning out the room. It was concealed, apparently." He brushes an invisible spot of dust from one corner, then adjusts it with the tip of his finger so that it's aligned perfectly with the edge of his desk. "I have already opened it. There's nothing of any particular sentiment or value, and I'm unsure as to why she felt the need to keep it hidden, though I suspect she was . . ." He trails off, and his lips bulge as he runs his tongue over his teeth. "She was not thinking clearly," he finally finishes, then looks up at me. "Stop fidgeting."

"What?" I hadn't realized how hard I was twisting the hem of my coat around my fingers. A button falls off and hits the floor with a soft *plink,* the thread trailing behind it like the tail of a comet. I force my hands together and press them against my thighs. "I'm sorry."

My father's jaw clenches, staring at the button for a moment before he returns to me and the box. "I wanted to give you a chance to look through it before I disposed of its contents."

"Oh. Thank you."

A pause. I reach for the box, intending to take it with me up to my room to sift through in privacy, but he snaps, "Open it now, please."

"Why?" I almost never question him, and even if this is the most toothless impertinence a son has ever given his father, it still surprises both of us.

It takes him a moment to compose an answer. "I'd like to see what you take."

"Does that matter?" I ask.

"Open it."

"I want to look through it alone."

Father takes off his spectacles and rubs a hand across his face with such force I'm seized by the fear that he will tear his thin skin. "Please, Adrian," he says, the words a sigh. The torn ribbon trembles on the desk, like the whole room moves at his whims. "Don't make this difficult."

I can't work out how wanting a moment in private with my mother's last worldly possessions is difficult, but I feel guilty as soon as he says it. I look down at the box again and realize she wrote her name on it. *Caroline Montague.* Her hand, always so light the nib barely made an impression, is sloppy and blotted, like she scrawled it in a hurry, but I can picture those same letters, slightly neater and with less of a slant, written in the inside cover of every book she ever gave me. Just before she left for Scotland, she bought me a new edition of *The History of Tom Jones, a Foundling*, as I had read the pages loose in my first copy.

Suddenly I feel as though I might turn to the study door and she'll be standing there, in her blue morning dress with her hair plaited, dirt from her garden beneath her fingernails, her eyes downcast as she explains she's going to bed early. I'll stop by her room after supper, and we'll look through her dictionary of flowers like we did when I was small, and she'll test me on how to spell their names, and suddenly the grief hits me like a hunger pang. Though I've devoted many sleepless nights since youth to anxiously concocting scenarios in which the people I love died and I was left alone, it's only now she's gone that I realize I was afraid of the wrong thing. It's not the moment the world splits in two, it's all the days after, trying to live a cleaved life and pretend you never knew it whole and don't feel the space of that missing piece that can never be repaired or replaced. Even the best facsimiles fall short.

It must be written all over my face, for my father says quietly, "Collect yourself, Adrian." I suspect I will get no more consolation from him beyond that oft-repeated admonition to fold up my feelings like an old shirt and tuck them in the bottom of the wardrobe, too unseemly for public display. But then he adds, "This may not be worth your attention."

How could my mother's last effects not be worth my attention? I want to grab the box and run, but my father keeps talking. "You know that your mother was a"—he searches for an appropriate word and finally finishes— "mercurial woman. And considering the circumstances of her death . . ."

"What circumstances?" I ask. Her death was unexpected, but not strange. She went to Scotland to take the waters, as she had done many times before. She was walking along the edge of a sea cliff on the morning of the summer solstice, so early it was still dark, and she misstepped. That was all.

"Adrian." Every time he says my name, it sounds more and more unpleasant, like it's a sour taste in his mouth that, even after he's swallowed, lingers. He looks down at the box again, then says, "We both know your nerves are delicate." He winces on the word, too feminine to describe anything about your only son without sparking shame. "I do not want this to upset you further."

Upset me more than my mother dying? My upsetness has already reached the brim, and a last gift, however unexpected, would hardly spill it over.

I reach across the desk and take the lid off the box.

He warned me the objects were of little consequence, so I'm surprised by how let down I feel to see this confirmed. There's a layer of fine paper like something a tailor might wrap a dress in, and beneath it, a set of gloves, fur-lined and too warm for the summer, even in Scotland. A mostly empty bottle of scent, its contents leaked out and gummed around an insufficiently stopped cork. A set of handkerchiefs she embroidered flowers upon. A small diary with scribbled appointments and lists.

Her wedding ring.

That's the first item I stumble over. There was briefly a concern of foul play raised in the investigation into her death because the ring was missing, but that was quickly quashed by the fact that she had been wearing a pearled necklace and diamond studs that were worth a substantial amount and much easier to steal than a ring. In the end, it was decided that some unfortunate combination of the sea currents and the natural changes of a body after death had conspired to send it to the ocean floor.

But here it was.

"Obviously, you are welcome to take that," my father says, following my gaze. "For Miss Davies, when you wed."

She put it in a box. She left it in her room. She stowed it away and then left. I had never seen her without her wedding ring—why take it off? And what were the chances the first time she removed it in almost thirty years of marriage would be before the walk that ended in her death? Something grates inside me, an old irritation flaring up again.

"Adrian," my father says, but I'm already pulling back the rest of the paper, revealing the last item, tucked in the bottom corner and wrapped in one of the embroidered handkerchiefs.

It's her spyglass.

It's such a shock to see it there that I shy, like I've reached into the dark and felt a spider skitter across my palm. I asked about it after she first died, but my father had been so intent on clearing her life from our home as quickly and efficiently as possible. He claimed it was not with her things sent down from Scotland, but I knew she had taken it with her. She took it everywhere. But he changed the topic so abruptly, and by the time I thought to ask of it again, it was surely too late. There was so much else to think of.

Now, as I pick it up, it feels like running across an old friend unexpectedly and far from home. Suddenly I can smell her powder—the special case that held the spyglass when I was small rested next to her puff on the dressing table. I remember sitting on her bed as she placed the case between us and lifted the lid with the reverence of offering a saint's relic to pray over. I was never permitted to look through it, which I suspected was due to the fact that it was broken. Two of the four extendable lenses were missing, leaving her with only the eyepiece and a second lens, with a long crack running down its side, bisecting the words engraved there.

When I was older, she took to carrying it everywhere with her, looped around her wrist or tucked in her pockets, its presence betrayed by the way one side of her skirt always strained at its fastenings from the weight. It was small enough that sometimes she even wore it around her neck. It never seemed strange to me. Some women have a favorite piece of jewelry they wear each day, some men don club rings and still carry the engraved snuff boxes their headmasters gave them at Eton. My mother had her spyglass.

She never told me where it had come from, though I couldn't remember her having it before she went to Barbados—a sudden trip to her childhood home when her father died. She had been there for almost a year, our house ringing with her absence in a way that, I remembered thinking upon her return, it never would again. She'd hardly told my father she was leaving, and hadn't written when she'd return—we learned when a letter arrived from Portugal that she was the sole survivor of a violent storm off the Iberian coast that had wrecked her ship back to England. I've always assumed that was why it was important to her. They survived together. The spyglass had always been such a part of her, I never thought to ask what it was or where it had come from or why it was so dear to her, the question as foolish as inquiring as to why she had fingers. *Why didn't I ask her?*

"I would prefer," my father says softly, "if you did not keep that."

I look up. "You said I could—"

"Please don't be pedantic, Adrian," he interrupts. "I want to be rid of it."

"Why? I want it. It was hers; I want to keep it."

He presses his fingers into the tabletop so hard that his nails mottle. "Nothing good came from her obsession with that spyglass."

"Why would she have left this behind?"

"She went for a walk—"

"She wouldn't have left her spyglass. She took it everywhere; she never left it behind. Never. She wouldn't have left it in a hidden box in her apartments." My chest tightens, panic clenching its fist around me with no warning. There's so much I should have asked her—why didn't I ask her when I had the chance? I spent so much time with her relishing the fact that we could sit in comfortable silence, and now I wish I had never stopped asking for every detail of her life. "Did she get this in Barbados?"

"I suppose." Father picks up one of her gloves and smooths the material between his fingers.

"Did it belong to her family? Was there more?"

"I don't know. Though that"—he gestures to the two broken pieces—"is all she ever had of it."

"Did she get it here? When she was in—where was she? Where did the ship wreck?"

"God, I don't recall. They took her to Portugal. I wasn't there."

"Why didn't you go to her? She's your wife—she almost died. You couldn't go to Portugal to meet her?"

"She had to stay in Porto for months—there was a court case. Something about insurance, we didn't know when she'd be finished. And I had a great deal to contend with at the time. You were unwell—"

"Was it my fault?" Was it? I don't remember it that way. I can remember being ten or eleven, too young to have an objective view of myself or the world around me. Had I kept him from going to her when she needed him?

"Not unwell," Father corrects himself. "But after your mother left so unexpectedly, you didn't like being alone. I missed a year of Parliament—"

"What was it called?" I interrupt.

He looks up, clearly annoyed at having to cut short his list of complaints about my boyhood self. "What?"

"The ship. The ship that sank." Why isn't he understanding me? I almost lean forward, the need to know—to be understood—so strong my body is tilting toward him like a magnetic pole. *I should have asked her.* "What was the name of it? The ship she was on. Do you remember?"

"Of course not," he sputters. "That was a decade ago."

"But she was on it."

"That doesn't mean I remember the name of her ship."

"It sank."

He stares at me, and I can't decide if he's being intentionally or sincerely obtuse. "I'm aware."

"So I would think that would make its name memorable. Do you know who has the other half?"

"Other half of what?"

"Of the spyglass!" I burst out.

My father—maddeningly—looks at me as though this is an absurd question, when it feels like one of the more reasonable queries I've ever posed, though I immediately begin to doubt it. Maybe the way I sound in my own head is nowhere near what others hear. "I will not have this conversation with you. Not until you have recovered."

"Recovered from what?" *Is something wrong with me?*

"Recovered your composure. You need to calm down."

Am I not calm? What's the opposite of calm? Hysterical? I don't feel hysterical—but these questions are urgent. Questions decades old that cannot wait a second longer. *That doesn't make any sense, you idiot.*

"This is not a matter for discussion," Father continues, though I've made no move to do so. Sometimes I feel as though he isn't talking to me but some imagined version of me in his own head, a son who is stronger willed and smarter and more assertive. He closes his hand into a fist on the desktop. Veins bulge beneath his papery skin, bruise-blue and throbbing. "Your mother was never the same after."

Was she different? I don't remember one version of my mother going to Barbados and a changeling returning in her place. She was affected, surely—anyone would be by surviving something like that. But whatever wound it left scarred and became skin. Just another part of her.

Unless she had been dying slowly for the last decade and I never realized it. Was that even possible? It wasn't cancer or consumption or some protracted illness that had taken her. Can it take a decade for someone to misstep on a morning walk?

"And," Father continues, "her obsession with that spyglass was unhealthy. I don't want you to grow ill as she was."

I look down at the smooth golden lens in my hand. He says it like the spyglass is a vial of poison she sipped from each day until it killed her, and now I too have raised it to my lips. "Was she ill?"

He pauses, and for a moment I think I've caught him in a lie. But then he says, "Not in a way most people would consider illness."

"How did a spyglass make her ill?"

His lips thin. "I did not say that."

"Am I ill?" My voice pitches as the struggle to breathe intensifies. "Why do you think this is going to make me ill? It's a spyglass, not a plague rat! Why would you say it that way?"

"Adrian, please—"

"Why don't you remember the name of her ship?" My halting breath is starting to get in the way of what I'm trying to say. Each word comes like a piece of glass I'm struggling to gag up. "That's important. You should know. I should have asked her. Can we—isn't there some way we can—can we find out?"

"Take a breath."

"I can't."

"Goddammit, stop that!" He slams his hand against the desk, so hard that the inkwell jumps in its stand.

"Why must you always make everything so difficult? You and Caroline both, you refuse to be disabused of even the most outlandish notions once they enter your mind."

I want to go above stairs, get into bed, and put my head under the covers, where no one is looking at me, or talking to me, or asking anything of me. I want to be swallowed up until I no longer take up any space. I want this panic to go away—or at least tether itself to a tangible source. I want to stop my thoughts, a task that feels as dangerous as jumping in front of a wild stallion.

Does everyone feel this way or is it just me?

Just me and my mother.

Father waits while I choke for breath. I see him cringing each time my lungs fail me. When I've finally started breathing again rather than wheezing, he takes his own moment to compose himself—I'm so goddamn envious he can do it in a moment—before he says in a more even tone, "You are not ill. You are grieving." The inflection he puts on the word makes it clear how unseemly he finds it. "Your mother, however, dealt with conditions that she chose not to make you aware of. She was never a well woman, and this spyglass became some kind of talisman for her. The sicker she grew, the more obsessive she became."

To my surprise, Father reaches suddenly across the desk and places his hand on top of mine. He lets go almost as soon as he touches me, and I have a sense we both deeply regret he moved at all. "I know you loved her, Adrian. I know she was important to you in a way I never will be. But you must understand: when she was with you, she was only a piece of herself. She was your mother, and she was who you needed, but that was not the entirety of her." He retrieves the lid of the box and replaces it, pausing once again to align the edges with his desk. "You may keep the spyglass," he says, like he's granting me an enormous favor. "But I don't want you obsessing over it like she did. Or obsessing over her. Or her death. And I don't want to hear of any more involvement with Edward Davies and his radicals."

"I can't avoid Edward Davies; I'm marrying his sister," I say, unable to keep the incredulity from my voice.

"If you are so keen to join them rather than bringing Miss Davies into our family and values, then perhaps we shall have to reconsider the engagement."

"No, please." My mind skips ten years down the road, to me, alone, or worse, with someone who isn't Louisa, one of the only fixed points in my future suddenly knocked off the map and my whole world struggling to recalibrate around it. "I promise, I'll be better. I will. Please."

"Then limit your engagement with Edward Davies," my father says. "And you'll let your mother rest easy. Do I make myself clear?" When I don't answer quickly enough, he snaps, "Indicate that you understand me, Adrian."

"Yes, sir. I understand."

"Very good. You may go."

I snatch up the spyglass and the wedding ring, then clamber to my feet. I have to hold on to the back of the chair for a moment to regain my balance before I turn for the door.

I'm at the threshold when, behind me, my father says suddenly, "It was *Persephone*."

I glance over my shoulder. "What?"

He has his elbows resting upon his desk, fingers pressed into his forehead. He still wears his wedding ring, a thin gold band he must have had polished recently, for it shines. "Or . . . no, it had to be *Persephone*. She misspelled it in every letter."

"What are you talking about?" I ask.

"That was the name of the ship she was on," he replies, then lowers his hands and nods once. The matter settled. "The *Persephone*."

3

Louisa sends a card the next morning, and I call upon her after lunch.

Imogene, the woman Edward has lived with for almost a decade, gives me a hug at the door, which I struggle to react to like I'm being embraced and not stabbed. "I heard you had quite a day yesterday," she says, rubbing her hands up and down my arms like she's warming me. "Was your father cross with you?"

"He . . . wasn't pleased," I say, the grandest understatement of the generation. "Where's Lou?"

"In the library," she says, though her hand on my arm is guiding me the opposite direction. "But Edward wants a word with you first. He's in the dining room."

Oh God, how can one sentence inspire so much dread? I start to sweat, though I've just stepped in from the spring chill.

Edward is sitting alone at the long table, unwigged and running a hand over his shorn hair as he reads a stack of documents spread before him. He looks up when I knock, and I realize that, atop all those pages is my Everyman pamphlet.

"Adrian!" He beams when he sees me, and I smile back. Somehow, in spite of being best known for rallying social reformers and raising hell in the House of Commons, Edward is still the most likeable man anyone knows. He's been arrested four times, twice put in solitary confinement, and can swear extensively in each of the four languages he speaks. But he's also easy to make laugh, and is also sincerely interested in any conversation on any subject with almost anyone. When he and Lou came for tea after we were first engaged, my mother walked him around her gardens for almost an hour—far longer than he had likely expected when he asked about her hydrangeas. I was ready to make apologies for her enthusiasm when he returned to Lou and me, but before I could, he said, with real fascination, "Did you know that pumpkin squash can be pollenated with a pipette when necessary for reproduction?"

Now, he stands for me as I enter his dining room, his smile too wide for his face. "How are you? Did your father give you a bad time about yesterday?"

"A bit," I say. The sight of my pamphlet has momentarily

distracted me from shuffling through possibilities of what it is he wants to speak to me about, which range from *You did not protect Louisa from the law; neither did you adequately stand up for our cause of reformation, rendering you completely useless* to *I changed my mind and decided you have ruined my sister before your wedding and I will now castrate you in the middle of the table; please lie down and hold still.*

As unlikely as the latter seems, my rabid-dog brain still gives it a good shake. Edward knows I often spend the night, and after a decade of him and Imogene living together unwed, I could challenge him on the grounds of both willful ignorance and hypocrisy. Though the plausibility of a worry has never stopped me from asking it to dance.

"Would you sit down for a moment?" Edward gestures me to the spot beside him at the table. I don't pull the chair out far enough and end up wedging myself into the gap between it and the table. I accidentally ram my shin into one of the legs and have to bite my tongue to keep from groaning in pain.

Edward folds my pamphlet so the title is visible, then holds it up for me to see. "Louisa had these printed for our rally last month at the Saint James Workhouse. She didn't mention you wrote it." He pauses, like I might confirm this. I do not, so he presses on. "I assumed she was the author, though between you and me, she doesn't write this well." He glances quickly at the door, to make sure she isn't within hearing, then grins conspiratorially at me. "Don't tell her I said that."

I stare down at the dark polished wood of the table and dig my nails into my thigh. "It was a lark."

"I wish anything I wrote on a lark was half as good as this."

"It's not good."

"I think it's brilliant. Lots of people do. We had more requests for it than we had copies printed. Most people had already heard of it before we offered it to them. I heard about it being read aloud in front of the Old Bailey last week."

I wonder momentarily what he would do if I went completely boneless and slumped to the floor beneath the table, then slithered away on my belly, out of the house and into the street, and no one ever heard from me again. I don't like his praise. I don't want it—somehow it only makes me feel more rotten about my work, like it's a drunk friend I have to make excuses for. "I'm sure they only took them to be polite."

"They took them because you have important things to say, and you say them so well," he says, and I curl my toes inside my shoes. "It's a skill to condense complex subjects into digestible talking points while staying conversational and witty." He beams at me, the apples of his cheeks rosy, and I wonder if Edward is ever unsure what to do with his hands, or feels too tall and like his own body fits him poorly.

"Was your father's request for your acceleration to the Lords approved?" he asks.

I debate for a moment whether I'm more anxious about his potential response to the truth, or the idea of lying to him. "We decided it wasn't the right time."

He knocks his knuckles on the table. "Damn, I was hoping to have you for the vote. You would be on our side, yes?" I try to look at him but panic at the last second and end up raising my face and then fully closing my eyes like a loon. It's too much to hope he didn't notice, and when I open my eyes again, he's running his fingers along the creased edges of the pamphlet. "Does your father know that your politics lean so strongly toward the Whigs?" he asks carefully.

"No," I say quickly. I wasn't planning to make that known until after he was dead, and even then, I hoped to be radical as quietly as possible. Lou's and my arrest rather spoiled that, though if Father remains dedicated to the notion that ignoring something will make it go away, I am more than willing to be ignored.

"Hm." Edward sets the pamphlet on the table between us, then leans back in his chair and surveys me. "Well, if we can't have you in person, perhaps you'd allow me to read this in the House of Lords when the bill is presented?"

Oh God, this is so much worse than being castrated. I can feel red blotches rising along my neck. "What?"

"The bill I'm supporting—the one for restructuring bail fees for the magistrates who run the workhouses? It seems likely it will pass in the Commons, and if it does, I've been granted permission to speak on it in the Lords. It's a small step, but it will open the conversation of larger reforms to the workhouse system. This pamphlet about the Saint James Workhouse and what you've seen there firsthand would make compelling evidence that may convince several—"

"No," I blurt before he can finish.

"Oh." He frowns in surprise, like it didn't occur to him that I might refuse. "I wouldn't put your name on it," he says, then adds, "though it would make a real difference if I could."

I shake my head, eyes falling again to the tabletop. It's so polished I can see my reflection in it, and I look away. "No, I'm sorry."

"Adrian." He hunches down into my eyeline, forcing me to meet his gaze. "You've written a treatise that could effect real change in your country. Your writing is accessible and smart and essential." His voice is so sincere, and he has no reason to lie to me or flatter me or puff me up unless he means it, yet I still can't make myself believe a single word he says. "You'll soon inherit a place of privilege that you can use for tremendous good. Don't you want to be part of this movement for change?"

And I do—I really, truly do. But I keep shaking my head.

"Is it your father?" he asks. "You know, you don't have to follow in the policies he's supported just because you'll take his seat."

"It's not him," I interrupt. "I'm sorry; I really am. But I . . . I can't. Let you."

Edward purses his lips, and even though I hate the idea of having my paper read in Parliament, I loathe equally how obviously disappointed he looks. However this conversation ends, it will be with me steeping in shame like embarrassed tea leaves.

But then he smiles and says cheerfully, "That's all right. Maybe the next one, yes?"

"Yes," I say, though I'm still shaking my head.

"Well." He shuffles the papers in front of him, and are we both now deeply embarrassed? Have I ruined things? Have I offended him? I almost reverse course just to patch up this imagined rift, but then Edward says, "You'd best go find Louisa. She'll be waiting for you."

He doesn't sound angry, but he's probably hiding it well. As I stand, it takes a great effort not to ask him if he's angry at me. He must be. But then he catches my eye as I pass him and smiles widely, and yes, I'm almost certain, he definitely hates me.

Louisa is folded up in an armchair in the library, her skirts rucked up about her knees as she reads Rousseau's Second Discourse with her head tipped so far over the arm she has to hold the book upside down. She's so occupied she doesn't hear me come in, and I make a game of seeing how close I can get to her before she realizes I'm there.

When at last I hook my finger around the spine and tip the book away from her, she startles so grandly she nearly drops it upon her face. "Good Lord, Adrian!" Before I can apologize for startling her, she launches herself upward and, still seated, throws her arms around my middle. In return, I press a kiss to the top of her head. "I've been going mad over you." She tilts her face up to mine, chin resting on my stomach. "Was your father upset? Did he say anything about the pamphlets? Here, come sit with me."

The chair isn't quite wide enough for us to fit side by side, so Louisa sits mostly upon my lap, both her legs hooked around mine. I take the Rousseau from her and read the frontispiece aloud. "'Discourse on the Origin and Basis of Inequality Among Men.' Isn't this mine?"

She snatches it back and presses it to her chest. "Perhaps."

"Did you steal this from my bedroom?"

"No, I absolutely asked you if I could borrow it." She pauses, then adds, "I think I asked. Maybe I forgot."

"You mean you stole it."

"I will give it back!" She presses the book over her mouth, peering out from behind it with her eyelashes fluttering. "Do you need it?"

"No, I'm back into *Tom Jones*."

"How many times have you read it now?"

"How many times have *you*?" I poke her in the stomach and she yelps with laughter.

"An equally embarrassing number as you, though yours is embarrassingly high and mine is embarrassingly zero. It's so dense!" she protests when I roll my eyes. "Long-form fiction is so tedious! That's why I like your pamphlets." She wraps her arms around my neck and settles with her cheek against my shoulder. "Did Edward ask you about it, by the by?"

"What a flawless change of subject."

"All I heard was flawless, to which I must agree, I am."

I laugh softly and kiss her temple. I keep my forehead to hers so I don't have to look at her when I say, "I told him he can't read it."

She sits up, face level with mine. "Really?"

I nod.

"Aw, Adrian."

"Don't say it."

"Say what?"

"That I'm wasting my voice and my talent and my ability to be a force for change in the country and I'll be a waste of a seat in the House of Lords."

"I don't think any of that." A pause, then she continues, effectively nullifying anything she had done to ease my mind. "But. You *do* have a great talent. And a great capacity to be a force for change in the government. I'm not saying you need to announce yourself as John Everyman tomorrow and begin declaiming liberal theses on street corners. But I want to see you and Edward set Parliament on fire. Metaphorically. Well." She reconsiders. "I wouldn't be opposed to a literal fire. Just a small one to wake everyone up a bit."

I tip my head back against the chair and stare at the bar of luminous sky visible through the upper windows. Today, the clouds are golden, sunlight folded into their creases so that honeyed light spreads across the sky. "I want to, Lou, I really do."

"Then what's stopping you?"

"I can't even hand out copies in the park without falling apart."

"But you wouldn't have to do a thing!" She sits up straight, arms still around my neck. "Let Edward read it—he won't put your name on it!"

"I can't." Edward may not name me as the author,

but *I* will know it's mine, and will absorb every criticism that will be lobbed at the anonymous writer. What if my pamphlets are mocked by satirists or quoted in cartoons or misquoted with incorrect grammar, or quoted with incorrect grammar because I have a tendency to invert my prepositions? What if I did spell *impoverished* wrong? And what if word somehow does get out that it's me? What if Edward lets it slip, or Louisa does, or someone I know hears the speech and recognizes the way I tend to rely overmuch on the phrase *simply put* when I write? What if one person recognizes me for the author? The scandal would spread through the peerage like a wildfire. And Father would find it harder to overlook than a tussle in the park with political literature nearby. He could rescind my title—there's no one else in our family line to take it, but I'm sure he'd give it to the crown before he'd see me favor the Whigs.

I want to tell her I need more time, but if I wait until I feel ready, I suspect I will be waiting for the rest of my life.

When I write, no one knows how scared I am, or how I struggle to speak aloud. As soon as Edward Davies puts voice to my words in Westminster, I'll lose my last stronghold.

Lou must realize that she's lost me to my thoughts, for she takes my hand in both of hers and massages my palm with her thumbs. "Adrian. Look at me." I meet her gaze and struggle to hold it, trying not to catalogue all the flaws she must be finding in my features. "It's all right," she says gently. "I shouldn't have said anything. I know it's hard for you. I promise it's all right. Edward isn't upset. Neither am I."

She cannot definitively know that Edward isn't upset, and there's a chance she's lying about her own state of mind and oh my God, why can't I believe her? Why must I recast everything ever said to me in the most unflattering light?

Louisa threads our fingers together, then presses her lips to my knuckles. "Is something else bothering you?"

How to pick only one of the many things that have been gnawing on my bones since . . . forever? It seems they can best be gathered into the wide-cast net of a statement: "I think there's something wrong with me."

Lou frowns. "What do you mean?"

"I think there's something wrong with . . ." I don't know how to select a specific location. It feels like my entire body is corrupted. "My mind," I finish at last.

"It's a brilliant mind." She traces the lines of my palm with the tip of her finger. "Why do you think there's something wrong with you? Being a bit shy isn't a symptom of some greater illness, I promise you."

"Sometimes, I feel . . ." I fist my hand around her skirt, struggling for words. How do I explain that I have thoughts that don't feel like my own, thoughts I cannot choose any more than I can choose my own name, and how each of them is an uninvited houseguest in my mind, eating my food and drawing on my walls and smashing the furniture so that, when they finally depart, I'm alone, but the damage remains? And now, the only person who ever seemed to understand that—who made certain I knew that our shared storms were weather and not climate—was apparently unwell in a way I somehow never saw?

What was my father's word? *Mercurial.* It made her sound planetary, like she was a being shaped in the stars. Someone not of this world.

Louisa stares at me, waiting for an answer with her eyebrows sloped. The truth to its fullest extent would make her fear me. Or think me too strange to understand. Or insane. But evasion will sour her to me, and God, I love Lou so much it makes me feel fragile. Isn't love meant to make you safe and strong and swaddled? What man happily in love has described himself as constantly terrified he's going to do something to ruin it? It's hardly the stuff of poets.

"You feel what?" Louisa prompts.

I feel like a shipwreck. A house fire nothing but bodies can be pulled from. So full of gaping boards and fallen walls that some days, there doesn't even seem a foundation worth rebuilding upon.

"Do you ever obsess about something?" I ask, hoping a more roundabout approach might make for an easier path. "Not books or plays or things like that but . . . Do you ever think about what would happen if you killed someone?"

Her eyes widen. "Good gracious, what?"

"Have you ever thought about it?"

"You mean, have I ever thought I might be murdered? I think everyone sometimes has wayward thoughts about death, particularly after—"

"No," I interrupt, trying not to sound too impatient. It's kind of her to try and rationalize on my behalf, but the deeper we wade into this, the more certain I am that I won't float. "I mean, do you ever wonder what would happen if you killed someone? Because sometimes I can't stop thinking about it."

The crease in her forehead returns. "Who are you planning to kill? You are the least likely murderer I know."

"I'm not planning anything—it's all entirely hypothetical. That's what I'm saying. But sometimes I have one passing thought about something that maybe might one day happen to me or you or the world at large and it starts rolling around like a snowball and getting bigger and bigger and picking up more thoughts as it goes and then I start to feel like it's actually happening, not like I invented it, and then I can't sleep or eat or focus on anything else . . . does that make any sense?"

Louisa considers this for a moment. "Forgive me for being reductive," she starts, and my heart sinks, "but . . .

can't you simply choose to not think about that? Think of something else! Distract yourself. Read a book or take a walk or—"

"I can't."

"What do you mean you can't?"

"I mean, it feels as though if I don't devote all my attention to whatever fake scenario I've come up with, then I won't be ready when it happens."

"But it won't happen."

"But what if it does?"

I know I'm speaking more strongly than she's accustomed to, but suddenly her understanding feels vital, that cracked hole left by my mother impossible to plaster over until someone says, *Yes, that makes sense and it happens to me as well. You are not alone and you are not insane or mercurial or whatever the hell you want to call it.*

"I suppose I've felt something similar," Louisa says carefully, "but not about hypothetical circumstances that might hypothetically lead to me murdering someone in a hypothetical future." She touches my left ring finger, running her thumb along the spot where I'll soon wear a wedding band. "Do you feel this way often?"

All the time. About everything. I'm already starting to fret about Louisa relaying this conversation to Imogene or Edward or literally anyone, who will then feel compelled to intervene and separate us and I'll never see her again.

Instead I say, "My father said something about my mother earlier, and it made me think."

"Obsess?" she asks, and I know she's trying to under-stand—*I know*—but just as suddenly as the urgency set in, it's replaced by deep embarrassment. *Why* can't *you stop thinking about these things?* When I don't respond, she prompts, "What did he say?"

Was it about my mother or was it about me? I can't even remember now—I'm not sure if the version I have inflated in my head by turning it over and over is what really happened or another fiction of my own mind. "It's nothing. I don't remember."

"It doesn't sound like nothing." Lou curls into my shoulder, and I press my chin to the top of her head.

Splinters of light fall across our faces, split by the rip-pled glass of the high windows. Panes the size of playing cards glimmer where the sunlight catches the raindrops still lingering there from the day before, turning each into a pearl. I think of days like this, after a heavy rain, when my mother and I would take off our shoes and run across the lawn, kicking up dew and reaching the pond out of breath and with our feet stained and striped with damp blades of grass. How she'd sometimes dismiss my tutors unexpectedly and take me to the banks of the River Dee, where we'd climb the tallest rocks and picnic by the water. The days she'd take me walking, and we'd sneak up to the windows of other manor houses to peer inside and judge the furniture. Waking in early spring to find her already up and outside with the gardener she brought in from Kew, plotting shrubbery and foliage in her sun hat and work gloves, the knees of her skirt stained with mud.

"I've been missing her," I say. "I always miss her, but it feels more lately. Like I'm doing this out of order."

"In my experience, grief is rarely linear," Louisa says, and her voice rumbles against my chest. God I'm so thin, she can probably feel my ribs. It's repulsive. "Nor is it guaranteed to get easier with time."

I let out a hollow laugh. "Oh God, doesn't it?"

"No," she replies. "It just gets different." She presses her fingers into my palm, and it feels like she's playing piano keys, a song into my skin, and I wish my first thought wasn't how she should find someone more worthy of her music. "After my mother died, I didn't cry for weeks. Even at the funeral. But then my aunts came to pack up her things and suddenly I was hysterical because they wanted to take her shoes."

I still have moments where I want to board the next carriage to Aberdeen and rush to where she was staying, certain I would find her sitting in the parlor reading a book, all of this some grand misunderstanding.

"I thought it was because I was young and didn't know better," Lou continues. "But when my father died, it was the same. Do you remember how badly I wanted to be done with the funeral? I think I expected that once we got this whole business of mourning him over with, he could come home. Losing someone does strange things to a person. We all know it will happen eventually, but there's no way to prepare for it, or to anticipate the tricks it plays with you. You can imagine the funeral, or arrangements or how someone might go, but beyond that, I don't think there's any way to *really* imagine a life without someone you love until it happens to you. Until it happens, it's hard to believe that things really die." She pushes my hair back from my face and kisses me gently. "There's nothing wrong with your mind, Adrian. You just miss your mother."

I should be glad that's all she thinks it is. Lou knows me better than anyone and she's never thought me strange or unnatural, so shouldn't that make it true? Why isn't that as loud as the part of me that wants to keep arguing and explain that this is something deeper, something that has been with me as long as I can remember, a favorite toy from childhood I still haven't stopped carrying around. I may be grieving, but there is something in me that is more than that. My father almost gave it a name.

Lou settles back against my shoulder, holding our hands up to the light. "Tell me what you'll write about next."

"I will write," I say, raising our cupped hands to my mouth to kiss the words onto her knuckles, "a declaration in support of the silk weavers' riots, and that stricter tariffs on foreign-made cloth are necessary to combat the growing overseas competition and maintain workers' rights amid industrialization."

"God, you have no idea how attracted I am to you right now." Louisa hefts her skirts up and climbs overtop of me, her legs on either side of my lap, and I let her take my face and kiss me deeply. I press her against me, my hands around her waist, and her fingers rake my hair. The familiarity of her touch, and the predictable, comfortable shape of our love, like the worn-in elbows of a favorite jumper, makes my muscles loosen. I can almost take a breath.

Lou suddenly stops and pulls away from me, her head cocked. "Adrian," she says with a wicked smile. "Do you have something in your pocket, or should I start working on my buttons now? It'll take me at least a quarter of an hour to get out of this dress."

"Oh God, yes." I had completely forgotten I had the spyglass. In our tangle on the chair, the tails of my coat have gotten twisted up so that my pocket is now folded between us. "I mean . . . yes, maybe start on the buttons as well, but my father was sent a box of things from my mother."

I didn't realize how necromantic that sentence sounded until I watch the confusion and horror and fear and excitement all play out over Louisa's face in unison.

"The spa in Aberdeen sent it," I clarify quickly. "She left it behind and they only just found it."

"Oh good gracious." Louisa presses a hand to her chest. "I wasn't sure how to take that." She slides off me and sinks backward onto the footstool as I straighten my coat. I pull the broken spyglass from my pocket and hand it to her. She turns it over for a moment before her face lights with recognition. "She always carried this with her, didn't she? I wondered what had happened to it." She tips the base toward the floor, like she's trying to eke a few final drops from an empty jug. "Did she ever tell you why? Or why it was so precious to her? Or how it came to be broken?"

I shake my head. "I think it was something from her home in Barbados—she brought it back with her after her father died. That's all I know."

"Do you know what it said?"

"What?"

"Just here." Louisa points to the small engraving along the side. *The Flyi* is cut in a curled script, the rest of the message lost with the missing lenses.

"I don't know. Or maybe I did once, but I don't remember." I wish I had asked her. There's so much more I wish I had asked her when I had the chance. So many things tucked up in the attic that I had always meant to take down someday and look at with her.

Lou runs her fingers along the edge of the lens

like she's looking for a hidden clasp or secret message scratched into the brass, then raises it to her eye. I flinch reflexively. "Don't—" She freezes, and I feel myself blush. "Sorry, she never let me look through it. Old habit."

"Well, you can't see anything anyway."

"Really?" I had thought there would at least be a distorted image, half its magnification missing.

"It's just darkness. It's strange. Look." Lou holds it out to me, but I shake my head. "What else was in the box?"

I consider telling her about the wedding ring but instead say, "I think there's more to her death than I was told."

Lou raises her eyebrows, but follows me down yet another turn in this conversational hedge maze without question. "Are we circling back to your fear of accidentally murdering someone?"

"No, not that." My eyes linger on the shaft of the spyglass, the crack I had always seen but never really looked at. I assumed she dropped it once, or it rolled off the edge of a desk or was crushed in poorly packed luggage. Looking at it now, as Lou holds it out to me, it seems like a violent wound, the scar from a fight. Like she clung to one half and someone else the other and they tugged and tugged until the spyglass spilt, throwing them apart.

The sicker she grew, the more obsessive she became.

Something had happened to her in that shipwreck. The way my father spoke of it made it sound as though losing her footing on an Aberdeen cliff hadn't been an accident or a terrible mistake. It had been an inevitable conclusion, the final saga of an epic poem. The hero's noble sacrifice not a question of if, but when. Maybe everyone had known how many pages were left but me.

"She never went anywhere without her spyglass," I say. "Even if she was just going for a walk, she would have taken it with her. Unless she knew something was going to happen to her. Or unless she knew someone wanted to take it from her. Or—"

"Or . . ." Lou interrupts, pressing the spyglass into my hand and wrapping her fingers around mine. I can feel the engraved grooves in the metal, those half-finished words. "Maybe there's nothing more to it." When I don't answer, she says, "I know what it's like to try to stuff up the holes inside you with anything you can find. But maybe she simply left her spyglass behind and went for a walk."

I shake my head. "She wouldn't." I can't explain the surety, but it suddenly feels foundational to everything I knew about my mother. She wouldn't have taken off her wedding ring, and she wouldn't have left her spyglass behind. "I've got to know what it was. And where it came from, and why it meant so much to her." *Meant so much*. The kindest way to describe an obsession.

Louisa runs her tongue over her teeth. "Adrian. I love you and I loved your mother, but consider—just consider—that maybe there won't be any answer to that."

I tuck the spyglass into my coat. I've only carried it for a day, and already the weight of it there feels familiar and tethering. I think of the thousands of times I saw my mother reach for it—in her pocket or tied to her waist or resting on the bench of the pianoforte as she played. Sometimes only one finger pressed to the smooth brass. I feel the urge to touch it now—though I can still feel the weight in my pocket, I'm suddenly worried it's vanished, same as she did.

One moment there, gone the next.

4

We first visit with a pawnbroker called Mr. Murphy, who tells us nothing beyond "It looks like a bit off one of those sailing things," and mimes extending a telescope. He then starts working on us to buy some of what quickly becomes clear is fenced merchandise. We leave in a hurry, and a few blocks later, Louisa remembers that his name sounded so familiar because he was so often called to testify against thieves at the Old Bailey. I rib her over this all the way to the Newgate Market, where Imogene knows a dealer who, Lou swears, is both professional and doesn't buy from thieves. He has no information about the origins of my mother's spyglass, but sends us to an antiquarian in Soho who in turn promises he'll ask a colleague who specializes in maritime goods, but then never sends a card.

I find two more antique shops in Belgravia—one that

deals primarily in scientific artifacts, which is where we are at last given some practical advice: make an appointment with a historian at the Sloane collection of the newly established British Museum, which I do at once, though it's another week before there's room in his schedule.

Louisa has an early supper planned the day of my meeting, but refuses to be left behind, and I similarly refuse to leave her, as she does most of the talking and the eye contact in these interactions. We arrive together at the mansion on Great Russell Street in the middle of a torrential downpour. Even the short path from the hack to the door leaves us shaking rain from our cloaks. We give our names to the boy taking deliveries in the front hall and are promptly escorted above stairs. The collections aren't open to the public and most are only half assembled. As we pass through galleries and offices, we catch a glimpse of the much-touted library, which, even at a cursory glance, is breathtaking in scale, and the hall of natural history, where a group of laborers is puzzling over the assembly of an enormous skeleton, still in too many pieces to be identifiable as any creature in particular.

The delivery boy shows us to a salon crowded with crates, their tops pried open but their contents still buried in straw, and stacks of books littering the tile beneath floor-to-ceiling shelves. The windows are still in the process of being installed, and several panes are covered with oiled butcher's paper to keep out the rain. A man is sitting at a desk across the room, making careful notes about what appears to be a bone-white tusk the length of an épée. He startles when he hears our footsteps, and quickly snatches up his wig from where it's resting upon his unlit lamp and smashes it onto his head.

"Your three o'clock, sir," the delivery boy calls, then leaves without another word.

The man stands, trying to push his wig back up his forehead as discreetly as possible as he approaches us. "Good morning. Afternoon? I suppose it's afternoon now. The day gets away from me." He extends a hand with a broad smile. He's ruddy cheeked and portly, with a Yorkshire burr that sits heavily in his vowels. "Rowan Buddle. I'm one of the trustees for the museum."

I take his hand, painfully aware of how damp my palm is. "Adrian Montague," I mumble.

"Montague?" He gives up on the wig and tosses it back onto his desk. The queue dangles off the edge, giving it the appearance of a sleeping cat. "Any relation to Henri Montague, the Earl of Cheshire?"

My stomach drops. I'm ready to bolt if this man gives even an inkling that he may know my father and subsequently report these investigations. "Do you know him?"

Mr. Buddle smiles brightly. "Not personally, no, but he was part of the coalition that opposed the British Museum Act. Claimed it was a gross waste of funding."

"Oh." I almost laugh in relief. "Well, he hates most nice things."

I immediately regret saying it—it had sounded like a flip jape in my head, but as soon as it leaves my mouth, it feels far too pointed a joke to make in the presence of a stranger, and I say it much too straight-faced for it to register as facetious. I'm about to apologize, but then Buddle snorts, and makes only a halfhearted attempt to cover it with a cough as he turns to Louisa. "And you, miss?"

"Louisa Davies." She gives him her hand. "Adrian's fiancée."

"Ah, felicitations." His smile goes somehow wider. "I trust you will be certain that he supports the British Museum once he has come into his inheritance."

"Depends how helpful you are today," Louisa says with her own brilliant smile, and I envy the way conversation is so easy for her. Sod that, I envy the way she's able to simply *have* a conversation without fretting about everything she says being taken wrong and the opinions others are forming about her, and then obsessing about them for days afterward. I'd settle for that.

We take the pair of chairs across the desk from Buddle. "Pardon the horn," he says, as an explanation for the javelin about which he was making notes. "It's quite fragile and not particularly mobile."

"It looks like you've captured a unicorn," Louisa says

teasingly, though Buddle replies in earnest.

"A narwhal, Miss Davies. The unicorns of the sea. There's a stuffed one on display in the natural history gallery. I'd be happy to show you—"

He starts to stand, but Louisa must sense how much I do not want to go to a second location with a stranger and pretend to be interested in dead animals, for she says quickly, "We're on a schedule, I'm afraid. But perhaps another time."

"Of course." Buddle settles himself down again, looking only slightly disappointed. "Now, what is it you have come to show me? I confess, my specialty is in the natural maritime but many of the donations we've received include personal artifacts of the collectors, so I've become very familiar with a range of seafaring miscellanea."

I withdraw the spyglass from the pocket of my coat and place it on the desk, careful to avoid the horn.

I suspect Buddle will take time to study it before making a pronouncement—perhaps pull some books for reference or a magnifier or even ask me if he can keep it for a few days to make a complete catalogue of its attributes—but instead he starts, like I've dropped a wriggling eel before him, and looks as delighted as a natural philosopher with a specialization in maritime life likely would be were he presented with an unexpected eel. "My word! This is extraordinary."

"Is it?" After so many false starts across the city, I had begun to worry no one but my mother thought so.

"May I?" He gestures to the spyglass, and I nod. He takes a set of fine white gloves from his desk drawer and pulls them on before picking up the lens, which immediately has me wondering if I should be showing it more care than toting it around in my pocket alongside loose coins and peanut shells. Perhaps I should get white gloves of my own. "What you have here," he says, tipping the lens toward the light, "is, obviously, two lenses of a captain's spyglass. They were often given as gifts upon the promotion of rank in the Dutch navy, and the captains would have the names of their ships engraved upon the side—you can see the first few here." He points to the engraved *The Flyi*, the letters split neatly as if the crack had been drawn there. "This is a family heirloom, you said?"

"Something like that," I mumble.

"Are your family sailors?"

"Not that I know of."

"Perhaps they were involved in the shipping industry, then? Your father's side is aristocracy, but your mother?"

"Her parents were plantation owners," I say, trying to ignore the bubble of guilt that rises inside me every time I think of it. I'm shocked Lou didn't refuse to marry me based solely on the fact that a good deal of my inheritance was earned on exploited African labor. "They sold sugarcane in Barbados. She came to England when she was seventeen."

"Do you have family in the Netherlands?" When I shake my head, he frowns. "Curious."

"Is it so unlikely it would have been acquired in Barbados?" Lou asks.

"Yes, in fact. This one dates somewhere around the early 1600s. It likely came from the workshop of the Dutch spectacle maker Hans Lippershey, who first applied for a patent on what we think of now as the nautical spyglass in 1608. He died in 1619, so I would imagine your spyglass lens here was made sometime in between. You can see the touchmark of his shop here, along the rim. Of course, the spyglass or telescope was already in existence before then, and he was one of several men across Europe to apply for the patent, and it was improved upon later by the famous Galileo Galilei. Your mother wouldn't have been likely to come by it in Barbados since it's Dutch made—and these are the sort of items that are passed down through families, not given to charity shops. Was it passed down to her?"

"I don't . . . I don't know."

"Do you know where the rest of it is?"

I shake my head again, feeling like a fool for my lack of information. Under the desk, Louisa squeezes my hand.

Mr. Buddle examines the piece of the spyglass, raising it not to his eye but instead to eye level. "When fully

84

assembled, it would have two additional lenses, though based on the thickness of this glass, I'd estimate it had a magnification distance of about six leagues. Fairly standard."

I didn't expect any of this. After the total disinterest by the antique dealers, I had begun to suspect there wasn't actually anything to be known about the spyglass—it was a trinket my mother had picked up at a seaside store, an item that held no real value except in her heart. I was already making peace with the fact that my mother's strange death wouldn't be solved by this particular clue, but here suddenly is more information than I know what to do with. I can't say what any of it means, but the fact that it exists—that there is something to know about it—sends a shudder of excitement up my spine. I sit forward in my chair, resisting the urge to snatch the lens back from Mr. Buddle's careful hands.

"I thought you specialized in sea creatures, Mr. Buddle," Lou says with a breathy laugh.

"I do," Mr. Buddle replies, and adds hopefully, "The offer to see the narwhal still stands."

"Then how do you know so much about a telescope?" Lou asks. "About *this* telescope in particular?"

"Well." Mr. Buddle sets the lens on the desk between Lou and me and removes his gloves, pausing only when the threads snag on his wedding ring. "It happens I did rather extensive research on this very item several weeks past. A gentleman brought in a description of this exact make and model of spyglass in hopes I could help him locate two missing lenses."

The hair on the back of my neck stands up. "Someone is looking for this spyglass?"

Buddle beams at me, like I'm a narwhal. "Quite an extraordinary coincidence, isn't it?"

"Did he have the other half?" I ask.

"If he did, he didn't show it to me," Buddle replies. "It sounded more like he had the same half you do and sought the same missing lenses. But he only brought a written description from a letter—I believe he said his mother sent it to him—and asked if I might point him in the direction of more information. Oh! And I found a reference painting. Just a moment." He retrieves a thick volume from the windowsill, its placement suggesting it was recently perused, and flips through to a marked page, then turns it around for Lou and me to see. The painting reproduced in ink is a still life—a skull atop a stack of books, alongside a wilted tulip and a burnt stub of a candle. Lying unfurled and resting against the base of the skull is the exact same telescope as my mother's—the details are unmistakable. Even with only the one lens, it would have been impossible to argue they came from different workshops. In fact, they look so similar—the engraving, the small notch on the rim of the lens, the touchmark—that it's easy to think that my spyglass is not only kin to, but the very one used for reference.

The title of the painting is printed in Dutch at the bottom—*Vanitas van de Vliegende Hollander.*

"Do you have an address for this man who was looking for the spyglass?" I ask.

The man looking for the same pieces I am, the man with a letter from his mother, a letter from his mother about a spyglass like mine, a spyglass my mother always kept with her. I can't make sense of it—my thoughts are moving so fast, even the words seem to rearrange themselves into an incomprehensible order. *Spyglass. Letter. Mother.*

"Somewhere here, I'm certain I do."

As Buddle fishes in his desk for his diary, Louisa puts her hand on my knee. "Breathe," she whispers, and I realize I've been bouncing my leg nervously, and the motion is starting to rattle my chair. It takes a great deal of focus to stop, even with Louisa's hand pressed there.

"Do you know what a vanitas is?" I ask. She looks at me quizzically and I nod to the book. "That's the name of the painting."

"Oh, I didn't notice." She peers at the title. After a trip to Amsterdam with Imogene, Lou had gone through a period of intense fascination with Vermeer, and it seems likely she'd encountered the term before. "It's a style of still life meant to represent the nature of life and death—ephemeral and inescapable. I think it's from the traditional Dutch schools of the Golden

Age—am I correct, Mr. Buddle?"

"I don't know much about the painting," Buddle replies, surfacing from his desk. "I was interested in the spyglass, not the image itself. Here's his card." He slides a paper across the desk to me—it seems closer kin to a scrap of newsprint wrapped around a fish than a calling card. Written upon it in aggressively poor penmanship are the words *Hoffman Enterprises, Exeter Street, Covent Garden.* "The proprietor's called Newton. I've had some dealings with his company before, and they're honest men."

I retrieve the spyglass lens and the slip of paper, studying the handwriting like I might recognize it. There's a small part of me I can't explain that's searching for a hint of my mother's penmanship in it, but there's nothing familiar about it. Nothing legible either. I *think* it says Hoffman—it could be Hossmum, for how little effort has been put into properly closing the loops, or Hollnunmn, for there seems an excessive number of hills at the end. I shove the lens and the paper into my pocket, resisting the urge to immediately touch them both to ensure they're still there.

"Now that that's settled"—Buddle folds his hands on the desk and beams at us—"Would you like to see the narwhal?"

By the time we leave the museum, the rain has turned from a downpour to a drizzle. Lou presses up against me in the carriage home to ward off the chill, and I wrap my arms around her, though I feel flushed, like I've been sitting too close to a stove.

I'm aware somewhere in the back of my mind that Louisa is talking, but I can't focus on what she's saying. I feel like I am looking at the world through breath-fogged glass, nothing around me as real or present or important as what's happening inside my own head. All I can think about is a letter about a spyglass sent to the offices of Hoffman/Hossmum/Hollnunmn/whatever those death throes disguised as penmanship had said, with a stranger who may have known my mother. I don't know who he could be—I don't know anyone called Newton. But perhaps that's the point. Perhaps we weren't meant to find each other until after she died.

"I need to meet that man," I say.

Louisa stops talking and blinks at me. "What man?"

"The one who's looking for my spyglass."

"He's looking for *a* piece of *a* spyglass," she corrects. "It may not be related to yours."

"But what are the chances there's someone else looking for the exact thing she left behind?"

"Well . . ." She squints onto the street as another carriage rattles by ours, the footman clinging to the back trying to wring water from his wig. "Quite high. It sounds like that Dutch fellow made a lot of them."

"Then what is the likelihood that there are two of

us, here in London, looking for answers about its origin at the same time under instructions from a mother? I know," before she can voice the counterargument I am certain is rising in her throat, "I know, I shouldn't make a mountain out of a molehill, but it's really the only thing I'm good at. And surely this is bigger than a molehill—a knoll at least."

"Perhaps," she says, though she doesn't sound convinced. "Try not to get your hopes too high."

"But what is the likelihood—"

She pushes away from me and takes my hands in hers. "Adrian. My darling. I will admit, there is the tiniest of chances that they might be related, but for your own sake, I think it's best you don't get worked up over it."

I frown. "What do you mean for my own sake?"

"Only that you have a tendency to inflate things in your own mind, and then you don't come down easy. I don't want you to be disappointed is all, if this doesn't have a thing to do with your mother." Lou presses my palms between hers like we're playing a child's game. I was too anxious about the impending meeting to eat anything earlier, and I know Lou can feel the tremor in my hands because of it. "Why don't you come have supper with Edward and Imogene and me tonight?" she asks.

"I can't. I need to go to Covent Garden."

"To that shop? Adrian, it's late. They're probably

shut up for the day. And it's raining. And it's in a terribly unsafe area. You shouldn't go alone. We can go first thing tomorrow. Please, I promise I'll go with you. I bet we can even bring Edward along. He'll protect us. And there's a bookshop near there he likes."

He may throw a good punch for a gentlemen's club, but I can't imagine Edward cuts a figure intimidating enough to ward away the gangs of Covent Garden.

"Come to supper with me," Lou says again, teasing out the words. "Then we can go back to mine and dry off and cuddle up and read."

There is literally nothing I want more, and she knows it. Minus the going out—I would have been content to take the meal at home rather than some noisy chophouse or social club—and perhaps a bit more than cuddling. Both suggestions I'm sure she'd be amenable to.

But she also knows me well enough that when I start, "I'll—" she finishes for me.

"I know, I know, you'll be thinking of it all night."

"I'll be unbearable."

"You never are." She presses a kiss to the tip of my nose. "You sometimes are, but it's why I like you. At least go home and warm up and think on it before you make any decisions."

The carriage jerks to a halt, and we both brace ourselves against the seat. I hear the squelch of mud as the footman jumps down from his perch, then calls that we've reached her address. "We're dining at seven," Lou says. "Please come."

I kiss her cheek. "If I do, you have to tell Edward he's not allowed to ask me about my pamphlet. Or if he does, you have to come to my defense."

She gives me a small bow. "I am, as always, your knight in shining armor."

"So long as that shining armor is easier to unfasten than your dresses."

She slaps my shoulder playfully as the footman opens the carriage door. "Adrian Montague, you scoundrel. You'll give a girl ideas."

5

In spite of my promise to Lou, I don't go home. I have the coachman drop me two blocks from Edward's townhouse, then set off on foot to Covent Garden. A hack there would garner attention.

True to its Londony self, the rain does not so much stop as it turns to a foggy mist, so that by the time I reach the address I'm more chilled than seems proportional to the dampness of my coat. The office isn't hard to locate—though it is, as Lou suggested, in a not overly savory area of town. On my way, I pass Chippendale's workshop, an open-air cock pit, and what is almost certainly a molly house all on the same block. A printer three doors down from the office has stacks of the second edition of Harris's List in their window, and I think I recognize a gent from my father's social club ducking out of one of the unmarked brick houses with his face tucked into the collar of his jacket.

The office itself is trim and looks well kept, the shutters newly painted and the bricks scrubbed clean. It's a stark contrast to the sagging waxwork that neighbors it, and I wonder briefly whether it's not an office at all, but rather a front for something illegal. The hanging sign above the door sways in the light breeze, a three-masted schooner painted above the very legibly written *Hoffman*. It would seem the gentleman looking for the spyglass at least hired someone with better penmanship to make his signs. Below it, hung lopsided in haste, is another sign, this one no more than paint slapped on a shredded scrap of wood: FOR SALE. INQUIRE WITHIN.

I open the door, expecting to hear a bell. Instead, the bell over the door flies off its peg and crashes to the floor. I stumble backward in surprise, nearly tripping back out into the street.

The office boy looks up from his desk in the corner. "Damn."

"I'm so sorry," I say quickly. "Would you like me to . . . ?" I look around for where the bell landed, though locating anything in this room would be a feat. In contrast to the tidy exterior, the office has achieved a level of clutter that most junkmen can only aspire to. There doesn't appear to be any actual furniture, just stacks of various objects cajoled into poor imitations. There's a coffeepot on a stack of books, the dregs cold and stodgy in the bottom of two mugs beside it. The office boy sits behind a desk that looks to be made entirely of documents, and the walls behind him are papered with maps, each marked with inscrutable lines in various shades of ink. Some are so marked up it's difficult to see what landmasses they were charting to begin with.

"Leave it!" the office boy snaps, and I straighten quickly. "Can I help you with something?" He sounds irritated, perhaps at the bell and perhaps at me and perhaps both in equal measure.

I'm so overwhelmed by the room and the logicless system in which so many things seem to be arranged that it takes me a moment to put words together. I have to close my eyes, just so that I'm able to focus before I finally turn back to the office boy, who is giving me such a look of concerned bafflement that I apologize without thinking. "Sorry."

"What for?"

"Sorry I"—I wave a hand at the office—"I was distracted."

He sighs, nostrils flaring wide enough to shove olives up, and I am yet again unsure what his annoyance is aimed at, but assume it's me. My shoulders slump, but I manage to stammer, "I'm here to see your proprietor about an object he's in pursuit of. A curator at the British

95

Museum gave me this address."

The office boy pushes his spectacles up his nose. "We're about to close for the day, but I can make you an appointment for later in the week." He opens his diary to a page that looks as cluttered as the office. "What did you say your name was?"

I don't have later in the week. I don't have time for any of this. I won't sleep until I've met this man, until I know why he's looking for the same spyglass I am and who he is. I won't eat. I won't think of anything else. I'll waste away waiting for a word from a stranger, even though, when it finally comes, if ever, it may be nothing.

But I say, "It's Montague."

The office boy huffs again. The lenses of his spectacles fog. "No, *your* name."

I stare at him, not sure if I've misunderstood the question or if it didn't make sense to begin with. "It's Montague."

"That's not—" He looks up from the diary and squints hard at me. I resist the urge to reach up and touch my face to make sure I haven't anything stuck or smudged or bleeding there. He flips the diary shut and clambers out from behind his desk. "Have a seat for a moment, will you?"

"Um." He pauses at the door to the back office, and I ask meekly, "Where?"

With another theatrical sigh, he manages to unearth a chair from under a leaflet of botanical drawings *and* the skull of some sort of enormous bird, and I have no idea where I am or what I have gotten myself into or whom I am about to meet. "Wait here," he instructs, then picks his way to the back office door, which he knocks upon once before letting himself in.

My heart feels like a wasp under a pint glass, and my breath comes in erratic gasps. Something is happening.

Think. Of. Something. Else.

He told me to come back later, until he heard my name. I have a sudden horrible vision of my father emerging from the back room and shouting "Aha!" as he snatches the spyglass from my hands and cracks it over his knee. Is this a trick being played on me? Or some kind of trap? It's impossibly hot in here. I struggle out of my coat, consider hanging it upon the rack, evaluate the stability of said rack and find it wanting, and instead ball it up and hold it in my lap, trying to use it to cover the nervous bouncing of my leg.

Think of something else. I look around. There's no want of distractions, but I am difficult to distract once I've started down the path of greatest catastrophe. The longer I pick my surroundings apart, the more it seems that the room has been cleaved down the middle, the side with the desk and the maps a shipping office recovering from some sort of beastly storm, the other a cobbled-together, half-disguised excuse for a living space. There are blankets rolled up in one corner, a washbasin and a shaving kit balanced precariously between them. Several socks are draped over the hearth screen, half of them darned, the other half practically unraveling with wear. A stack of books is wedged beside the coal bin, the top volume labeled as an atlas of cursed places, and beside that, a battered violin case with several holes peppering its side.

My fingers are going numb. I can't tell if it's dread or panic or both or neither, but the office boy has been gone for too long—I think. My sense of time feels unreliable. But I am suddenly certain that I should not be here. I need to go. I stand up, ready to flee before something terrible and unknown happens, just as the door to the back room opens again.

A man appears, immediately trips over a crate in front of the door, and curses. "Son of a bitch. Who put that there?" he demands, doubling over to massage his shin.

The office boy, who darted through the door behind him, glances up as he resituates himself behind his desk. "You did, sir."

"Oh." The man glares down at the offending crate, then at his office boy. "Don't let me do that again."

"Yes, sir."

I freeze, my hand resting on the door knob, as the

man straightens his jacket, then turns to me.

For a moment, I can't make sense of what I'm seeing. It feels like waking in the middle of the night and trying to convince yourself the shadows at the end of your bed really are just the furniture, not a restless ghost at your window.

But this—this *must* be a ghost. I close my eyes hard, then open them again, but he's still there.

He looks like my father. Younger, and trimmer, and leaner in the face than my father ever was, but *he looks like my father.*

He looks like me.

The same coffee-dark hair, and, though his is starting to salt around the temples, it's still thick and curls handsomely, just like mine. He's missing his right ear, and one side of his face is webbed with faint red scars, giving his skin the look of porcelain broken and then glued back together, but I can see my father's jawline. He's built like my father as well—short, but sturdy. Broad shoulders—I have those too. And the same Grecian nose and veined blue eyes. My mother's eyes.

When the man sees me, he too goes eerily still, and I realize I must be the same phantom in the mirror that he is to me. I half suspect that, were I to raise my hand or bend at the waist, he would do the same, my strange reflection. We are two ghosts, staring at one another, not sure which of us is haunted and which is haunting.

Then he says, "What are you doing here?"

And his voice is nothing like what I expected. It's flat. Emotionless. Not even the sort of pomp and formality one might use when addressing a stranger—this is the sort of careless affectation reserved for someone already known. And disliked.

In return, I can only stare at him, stars blinking at the corners of my vision. I don't know what to say. I don't know what I would say if I could. I can't feel my hands anymore. I might be swaying.

He folds his arms and surveys me coldly. I have no idea who this man is, other than possibly a painting of myself twenty years in the future, but he's staring at me like I'm a slug turned up in his newly tilled flower bed. Poppy-red splotches rise along his neck, betraying the distress he's trying to mask with that overreached impassivity.

I don't know what to say. I don't know what he wants of me or who he is, though something in my bones knows it. His must be telling him the same.

The office boy glances slyly up from his ledger, like it's possible to be subtle about eavesdropping when there's nothing but a skull separating the three of us. The man must notice too, for he shoots the boy an irritated look. "You're done for today, Marvin. Go home. We'll see you next week." As the office boy slides off his stool and retrieves his coat, the man snaps at me, "Come on, then," and turns toward his back office.

I consider running again. I could leave right now and still meet Lou for supper. I don't have to know this answer. I don't even have to stay long enough to ask the question. But I have a sense a grave was overturned the moment I set foot in his office, and I'll be haunted until I know who this man is.

As I follow him, I trip over the same crate he did.

The back office is in the same state of stressful disarray as the front. I start to shift papers off the chair beside the door, but several cascade free and land in a haphazard pile. The man's eyes flick in my direction, so instead of making an attempt to shift the stacks again, I just sit on them. His jaw tenses, though I think more in response to the fact that I sat myself rather than that I did so atop his paperwork.

He doesn't sit. Instead, he plants himself against the opposite wall, as far from me as possible, and I think again of my father, and the way he is never without a desk between us if he can help it. "What do you want from me?" the man says flatly. He has his arms folded, his mouth set in a hard line that leaves no room for assuming he's anything but hostile.

"Nothing," I say quickly, then realize that's the opposite of the reason I've come. "I mean, I had a question about . . . we went to the British Museum and . . . they gave me your . . . your address . . . I'm sorry, but . . . have we met?"

He gives me a pointed look, and I feel as though he's waiting for me to crack a smile and reveal a jape he does not think is funny. When I don't, he says, "Are you in earnest?"

"You seem to know me," I say. "Or at least have some kind of feeling about me—but I'm not sure who you are."

He stares at me for a moment, like I'm a book written in a language he doesn't understand but is trying to read anyway. Like he can't make sense of me. At least we have that in common.

"For Christ's sake." He wets his lips and stares at the ground for a long time. His shoulders rise with a deep inhalation that makes me realize I've been holding my breath.

Breathe, Adrian.

Then he looks up at me, and somehow, I know. Even before he says it.

"My name is Henry Montague," he says. "I'm your brother."

6

I speak without thinking, which results in the first words that leave my mouth being, "Are you certain?"

His lips twitch, though I suspect in prelude to a grimace rather than a smile. "You are Adrian Henry Laurence Montague," he says, and I immediately cast backward in my memory, trying to remember whether or not I gave him my name, though I'm almost certain I didn't, and if I had, certainly not the middle bits. "You were born—God, let's see, it would have been January the . . . fifteenth? Sixteenth? Am I close?"

"Fifteenth," I murmur. I feel dizzy.

"And that would make you"—he does a quick tally in his head—"nine and ten years. Your parents—our parents are Lord Henri Montague and Caroline Montague, née Braithwaite. You must have been raised in Cheshire, same as I was, about an hour's ride south of

Chester, Wrexham to the west. Close to a five-hundred-acre property, though I may be misremembering. The house is gray stone with a columned facade, a pond adjoining the main garden; you would have slept on the second story, eastern corner, above the hedges that would always die before they bloomed, though she may have replanted—"

"Stop."

This must be a joke. A trick. Some kind of elaborate hoax—for the first time in my life, I'm dying to be laughed at for being gullible. I don't have a brother. Or—he must be illegitimate. Though I can see both my parents so clearly in his features. And unless he were their child, he never would have been raised in the manor—or even spent any time near enough it to be acquainted with the details of the house and the grounds. But surely someone would have said something to me before now. There would have been some clue, some hint, his name carved into a windowsill or written in the frontispiece of a book.

Perhaps there was, and I had simply never known what I was seeing.

"Am I right?" he asks. When I don't answer, he looks up at the ceiling and drags a hand down his face with a sigh so heavy it should have dropped through the floor. "Why are you here? Can I interest you in investing some of your certainly not insubstantial fortune—you're welcome, by the by—in a shipping route to the West Indies?"

I have no idea what to say. I can't find my footing enough to move. I'm staring at this man—this stranger—my brother—and I cannot understand the convergence of those things. Henry must sense I've lost my tongue—and perhaps also sense the sincerity of my protestations of ignorance, for he says, still flat but less openly mocking, "How did you find me if you had no knowledge of our relationship?"

If there is more clinical phrasing to be used, I can't come up with it, though I'm grateful for a question I know the answer to. "The museum."

"What museum?"

Before I can reply, we're interrupted by the sound of the front door opening. I sit up, thrilled for a conversational intermission—the devil himself would have been a welcome intrusion, so long as it gave me time to collect myself. Henry glances at his office door, and a moment later, a dark-skinned man in a rough coat enters, his cloud of curly hair pulled back into a knot at the nape of his neck. "Monty, why is there a skull with the . . ." He catches sight of me and breaks off, looking between us. "Sorry. I didn't realize you had a meeting."

Henry—Monty—what?—sighs. I swear, even that small twitch is enough to make the dimples in both his cheeks pop out. I only inherited one from our father, but he appears to have the matching set. "Johanna sent it. I believe it's meant to be some kind of present. Or possibly we are meant to keep it for her until she's next in London. It's always so hard to tell, and it has arrived so near to your birthday."

"I would imagine the latter." The dark-skinned man takes a wide stride over the pile of papers I inadvertently scattered and extends a hand to me. He has a broad smile, which is deployed in full as he says, "Good day. I'm Percy Newton."

I take his hand numbly, realizing that my brother never offered me his, and yet here is a stranger who, with one small gesture of courtesy, has already been far, far kinder to me than my own flesh and blood still glowering at me from across the room. "I'm Adrian." I don't dare give my last name for fear that Henry will set me on fire.

Though my omission doesn't seem to matter. Mr. Newton's grip shifts in mine, like his bones turn to pudding. "You're . . ." He looks to Monty, then back to me, and I realize he knows me too.

His whole face lights with delighted astonishment. "Good Lord. Adrian Montague."

Suddenly I feel like I'm about to cry. "I should go," I mumble.

"No, don't," Mr. Newton says, at the same time Henry says, "That's probably best."

Mr. Newton shoots Henry a stern look, then says to me. "Don't go, please. I mean, my God, you're Adrian!"

He looks to Henry and holds up a hand in presentation, as though there was a chance I hadn't yet been noticed. "Monty, it's Adrian."

"Well spotted," Henry says flatly.

"Did you . . . ? Have you just . . . ? Oh my God!" Mr. Newton lets out a breathy laugh. He's more flushed than Monty, and I feel, for a moment, a bit less like a rotted fish carcass some feral cat deposited on their doorstep. To Percy Newton, I suspect I am at least a fresh fish. "What are you doing here? I mean obviously you're here to see Monty. This is so . . . my God, I knew you when you were a baby. Though I don't suppose that really counts, as one can't truly know a baby; notoriously poor conversationalists, babies. Back then we all called you . . ." He stops, seems to swallow whatever he was about to say, then finishes instead, "Adrian. We called you Adrian because that's your name—what else would we call you?" He must mistake my general discomfort for confusion, for he says, by way of explanation, "I grew up with your family—with Monty."

"Oh." I try to infuse my voice with even a drop of enthusiasm and fail entirely. I sound petrified.

"Are you acquainted with the Powells?"

"Mathias Powell?" I ask. He has a son my age, one of the many lads currently touring the Continent, and three young daughters all with honey-gold hair. None of them bears even a passing resemblance to Mr. Newton except for the freckles, but his face breaks into a wide smile at the name. I wish Percy Newton were my brother instead of the brooding twat still glowering at me.

"He's my cousin. His father raised me. My God, this is . . ." He trails off, seeming to notice Henry's set face for the first time. I hope he might tell him to stop being so sour, but instead his own smile fades, concern clouding over.

And now they both hate me. I stare down at my feet and swallow hard.

Mr. Newton pivots back to me, his smile in place once more and only slightly more fixed looking. "Is there a reason you've come to see us, Adrian?"

You could leave, I remind myself. *You could walk out of this office right now without a word and never think of this again.* But instead I mumble, "We got this . . . this address from . . . the British Museum . . ."

"We?" Mr. Newton asks, and I cringe at the error. I now sound even more insane, like I have an imagined equipage accompanying me.

"My fiancée and I."

"Good Lord, you're engaged?" He presses a hand to his forehead with a laugh. "I feel so old." He smiles again, and it is so sincerely kind that it has the adverse effect entirely and I feel my eyes well up. I look to the side quickly, like there's anything subtle in a sudden head whip.

If he notices, Mr. Newton is too kind to comment. "Why did the British Museum give you our address?"

Before I can respond, Monty reaches suddenly forward, yanks open his desk drawer and roots around for a moment before he retrieves a letter and holds it up. I recognize my mother's handwriting on the front, not much steadier than it had been in the final pages of her diary.

Mr. Newton looks from the letter, to me, then back. "Monty, what is that?"

"A letter from my mother," Henry says. He's still looking at me. The collar of my shirt itches against my skin.

Mr. Newton blinks, and I realize that, if he grew up with my brother, he must have known her too. "You were . . . communicating with your mother?"

You were communicating with my mother? I want to ask it too. *And she never said anything? You've been here all this time, and she knew it and never said a goddamn thing to me?*

"No," Henry replies firmly. "She had a question about some trinket she owned and I had Rowan Buddle look into it for me. The gent who bought the narwhal from us."

"You didn't tell me," Mr. Newton says, and I wonder what exactly is the nature of their relationship that this is the sort of thing that would merit disappointment at omission.

Henry shrugs. "Nothing to tell. After she died, I didn't pursue it further."

He holds my gaze a little too intently, and I realize he's lying. The spyglass isn't a subject he dipped into years ago on a whim. He has been at the museum recently enough that Mr. Buddle still has the page with the reproduction of the vanitas flagged. He sent Mr. Buddle diving into his archives searching for answers. My brother has been looking for the spyglass too, even after she died.

"Am I right?" he prompts.

I withdraw the broken spyglass from my pocket and hold it up for him to see. He purses his lips, and I can't tell if he's disappointed or relieved.

"How did you know she died?" I ask.

"There was a notice printed in the paper," he says, and he might as well be recounting the past week's weather for all the emotion in his voice. He unfolds the letter, then says, "So I'll give you a quick summary and then you can go."

"Could I . . . ?" I start to reach for the letter, desperate to read it, then realize what he said and stop. "I can't go."

Monty nods toward the door leading to the front office. "Straight back the way you came. You won't get lost."

"Monty," Mr. Newton says, his voice edged. Monty gives him a wide-eyed *What?* look, to which Mr. Newton replies, "Stop being a prick."

Monty looks away, his neck going red.

I can feel myself blushing too. I'm struggling to comprehend the way my entire world has recalibrated since I walked into this office, and I still fear I may be sick or cry or faint at any moment simply because I'm so overwhelmed, but I know what I need to do. My mother kept this spyglass all these years for a reason. It was important to her, and the last thing she did on this earth was choose to leave it behind. And now here I am, my spade barely sunk in past the surface and already I have turned up a lost sibling.

I have a brother.

"I want to talk to you," I say.

Henry crosses his arms. "Why?"

I didn't anticipate that would require explanation. "You're my brother."

"And that makes us what, exactly?"

"Well. Related."

"Does that matter?"

"It does to me," I say, looking to Mr. Newton for support, but he's fixated on Henry. "I didn't know you existed until now, and I can't . . . I can't just leave like we never met. We can . . . can I . . . can I buy you a meal? Or a drink or—give me as long as that takes. One meal. Or just an hour. Or less, if you're . . . busy." I need to stop negotiating myself down or I'll end up agreeing to three words and a firm handshake before I've given him a chance to agree. "Please, one conversation. I didn't know you existed until today and I'm trying to . . ." I flap a hand at my face, like that might indicate my attempts to get my head on straight. "Don't you want that too?"

Henry stares at me for a moment, then says flatly, "No."

"No to . . . to which bit?"

"All of it." He leans forward, palms flat on the desk, his elbows locked. "I don't want a meal, or a drink, and I don't want you to come back at a more convenient time. I don't want to know you, and I don't want you to know me. If I did, I would have come looking long ago. Has it occurred to you that just because you were ignorant of my existence, that doesn't mean I was of yours? This may have been happenstance from your perspective, but I've spent two decades making certain this meeting didn't happen. Your parents chose not to tell you you had a brother, and your brother chose not to make himself known to you, and the fact that you wandered in here looking for some sentimental token of your mother's life doesn't change that."

"Monty, stop." Mr. Newton reaches for Henry's arm, but Henry turns away, staring determinedly at a spot on the wall. He rolls his neck like a boxer stretching out after a punch to the jaw.

Mr. Newton looks between us, forehead creased, then

says gently to me, "Perhaps you might come back and see us another time? Then we can all have some time to . . . adjust." His voice is so kind, but at this moment, it feels like being smothered with a compassionate pillow. Bless this gentleman, who is clearly trying so hard to make me feel like less of an imposition when all it's doing is making me feel like more of one.

I stare at Henry. He won't look at me. I want to scold him, or shout at him, anything from *How dare you be so unkind to me?* to *At least I'm taller than you are!* I can't walk away from this. I'm afraid if I leave, these men and this shop and this family I didn't know I had will have vanished completely, Eurydice cast back to hell the moment I turn to be certain she was ever there. I should stand my ground. I should stay. I have as much say in this relationship as he does, no matter how hard he is working to make me feel otherwise.

But he doesn't want me. He never did.

So all I say is, "Another time."

"Are you around next Sunday?" Mr. Newton encourages. "We've business in Southampton this week, but perhaps we might meet up after." When no one says anything, he prompts with obvious emphasis, "Monty? What do you think?"

Henry—Monty—I sincerely have no idea what his name is—looks as though he's been asked to select a date for his execution. "Must we?"

"Don't," Mr. Newton says quietly, and they stare at each other for a moment. I can sense some unspoken conversation passing through the air between them. When Henry says nothing more, Mr. Newton turns to me. His smile is truly starting to test the limits of his face. "Brilliant. We'll see you back here then." He reaches out a hand to me again and starts to say, "It was so lovely to meet—" But I leap to my feet, strangling the spyglass lenses, and dismiss myself before I am forced to shake hands with a man who is not my brother.

I grab my coat from the chair by the door and stumble outside, ignoring the clatter as the bell once again flies from its hook. The wind catches the door and slams it behind me, and I startle like I've been grabbed around the throat. As much as I would like to make a defiant stride down the street and out of sight, my legs are shaking too badly for me to go more than a few steps. I slump backward against the wall, the bricks snagging the wool of my jacket. The sun has set behind the storm clouds, and the sky over the rooftops is livid purple, the color of a fresh bruise.

I press my face into the crook of my elbow, trying not to let it all swallow me.

It has to be a lie. A trick. He knew so much about me, the sort of details only a con man would know in an attempt to overcompensate. He's an actor. A liar. This is extortion—*for what?* This will be extortion. It's a drawn-out con. That involved sending me away.

Or he's telling the truth.

Which remakes my entire world in a way that seems impossible to have happened in anything less than centuries. Cards reshuffled. Curtains pulled back so new light falls on dark corners of a room that have never before seen the sun. Or perhaps the opposite—perhaps the drapes have now been drawn around me. I'm not sure if this is darkness or daylight. Do I run from it or to it? The shadow this day casts feels so enormous I can't see where it ends.

Maybe my father never knew. Maybe it wasn't a choice, but true ignorance on his part. And my mother . . .

Sand is funneling into my memories, cracks and crevices I didn't know existed until they were filled, suddenly forming a complete picture of my childhood. How lucky for my parents they had a younger child who was too shy to ask questions and never spoke to anyone unless he had to—it must have made this secret so much easier to keep. They must have stripped portraits from the walls before I was old enough to remember they were missing, burned a wardrobe of clothes, papered over the places he had left fingerprints. Wiped clean their memories of his favorite spot in the garden, the riding trails he followed along the River Dee, the dish he requested be served on his birthday, the act of forgetting and pretending becoming so intertwined they didn't know them apart. I wonder how many times my mother had to bite her tongue when I smiled, resisting the urge to say *You look so much like your brother.* I wonder if I was a replacement. If they threw him out. If he left or if they forced him out. What he had done that had prompted either of those. Maybe it was his absence that drove my mother inside herself; the only place she could keep company with both her children was inside her own heart.

And now, here I am, with a brother who didn't want to be found and a truth I can't unknow. No matter what happens, from this moment, nothing will ever be the same. I can't drop the curtain on this drama of Shakespearean proportions and pretend I never witnessed it. I can't do what my parents did.

Voices are raised suddenly in the office behind me. Or rather, a voice—it's only Henry shouting. I can hear him moving across the room and toward the street. I realize I should go a moment too late, just as the office door flies open and Henry charges out, his coat swinging over his arm. Behind him, I hear Mr. Newton call, "Please, don't—"

But Henry slams the office door, turns, and nearly collides with me.

He jumps in surprise. I saw him coming, but still flinch for no other reason than that my body is so overwrought that a stray dust mote would have caused me to piss myself. My hands fly up involuntarily, like I'm ready to defend myself from him.

It's far more exaggerated than such a small start has the right to be, but Monty pulls back at once. He raises his own hands, like he's approaching a wild animal, and oh God, I *feel* wild. Maybe this is why he stayed away. He didn't want to meet his feeble-minded brother.

We stare at each other. I lower my hands slowly, forcing them into fists so I won't start pulling at the front of my jacket. I open my mouth, ready to excuse myself *again*, but then he looks me up and down, the disdain in his face not disappearing, but at least diluting, like watered paint. "Do you have somewhere to be?"

I'm not sure if it's meant to be a snide jape to send me scurrying off, or if he's sincerely asking. I don't have enough air in my lungs to speak, so I shake my head no. He glances back at the office door, as though he's debating whether or not standing here with me is more or less painful than walking back to his argument with Mr. Newton. He drags a hand over his face and mutters something that sounds like "Son of a bitch." Then he puffs out his cheeks, ruffles his hair, and tosses his coat over his shoulders. "All right, let's go, then. There's an alehouse two streets from here that serves quality pies." From his pocket he retrieves a lumpy knitted hat that looks like a hedgehog and jams it on his head. Even donned, I'm not entirely sure it's *not* a hedgehog. He starts down the street, and when I don't follow, glances over his shoulder at me. "Come on, then."

I don't move. "Come on where?"

He sighs, and in a tone that reeks of the unspoken *against my better judgment*, he says, "I'm going to let you buy me dinner."

7

The alehouse is not, strictly speaking, the most respectable establishment I've ever dined in. The floor is alternately sticky and splintered—there's an honest-to-God hole through it near the hearth, deep enough to see the foundation. I watch a man lean over it at an angle that gives me secondhand vertigo to light his pipe in the embers of the fire. A crowd is gathered near the bar over a game of tabletop skittles, their vocabulary stunningly vulgar and audible even over the fiercely dissonant jig being played in repetition by a pair in the corner, the fiddle player squeezing out the high notes like kidney stones. Painted women linger along the rails of the stairs behind the bar. One of them winks at me, and I trip over my own feet, nearly smashing face-first into my brother.

The barroom is so packed and hot and rotten smelling and possibly also rotting that I have a sense Henry picked this place intentionally to make me as uncomfortable as possible. And as much as I don't want to let him put me off, I am. Very much. It's hard not to think of who sat here before me as my breeches stick to the seat of the chair I pull up to the scarred pub table.

"This is nice," I say, as a drunk woman passing accidentally pours half a glass of gin onto our table. Henry snorts.

Several excruciating minutes pass between us in silence. Henry sits with his back to the wall, hands folded on the table. I am trying to focus on him and not how badly I want to ask him to swap seats with me. I don't want to explain that sometimes I grow panicked someone is sneaking up behind me when I can't see the door of the room I'm sitting in, and the itch is starting on the back of my neck. While Henry is already so tense and obviously unhappy about solely my existence that I'm sure one unorthodox request wouldn't cause him any more discomfort, I'd rather just be his brother for now. Unwanted brother, yes, but not his strange, obsessive, anxious, sweaty, awkward, unwanted brother.

It must be at least ten full minutes of silence before I get up the courage and the breath to finally say to him, "Would you like a drink?"

He doesn't look up from his clasped hands. "No thank you."

"I'll cover the bill."

"I said no thank you."

I tuck my chin to my chest and look down too. Silence again. If I can't breathe and he is determined to remain silent, we may simply run out the clock on this coerced interaction. I glance up at him. He has his face turned away from me, staring at the table, like he's making a show of not giving me his full attention. His knuckles have gone white from the strength of his grip. He can't possibly be nervous too, can he?

He didn't ask for this either. But at least he knew it might someday happen. At least he knew I existed.

He presses a nail into the skin of his left ring finger, and I realize he isn't wearing a wedding band. Suddenly I'm flooded with the urge to ask him everything. I want to know everything I've missed. If he's going to be an ass, I at least want to know *why* he's an ass. I want to know how he takes his tea and which room he slept in back home. I want to know the books he's read more than once, if he believes in God, if he's ever been in love, if he went to Eton, what subject was his best. I want to know about the days in his life he didn't think he'd live through, and the ones where the stars felt dull and pale in comparison to his own happiness. I want to know if he remembers our mother. I want to know if the inside of his head looks anything like mine. I want to know why he thinks my mother carried a cracked half of an antique spyglass, and why he went looking for answers about it too.

But before I can voice any of this, he says, "It's not actually your money, though, is it?"

I falter. "Excuse me?"

"Whatever you'll be using to fund this meal—it's your father's money, correct?"

"Well. If you want to be—"

"It's a yes-or-no question."

"Yes, I suppose."

"That changes things." As one of the men from behind the bar passes us, a stack of dirty plates balanced in the crook of his elbow and two empty mugs hooked around one thumb, Henry waves him to a stop.

"Oh, I think you're supposed to go to the bar—" I start, but Henry has already called, "Hullo, Jack."

The man stops, a splash of ale from one of the mugs he's carrying sloshing out and coloring his apron. "Monty," he says, his tone most generously described as trepidatious. "You've got a new friend." Jack nods toward me.

"No, no," Monty says quickly. "No, he's . . . no he's not." His neck goes red, and I swear the barman smirks the tiniest bit at having flustered my brother. *My brother.* Will it ever not feel strange? "Tell me, Jack—do you sell whole cakes?"

I almost fall off my chair. Jack glances between us, his tower of plates wobbling. "Do you mean tea cakes?" he asks. "Or Chelsea buns?"

"No, like a butter cake. Something large, and with icing. The sort you bake in a tin." Henry indicates the desired size with his hands—the girth is close to that of an obese housecat. "Or maybe instead a great big pie?"

"You want . . . a slice of pie?" Jack asks, looking to me for a translation though I'm as clueless as he is.

"No, I'd like an entire pie," Henry replies cheerfully. "Something with fruit, if you have it. Or gold leaf, if that'll run up the bill. Let me get a whole pie, every cake you have—the big ones—a pot of coffee." He looks at me. "Do you want a pie as well?"

I'm so stunned that all I manage in reply is "I'm not that hungry."

Henry screws up his face like he's considering a difficult choice, then says to Jack, "Best do two anyway; I'll want something savory. So that's a pot of coffee, all the butter cakes you have—mind you that's *all* the cakes, not *a lot* of cakes, *all* of them. Then shall we say a veal pie and perhaps a lemon mince? Or hot apple? Or both?" He looks to me, like he'd care for my opinion if I had one. "Both. And maybe some cold meats, a variety of cheeses—none of that chewy nonsense, though, just the really expensive soft ones—a fruit selection, a whole shoulder of beef, pheasants—do you serve pheasant?— God," he looks at me across the table like he's just had a brilliant idea. "Why didn't we go to a chophouse? Those are much more expensive."

I give Jack an apologetic smile. "We'll just have coffee. And a pie," I add quickly, when Henry looks disappointed. "We'll take a pie."

We must sound like lunatics, though Jack seems familiar with my brother's particular vintage, at the least.

He seems less confused than exasperated. As Jack departs, Henry settles back in his chair, suddenly more at ease now that there's pie in his future. "Should have asked for a jug of cream for the coffee. And for the pie, come to think of it. I bloody love a good pie. Can't remember the last time I had one."

I resist the urge to ask if, that last time, he had ordered and then eaten the *whole* pie. But if his affection can be bought so easily, I don't intend to be tightfisted. I sit up straight, tugging on my waistcoat. The back of my neck itches, and I resist the urge to glance over my shoulder at the door. "So. Henry—"

"Jesus, stop, please, don't." His face pinches like I've just called him something far worse than his own name. "Monty's fine."

"Oh." I try to meet his eyes, but look away almost as soon as I do, staring instead at the fraying shoulder of his coat. "I could call you Mr. Montague, if Henry's too familiar. Perhaps—"

"For God's sake, it's Monty," he says firmly. "That's all I've been called for years."

I nod, still not looking at him. "All right then. Monty."

"You're welcome to take Henry for yourself." He scrapes at a trail of crumbs fossilized to the tabletop with his fingernail. "Where'd they get Adrian from, anyway? I'm sure it was mentioned at your christening, but I must confess, I was either drunk or asleep. Or both."

"You were at my . . ." I want to look to the door so badly. I slap the back of my neck like there's a fly there, as though that can banish the discomfort. *There is so much we do not know about each other,* I think as I stare at this familiar stranger across from me. Then wonder if it's just me in the dark. How much does he know about *me*? "From Hadrian."

"Like the wall?" he asks.

"Like the Roman emperor," I say, then add, "*And* the wall. He built that."

"Good Lord." Monty flicks the crumbs he pried loose onto the floor. "His Lordship really hoped you'd be his prize-winning stallion, didn't he? And I hadn't even left yet."

My posture wilts.

A bar boy appears suddenly and sets a pot of coffee and two ceramic mugs between us. "Jack said to tell you your . . . pie . . . will be along shortly," he mumbles, then vanishes again.

"Well then." Monty picks up one of the mugs and raises it to me, though it's still empty. "A toast to your father and his favorite son."

Then he drops the mug.

When it shatters, the entire bar turns to look at us, in that momentary hush that always follows the sound of something breaking. Monty, eyes still fixed on me, gives an overexaggerated gasp. "Oh dear, so clumsy, guess we'll have to pay for that."

I grit my teeth. The poor lad who brought us the coffee rushes out from behind the bar again to retrieve the shards and bring Monty a new mug. "Add it to the bill," Monty tells him as he sets the new mug down, then he immediately pushes it off the edge of the table so it breaks as well. "Don't know what's wrong with me today," he says, and reaches for my mug. "Best pay for that one too." The bar boy—now on his hands and knees beneath our table—braces himself like Monty's about to crack the next mug over his head. Behind the bar, Jack is glaring at us, and I have a sense he'd like to take one of the sharp shards collecting on the floor and stick it through my brother's eye. You take the right, I'll get the left, I think.

"Stop it!" I snatch up my mug before Monty can send it to its death and clutch it to my chest. "I didn't know about you!"

"How?" He pushes himself forward on his elbows and leans across the table toward me. "How could you *not* know? It's a good act—you're selling it, truly, but there's no chance—"

"No one told me!" I say. "No one has ever said a word about you! Just because you're an ass who never gave a fig about me, doesn't mean I am too."

And maybe it's something in my voice, or my face, or maybe he realizes I am not the kind of person who is capable of keeping up a pretense, for that obnoxious, mug-breaking grin suddenly falters.

The table rattles as the bar boy bumps his head against the underside. "Sorry, sorry, pretend I'm not here," he says, backing away with his hands full of shattered mugs. I look down. The toes of my shoes are dusty with clay.

"I didn't know that office was yours," I say. "I wouldn't have shown up with no word if I had. What kind of bastard do you think I am?" His eyebrows flicker upward, and I keep talking before he can answer—or I can fill it in for him. "And I'm sorry—I really am—but I don't know if you're upset because I never came to find you, or because I have now."

Before he can reply, Jack arrives with cutlery, yet another new mug, and a hot apple pie the size of a wagon wheel, its steaming top studded with black bay leaves. Had Monty not destroyed our mugs for us, they would have been knocked off the table as he slides it into place. I rescue the coffeepot before it tips. Monty looks disappointed. "Would you like plates?" Jack asks, though it's a performative question, as there's no room for them.

"Or"—his eyes glance off the surviving coffee mug—
"less fragile drinking vessels?"

"No, I think we'll do just fine like this. Cheers, mate."
As Jack leaves, Monty sticks his fork into the middle of the
pie and scoops up a bite that is entirely filling. "Eat some,"
he says, sliding the second fork across the table to me.
"Believe me, pie is going to be the only way to get through
this conversation, particularly if we're doing it sober."

"You could order a—"

"Don't." He hacks a piece of crust off and spears it.
I look down at the pie. The colorless filling bulges out
between the lattice strips, fatty reservoirs pooling along
the crimped crust. I feel sick.

There's another period of silence in which we alter-
nate between making careful examinations of the pie
and swallowing enormous mouthfuls of coffee, though
it's both too hot to drink and has a viscousness to it like
saliva. "So," I ask at last, then realize I have no idea
what I intend to follow that so with. I take the first conversation path I stumble upon, which leads me straight
off a cliff. "What's your . . . middle name?"

Monty snorts, which is . . . not the worst reaction,
I suppose. He looks up at me, and I swear his mouth
quirks, which is at least in the neighborhood of a smile.
"Eat some pie," he says again. "You look about ten
pounds soaking wet. Isn't he feeding you? And you're so
goddamn tall."

I scrape at a spot behind my ear until I feel the skin start to come away under my fingernails. "Sorry."

"What are you sorry for?"

"I . . . don't know." I shove a bite of pie in my mouth as an excuse not to answer. It feels like a slug all the way down my throat, and I struggle not to retch. When I look up, Monty is watching me, though it's not a glare this time. He's actually looking at me, like I am a human being sitting across a pub table from him eating a pie. Which is somehow worse. I press the tines of my fork into the palm of my opposite hand until the skin goes numb. I feel too tall. Too skinny. Like my clothes sit oddly on my body and all I am is a collection of parts encased in skin, a rag doll poorly sewn, with its limbs all sticking out at odd angles.

"I thought," Monty says, stabbing at a shaving of sopping apple, "that he would at least have told you I was dead. Or some other such story. I didn't think he'd want to make certain no part of me existed in your life. I don't care that that's what he chose, it's just not what I expected." Perhaps I'm imagining it, but he actually looks a bit unstrung by this. I want to apologize again, though I'm not sure what for. For careening into his life like a stray bullet and doing just as much damage?

"Why didn't you ever come home?" I ask tentatively. I feel like I'm testing how hard I can press on a mouse-trap, a bit more pressure and a bit more, knowing it will snap but not sure when. "Or write? Or, why did you leave home—did you leave? Or did something happen? Were you forced to? Is that too personal? You don't have to tell me. Sorry."

"Well, that was a journey." He takes another jab at the pie with such ferocity that the table legs jump. "I left, when I was about your age."

I wait for more. When he doesn't provide it, I prompt, "That's all?"

"That is all."

"But. People don't . . . do that. They don't just leave their families and their futures and their land and their titles."

"I thought you said I didn't have to answer that if it was too personal."

I clap my hands over my mouth. "Oh, no, of course not. I'm so sorry."

His mouth twitches again, so close to smiling that I realize he's jesting. "Your family and I didn't get along."

"They're your family too."

He laughs hollowly. "Is that what you call a father who beats you senseless and a mother who closes her bedroom door and pretends not to hear it? Family?"

I almost drop my fork. "What?"

He looks up at me, a thin crease appearing between his eyebrows. "Did he never—" He breaks off suddenly, shaking his head. "You know what? Doesn't matter." He ruffles his hair again with a laugh that rings like a marble in a jar. "Nice to know there's a part of our family legacy that will always be solely mine."

Father has never raised a hand to me. I can't imagine him beating anyone—it's not the way he hurts people. I try not to stare at the web of scars on the side of Monty's face, the small cleft in his bottom lip, hardly noticeable unless you're looking for it. I want to ask, but instead I say quietly, "I'm sorry. I didn't know."

He stares down at the table and says nothing.

The dollop of apple I've loaded onto my fork with no intention of eating slides off and lands on the table with a wet plop. "Did you . . . ," I venture after a moment of consideration, "never speak to them after you left?"

"I saw Caroline by chance, once." He picks up the chunk of apple I dropped and tosses it back into the pie. "She was seeing a doctor at Saint Luke's, and Percy and I were there at the same time."

"Saint Luke's, the . . ." I feel as though I need to lower my voice. "The lunatic asylum?"

"No—I mean, yes that's what it is but we were . . ." He scratches the back of his head with his fork. "Percy has a condition and there's a physician there who advised us—him—on a possible treatment. He's not insane," he adds quickly.

But my mother was? "Did you speak to her?"

He shrugs. "Only for a moment. We went through

all the niceties, you know—what have you been up to for the past twenty years, why do you have one less ear than you did the last time I saw you, are you here for the leeches or the cupping or that procedure where they drill holes in your head to let the bad spirits out? I told her we were—I was—living in Covent Garden, and a bit about the company. And then a few months later, this letter arrived asking if I could help her find out more about an antique spyglass."

"When was this?" I ask.

"The letter came . . . let's see, last spring? It must have been before the summer solstice."

"Why do you say it like that?"

"She mentioned it in the letter—it sounded like she needed the information by then. It was odd."

"She died on the solstice."

"Did she? I didn't . . ." He trails off, then takes a sip of the jammy coffee. "She seemed worse off than I remembered her."

"Worse off how?" I ask. The legs of my chair squeak against the floor, and I realize I've pressed myself so close to the table that I've tipped my chair onto two legs.

He shrugs. "You know how she was."

"She was kind," I say, and it comes out more defiant than I mean it to.

But Monty nods. "She was. She was quiet and kind and good to the staff, and kept a lovely garden. Which I vomited into. Several times." He flicks his eyes skyward. "Sorry, Mum. But she was always a bit . . ." His eyes drift over my shoulder without focusing on anything as he struggles for a word. "It was all too much for her," he finishes.

"What does that mean?" I ask.

"Jesus, Adrian." He presses his fingers to his eyelids. "What do you want me to say?"

"You think she was insane?"

"No."

"You saw her at a hospital for lunatics."

"Well, I was there too. Insanity is a broad spectrum." He swipes his bottom lip with his thumb, then says, "I remember that sometimes she couldn't leave the house. She would lock herself in her room and refuse to get out of bed. She woke the whole house once in the dead of night because she was convinced—really truly honest-to-God convinced—a gang of robbers was about to break in and murder us in our beds. Father had to send for a doctor to have her sedated, it was all so . . . real to her. Things were real to her in a way they weren't to other people. Maybe that's what it was."

That's what what was? The reason my mother was being treated at an insane asylum? I feel like I'm seeing a theater set from the other side, rigging and sandbags and actors waiting in the wings destroying any illusion of truth to the story being told. It shouldn't change

133

anything. It doesn't change anything. It doesn't change anything she was, or anything she taught me, or any shades of myself I saw in her or the fact that when I was younger, I had woken her in the night sometimes because I too was afraid of robbers and thieves and gangs in a way that made the danger feel so real. Neither of us could rely on our minds to convey what was real and what was an invented threat.

"Why did you keep looking for the spyglass?" I ask.

"*I* wasn't looking for the spyglass, I was looking for information about it on her behalf."

"But you knew she was dead, so why keep searching?"

He freezes, fork halfway to his mouth, then says, "All right fine, that was a lie." He sets down his fork, then digs around in his coat pocket for a moment before coming up with Mother's letter. My heartbeat, which had just started to find a comfortable pace for the first time since I saw Monty, takes off again like a spooked horse. I fist my hands, resisting the urge to snatch the crumpled paper from him as he unfolds it.

"Let's see . . . it says she was happy to see me, I'm still the best looking of her sons, maybe I could help her because of my line of work—"

"What does that mean?" I interrupt.

His eyes flick from the paper to me, annoyed at having been interrupted. "We—I own a shipping company."

"What do you ship?"

"Lots of things."

"What was she interested in?"

He sucks in his cheeks, and how badly I want to shout that if he's going to keep being a shit, he shouldn't have agreed to this at all. "We've done a good amount of work with rare and precious artifacts. Some of which have peculiar properties."

"What do you mean?"

"God, you ask a lot of questions." Rather than lift his fork again, he pinches the piece of pie speared on it between two fingers and drops it into his mouth. "Well, the last job I did personally was overseeing the transport of the autobiography of an executed convict that was bound in his own skin."

The few bites of pie I've managed to muscle down bubble back up, and I have to swallow hard to stop myself vomiting onto the table. "What?"

He shrugs. "Supposedly if you read aloud from it, you'd die a terrible death within the next fortnight. Two previous owners had already met their end that way."

"Did you?" I ask, my voice hoarse.

"Read from it? God no." He pauses, then adds, "I'm not much of a book person."

I ignore how obviously pleased he is with himself for that joke. I can't stop staring at my mother's writing on the paper in his hand, her letters forming his name, *Henry Montague.* I had seen her write it before—it was my father's name too. But here, it looks different, new words in a familiar language.

"So Mother asked for your help with her spyglass because you know about cursed objects?"

"She didn't say it quite like that." He returns to the letter, skimming the page until he finds where he left off. "'During my return crossing to England, I came into possession of one half of a broken spyglass'—bit of description of the spyglass, something about the crack. She's looking for the missing lenses, needs to return them to their owner."

"Who's the owner?"

"She didn't say."

"Where's the rest of it?"

"Also a mystery. I think she hoped I might help her on that front."

"Did she mention the wreck?"

He looks up. "What?"

"She went to Barbados when I was younger," I say. "Her return to England was on a ship called the *Persephone*, and it wrecked. She was the only survivor—she was rescued off the coast of Portugal."

"Really?" He looks down at the letter again, eyes skimming it. I keep hoping he'll pass it over and let me read for myself, but instead he folds it in half and tucks it back into his coat. "That's interesting."

I swallow, about to ask what exactly is interesting

when another worry interrupts it. "My father told me she was sicker after the shipwreck."

"Well, I'd imagine it was rather traumatic—"

"Not like that," I say. "All that too-muchness. It got worse. I think something happened to her—not just the shipwreck, something more. Something tied to this spyglass."

Monty picks at the pie crust with the tip of his fork.

"Can I read the letter?" I ask before I can stop myself. "I think it would help—"

"Best not." He takes a thoughtful bite. "You know," he says after a moment, "I sort of thought that if you ever did show up, it would be to murder me."

"Murder you?" I squeak. "Why?"

"You're the second son now—your title is in jeopardy! Your land! Your inheritance! Your lordly honor! All those things men of your stature care so very much about. Not literal stature. But really—how tall *are* you?" I must look horrified at his accusations, for he amends, "Don't worry, I haven't any interest in my claim. But if you're so inclined, we're notoriously bad at locking our doors, and I sleep very soundly. All it would take is a quiet step and a pillow over my head and the job would be done. Consider that advice gratis." He drains the rest of his coffee, then stands. "So, I suppose I'll see you then."

"See me when?"

"When you come to murder me." He slings his coat around his shoulders, fishing around for that strange hedgehog hat again. "I'd say it was good to meet you but honestly it's been really goddamn stressful, so let's leave it here." He starts to walk away, then seems to remember his pie, reconsiders, and hefts the entire thing from the table. I'm shocked its weight doesn't pull him over.

I stand too—stumble, rather, my knees knocking so hard into the table I nearly break the mugs he spared. "You can't go."

He turns, walking away from me as fast as a man can hope to while hauling half his body weight in pie across a crowded barroom. "I have pressing plans I need to attend to, which is to demolish the rest of this pie in bed with no trousers on."

"Can we at least see each other again? Or can I write you? Or something?"

He stops and stares at me, running his tongue over his teeth, and I think for a moment he might sincerely be reconsidering, but then he says, "Adrian." And the downturned end of my name alone makes my heart sink. "You seem like a very"—a too-long moment of silence as he fishes for a flattering descriptor, comes up empty, and casts a broader net—"young man. But I've worked for a long time to be free of your family. Forgive me for not wanting to risk proximity once more."

"What about the spyglass?" I ask, my voice pitching.

"What about the *Persephone*? What about why she died?" I want to go home—I want so badly to be home *and* in bed or, better yet, at home and in bed *and* years in the future when I do not feel like an open wound. I'm gripping the edge of the table with shaking hands. "You can't say it doesn't matter, because you kept looking. Even after you knew she was dead. You're still looking for answers about her and what she left behind, and so am I. We might as well do it together."

Monty laughs. "Where do we start? She came by a spyglass on a ship that wrecked somewhere off the coast of Portugal. That hardly narrows it down."

"Then I'll go to Portugal."

Monty raises an eyebrow. "Really? Forgive my assumptions, but you don't seem the type to chase a whim across the world."

"Well, maybe I can be." I try to square my shoulders and stand as straight as possible, but Monty's frown deepens and I slouch again, though still manage to say with some authority, "And it's not a whim; it's our family."

"You didn't know you had a family until an hour ago," Monty replies dryly. "Look, it's not going to be as straightforward as you show up in Portugal and a kindly stranger escorts you to a museum exhibit about the wreck of the *Persephone*."

"I know that," I say hotly.

"You're probably going to be chasing records all over

the country. And she might have been picked up on one of the fishing islands off the coast and then brought to a port, which would change records, and jurisdiction. And if you want to find the wreck itself—"

"Do I?" I ask. This is getting very big very quickly.

Monty shrugs. "What I'm saying is you can book passage to Portugal and then arrive and find you're as lost as you were here, but now you've got to pay for seedy inns and unreliable transport."

"Then I'll hire a ship. And a captain—someone who knows the waters."

"Christ Almighty." He heaves the pie back onto the nearest vacant table and then stretches his arms like he's been carrying an enormous weight. "Don't do that—I know someone."

"Someone you work with?" I ask.

"I have, in the past, though mostly he sails with Felicity now."

"Who's Felicity?" I ask.

Monty stills, like a rabbit that's heard the snap of a twig beneath a hunter's boot. "What?"

"You said your captain sails with Felicity. Who's she?"

"I don't know. No one." He looks like he's going to snatch the pie and make a run for it. I take a step toward the door without meaning to, ready to head him off.

"Well, which is it? Who's Felicity?"

"She's . . ." He tilts his head upward and blows out an exasperated breath. "Damn it, whyyyyy? She's your sister. That's the last one of us, I swear," he adds quickly. I must look stunned, though the news of *also* having a sister after discovering I have a brother hits less hard. *What's one more?* It's the same logic as finishing off a tin of biscuits when you've already eaten half of them, but I try not to dwell on that.

I settle on the most practical question in the wake of this new revelation, and ask, "Does she work for your business as well?"

"No. Yes. Sort of." He breaks off a piece of the pie crust. "Sometimes. It's complicated. But she could get us a ship. Get you a ship," he corrects himself quickly.

"Oh. All right, brilliant. Where is she?"

"You won't like it." Does he sound gleeful about this or am I imagining it? "She's in Morocco."

"Morocco," I repeat. "As in . . . Africa?"

"No, Cornwall."

"Oh, thank God," I start, but Monty interrupts me.

"Of course Africa, you goose. Rabat, specifically."

My chest compresses again. "Why is she in Africa?"

"It's so complicated."

"Well, try to explain it," I snap, my voice rising in spite of myself. "Whether you do or not, I'm going to find Veronica."

"Felicity."

"Right."

"We're definitely calling her Veronica, though, starting now." He sucks in his cheeks, the flickering lanternlight and its shadows conspiring to highlight the fine bones of his face. "What do you think this will achieve, exactly?"

The question drips through the sieve of my anxiety. *What are you chasing?* I chide myself. *A spyglass? A memory? A sister you've never met and a brother who pretended you didn't exist? A family that fell apart before you were born and doesn't want to be put back together? A mother who was losing her mind? You think that's worth following halfway around the world when, more than likely, there isn't even anything to find?*

But there is something about this that pulls me. It feels like following a figure down a hallway, seeing the shadow of a skirt disappear around every corner, just out of reach. I can't stop now or I'll always wonder.

She had two other children I never knew of. She was seeing a doctor for madness.

Something made her sick. Something killed her. Something to do with a shipwreck and a spyglass.

"I want to know how she died," I say, then correct myself. "Why she died. I have to know what happened to her."

And if it's going to happen to me.

"You cannot go to Morocco," Monty says, "for purely practical reasons." I open my mouth to protest, but he

142

interrupts. "Have you ever traveled alone? And to be clear, by alone, I do mean with no valet or footmen or someone to read a map for you. Have you ever had to carry your own bags or purchase a ticket for a stage-coach or reserve a room at an inn? Have you ever done it in a country where you don't speak the most common language? Have you ever had to cook a meal for yourself? Or boil water? Let's start there—do you know how to boil water?"

Oh God, he's right. He's so right that my palms start to itch. I've left England once, and it was only to go as far as the coast of France for a summer holiday in a house of servants my father hired. Even London flattens me. I speak French well, but I don't know what the language of Morocco is, or if that language even uses the same characters as ours. And while I'm certain that, if pressed, I could work out how to boil water, the process is currently escaping me.

And then it occurs to me. "You have."

Monty glances up from mashing a bite of pie between his fingers. "I have what?"

"You've traveled, haven't you? And boiled water."

"Now, let's not get carried away—"

"You could come with me."

He laughs again, more pointedly this time. "As jolly as it sounds to spend weeks trapped on the open sea with you, I have responsibilities here."

"What about Mr. Newton?"

His mouth goes taut. "What about him?"

"He could handle things while you're gone," I say. "You two seem to be good partners." Monty opens his mouth, then closes it again, like he was about to correct me but thought better of it. "Please," I press on. "I'll pay for everything."

He flicks the piece of pie back into the tin, then wipes his fingers on his trousers. "I can't. For at least a dozen reasons."

"Such as?"

"Such as I don't want to. And such as if your father found out it was me who secreted you away from his home—"

"I won't tell him. No one will know. Please come."

Monty rubs his temples, the same way Father does, and I can feel him doing some sort of arithmetic in his head, weighing how guilty he'd feel if I died from lack of boiled water off the coast of Portugal versus how much of a hassle it would be to be the one boiling the water for me. It's obvious which side comes up wanting.

He looks me up and down, and I pray that, for the first time in my life, my general wretchedness and pitiable demeanor work in my favor. "Let's say this," he finally concedes. "You find a ship, and you book passage for us both—and I'd like to travel first-class, please, none of this steerage nonsense—and you send a card to our office with the departure details and another pie and also prove that you've learned how to boil water, I will"—he pauses, and my heart stutters against the silence—"consider it."

"All right. That's . . . that's fine." It's not fine—a definitive yes or no would really be preferable. Not having to go to Morocco at all would be most preferable. But it's fine. It's better. Better than nothing. Better than what I had this morning.

It's going to get better.

It has to.

8

The *Hotspur* is ten minutes from departure, and Monty is nowhere to be seen.

Meanwhile, I am waiting for him at the dock, about to have a nervous collapse.

I have never been on any extended sea voyages, beyond the Channel crossings to our holiday house in France, and the two weeks that have elapsed since Monty and I met and I proposed this mad journey have hardly been adequate time to prepare myself. The size of the harbor at Woolwich alone is terrifying. I haven't even begun to consider the ocean beyond it. There are too many people. Too many noises. Too many smells and so few of them pleasant. There are so many ships of all sizes, their masts foresting the horizon and the muddy water of the Thames bubbling and frothing like a boiling kettle against their hulls. Green passenger boats dart between them, followed by tiny fishing vessels, weighted with a catch to be delivered to Billingsgate. Along the surface of the water, the dark silhouettes of eels flutter. The crowd gathering to see off the *Hotspur* alone seems to be the equivalent to the population of the entirety of my county. There are passengers, crew, cargo, livestock, all in various states of being loaded aboard.

Lou offered to come see me off, but I was concerned that if she did, I wouldn't find the nerve to board the boat. Or at the least, not leave without dragging her after me. And while Lou made it clear she was also more than willing to go to Morocco, whether or not there was a good reason for her company, I insisted she stay behind. I don't know what waits for me on the other end of this voyage, but something in my gut is telling me it will be the scene of a crime, and I'd rather have some time to clean up the blood on my own.

I left a note for father claiming to have gone back to Cheshire. It's a lie that won't hold for long, but if all goes well, neither will this trip. Several weeks at sea is not an insubstantial amount of time, but it's no Grand Tour. It's no running away from home. It's no abandoning your family without a word or a note or a visit even though you knew you had a little brother you'd left behind.

I wait by the gangplank, feeling too tall and too visible and strangling the strap of my pack—I keep adjusting it on my shoulder, and I can feel it starting to rub me raw. I have been here for almost an hour, my paralyzing fear of being late to anything compelling me to leave the house long before they were even allowing passengers to board. It's unreasonable to expect that Monty shares that same idiosyncrasy, but ten minutes is cutting it very fine for a voyage of this sort. Isn't it? Maybe it's not. I try not to stare at the harbor clock looming over the nautical records office. Someone steps on my foot, and, when I shy, a boy darts into my path, shoving a rate map for crossings into my hand before I can refuse, and *what am I doing here?*

What am I doing here?

I cannot go to Morocco. I cannot get on a boat and sail toward an unknown destination without telling my father, and with nothing but a knapsack of belongings. No one but Louisa knows where I am, and my only company is my brother, who hates me and has possibly changed his mind and is not coming at all. Oh God, what if he doesn't come? The only thing worse than extended travel with him is extended travel alone. Something terrible will happen on the voyage; I'm so sure of it all my muscles tense, like I'm bracing for a punch. We'll be attacked by pirates. We'll be stranded by windless sky. We'll run out of food and have to resort to eating rats. Or each other. I'll get gangrene. There will be a mutiny. We'll run aground. Sharks will bite so many holes in the ship that we will sink, and I know that last one is not physically possible but somehow it still has equal billing with the other calamities crowding for my attention.

It is so much easier to give into them than to try and fight them off. It's a relief, like letting go the lead of a dog that's been wrenching your shoulder with the force of its pulling. But now I have a dog to chase, and I'm running in circles after every catastrophic scenario, struggling to breathe.

And even if I do reach Rabat, I won't know anyone there. What if no one speaks English? I'll be lost. I'll be without a home. My luggage will be stolen. I will find nothing I like to eat. I'll eat something and become sick from it. There will be a hurricane that will wipe the whole coast off the map. A fire. An uprising. How will we get from the dock to our accommodations? What if I'm murdered? What if I'm murdered while accepting help from a seemingly friendly stranger on my way to my accommodations? They'll never find my body. I'll develop a fever. Fall prey to a snake attack. Are there snakes in Morocco? Why didn't I read about this? I had halfheartedly bought a copy of *A Short History of the Barbary Coast*, which is anything but short and I have yet to crack it open, the devil of my own invention being preferable to the confirmation that any of it is real. I didn't even bring it with me, for God's sake. The only book I have is *Tom Jones*, tucked in between the three sets of shirts and breeches, two pairs of socks, and the Monmouth cap that are now the only things in the world I can call my own.

I can't breathe. Everything is so loud, and I'm folding in on myself. It's like I can feel my skin pulling away from my bones. I should have packed more socks. I should have read that goddamn book. I should have told my father where I was going. I should have told Edward. I should have told *someone* besides Louisa.

There's a clatter nearby when someone drops a tin cup, and the sound of metal striking cobblestone makes me start so badly I bite my tongue.

I can't do this. I can't go. What am I doing? Why did I agree to this? What made me think I could possibly do this? I'm stupid and small and pathetic and not brave or strong or smart enough to undertake a venture of this size.

I can't go. I can't do this. I have to go home, I want to be home.

I turn from the ship and start down the dock, away from the *Hotspur.* I try to walk at a natural pace, though the press of the crowd slows me down, which only makes me more desperate to get away from here. In an attempt to break from the throng, I slip into one of the shop-lined lanes that form the border between the city and the harbor. Cellar doors thrown open along the path display meats and vegetables, their rotted predecessors from the day before mashed into the mud. A bony cat with only one eye hisses at me when I draw too close to the turnip he's nursing. In my rush, I nearly knock over a shopkeeper coming up from the cellar of his shop, a sack of raw indigo under each arm.

By the time I reach the end of the lane, I'm almost running. I lurch around the corner, down one of the covered closes between a fish market and an alehouse. I don't have enough breath to voice my apology. I feel like I'm hiding from the *Hotspur* itself, as though being out of sight of the harbor will give me an excuse not to leave. I'm so hasty I don't look where I'm going, and I collide with a pair of lovers pressed against the close wall, kissing deeply.

It's not a gentle collision. My frantic approach combined with their placement means that I essentially tumble straight in between them, like I'm cutting in at a dance. Except mortifying and inappropriate and so much more tongue involved.

The gentleman swears as I step hard on his foot. He grabs me under the elbows, though I suppose that's more out of instinct than any actual care for my well-being, and I nearly pull him over with me. As soon as he feels himself start to tip, he lets me go, and I crash to the ground alone, landing hard on my backside.

I'm apologizing before I've even properly finished falling. "I'm so sorry. God, I'm sorry, I'm so sorry."

"Watch where you're going! Jackass."

I freeze. Even my panic seems to place itself on a temporary hold at the sound of the voice. "Monty?"

He turns, and yes, it is indeed my brother propped against the wall, his hair tousled and his shirt untucked.

"Christ." He covers his eyes. "Adrian."

Beside him, an equally askew Percy Newton gives me a sheepish smile. "Good morning."

I look between them, trying to make sense of the scene I have literally run into. It only takes a few seconds of mental arithmetic, then I feel my entire body go red. Monty's face is also splotchy, though that may be from the scrape of Percy's stubble.

"Adrian," Monty says, then again, "Adrian." like he's forgotten every other word he knows. Percy is straightening his coat and pushing his hair back into place, but Monty makes no effort to put himself back together. He seems as disarmed by my sudden arrival as I am by the sight of him and Percy together. "How . . . ?" He pauses, considering his next words carefully. "How much did you see?"

I have no idea how to answer that without dying of embarrassment, so instead I blurt, "You're coming."

"No, I'm fornicating in a fish market alleyway because feral cats really get me going." When I stare blankly at him, he rolls his eyes and says, "Of course I'm coming. I told you I was."

"You said you'd consider it."

"Did you?" Percy says accusingly, and I suspect he got a different version of this story.

"Did I?" Monty scratches the back of his neck.

"I sent a card. And a pie. You never replied."

Percy knocks his shoulder against my brother's, and somehow even that feels obscene. "You cad. You didn't have to leave him wondering."

I have no idea where to look or what to do with my hands. "And you're late," I finally say.

"I am not." Monty squints upward, like he's trying to read the time by the sun. "It's still quarter to the hour."

"It's five till," I reply.

"Is it?"

"At the earliest."

"Still. I'm not late."

"Adrian, are you all right?" Percy asks. I think he's inquiring after my fall, then realize I'm still gasping and shaking, my eyes leaking tears—I hadn't realized I started crying. I swipe my face with the back of my hand. Percy looks so sincerely concerned I almost tell him that no, I am most definitely not all right, and I'm starting to grow concerned I may never be again.

"Of course he's not all right, he's just had a bloody great shock," Monty mutters.

Percy glares affectionately at him. "Shut it," he says, then adds, "and do your trousers up."

Percy holds out a hand, but I scramble ineptly to my feet on my own, shaky as a newborn foal. The panic rears again at the thought of someone having to be witness to it. Or of being touched. I feel like my skin is on fire where his fingers brushed me. "I'm fine," I say. "Really. I'm all right. Just . . . a bit anxious."

"Of course you are," Percy says. "Sea travel is daunting. God's wounds, *I'm* anxious and I'm not even going. It's natural."

"Right. Natural," I say, though I feel anything but.

"It's going to be fine," Percy says gently. "You'll be two weeks at sea, maybe three. That's hardly any time at all. And Monty will take care of you. Won't you, darling?" Monty gives a noncommittal grunt without looking up from the buttons of his trousers. Percy smiles at me, like my brother offered a brilliant and articulate response. "You'll be all right."

"Of course," I say, though I have been assured of the same in far less upending circumstances and never believed it then either. Precedent is cold comfort.

"If you two are finished," Monty interrupts, "Adrian, do you think you might . . ." He glances at the corner, back the way I'd careened from. I stare at him, not understanding. He lets out a tight sigh with his back teeth clenched. Father's sigh. "Would you give us a moment? Please?"

"The ship is—"

"I'll be there," Monty interrupts, his voice tight. "I just need . . . please."

"Right. Yes." I give Percy a stiff nod. "Good-bye, Mr. Newton. It was good to have met you."

He starts to offer me a hand, seems to reconsider

based on its most recent activities, and instead tucks it into his pocket. "Safe travels, Adrian. Keep Monty out of trouble for me. I hope to see you when you return."

I wait at the end of the alley, trying to look as casual as a man can after walking into his brother groping for trout. When Monty joins me at last, he looks only slightly less ruffled—though his trousers are blessedly fastened—and his eyes are red, though he shields them with a hand raised on the pretext of blocking the sun. He's dragging a traveling case so battered that it looks as though it was recently exhumed from a burial site, and the laces of both his boots are untied.

We stand side by side, neither of us looking at the other. Both our necks are bright red in mirrored patches.

Finally, Monty says, "So. Are you going to be a shit about that?"

"No," I say. "Why would I be?"

He gives me a sideways glare, and in return I smile at him like a moron. His face softens, and for a moment, I think he might actually smile back. Then he looks up at me, and my height seems to remind him how much he hates me, for he glowers again and hefts his traveling case.

"Well then," he says, "what the hell are we standing around here for? We'll be late."

9

As the *Hotspur* is primarily a cargo vessel, the only passengers on board are first-class, meaning we each have our own cabin, small enough that I can touch both walls with my arms spread, outfitted with a bunk, straw mattress, linens, lamps, a writing desk, tin cutlery, and a chamber pot, into which I spend the first few days of the voyage being sick. Sailing does not agree with my stomach, which is an unfortunate discovery to make three hours into a weeks-long journey.

The sailors seem to always be busy, and they keep to themselves, but the other passengers I meet are friendly, though their competitive-bordering-on-hostile whist tournaments are too much for me to even watch without feeling like I'm going to chew my fingernails off. The food is terrible—salted meat tough enough to sole a shoe, hard biscuits, and suspiciously gray cheese. Some of the sailors catch fish off the side of the boat and cook them, and the best meal we have is the night they slaughter one of the pigs from the livestock deck.

While the distance is long and I could do with fewer maggots poking their heads out of my breakfast, I find that I don't mind being at sea. When I finally get my sea legs and the nausea abates, I'd almost say I enjoy it. I love the way the unblemished sea surrounds us, the same color as the sky so that, in some disorienting moments, it feels like we're suspended in midair. The waves break toward the horizon, crested with white lips of foam. Gulls float by, riding the breakers and waiting for a reason to dive. I love the sea. I don't even mind the ship. I have a cabin I can retreat to when anxiety starts to close its fist around my chest, but enough people around me not to feel lonely, people who generally don't question my fondness for sitting on the edges of groups and listening to others talk rather than joining in.

In spite of our limited quarters, I don't see much of Monty until I go looking for him. The day after we met, I started a list inside the *Tom Jones* cover of all the questions I wanted to ask him in case we found ourselves in forced proximity. At the time, and with each addition I made, it seemed a way to release all the pent-up emotion of discovering I had a brother. It was a plan of how exactly I was going to approach our acquaintance, and I love a plan. But when I find him one morning on the fo'c'sle deck, wedged with his back against one of the propped hatches leading below and sunning himself like an ill-tempered cat, it feels so foolish I nearly throw *Tom Jones* overboard and retreat back to my cabin.

I can't tell if he's sleeping—he has a wide-brimmed straw hat tipped over his face, and he doesn't react as I approach. I stand silently beside him for far too long to be anything other than extremely unnerving, debating whether to wake him. My palms are starting to sweat in such enormous quantity that I'm afraid it will soak the book's cover and my hard work will be ruined.

Better do it quick, before I lose what little nerve I have. "Monty?" I touch his shoulder, hoping to wake him gently. Instead he screeches like I slapped him across the face. I screech too, nearly throwing *Tom Jones* in alarm.

He whips off his hat, realizes it's me, and claps a hand to his chest. "Jesus Christ!"

"I'm sorry!"

"Where the hell did you come from?"

"I'm so sorry. I was trying not to startle you awake."

"Well, good job." He fans himself with the brim of his hat. "Dear Lord."

"Sorry."

There is a moment of panting as we both recover our senses. Finally, Monty says, "You didn't wake me; I'm deaf on this side." He taps the space above his missing ear. "Can't hear a damn thing."

"Oh. Sorry." Why am I apologizing? He didn't tell me that. I didn't know. *You don't need to apologize for everything*, I remind myself, and then, of course, say again, "I'm sorry."

Monty grunts. A pause. Then he asks, "How's the seasickness?"

I try not to sound surprised—I hadn't realized he knew I was unwell. "Better."

"Ginger broth helps."

"Does it?"

"Sometimes."

"I'll try that."

Silence, and I curse myself for not parlaying his niceties into a real conversation. Why does every interaction with him feel like we're a pair of acrobats, me leaping with my hands outstretched, trusting I'll be caught, and him turning away, or not noticing I jumped at all? Monty settles backward again, slapping his hat on like he intends to actually go to sleep now. Before he has the chance, I tip the cover of my book open to the blotted list I scrawled in the front cover, then stand over him like I'm about to read a sermon. He pushes his hat up with one finger and casts me a wary eye. "Is there something I can help you with?"

"I thought we might get to know each other better."

"Why?"

"Because we're brothers."

"So were Cain and Abel." I must look shocked for he adds, "I'm not going to feed you to a den of lions. Obviously I'm Abel in that story. He was the handsome one, wasn't he?"

"It's not really a story about handsomeness," I say. "Or a lion's den."

"Isn't it? Christ, I hate the Bible." He catches sight of the inside cover of my book and sits up. "Oh my God, did you make a list of questions for me?"

"What?" I snap the book shut so hard the breeze ruffles my hair. "No."

"That's adorable. Can I see it?" He snatches *Tom Jones* before I can stop him, then props it open against his knee.

"No, don't—" I start, but he's already reading them aloud.

"'What's your favorite book?' Well, not the Bible. 'What was your favorite thing about Cheshire?' Leaving it. 'Are you married to . . .'" He stops, his eyes scanning the rest of the list.

I can feel myself going red, and my eyes sting. I hate myself for thinking this stupid idea would yield any results, and that Monty has yet again gotten a rise out of me, and how easily and involuntarily I cry.

"Adrian, this is—"

I press the heels of my hands against my eyes. "I know, it's daft. I'm sorry."

"It's not," he says. He looks up at me, and his gaze is . . . not openly hostile. Maybe it's the light, but for a moment, he appears almost touched. I wish I could know this version of him, this person I'm sure is somewhere nearby. He clenches his jaw, weighing his next words. "You're not what I expected you to be. That's all." He runs a finger down the list, doing a quick count under his breath, then says, "This is excessive. You have nearly one hundred points here."

"Do I?" I hadn't realized I'd gotten so carried away. Though I had been adding to it almost daily, obsessed with the idea that all I had to do was find the right question, and whatever I came up with next would be the one that would crack him open like an egg.

He flips the cover shut, then extends the book in benevolent presentation. "You may pick three questions to ask me, and then I'm going to sleep."

"Only three? Um." I hadn't been prepared to have to narrow it down so drastically. I hoped one might naturally funnel into another, and another, and then soon we would be conversing without assigned topics. Which, I realize now, may have been a bit too great a thing to hope for. Should have aspired to something smaller, like world peace.

I scan my list, trying to pick the least silly questions, though they all feel silly now.

"Choose faster," Monty grumbles.

With great practicality, I settle upon the first one and ask, "What happened to your ear?"

"Is there something wrong with my ear?" he says, expressionless.

"And the scars." I gesture to the side of my own face mirror to his before I can stop myself. "You know."

"I'm aware." He pushes his hat down lower on his forehead. "See, I could never have been a lord. My face isn't parliamentary enough. Though I did consider becoming one of those masked vigilante nobles with a double life you read about in adventure stories. Rob the rich and give to the poor. Or keep it. Rob the rich and keep it for yourself. Why does no one ever write about those heroic exploits?"

I can tell he's avoiding the question, but I hold firm. I was promised three answers, and by God, I will get them. "What happened to it?"

He pushes his hat back to the crown of his head so the sun falls full on his face. He has the remnants of youthful freckles across his forehead, countered by the crease between his eyebrows that hangs about, even when he relaxes. Or perhaps my presence makes him so tense he *can't* relax—that seems more likely. "I was shot in a catacomb that collapsed on top of me while searching for a magical heart inside a half-dead woman. Next question."

I snap the book shut, suddenly peevish. "If you don't

want to tell me, just say so."

He shrugs. "Believe what you'd like." A pause, then he adds with a treacly sweetness, "I'm just hoping we get to know each other better." He can't resist a smug smile. Those dimples make me want to throw something at him. Clearly he's not going to tell me anything real. He's going to spin it all around and mock me and my preciousness and naivete. My brother hates me. That is the fact, and perhaps I need to make peace with it as soon as I can. I didn't promise to pay his passage back to England, after all. I could always dump him in Rabat.

But the spyglass is heavy in my pocket. I swallow and dive back into the list. "When did you leave home?"

"Just after you were born." He picks at a loose thread on his shirt cuff, wrapping it around his finger until it snaps. "I was . . . eight and ten, I think? It was mostly by accident. Percy and I took a Grand Tour and got lost and then we both had our reasons for not wanting to go back. So we went on being lost."

"Do you ever wish you'd stayed?" I ask, hoping this might pivot naturally into a conversation that could lead to an excavation of our shared experiences, followed by familial bonding.

But instead, he answers bluntly and briefly. "Never."

"Oh. Um. All right then." I glance down at the list again.

"That was three."

I look up. "No it wasn't!"

"Face, leaving, regrets." He ticks them off on his fingers.

"The last one doesn't count," I protest.

"It was a question."

"It was a follow-up!" I say. "I was trying to make conversation!"

"I didn't agree to conversation. I agreed to answer three questions." He pushes his hat over his face and settles his hands across his stomach, the posture of a man about to take a nap.

I stand next to him for a moment, my eyes squeezed so tightly I can see stars. I wish I were a different man. I wish I were the sort to argue, to fight, to stand my ground and tell him off for being needlessly cruel. The sort of man who could pull his socks up, or better yet, the sort whose socks never slipped. Who was always well pressed and unruffled and sure of his own stride, and did not waste so much time with this endless self-contemplation. I wish I was any kind of man instead of the kind I am.

But I'm me, so I turn and start to walk away from him.

But then I hear Monty call, "Come back here."

I pause, one foot on the top step leading to the lower deck. "Why?"

He holds out a hand to me, hat still over his eyes, and

wiggles his fingers. "It's my turn."

"Your turn to what?"

"Ask you three questions. Give me your book."

I hesitate, mentally reviewing my list and trying to remember if there is anything on there that will lead to a conversation I don't want to have with him. Something I was ready to ask him but not yet ready to reveal myself. Unfair? Perhaps. It would be more unfair had he given me a clear answer to my one of my three questions. Or three questions, full stop.

He flexes his fingers again. "Come on, give it here."

Reluctantly, I surrender the book. Monty sits up, pushing his hat back and scanning the inside cover with his elbows resting upon his knees. "Let's see, let's see . . ." He flips the cover closed and looks up at me. "Is this trip a pretense to avoid something?"

"That's not on there."

"Yes it is, right here." He flashes the list at me so fast I couldn't possibly read any of it. "You're getting married. You're going to step into estate management and parliamentary duties. What a perfect time to chase the origins of a family heirloom halfway across the world. And what luck, there's also a mystery that goes with it." He spins the book flat between his palms. "Is that it? Is it adulthood in general that you're avoiding or maybe Parliament specifically? Are you allergic to banal conversation? Does the idea of endless hours of political debates not thrill you? I've heard it's better than sex."

"It does, actually," I say, then amend. "Thrill me. Parliament, I mean. Not the . . . sex is also good."

He raises an eyebrow. "Are you . . ." I am so certain he is about to say a virgin that I nearly whimper aloud, and he must know it, for he lets the silence go on far longer than necessary before he finishes, with a small smirk, "political?"

Thank God. "Not overly."

Monty flips the book around so he can see the spine. "Fielding's quite a liberal writer. Are you a radical?"

"I think you've exhausted your three questions."

"This will be my last, then."

I consider leaving. Let him keep the book and I'll go back to my cabin and not come out for the rest of this voyage and never try to speak to him again. Though it's nothing particularly sensitive we're discussing—he's worked so hard to remove himself from our family circles that there's no chance he'd leak my political alliances to anyone to whom they'd be relevant. It's more that any conversation about myself makes me feel like a skinned orange, the only shield between myself and the world stripped back by sharp nails until I can be halved and squeezed.

"I wouldn't say a radical," I reply. "But neither is Henry Fielding. I don't think calling for a country's

166

poorest citizens to be treated with basic human dignity is a radical notion."

"Many would disagree. Particularly the men who benefit from that lack of human dignity granted to the poor. Like your father." He thumbs the book, skipping to the end to check the page count. "Good God, this is so long." He flips *Tom Jones* around and wedges it under his head for a pillow. "What will your cause be in Parliament? Or do you intend to spend your tenure sitting quietly in the back reading erotic novels? Because if so, might I recommend some excellent leaflets with very open ideas about the gender of a bedfellow. And much shorter than this brick."

"Father is very involved in the expansion of the workhouse system."

"I didn't ask what your father's cause is."

I pause and realize biting back my real opinions has become a reflex more than a choice. "A reconstruction of the workhouse system," I reply.

He pushes himself up on his elbows and studies me. One eyebrow is split by the scars, so it looks perpetually cocked. "Go on."

And why not? Why not tell someone who isn't Louisa what I really think, for the first time in my goddamn life?

"Father is a patron of several," I reply. "One in particular in London—the Saint James Workhouse. He's raised loads of money for it and touted it as some enormous charitable accomplishment, but it's hellish. The way they treat their residents is horrifying—and he knows it. He just doesn't care, because supporting it makes him look charitable, and because he's given a portion of the occupancy taxes."

Father took me to see it before it was occupied, and even then it felt haunted, like a place about to be destroyed, not one meant for habitation. I went back a second time with Louisa and Edward and several men in his party—not under falsified pretenses, per se, but also not entirely truthful ones either. Edward told them we were parishioners come to give service on advice of our bishop, and we were practically dragged inside. The eight wards that had been empty when I walked through with Father were packed so full there weren't enough beds for the workers, nor truly enough room for all the beds they had managed to squash in. The food was so stale it was inedible, and the few provisions magistrates were required to provide their residents with—soap, candles, and a set of clothes—looked as though they had lived at least a dozen lives before being handed out and fought over. There was sewage on the floor, children screaming for mothers who had died in the night, gray-faced men missing fingers trying to lift hammers to break stones. Flies hovered in thick, fetid swarms. On our walk back to Mayfield, Edward bought Lou and me each a copy of

Henry Fielding's "A Proposal for Making an Effectual Provision for the Poor" from a Grub Street printer, and even his sentiments had felt too meek in places.

"You can't see people treated that way and then sit by and do nothing," I finish.

"And yet so many men do," Monty replies. "That's a bold stand to take against your father's work. What does he think of you burning his legacy of charity to the ground?"

"The workhouse system doesn't give a fig about charity," I reply hotly, then add, "He doesn't know."

"Oh, defiance!" Monty claps his hands together in delight. "I love it. When will you spring the news on him?"

"Hopefully never."

"That's disappointing. I was hoping you'd have him rolling in his grave before he was even in it. What's the good of ideas if you don't share them?"

"I do share them," I say. "I write political pamphlets."

"Do you really?" He loops his arms around his knees and leans toward me and oh my God, are we having an actual real conversation about ourselves? Did my list actually work? I hate it—I had meant for this to be about him, not me—But. We. Are. Actually. Talking. I bite back a grin, afraid I'll break the spell. "I hope they're horrifyingly liberal. Are they under your own name?"

"God no," I say. "I have a pseudonym."

"Have I heard of you? Dear Lord." He clutches *Tom Jones* to his chest. "Are *you* Henry Fielding? Should I have you inscribe this?"

I snatch the book back. "They're daft. Just silliness, really. Something to do until I take my seat. I'm not a real writer." He goes on staring at me, waiting for an answer. I swallow.

"I write as John Everyman."

His teasing smile falters. "You're joking."

"It's daft, I know, I came up with it on a whim—"

"Adrian!" He punches me lightly in the arm, and I realize with a jolt that he knows them. I can't decide whether that makes me proud or panicked. "You *are* famous. Sod Henry Fielding."

"I'm not," I mumble.

"Someone threw one of those pamphlets at Percy when he was walking through Hyde Park a few weeks ago and he brought it home."

"Did you read it?" I ask, trying not to sound as horrified as I feel.

"Yes! Well." He scrunches up his face. "Percy did, and gave me a very thorough summary. I'm not much for reading."

"It was two and a half pages."

"God. Liberal political pamphlets." He looks me up and down with that same sly smile as before, but this time, it feels like I'm in on the joke. "I didn't think you'd be a hellion." He leans backward against the hatch, letting his hat fall over his face once more. "Careful," he says from beneath it, "or I might start liking you after all."

Rabat

10

The journey to Morocco seems to be going well, I say, as a passenger with no understanding of seafaring. But the skies stay blue and the wind at our backs as we push south. It doesn't take a trained sailor to assume those are positives.

But the mood among the crew shifts in the opposite direction, like we've crossed an invisible demarcation. One morning twelve days into our voyage, I emerge from my cabin to find that same blue sky and gentle breeze, but the sailors gathered around the main mast. The salt smell that always thickens the air is smothered by an herbal haze, and I realize one of the sailors is carving a symbol into the wood of the mast with a poker, the end glowing red. When it cools, he shoves it into the brazier burning at his feet, smoke spewing up in a column and trailing behind the ship like a pennant.

Monty is leaning against the banister of the stairs leading to the upper deck, watching this strange ritual with a mug pressed against his chin. I'm not sure whether he looks amused by the sailors or his face simply rests in disdain.

He barely glances at me as I approach, but when I sit on the bottom step with my own coffee balanced on my knee, he asks, "You're not hiding that book somewhere, are you? I haven't thought of a favorite color yet."

"It's too big to properly hide."

"Ha! See?" He nudges my shin with his toe. I try to take this as a gesture of affection and not be repulsed by his bare feet in such close proximity to me. "Even you admit eight hundred pages is longer than a book has any business being."

"What are they doing?" I ask. In spite of our conversation, neither of us has looked away from the men gathered around the mast. The poker has been withdrawn again, its end now white-hot, and the smell of burning charcoal fills my lungs as the man sets in again.

"Being superstitious," Monty replies, taking a sip of his coffee. "Sailors are always looking for ways to shield themselves against the dangers of their profession."

"How is that a shield?"

"They're burning a stave—it's a rune from somewhere up north. It's meant to be protection."

"Protection from what?"

Monty shrugs. "The charms are never very specific. Makes it easier to explain why they fail to ward away anything." He takes another drink. "Well, that's disgustingly cold." He pushes himself straight, then leaves me without another word.

I sit alone and watch the sailors until they finish. They leave behind an eight-armed cross, veins and spikes carved from its center that then jut into more lines. It looks like a snowflake caught on a mitten and held close to the eye the moment before it melts.

Some of the men touch it every time they pass. Others leave small offerings at the base of the mast throughout the day—tobacco and ivory dice and cannikins of grog. One man even pulls out his boot laces and wraps them around the stave. I don't ask what dangerous land we crossed into that morning. I don't need something else—imagined or not—to fear.

As we draw closer to the Barbary Coast, the weather warms until it's pleasant enough to be on deck without a coat. Over the rail, I catch glimpses of the silky backs of porpoises as they surface amid the waves. Sometimes pods follow the ship for miles, laughing and chattering as they chase us across the world. At night, the moon on the clouds makes rainbows of the darkness, and the stars clutter the sky, their light enough to keep me sleepless.

Whatever dangers the sailors meant to ward away with their etched stave, it must prove effective, for we dock in Rabat late in the night two weeks and three days after our departure. Monty and I go straight from the ship to a seaside inn. We take a day of recovery, most of which I spend trying to remind my body what it's like to stand on ground that isn't pitching, and the next morning meet first thing in the dining room before we make our way into the city to find our sister—I'm too anxious to eat, so I tell Monty I finished my meal before he came in hopes he won't nag me about it. I keep having uninvited thoughts about unfamiliar food, and although I know there is nothing wrong with what I'm offered, my brain refuses to be argued with.

"So we aren't actually going into Rabat itself," Monty says as we leave the inn and start to walk to the north. "About a mile from here, the Bou Regreg River drains into the Atlantic, and on the other side is a city called Salé—well, it used to be a city. Now it's a part of Rabat. But it operates as an independent port."

A school of cobalt-blue fishing boats is moored along the dock, their sides clacking together as the waves rock them. "Why are we going there?" I ask.

"Because that," Monty replies, "is where the pirates live."

We hire a rowboat to take us across the river, and from the water, I watch the sand-colored garrison that dominates the opposite coast draw closer. The walls rest on the edge of the sea, their foundations nearly hanging over the Atlantic. The city itself climbs the hills above it, the silhouettes of minarets and domes and whitewashed stone houses peeking over the walls. Cannons poke out between the ramparts, each of them a slightly different style and bearing a unique crest. Green flags emblazoned with a split scimitar snap in the wind off the water.

"Is the whole city made up of corsairs?" I ask in English.

"Mostly." Monty says, grabbing the side of the boat to steady himself as we strike an errant wave. "Some more active in the business than others, and some who only handle the bits of piracy that happen on land. When the Spanish exiled all the Muslims, a lot of them came here, and more than a few wanted revenge on the Spanish, so they started raiding galleons with the support of the Moroccan crown."

"Why would the crown support piracy?" I ask.

"Because the king gets ten percent of their take. And he's descended from exiled Muslims, so he also hates the Spanish. Who doesn't, really?" The sun strikes the water, turning it to a diamond field stretching between us and the shore. I shield my eyes. "Now they'll raid any ship in their waters, Spanish or not, and more outside pirate fleets moved in because they knew they'd be protected."

"So it's a pirate republic?" I ask. In spite of how morally opposed I am to piracy, the concept itself is fascinating.

"More or less," Monty replies. "Though I have a sense your definition of *republic* is more technical than mine."

"Is that what the sailors were hoping to ward against?" I ask. "Pirates?"

But Monty laughs. "They'd need a hell of a lot more than a few staves to keep them away."

As we approach the dock, a man on the shore throws our boatman a rope, and he catches it with an arm covered in black-inked illustrations. Monty catches me staring and clicks his tongue until I tear my gaze away. "Remember," he says quietly. "Everything here is stolen, and everyone is armed, so try not to stare."

We enter the city through a stone archway covered in ornate carvings. The buildings lining the street are washed in white or the same blue as the sea, the paint cracking in places to reveal the peach terracotta beneath. Monty assures me he knows where he's going, leaving me nothing to do but follow him and marvel at the palm trees with their wide fronds and hairy trunks, which I have never seen growing outside the royal conservatory. Without him as my guide, I would not only be lost, but likely stupefied. The smells alone are overpowering— sand and incense and mules and goats tied up outside blue-doored houses, spices tossed in bright clouds across mutton turning over open fires. Even the smoke smells different, flames devouring wood that doesn't grow in England. I've never been to a city that didn't reek of sewage and soot, nor one where the predominant color wasn't gray. I wish Lou were here to see it all with me— she loves London in all its filthy glory. A place like this would charm her to bits. I allow myself to entertain a brief fantasy of bringing her here someday, walking these streets hand in hand and showing her the spots I already knew. I would be confident and lead the way, and I'd know the best foods, and wouldn't worry they would make me sick. I'd take her to lookouts and galleries without questioning my own taste, and I would not apologize if we grew lost or feel guilty if every schedule we made was not followed to the minute. Perhaps we'd travel without a schedule at all.

All obviously impossible, because that version of me will only ever exist in my own imagination.

As Monty leads me through the narrow brick walkways climbing at impossible angles, we are more than once forced to stop to let donkeys with wide panniers on their backs pass us. "So it's a bit of an unorthodox living situation that our Veronica is in," Monty tells me, his words punctuated by gasps. We're both out of breath from the climb.

"I thought she was called Felicity."

"She is, but now we're calling her Veronica." He swats a fly off his forehead. "Her life is unnecessarily complicated."

If only we'd had weeks alone on a boat with nothing for

you to do but explain this before we docked, I think. "Is she part of one of the pirate fleets here?"

"She is indeed. They're called the Crown and Cleaver."

"Are they dangerous?"

"No, they're actually known as the cuddliest fleet in the Mediterranean."

I consider crossing my arms petulantly, but their momentum may be the only thing carrying me up this hill. "You're mocking me, aren't you?"

"I am," he replies solemnly. "So Ronnie fell in with the daughter of the commodore when we were younger—"

"What does the commodore do?" I ask.

"Oversees the affairs of the entire fleet. There are governors in each port city who are more involved with local business, and they report to the commodore, who is usually at sea or in their court city. The Crown and Cleaver are mainly based in Algiers, but they have a significant presence here." He points with two fingers to one of the towers that jut up from the city walls.

"Are they the official ruling government?" I ask. "Or more like the gangs of London?"

"More formal than the gangs—every fleet has accords and contracts all their sailors sign, which are enforceable under the law. The London gangs can only dream of being as organized as the Berber pirates." He swats at another fly and nearly smacks me in the face. "So Felicity—"

"Wait, that *is* her name?"

"Yes, please keep up. Felicity is quite chummy with this fleet and they let her do things with natural philosophy in their waters. She used to live in Amsterdam but then came back here to focus more fully on her research and—hold on." He pauses to catch his breath. The street is quiet, but I can hear the call to prayer from a nearby mosque echoing over the rooftops. "The point is," he says after a moment, "last I heard, she was based out of Salé, and even if she's at sea or changed locations, the Crown and Cleaver can direct us from here."

"And once we find Felicity—"

"Veronica."

"—she'll have a ship for us to take to Portugal?"

"Yes." Monty nods once, then adds, "Hopefully."

"What—" I start, but he's already walking again, and I have to jog to catch up. All of this would have been so helpful to know in advance. I berate myself for not asking, though even my arsehole brain acknowledges there is no way I could have possibly anticipated adding *Is my sister allied with an African pirate duchy and how much pirate interaction will this trip include?* to my list.

Monty considers a fork in the path for a moment, then settles upon the right. "So that's the situation. Any questions?"

"Are they a democracy?"

He stops walking so suddenly I step on the back of his shoe. "What?"

"The pirate fleet. Is it a democracy? Or, democratic monarchy, if they have a commodore, I suppose. Or is each territory self-governing? Like a city-state." When he doesn't answer, I add, "Do you know anything about the wealth distribution, or their welfare system?"

He stares at me, then shakes his head and keeps walking. "You're so strange."

In spite of the temperate weather, I've sweated through the back of my shirt by the time we cross the medina toward the palatial compound that dominates the city center. The narrow paths are crowded with stalls, chickens wandering between them, occasionally startling with a squawk and aborted attempt at flight. Men with long beards sit on unmarked barrels, drinking black coffee in the shade of the mosque that adjoins the square. As we pass, I peer at a few of the stalls. The goods laid out encompass every conceivable area of commerce—textiles and firearms and whittled flutes and sacks of loose tea leaves on ornate carpets. Gourds strung along the walkways make hollow music against each other whenever brushed. A woman with her face covered is collecting golden oil from a roughhewn stone press. A few vendors, without customers to occupy them, shout prices at us as we pass. One man selling an astonishing variety of seeds, nuts, and dried fruit from baskets so large I could comfortably curl up in any of them starts chattering at me in a language I don't understand. I feel rude ignoring him, so I give a little wave, but Monty slaps my hand out of the air. "Don't do that," he says. "Remember, pirates. Stolen."

"They're dates."

"Pirate dates."

I resist the urge to roll my eyes. It's hard to work out just how dangerous and piratical this city actually is when Monty seems prone to theatrics, but I don't have enough actual knowledge to judge for myself.

On the other side of the market, we enter the palace through a series of narrow hallways. The passage opens into a breezy courtyard, lined with vaulted colonnades and domed by intricately carved ceilings. The pillars look like soft taffy twisted by children's hands, and the walls are tiled in green and gold. In the center, a fountain burbles pleasantly, and potted ferns tumble from the upper balconies.

On the opposite side of the courtyard, two men with cutlasses guard a doorway, and though my instinct upon seeing armed soldiers with biceps the circumference of my waist is to go the opposite direction, Monty walks straight up to them with a smile. "Hello, gents."

If he expected them to recognize him, he must be sorely disappointed.

The taller of the two men says something in a language I don't understand—couldn't even identify, but assume it's the same as what's written on the city walls—and

Monty answers him in French. "We are friends of the Crown and Cleaver. We're looking for Felicity Montague."

The guards don't move. Neither does Monty. Even his smile doesn't slip. I glance at him, trying to work out what silent standoff is playing out.

The taller guard finally speaks, first in his language, then in French. "Your ink."

"Yes, I've got it," Monty replies, too loudly.

"I need to see it."

Monty squints at him. "Do you, though?"

"Does he need a passport?" I hiss to Monty in English. It's the only relevant ink I can think of.

The guard laughs, and I have a sense he understands me, though he continues in French. "You can show me now, or I can carve our crest into your corpses."

My heartbeat skips, and I immediately reevaluate just how dangerous this beautiful city is. "Monty—"

"It's fine," he interrupts, though he's still looking at the guard.

"What does he need? Just give it to him!" I'm ready to turn and run should either of these guards even look as though they're contemplating drawing their cutlasses. What is my sister mixed up in that the first level of access involves armed men throwing around threats about disfiguring our murdered bodies? Why didn't I ask more questions on the walk here? Though even knowing pirates were involved, *How many cutlasses will there be?*

186

would never have occurred to me. It also never occurred to me, I realize, to ask Monty for any sort of identification that he is in actuality my brother—suddenly I have a vision of an elaborate con involving leading an unsuspecting English nobleman to a foreign country under false pretenses, then robbing him blind, holding him for ransom, and eventually slitting his throat, all because he was lonely for a family.

It could happen.

The second guard is staring at me now, and I realize how fast I'm breathing, and how little air seems to be getting into my lungs. I'm working myself up again with nothing but my own fictions. *God, Adrian, pull yourself together.*

Monty glances at me as well, and I must be more obviously falling apart than I thought, for he turns to the guards and says, "All right, yes, fine, here's my ink."

To my astonishment—more accurately, horror—my brother then turns his back to the enormous men with very sharp swords and drops his trousers. It's so presentational and deliberate I'm not sure whether I should look or not. Both guards certainly do. Though less at his buttocks and more at the blue symbol inked there, a crown overtop a blade.

"Finished?" Monty asks without turning around.

"A moment." Monty has his back to the men and no way of seeing that the guards are no longer staring at his ass and have simply left him peacocking while they laugh behind their hands.

He finally glances over his shoulder, realizes he's being made the fool, and straightens, pulling his trousers up. "For God's sake."

The guards are still laughing, but one of them manages to get out, "Who is it you said you're looking for?"

"Felicity Montague. She's under the protection of your commodore. Last we heard, she was living here."

The guards confer for a moment, then instruct us to stay where we are while one of them disappears through the door.

Monty catches me staring at him as he pulls up his trousers. "Shut up."

"I didn't say anything."

"I was nineteen, all right?" he says. His neck has gone red. "It seemed funny at the time."

"I'm nineteen, and I don't think it's funny."

"Yes, well, some of us use bawdy humor as a way of coping with our emotional turmoil."

He's still struggling with his buttons when the guard reappears, now with two more men and three women flanking him, all outfitted in similar liveries. It doesn't look like a welcoming committee—more like a militia. I take a step back without meaning to.

Monty frowns. "What's going on?"

The tall guard says something in their language, and

points between us. Before I understand what's happening, one of the men has grabbed my arms and twisted them behind my back with such force it steals my breath. I try to pull away, but he hooks a foot around my knees and yanks them out from under me. I slam into the ground, my chin striking the mosaic stone. Another guard has a hold of Monty, who is trying to both finish doing up his trousers and resist capture, two activities that are fundamentally incompatible. I lose sight of him as the man holding me grabs my neck, pushing my face into the ground, and another forces a beam over my shoulders. There's a concave to fit over my neck, and manacles on the ends that they clamp my hands into, and dear God, what sort of medieval nightmare have I fallen into where men with cutlasses chain me to a pillory? They're going to execute us. They're chaining us to blocks to chop our heads off.

Monty is being outfitted with a similar torture device, and he's forced to surrender his grip on his trousers as his arms are forced into the manacles. They drop around his ankles. He's putting up a good protest, both louder and peppered with more curse words than I would have the gumption to use to guards with muscles this large and sabers this sharp, particularly while less trousers. "Montague!" he keeps shouting. "Felicity Montague! I know you know us! I've got the goddamn ink—why else did I show you my ass?"

"Monty—" is all I manage before one of the women grabs the beam I'm chained to and hauls me back to my feet. My arms are pinned in place parallel with my head, and the angle makes the muscles in my shoulders burn. The guards search us roughly for weapons—from Monty, they take a small knife, a pipe and tobacco case, a used handkerchief, and half a biscuit of hardtack. "Don't throw that away," he says as one of the men sniffs at it. I am relieved of my passport and documentation, money, and, most importantly, the spyglass. The guards pass it around curiously before one of them stows it with the rest of our possessions.

We are then pushed forward down the passage the guards came from. The light is poor—only a few unshaded candles stuck into iron sconces dot the walls. The stone is washed white, and painted all over with the same unfamiliar language that's in the streets.

I try to go as cooperatively as possible—perhaps, instead of being executed, I could be a prisoner for life, that would be preferable—maybe—I have no idea, having never considered that particular devil's bargain. Behind me, Monty's progress is impeded by his trousers, which are still around his ankles.

The hallway opens onto a balcony overlooking an octagonal room, closed off and steamy. It's framed with the same arches as the courtyard we came from, these tiled in deep sapphire and each with a lamp dangling from its center, their colorful glass panes angled to cast light all around them. The walls are tiled too, intricate tessellating patterns speckled with condensation. Fountains are built into the walls at either end of the room, draining into tiled tubs built into the floor. Steam rises from the long slats between them. In the center of the room is a raised stone platform, surrounded by a small moat of crystal-clear water. The stone looks lustrous, like it's been polished for the last thousand years.

The guards lead us down to the main floor. The steam envelops us, leaving me feeling hot and dewy almost at once.

My clothes stick to me in a way that makes me too aware of their seams and the shape of my body on display. As we walk the narrow aisles between the baths, the women soaking there peer up at us curiously. Most of them seem unbothered by the presence of men among them, though I realize that aside from the guards escorting us, all the sentries around the perimeter are women, their hair covered and twin swords at their waists.

One of the guards stops before the stone dais and extends a hand to the woman reclining upon it. Steam curls around her limbs and pearls on her skin. She ignores his hand, and instead slides to the edge of the stone and sits up. She's completely naked, and I look away, blushing, though she seems unbothered by it. One of the guards hands her a cloth to dry off, and I hazard a glance, only to find that she has simply tossed it over her shoulder. I try to look without looking. Her skin is olive, and her dark hair cascades down her back, its ends spattered with what looks like clay. She has wide hips and a soft belly, and her skin is flawless. She looks like a Venus carved from stone and leafed in copper.

Monty and I are both shoved to our knees before her as she takes up a long-stemmed copper pot and pours a stream of golden oil into her hands. It drips between her fingers like honey and runs down her legs and into the water. We are forced to crane our necks at a cramping angle to see her, though I'm still not sure where to look. She's so comfortably disrobed that it makes me somehow more uncomfortable with it. Monty has lost his trousers somewhere along the hallway, and the tail of his shirt barely covers his most vulnerable bits.

As the woman begins to slick the oil up and down her arms and shoulders, the guard who searched us drops the contents of our pockets on the stone beside her. She doesn't look at them, but continues to massage her skin as the guard speaks to her in their language, presumably giving an account of how we came to be kneeling and chained and trouserless before her. When she pulls back her hair, I notice the same symbol Monty has on the back of her neck.

Something the guard says makes her cock her head, and she holds a hand to halt him, then turns her glittering eyes to Monty. "You're one of the Hoffmans," she says in French.

"I'm not *a* Hoffman," Monty replies. "I work for them. I run their shipping office in London. Who are *you*?"

"Basira Khan," she replies. "I am the Crown and Cleaver's governor of Rabat."

"Congratulations," Monty replies. "Now please release us. I showed your soldiers my ink—we have an alliance with the Crown and Cleaver. We're looking for Felicity Montague—"

Basira spits on the ground and Monty and I both jump. "That whore," she hisses.

Monty looks taken aback. "Well, that's . . . new."

"That traitor." Basira snatches a billowing kaftan offered by a servant girl and pulls it over her head. "If I see her in our territory again, I'll cut her throat myself."

"Are we talking about the same Felicity?" Monty asks weakly.

Basira flips her hair from the neck of her caftan and stands, beckoning another servant girl over to her with a teapot. "And the throats of any of the men she sends into our territory."

"To be clear, she did not *send* us," Monty says. "We came looking."

"Well, you will not find her here. She broke the accords set out when she was welcomed into this court."

Basira takes a delicate gold cup from the tray offered her and raises it to her lips, but pauses to add derisively, "I never wanted her here—her or that other European girl. All white women are the same. They think they're oppressed by you men so they look for somewhere else to be queen. And now there's you—more white men with Felicity Montague."

"We're not *with* her!" Monty says. "We came here trying to find her, not carry on whatever traitorous whorishness she has committed."

Basira stares at us, eyes narrowing, then sets down her tea and says, "Felicity Montague is gone."

"Gone, as in . . ." Monty looks as though he isn't sure he wants the answer. "Is she dead?"

"Gone, as in banished," Basira replies. "She was put on trial, and the governors of the Crown and Cleaver voted to have her marooned by Commodore Aldajah for her crimes. Crimes her allies will answer for as well."

"Look here." Monty tries to stand, overbalances with the additional weight of the board strapped to his shoulders, and tips, catching himself on one knee like he's proposing marriage. The tails of his shirt ride up perilously high. "Obviously there's been some mistake."

Basira makes a show of turning away from him, clearly not listening, and starts going through our things with what feels like a deliberate invasiveness—she licks her fingers as she turns the pages of my travel documents, then sticks Monty's pipe between her teeth.

"First, that's a personal item," Monty says, unable to quash the indignation in his voice as she chews the stem. "Second, I didn't know about the whorish Felicity Montague doing crimes and being marooned, or we never would have come. We are trying to find her—and now we know she isn't here, so you can let us go." Basira presses her fingernail into the black tobacco in Monty's case, then raises it to her nose and inhales. Monty grinds his teeth. "Is Sim here? Let me speak with her—she knows me. We'll get this sorted."

"The commodore is at sea," Basira replies, testing Monty's half-eaten biscuit on her tongue. "Protecting us from the enemies Miss Felicity Montague welcomed into our waters."

"What article of your accords did she break?" I ask. I ask. Basira and Monty—as best he can with the manacles—look at me in surprise. Basira may have thought me mute. Monty might have forgotten I was here at all. I swallow, steeling my courage so my voice comes out as more than a whisp. "Your fleet operates under a set of predetermined laws that all the sailors agree to abide by. I'm assuming that, in return, the accords assure them some basic rights."

Basira drops Monty's pipe back onto the pile of our possessions. "Yes. What of it?"

"To have a fleet your size, I assume your code includes

some sort of clause about the right to a fair trial—particularly since you mentioned Felicity sitting before your governors to be judged. Or something to protect your sailors from a demagogue or tyrannical captain targeting them for unfair punishment."

Basira folds her arms. It may just be the angle of her tipped-up chin, but her smirk suddenly looks more like a smile. "What's your question?"

"Not a question," I say quickly. "Rather a request that you abide by your own code. Monty is a member of your fleet. Or, at least he has the ink. Which means he signed these accords as well, which means that he is entitled to a fair trial for entering your court unwelcome, during which he can present his facts and receive a judgment voted upon by more than one woman. Do you have a copy of the fleet contract we can review?"

I don't know if any of this is true—I'm cobbling together the scant details Monty offered, plus what Basira has said about Felicity, then doing my best to channel these facts through an impression of Edward Davies—speak with authority and charm in equal measure. I've met enough members of the peerage to know that, even if you don't know exactly what you're talking about, a few official-sounding vagaries and a confident tone often more than does the trick.

"Are you his solicitor?" she asks, and I shake my head. "And yet you know so much about our laws."

"No," I say. "But I'm familiar with governmental structure. Yours seems to be a constitutional monarchy, with your commodore standing in for the king, though without total veto powers. The success of such a regime requires a preordained series of guidelines for your citizens to follow. Without some kind of constitution or declaration of rights, you have anarchy. Your operation seems far too well organized for that." There is, of course, likely a good deal of corruption. No government is without that rot. But now doesn't seem the time to mention it.

"You want to be put on trial?" she asks.

"Yes," I say, with more confidence than I feel. "So long as we are given a chance to plead our case and judged fairly on our own situation."

Basira considers this for a moment, then points a finger at me. Her skin glitters with oil. "But *you're* not a member of the fleet. You never signed our accords. Or else you'd know there's a provision warning sailors against bringing strangers aboard our ships without permission from the captain."

"We're not on board your ship," I reply, trying to sound calmer than I feel. *Be Edward!* God, if I survive this, Parliament will be easy. "We are visitors to the city of Salé, which, as I understand it, is home to many pirate fleets. If you hold us in particular contempt, we would like to face the same assembly that sentenced Felicity

Montague for judgment. Clearly their ruling was fair, as she broke the laws and was banished." I really would prefer not to sit in prison for months to then be put on trial before some sort of pirate council, but I'm hoping Basira also won't want to go to all that effort for two blokes with one set of trousers between them and will let us go. Having to assemble any governing body is often more trouble than it's worth. Particularly if some of them are pirates at sea.

Basira laughs. "No, you're not a solicitor." She picks up my papers from the pile of our things, skimming them like she might find confirmation there. "You're a politician." She doesn't sound quite as authoritarian as she did before—instead, she seems amused. I will take amused. I am happy to be amusing if it gets us out of here alive. "Felicity Montague could be a politician too. She loved to talk until she stopped making sense. So many words for a woman with so little to say. You would think she . . ." She trails off suddenly, staring at the spyglass she uncovered when she picked up my documents. She drops my passport—straight into a puddle of water, and I debate momentarily whether I should say something—and reaches for the spyglass.

"Why do you have this?" She holds it up to the light with the sort of reverence usually reserved for religious relics.

"It was my mother's," I say. "She gave it to me."

"Who is your mother?"

"Caroline Braitwaithe Montague."

"Is she a treasure hunter?"

I glance at Monty as best I can. "Not that I'm aware of."

"A pirate, then." She tests the weight of the spyglass in her hand, then flicks the lenses open and holds them to her eye. "She was a thief, at least."

"I don't think so," I reply.

Basira lowers the spyglass and points it at me. "If not by thieving," she says, "how did she come by the spyglass belonging to the captain of the *Flying Dutchman*?"

11

Basira looks disappointed when I don't faint or scream or expire at her pronouncement. A flag goes up in my mind, some memory too distant to see clearly, but the name inspires nothing else. Monty looks equally at sea.

Basira lets out an exasperated sigh at our ignorance. "Isn't that what you call it in English? Or is it *de Vliegende Hollander* in your stories as well?"

Vliegende Hollander. The museum, I realize suddenly. That's where I saw it. The vanitas Buddle had shown us in the book had been called the vanitas of the *Vliegende Hollander.* The vanitas—the death painting—with our spyglass in it. I didn't think to ask the meaning of the title. I didn't know it would matter.

"You really don't know the story?" Basira asks, looking between us. Monty gives a noncommittal grunt, but I shake my head. "The *Flying Dutchman* is a ghost ship cursed to sail the seas for eternity, ferrying the souls of dead and drowned sailors from this life to the next. To see the *Dutchman* is a sign."

"A sign of what?" I ask.

"Death," Basira replies. "The *Dutchman* only appears to take you with her. Fathoms below." She looks down at the spyglass, running her thumb along the words carved there, and the letters spell out the rest of the name in my mind.

"How do you know that's from the *Flying Dutchman*?" Monty asks.

"It's engraved on the side," I say quietly.

Monty scoffs. "Anyone could have done that. Anyone can label anything. I could get *Flying Dutchman* tattooed on my ass; doesn't mean I'm also its property."

"Your ass is getting rather crowded." Basira runs her finger along the lens, pausing at the sharp cracked edge, then examining her finger as if looking for blood. "The *Dutchman* was an ordinary ship once, before the captain made a bargain with the devil. Now, it's a cursed vessel that carries only ghosts." She sets the spyglass onto the dais beside her, and perhaps it's my imagination, but I swear the droplets of water collected on the stone skitter away from it, as though repelled. "Nothing taken from the Dutchman would come without a price. Perhaps one paid by the thief. Perhaps by her children."

Basira stares at the spyglass in a way that makes

me think I'm not the only one who saw the water dance away from it. "Did your mother die at sea?" she asks.

I shake my head.

"She was in a shipwreck. When she was rescued, she had that with her."

"Well then. She must have been a brave woman to rob the captain."

"I don't think she robbed anyone," I say.

"That does not mean she wasn't brave."

The words settle upon me like a fine down of snow and I twitch, trying to dispel the cold. I drop my gaze, unable to look at her any longer. I feel like I need to defend my mother—against what? A compliment? She wasn't a brave woman. Not remotely. She was pulled from the ocean with only this spyglass and never set foot near the sea again.

Until she drowned in it, alone on a seaside cliff in Scotland.

Before I can speak, Basira pulls her hair over her shoulder and wrings it out. It's so long that when she takes hold of the end, she can stretch her arm out straight without sacrificing her grip. "I will release you."

Monty lets out an audible sigh of relief and cranes his neck, searching the room for either the guards approaching to unshackle us or where he left his trousers.

But then Basira adds, "On a condition."

"We'll hear it first," I say.

She snorts. "You think you are in a position to make demands of *me*?"

"I know: it's very typically English of me."

To my surprise, she laughs, waggling a finger. "I like you." Her eyes glance off Monty, but she doesn't offer him the same praise. "Leave my court and return to England," she says, then adds, "And give me your spyglass."

"No," I say at the exact moment Monty says, far too gratefully, "God, yes, take it."

"Why do you want it?" I say, fighting to keep my voice even. Be Edward. Be a politician. Never show your hand.

But she's keeping her cards equally close to her chest. "If you think the *Dutchman* is just a story, then all you have is a family heirloom. Leave it with me as a show of your loyalty to my fleet and how sorry you are for your associations with Felicity Montague."

"No."

"Adrian," Monty says quietly. I have a sense that, were we not incapacitated, he would kick me. I don't look at him.

Basira arches an eyebrow. "No?"

"That spyglass is mine," I say. "And I owe your fleet nothing. I have no loyalty to you or your company. From my perspective, all that has happened here today was that I came to find my sister, was assaulted, robbed, and imprisoned by strangers, and then extorted into giving up the last possession I have of my dead mother's."

"It's not fair, is it?" She bends over, hands on her knees so she's peering into my face. When I meet her eyes, she gives me a wide smile like one a nanny might give a child after teaching them an important lesson about growing up.

"If you truly value loyalty," I say, my tone quavering, "then you'll respect the loyalty I have to my family. And my mother, and what she left behind for me. I'm not going to leave it with you, no matter where it came from. It was hers—now it's mine, but it was . . . it was hers! You can't take it from me! I realize that's almost the literal definition of piracy but—"

"Adrian," Monty says again, and I realize I'm growing agitated. My face is hot, and I'm suddenly aware of the manacle over my neck as the cage that it is. I fight the urge to thrash it off.

It's just a spyglass. It's just a trinket. It's not her, it's not your memory of her, it's just a spyglass. So why does the thought of being without it feel akin to being asked to leave a limb behind? I keep thinking of what my father said, that the spyglass had made my mother sicker. *I did not say that.* Had he? I can't remember now, but I can hear those words in his voice so clearly.

Basira straightens, watching me with what I assume must be disgust. But when she speaks, her tone is gentler.

"Don't lose your head. I won't take it." She snorts, like this was all a joke. Maybe it was until I started to burst apart at the seams. "I don't give a damn about your telescope and I don't have time to waste a cell on you. I want you gone. You will both be on the next passenger ship north—I'll personally make sure your names are added to the log, and my men will escort you. Where are you staying?" I can't remember, so Monty gives her the name of the lodging. Basira tosses back the sleeves of her kaftan, then says, "The seas are in enough disarray without any interference from the English. Leave Salé and stay away from the Crown and Cleaver. Do you agree?"

But what about my sister and our ship to Portugal? What about the *Flying Dutchman*? What about the fact that we came halfway around the world and I refuse to turn back without answers? What about this spyglass and my mother and my broken family scattered across the world, from a marooner's island to a lonely cliff in Scotland?

Before I can answer, Basira bends down so our faces are level. She puts her hands on my cheeks, and though I am generally averse to physical touch when it is both from a stranger and unexpected, I don't flinch. Her skin is dewy, and she smells of nuts and citrus, a warm summer aroma.

"Go home, little ghost," she says quietly, and I'm not sure if anyone but me can hear her. "You don't want to tangle with the *Dutchman*."

I hadn't been planning to. I only learned of this sto-rified ship a few minutes ago; the idea of pursuing it, or any reason why I might, had never entered my mind. But all I say is, "I'm not a ghost."

She smiles, stroking my temples with her index fin-gers. "There's something about you, though. Just like that spyglass. Something in you about to overflow." When her hands leave my face, I can still smell the oil from her palms. "You aren't enough to contain it."

Monty and I are escorted from the palace by Basira's guards and dumped onto the city streets, Monty still trouserless and me rattled and jumpy. I keep compul-sively reaching for the spyglass, once again in my pocket, certain I'm going to drop it or lose it without realizing. Sometimes, even with my fingers wrapped around it, I doubt it's there.

"Do you know what she was talking about?" I ask Monty before the guards are even out of sight. "The *Flying Dutchman*—what is that? What's the story? You knew what it was—I know you do! Do you know why she'd think our spyglass—"

"Adrian," Monty interrupts, but I have more I want to ask—it feels so urgent I have to press my teeth together to stop myself from talking. It's all rattling around my brain like dice about to be tossed, and if I don't give adequate attention to every strange notion—if I miss any of this, leave any stone unturned or question unasked—I'm sure the one that gets away will be the one I regret ignoring. That will be the winning hand I could have thrown.

Monty tugs down the tails of his shirt as a veiled woman passing by grabs her child by both his hands and drags him away from us. "Have you eaten today?" he asks me suddenly.

I wasn't expecting that. How can he think of anything other than the ghost ship and the spyglass? "I . . . probably."

"Hold out your hands."

I do, not sure what he's looking for, until I notice the tremor. I fist them quickly and shove them into my pockets. "I'm anxious."

"*You're* anxious? At least you've got your trousers." He holds up a hand to shield his face from the sun, scanning the medina street ahead of us. "Why don't you go find something to eat and I'll find clothes and we'll meet back here in half of an hour?"

"No!" I almost grab his arm, grasped by the sudden surety that he's using this as a ploy to abandon me. Even if it's not, I can't be alone right now. Particularly not in an unfamiliar place, and with a responsibility. I want to die at the thought of having to ask "What's that?" about every item beneath a bakery counter while the shopkeeper laughs behind his hands, then try and work out exchange rates and money while people queue up behind me, growing increasingly annoyed. "Please don't leave me alone," I say, trying not to cringe at how pathetic I sound.

Monty sighs and rubs a hand over the back of his neck and I realize he probably wants some time on his own because being around me is an exercise in patience and now he's even more annoyed than before and I should have just grown a goddamn backbone and got us something to eat, a task literal children are capable of. I almost apologize and tell him not to mind me, but then he tips his head down the street and says, "Come on then—trousers first."

We don't share a single language in common with the vendor who sells Monty a wide-legged pair of seaman's duds, but whether or not he understands the circumstances that led to it, he's still clearly amused by Monty's lack of trousers. And, I suspect, hikes the price considerably due to our necessity. Trousers secured, we buy cups of mint tea and flatbread and brochettes—spears of salted meat that are sold off the same grill as steamed sheep heads, which puts me off a smidge—and pastries shaped like horns that smell of orange and cinnamon.

We find a quiet street off the medina and crouch on the stoop of an abandoned shop front to eat. Above us, a palm tree sheds long strips of shredded fronds onto the street each time the wind shifts.

I'm trying to eat—I really am—but my stomach doesn't feel steady—and not just because of those beady sheep eyes in their severed heads. Monty discovers a hole in the crotch of his brand-new trousers, and I have to remind him three times that picking at it will only make it bigger before he gives up. "Bloody idiot," he mutters, and I'm not sure if he's talking about the shopkeeper or himself. Or perhaps me. Probably me.

He wipes his greasy hands on the tail of his shirt, then drains the rest of his tea. "So." He sets the mug on the ground between us. "Felicity is probably dead."

I glance over at him. He's got his elbows resting on his knees and he's staring hard at the opposite wall of the alley, trying to play it all off as dead casual, but the set of his jaw betrays him.

"That's not good," I say quietly.

"Not ideal, no."

"I'm sorry."

He massages his shoulder, wincing when he reaches the spot where the manacles rubbed. "It's disappointing, isn't it? You don't realize how much you like someone until they're marooned and left for dead."

I hesitate, not sure how much he does or doesn't want to linger on this subject. "What about Portugal?" I ask tentatively.

He looks sideways at me. "You are still so intent on finding this shipwreck?"

More now than ever, I want to say. Basira Khan had all but confirmed that something about that wreck could haunt a person. Perhaps their whole bloodline.

Monty shoos away a stray cat wandering toward us, its eyes fixed on my untouched brochette. "Weren't you just explicitly warned by a terrifying woman to go home?"

"She wasn't terrifying."

"Intimidating, then. She was intimidating."

"They're not the same thing."

"Definitely not. Though there's some overlap. Felicity is both intimidating and terrifying. Was. She was. God." He tears off a strip of his flatbread, staring down the still lingering cat as he eats it, like the eye contact might better convey how our food is very much not for it. "Are you really *still* going to make me go to goddamn Portugal?"

I slump backward against the wall, unsure if I'm more annoyed that he's being a prat or that I'm letting it get to me. "I didn't *make* you come here."

"No, you just got lucky I needed a holiday."

"You don't have to come to Portugal."

"But I assume you're still going."

I toss a piece of my brochette to the cat, who sniffs it carefully before turning its wide eyes to me as if to say, *I'd prefer chicken.* "I can take care of myself."

Monty reaches over and slides the next piece of meat off my skewer. "Course you can. You should have given it to her."

"The spyglass? She said it didn't matter."

"That was absolutely a lie. She changed course because you looked as though you would set someone on fire if they tried to take it from you. Possibly yourself."

God. Had it been that obvious? Shame soaks into me like a stain. "I'm sorry."

Monty shrugs, helping himself to another piece of meat. "It worked."

"I thought she was testing us." I pass him the rest of the skewer, then hold out my hand for the cat to lick my fingers. "If I'd told her I loved my shoes, she would have asked for them." Suddenly the weight of the spyglass in my pocket feels so heavy and obvious that everyone who passes by must be staring at me and this treasure hidden in my coat. "Do you think it's valuable?"

"Against my better judgment, I think it's . . ." He pauses, chewing. I think he might take another bite to buy himself more time, but then he says, "The Crown and Cleaver doesn't waste time. If Basira Khan wants it, there's a reason. I just can't for the bleeding life of me think of what it might be, and I'm concerned that by the time we work it out, it'll be too late."

We sit in silence for a while. A few more cats wander over and similarly turn their noses up at my offering. One gets close enough to lick the inside of Monty's empty mug before he urges it away with his foot. Every inch of my skin feels irritated, like I've been hit by a gust of sandy wind. I scratch my neck, then my arm, then rub my palms against both my thighs, resisting the urge to dig my nails in.

"Stop that," Monty says suddenly.

"Stop what?"

"Trying to rip your own skin off. You're making me nervous."

"Sorry." My tea is mostly cold by now, but I clamp my hands around it anyway and curl over it, like I'm huddling for warmth. "Did Mr. Buddle show you the painting when you saw him at the museum?" I ask Monty. "The vanitas?"

It takes him a moment to find the memory. "Oh. Yes. I forgot about that."

"I think the title was something about the *Flying Dutchman*."

Monty frowns down at the cat rubbing against his shin. "Are you certain?"

"You think I'd lie?"

"No, but I think you might . . ." He hesitates, reaches for his tea, then remembers its empty. "Sometimes our memories shift to be what we need in the present moment."

"I'm sure of it." Am I? I have a thousand reasons to doubt my own mind. I press the mug to my forehead. Am I trying to put together a puzzle that doesn't exist?

Did I almost get thrown in prison by pirates over nothing but a family trinket that my mother manifested her insanity onto? "What did she mean that the seas are in disarray?" I ask.

"Not a clue. Though everything feels a bit . . . dunno. Upside down lately. Felicity's gone and Mum died and you've shown up and the company . . ." He trails off, rubbing a hand over his chin. He stopped shaving our last few days at sea, and his jawline is pebbled with dark stubble.

"Are you selling it?" I ask.

"How did you know that?"

"There was a sign in the window when I came."

"God, you're aggravatingly observant." He rubs his bare ring finger, then says, "We are, unfortunately."

"Why sell if it's unfortunate?"

"Financial necessity. Our profits took a rather significant dip a few years ago, and we've never really recovered. Actually." He reaches down and thoughtfully strokes one of the cats on the head. It leans into his hand, purring. When another cat comes too close, it gets slapped across the face by the first. Monty chuckles and offers it a piece of meat.

"Actually what?" I prompt. I've been mentally eating off my own fingernails in anticipation of the end of that sentence.

He glances at me. "What?"

"You said *actually*, like you had more to add. What was it?" My tone is too urgent. My hands are still shaking. I'm suddenly embarrassed by the sound of my own breathing. Shifting my posture feels showy and obtrusive, like I'm trying to draw attention to myself.

"Nothing," he says, though I'm sure it's not nothing. "I was just thinking."

"Oh. Sorry. I didn't mean to . . ." I have no idea what I didn't mean to do but I can't stop myself from apologizing so I say again, "Sorry." Sorry I'm here. Sorry we both are. Sorry my sister is dead and his business is ruined and Mum is gone and my thoughts don't make sense and I can't do a goddamn thing about any of it.

"If you want to go to Portugal," Monty says slowly, "we can charter a ship."

"What about Basira Khan's instructions?"

"Well, obviously we'd have to ignore those."

"Do you have a ship in mind?"

"I do, actually." He tosses the finished skewer into his mug, then stretches his hands over his head, fingers linked. "It was in the harbor when we arrived."

"A Crown and Cleaver ship?" I ask.

"They are now," he says, "but they sailed for Hoffman for a long time, under the protection of the Crown and Cleaver, not as members of it."

"And you think they'll be willing to go against Basira Khan's orders?"

"If it's still captained by the same bastard as it was the last time I saw it, I think he can be persuaded."

My heart soars, and I practically leap to my feet, ready to sprint all the way down to the harbor and row us across the sea. "Then yes. Yes, absolutely yes, let's . . . yes. Let's go to Portugal."

Monty blinks up at me, unmoved by my sudden burst of enthusiasm. He scrubs his hand over his eyes, then stands up. There's a sharp ripping sound, and the entire crotch seam of his pants splits. "Christ, I'm too old for this."

12

The captain of the ship Monty calls the *Eleftheria* is an hour and a half late to our meeting. We wait for him in a teahouse in Rabat, sitting on understuffed cushions and drinking cup after cup of warm mint tea until my sinuses feel cavernously clear and I have to piss so badly it's hard to sit still. A wall of glass on the opposite side of the room from our low table splashes colored light across our feet. Then our shins. Then our laps as the time passes. When the teahouse door finally opens, there's a diamond of green light on my face, and I swear I can hear an entire pot's worth of tea sloshing around in my stomach.

A wiry young man who looks only a few years older than me enters, spots us, and waves. Monty leaps to his feet with as much enthusiasm as a man can when hobbling up from sitting practically inside a mostly unstuffed pouf, and they throw their arms around each other. The young captain nearly lifts Monty off his feet with the strength of his embrace, and in return, Monty musses his hair affectionately, then takes his face in both hands for a better look. I feel a sudden stab of envy, knowing now that Monty is capable of a warm greeting after a long time apart, he just chose not to offer it to me.

"Come sit down, sit down." Monty encourages the captain toward our table. He sinks onto the deflated pouf beside mine, which expels a gasp of musty air, as Monty returns to his.

"God, it's good to see you." Monty gives the captain's shoulder a playful shove, and only remembers I'm there as well when I get in the way of this. "Oh, introductions." He seems to consider standing again, then decide I'm not worth his knees. "Adrian, this is Georgie."

The captain clears his throat. "It's George, Monty. No one's called me Georgie since I was small."

"Oh, damn, sorry." Monty presses his fist to his forehead. "Old habits. Scipio always called you Georgie."

"Scipio was the only one permitted." He smiles sadly, and Monty touches a hand to his heart, and why am I here? I don't want to be here watching Monty pick a different little brother he'd rather dote upon and trade hugs and memories and fond smiles with, and also I really have to piss.

"All right then." Monty again extends a presentational hand between us. "Adrian, George. George, Adrian."

George holds out a hand to me, and as we shake, I can feel him scrutinizing my face, noticing the same dark hair and easy-to-draw nose as Monty has.

"He's my brother," Monty says before George can ask. "In spite of our vigorous efforts, Percy and I have still not managed to procreate."

"You never told me you had a brother!" George laughs and claps me on the shoulder. I almost vomit. "Good to meet you, Adrian." A server passing by pauses to refill our cups and pour a new one for George, who gulps it down, then picks out the mint leaves and chews them with great relish. He has a puppy's energy, ravenous and curious and bounding through the conversation. The fact that he's not wearing shoes only adds to this effect. It feels like he outgrew them just before he arrived. "Sorry to keep you waiting."

I hate waiting; I hate lateness, whether it's mine or others'; I hate a schedule being altered without forewarning, even when that schedule is only in my own head and there aren't any following events to affect and also is there something in this tea that is making me bounce my leg so aggressively I feel like I'm rattling the lantern over our heads? Maybe I just have a severe intolerance for uncertainty, like some people have an intolerance for raw nuts or bee stings.

But I nod, like it's fine, and Monty says, "So long as

it was because you were snogging someone pretty in the alley—that's the only acceptable excuse."

"Is Percy here?" George asks eagerly, looking around the teahouse like Percy may suddenly step out from behind one of the frilled screens.

"No, he's keeping house back in England. Dear Lord, I mention snogging and you immediately ask after Percy? You're not even subtle about it." Monty gives George a teasing smile, one that, I notice with another stab of envy, is absent of any actual mean-spiritedness. What would it be like to be in on a joke with Monty rather than the subject of it?

George grins in return, helping himself to half the squares of baklava arranged on a plate in the center of the table. He has a chip in his front tooth, like the folded corner of a page. "Have you ever met anyone who isn't in love with your husband? He's a goddam saint."

"He's not . . ." Monty tucks his bare left hand into his pocket. "Not my husband, George."

"Maybe not legally."

"Not—no. Not in any way. Legally or otherwise."

George's eyes widen. "You've not separated, have you?"

"Of course not," Monty replies, though he doesn't sound entirely confident in that assertion.

"Or . . . does he not know?" George inclines his

head toward me, like I can't see him, and I wish I had let Basira throw us in prison just so this discomfort could have been avoided.

"No, no." Monty picks up his teacup, trying to recover his previous composure, but it's like watching a man pull on a coat without realizing he's missed the armholes. "Adrian has given me his blessing to continue living in sin with Percy."

"So what happened?" George helps himself to the other half of the baklava. "I thought you were going to ask him to marry you."

"Can we discuss this later?" Monty presses his teacup to his lips and mutters into the rim, "Or maybe never?"

He then takes an aggressive swig of tea just as George says, "Well, if you don't propose soon, I will."

Monty chokes, and the conversation stalls for his coughing fit. I'm relieved to not have to sit and listen to them reminisce about people and places they've been together without me, Monty probably showing George how to tie his shoes and ruffling his hair and teaching him the sort of things older brothers are supposed to pass down—I can't think of any at the moment, but that's most likely because I never had a brother.

I wait until just before Monty seems recovered, then say, "We need to talk business with you."

George stretches his long legs under the table. He's tall, even sitting down, enough that I don't feel quite so overgrown. Though he looks made of far sturdier stuff than I am. The muscled moons of his shoulders round out his linen shirt. He has the Crown and Cleaver mark tattooed on his forearm, and I have a strong suspicion that literally everyone who sports it chose better placement than Monty. "Is this about Felicity?" he asks.

Monty stops dramatically clapping his own chest and looks up. "Do you know what happened to her?"

George shakes his head. "Just that she was banished. I was at sea when it happened, and the court has been tight-lipped about the details of what exactly she did. This new commodore, Monty, I swear—"

"But she's gone?" Monty interrupts.

George glances down at his hands. His joints are round and nobbled, like a foal's. "I'm sorry. I should have written, but Sim said she would and—"

"Stop." Monty reaches out and gives George's clenched hands a quick squeeze. "It's all right."

George nods once, and Monty pinches the bridge of his nose then looks up, composed as a sonata. "Right," Monty says. George is still staring at the floor. "So. You've still got the *Eleftheria*?"

"For my sins," George replies.

"Then you can take a private charter."

George looks up. "Who's chartering us?"

"We are," I say.

"But it needs to stay quiet," Monty adds. "It can't get

back to Basira Khan. For your sake as well."

"Are you putting my crew in danger?" George asks, and I say, "Yes," at the same time Monty says, "No!" We look at each other. George calls for more tea.

Monty and I cobble together an abridged version of the events of the last few weeks, and I show George the spyglass. He turns it over as Monty finishes the story by saying, like he had nothing to do with it, "So Adrian's got it in his mind that finding the shipwreck our mother survived will shed some light on this already well-lit situation."

"It's not—" I would have kicked him under the table had it not been so low to the ground. "Have you heard of the *Flying Dutchman*?" I ask George.

"Of course," he says. "Every sailor has."

I shoot Monty a triumphant look, though it wilts quickly in the face of his indifference. "Basira Khan told us the spyglass might have come from there."

"From the *Dutchman*?" George asks.

He sounds as skeptical as Monty. "Is there something wrong with that?" I ask.

George shrugs. "No, but it's a bit like being told you'll pay coins minted in El Dorado. You've pulled something from a story."

"Do you think she was trying to trick us?" I ask.

"No, I suspect she meant it. Doesn't mean it's not a story." He pushes back his shirtsleeves, which have slipped down to his wrists. The inked symbol of his pirate fleet looks like blue veins under his dark skin. "Khan grew up raiding tombs in Egypt and claims her father died from a pharaoh's curse. She's the sort of person who takes superstitions very seriously. I was a deckhand under her banner when I was younger, and she'd flog men for whistling. Bad luck," he explains when I don't react. "Couldn't pass the salt either or she'd break your fingers."

"That explains why she was so interested in the spyglass," Monty says.

"Doesn't mean she's wrong!" I protest.

"So you're chartering my ship to chase the *Flying Dutchman*?" George asks.

"No, we're chartering you to help us find a ship supposedly sunk a decade ago by the *Flying Dutchman*." Monty raises his glass to me in a cheers, and I have a sense he intentionally made that sound as stupid as possible.

But George doesn't seem put off. He flexes his feet against the matted rug, cracking his toes. "Better than diving wrecks here."

"Is that what you do for the Crown and Cleaver?" I ask, and George nods. "Do you look for treasure?"

"Sometimes it's treasure," he says. "Usually much duller. When a Crown and Cleaver ship goes down, we dive it and try to recover what we can—or sometimes when we sink an enemy without collecting all the cargo they send me and my men to survey what's left."

"Are there many wrecks?" I ask.

"More lately. The last decade has not been good to the Crown and Cleaver. The Atlantic has gotten dangerous. At least where we sail."

"Dangers like English ships?" Monty asks.

"Sometimes. But it's more than that. The currents are changing. Winds come from the south and storms from nowhere. The migration patterns of the dragons have changed as well." I assume that to be some kind of sailing metaphor I don't understand, but don't ask. George looks at Monty. "Scipio noticed it too. He was always going on about having to remap the ocean because the shipping routes weren't safe any longer. And there's more fighting among the pirate clans than ever." He swipes his teacup off the table. "The Crown and Cleaver has its share of internal conflict."

"Who's Scipio?" I ask.

George and Monty share another annoyingly knowing look, and there's a moment of silent debate between them before Monty finally says, "He was a friend of ours. A sailor. He captained the *Eleftheria* before George, until he died several years ago. He practically raised George. Me as well, I suppose." He tips his mug skyward. "He was a good man."

"The best of them," George says, with his own salute.

He drains his teacup, then slaps it down eagerly on the table. I suspect he has as difficult a time as I do sitting still, but likely for different reasons. "We're leaving in a fortnight for a dive," he tells us. "That will be the best time to go if you want to avoid detection."

"It has to be sooner," Monty says. "Basira Khan wants us out of Rabat, and she's having us escorted aboard one of her fleet vessels north."

"I wouldn't advise you set foot on any vessel arranged by Basira Khan," George says. "She's too closely allied with the commodore. And your family name isn't a welcome one."

"Might you leave sooner?" I ask.

"I can try to fabricate a reason," he says. "But it will go through the governor, and she knows Monty and I are friendly. She may guess you've contacted me."

"So what if I have?" Monty says. "Is it a crime to get tea with an old friend?"

"It can be if their surname is Montague." George stands and stretches with his hands over his head. "Where should I send word when we have a departure scheduled?"

"Wait, are you going?" Monty looks disappointed that he has to be alone with me again.

"I need to be off. I have other business." George climbs to his feet, clamping an elbow around Monty's neck and planting a friendly kiss on the top of his head.

"Don't look so glum. If you're sailing with me, we'll have plenty of time to catch up. I'd hate for us to grow weary of each other before we even leave port."

Monty narrows his eyes at George. "You've got a girl waiting for you, haven't you?"

George grins. "Is that your guess?"

"Probably the same girl who made you late."

"Very close." This time, it's George's turn to tousle Monty's hair. "But he's a lad. Jesus, Monty, don't be so narrow-minded."

By the time we leave the teahouse, the sun is low on the horizon, steeping in the water so that the sea is infused with soft golden light. As we walk back to our inn, we pass tanneries with their shutters closed for the day. A blacksmith throws sand upon his open forge, and the flames hiss and whine, as though in protest of being snuffed.

The night is temperate, and the wind off the water barely a breeze, but Monty has his hands in the pockets of his trousers—the demolished crotch seam sloppily mended before we met George—like he's trying to keep warm. We've nearly made it back to the inn and I am about to call this silence companionable rather than stony when he says suddenly, "You needn't tell everyone you're hunting ghosts."

Is that what we were doing? We had clearly walked

away from this day with two very different understand-ings of our assignment. "I'm not hunting ghosts."

He releases a heavy breath, and I realize he's irritated with me. It was stony silence after all. "Well, don't tell everyone you meet about the *Flying Dutchman*, then."

"I thought you trusted George."

"It's not about trust—I do, by the way. But claiming you've got a piece of a spyglass from a legendary ghost ship makes you seem a bit . . ."

Insane? He doesn't finish but I hear the word.

I wish it made me angry, but I'm just embarrassed—I shouldn't be embarrassed. I'm embarrassed of myself because Monty is embarrassed of me. It's pathetic. It doesn't make any sense. I resist the urge to reach into my pocket and make sure the spyglass is still there. Even though I can feel its weight. My fingers twitch.

"It may give people the wrong impression of you," Monty finishes at last. When I don't say anything, he prompts, "Adrian? Are you listening?"

"I'm sorry," I say before I can stop myself. I can feel the seams of my shirt scratching my skin. The back of my neck burns, and I wonder if it's possible to develop a rash from manacles.

"What for?"

"I don't know." When I close my eyes, I see spots, the same diamond patterns as the light off the waves. "Sorry I made you come all the way here."

"Stop saying that." We've reached the inn now, and he pauses on the two steps leading up to the door. "You didn't make me. I chose to."

"I'm sorry I put you in danger," I say. "Or . . ." I can't think of another thing so I say again, "I'm sorry."

"You say sorry too much. You don't have to apologize for voicing your ideas or having them to begin with. Or for anyone else's choices. For God's sake, you'd apologize if someone poured soup in your lap." He rubs his temples again, and in silhouette against the gathering darkness and the light from the inn windows, he looks like an exasperated father scolding his errant son. "It's really goddamn annoying."

Before I realize what I'm saying, I mumble, "Sorry."

Monty claps a hand over his eyes. "Jesus wept."

"I can't help it!" I reply.

"Of course you can help it, just think for a goddamn second before you say something and ask yourself: Is this a situation in which I have done someone wrong and need to proffer an apology? And if the answer is no, which I promise you it will be almost every time, don't goddamn apologize."

"I don't always know," I reply. I can feel my neck reddening, and I have a sudden urge to push a finger into my palm hard enough that it breaks all the way through and out the other side. Instead I close my hands into fists, my thumbnails boring into the knuckles of my first fingers.

"And I'd rather not obsess about whether or not someone is holding a grudge against me."

"So what if they are? Why does what other people think of you matter so greatly? Usually if someone doesn't like you, they shouldn't matter to you, and if they do, they'll tell you they're upset and you can make it right."

I don't say anything. I'm staring at the ground, my chin pressed against my shoulder. The material of my shirt is so scratchy and hot, it *must* be giving me a rash.

"Adrian," Monty finally prompts, and when I still don't say anything or move, he adds, "Are you going to look at me?"

I laugh without thinking. "You sound like Father."

Monty pivots sharply from me, shoulders rising. I swallow. Now that I have something I should apologize for, I don't make a sound. He rubs a hand over his cheek, like he's massaging a bruise, then says, his voice peevish, "How about thank you instead of sorry? Thank you for tending me all the way here and making sure I don't starve or worry myself to death. Or maybe thank you for taking eighteen years of getting knocked about so you didn't have to? I was apparently such a disaster that even the mess that you are looks good by comparison." He starts to turn away, then seems to think of something else to say, and spins to face me again. "You know, when I was your age, I didn't have anyone to play nursemaid when I went off on a magical quest to justify my insanity—I had to drink myself stupid and try to work up the courage to slit my wrists."

I'm going to be sick. I consider pushing past him to get inside, but he might grab my arm or step in my way and I might end up punching him in the nose without meaning to like I did with Richard Peele, so instead I turn away from him, back to the street.

"Adrian, wait," Monty calls, but I keep walking. My eyes burn. I don't care if he knows he hurt me, and I don't care if he regrets it—I hope he does. We've had maybe two nice moments since we left England and survived imprisonment by a pirate governor and I saw his ass more than I would have liked and I stupidly thought that meant we shared some kind of comradery or at least might have bonded over the ordeal of it all.

"Adrian, stop. Where are you going?" Monty calls. Not an apology—though any sincere apology would be pointless, as it would require him to change his entire personality. "Adrian!"

"I've got to piss," I snap over my shoulder, the words punctured by my uneven breath. Why am I suddenly wheezing? I can't get a deep breath no matter how hard I try, and every aborted attempt just makes it worse, a reminder of my body's failings.

I keep walking until I reach the end of the street, out of sight of our lodgings. I stop in a space between two shops, dotted with patchy grass and overlooking a steep hill that rolls into the sea. Below me, a group of children plays in the waves, leaping into the white crests with their arms spread and shrieking with laughter as the water carries them back to shore.

I sit down and put my hands on either side of my head, wondering if I can press hard enough to squeeze out the noise. Maybe I can pop my own head like an overripe grape and then finally I'll stop obsessing about everything for once in my goddamn life. Maybe I will stop trying to force Monty to feel anything for me other than contempt, or hang all my stupid hopes on the one small hook that he someday might. It's like trying to hear the words *I love you* in the rattle of a shaken jar of buttons.

I take the spyglass from my pocket and hold it up to the sea. In the twilight, the crack down the side looks like a trench, bottomless and dark. Anger strikes me suddenly, like an idea rather than an emotion. If this was important, why didn't she tell me? Long before she went to Scotland, if she knew there was a chance she had crossed paths with something cursed that might soon come calling for me as well, she could have at least mentioned it. If there was something I was meant to do or find or protect for her once she was gone, she should have goddamn told me. I shouldn't be here. This shouldn't be my responsibility.

It feels like an act of tremendous rebellion to raise the spyglass to my eye and peer through it. I don't know what I expect to see there, what forbidden images she kept from me. But there's nothing. Not even a distorted view of the horizon. Just darkness. I drop the spyglass back into my lap. I want to fling it into the sea. I want to be rid of it. I want to be rid of carrying her around with me like stones in my pockets. But I also want to rub them smooth with my thumbs, hold them in my hands so they don't fall out along the path. I'm not sure if it's worse to remember or forget.

I sit on the overlook until the stars begin to appear, peppering the sky like straight pins stuck into dark fabric. The breeze off the water turns chilly and picks up handfuls of sand from the beach that sting my eyes. If I had found a better place, I might stay there all night. Instead, I stand up, brushing seagrass from my trousers, then turn and head back for the inn.

It is somehow both a tremendous relief and a tremendous disappointment to arrive in the common room and find that Monty has not waited up for my safe return. The innkeeper is asleep behind his desk with his head down, and the barroom is empty. The whole place feels too dark and too empty, like I'm the only one here. My skin crawls. I climb the stairs carefully, feeling with each toe before I step for fear of tripping, then let myself into my room.

It's ransacked. My knapsack has been turned inside out and sliced across the bottom, leaving a ragged tear. Every garment I packed has been scattered, as though a clothesline was caught by the wind. The sheets have been pulled off the mattress, every drawer in the small bureau pulled out and the bureau itself cracked open. *Tom Jones* sits pages-down on the floor, its spine broken. It looks like a bird shot from the sky.

I freeze, my hand still on the knob. Have I been robbed? If so, the thieves must have been sorely disappointed, for all my banknotes and travel documents were with me. The only thing they could have taken was socks and a tin of English tea. Was it just *my* apartments that were targeted, or the whole place? Surely someone heard this robbery in progress—we stopped by before we went to meet George, so whoever did this must have been here not that long ago. There must have still been people in the bar, or someone in an adjoining room must have been woken by the noise and come to investigate.

Monty.

I slam the door to my room and dart down the hall to his. "Monty!" I pound open-handed on the door. "Monty, wake up. I think I've been robbed. Someone's been in my room. They went through my things. Monty!"

The door swings open, and I'm face-to-face not with Monty but a man with a scarf pulled up to the bridge of his nose. He has a cutlass drawn. Behind him is a second man, pinning Monty against the wall with the flat of his own cutlass blade. My brother has his hands up in the universal gesture of *don't shoot*. Though *don't stab* is more appropriate here.

Monty gives me a little wave, hands still raised. "Bandits, yes, definitely aware."

The man who opened the door reaches for me, and I dodge without thinking. Before he can follow, I slam the door. He's not all the way clear of the frame, and there's a crunching noise as it strikes him in the nose. I hear him howl in pain but don't hang about to check the damage. I turn for the stairs and run, sprinting down them two at a time. I jump the last few and land wrong on my ankle, losing my footing and pitching hard into one of the bar stools. They fall like dominoes, one after the other. Above me, I hear a door slam and the heavy treads on the stairs as one of the bandits chases me. I don't have time to run—nor truly anywhere to go—so I crawl behind the bar, pressing myself into the darkness beneath a rack of the kind of small cups our mint tea was served in.

On the other side of the bar, the footsteps stop. I can feel the bandit scanning the room, searching for me. I hold my breath, though I know this is a rubbish place to hide. It won't keep me for long. There's a wet snuffle, then the sound of him spitting. I must have gotten his nose with the door—maybe not hard enough to break it, but it had bought me some time that I now had absolutely no clue what to do with. I try to think small, dark, invisible thoughts as I pull my knees tighter against my chest.

"Come out." There's a *swoosh,* then a waterfall of breaking glass against the floor. He must have swept all the cups sitting upside down at the end of the bar off— most likely with his cutlass for greatest effect. "Where are you?" he calls in a mocking singsong. There's another slash, and one of the lamps overhead shatters. I start to crawl along the bar, toward the opposite end nearer the exit. Why hasn't the innkeeper woken up? Why hasn't literally anyone in this whole goddamn place come to my aid?

"Come out now and I may not have to kill you." There's the clatter of a table overturned. "She never said I had to. We can come to an arrangement."

I nearly crawl straight into the end of the bar—it's just a wall. Nowhere to go except over and straight onto the end of his cutlass. I look around desperately, searching for something—anything—to defend myself. I don't know *how* to defend myself, particularly with something I might find behind a bar, but I'm not going to wait here quietly until he finds me.

Then I see it—a machete hanging from a hook under a wine rack. I saw one of the bartenders using it that morning to halve coconuts and then pour their water into pewter pitchers for each table. I slide the leather strap off the hook as quietly as I can. It's much heavier than I anticipated, and I need both hands to lift it.

Another table overturns, and I twist around to peer over the bar as best I can without being spotted. The man has his back to me, crouched down as he slides his cutlass under the benches lining the wall. There won't be a better moment. I heft the machete onto the bar top, then swing myself up and over. I hoped some roguish grace might suddenly possess me, and I would leap over the bar and swing my own weapon at him in one elegant move. Instead, the bar top is much higher than anticipated and I catch my toe on one of the taps, which starts to spew warm beer across my trousers. The bar top instantly goes somehow both slick and sticky beneath me, and I end up splatted across it, the machete teetering precariously on the edge.

"Gotcha." I hear the swoosh of the cutlass, and I lunge forward, grabbing the handle of the machete, and roll, straight off the counter. I crash onto the barroom floor, the machete flying out of my grip and sliding beneath the toppled stools. There's a crack, and when I look up, the bandit has stuck his sword into the bar top where I had just been so hard he's struggling to get it free. I lurch forward on my hands and knees, searching for the machete, shoving the fallen stools aside until I find it. I turn, clutching it in both hands, just as the bandit yanks his cutlass free.

We face each other. His scarf has slipped off, and his chin is dark and wet, a cracked front tooth winking out from between the greasy blood coating his lips. I am the only one out of the pair of us who has to use two hands to hold my weapon, and I suspect private fencing lessons with tipped blades and padded suiting are going to be less helpful than whatever on-the-job training this man has had with his sword.

He swings at me with a yell, and I throw up my machete, blocking the blow. When the blades strike, I feel the clang all the way through me. I swear my teeth knock together. He slashes again, lower this time, but I block that one as well, though it pushes me backward a step. I can see the strategy straightaway—he could swing all night and never tire, while I'll likely take about three more solid hits before I lose my grip. He doesn't have to fight me; he just has to outlast me. Be the aggressor longer than I can defend myself.

So there's only one solution.

Before he can swipe at me again, I raise my machete and, with a primal enthusiasm I didn't know I possessed, run toward him, screaming like a wild creature. I consider trying to actually apply any of the skills I learned in my fencing lessons, but when faced with this man and his cutlass, I can't remember a parry from a riposte, so I just swing. He dodges, then dodges again, caught off guard by my ferocious, if inept, attack. He steps backward, right into the spreading puddle of beer, and slips, falling backward onto one of the bar stools. His scarf comes loose and flutters to the ground, revealing the blue-inked symbol of the Crown and Cleaver on his neck.

I swing at him again, but he thrusts one of the stools in front of himself like a shield. The cushioned seat must be harder than a coconut, for my blade bounces off it and I lose my balance.

A gunshot from the floor above us splits the air suddenly. The bandit and I both pause, united for a moment in wondering which of us just lost our ally. Then he swipes at me again, hacking gracelessly with all his strength. The machete flies out of my hand when his cutlass strikes it and slides across the barroom floor with a metallic scrape. I stumble backward. My foot catches the splintered remains of one of the tables, and I trip, my already throbbing ankle twisting under me.

The bandit pulls himself to his feet with a hand on the bar top and lurches toward me. I swear he's a foot taller than he was when he opened the door to Monty's room. I crawl backward, managing to wedge myself beneath one of the benches, but he grabs the edge of it and tosses it aside like it weighs nothing. It splinters when it strikes the bar. Before I can move, he puts a foot on my chest, pressing down hard enough that all the breath goes out of my lungs. "Nowhere else to go."

"What do you want?" I gasp, the words barely audible.

"You know," he says. I have a guess, but would rather not give him ideas if I'm wrong, so I shake my head. "Your spyglass," he says. "You can give it to me now, or I can rip it from your corpse."

"Now surely those aren't the only choices," someone says from behind us.

The bandit turns, foot still on my chest, and I raise my head. Monty is standing at the base of the stairs, holding an antique pistol like he almost knows how to use it. His nose is bleeding, and the bridge looks flatter than it was before, but he's on his feet. And armed. Better than I'm doing.

The bandit raises his cutlass and bares his teeth at Monty. In return, Monty pulls back the hammer on the pistol. "Yours might be bigger, but I'll wager mine works faster." Even in this, the direst situation of my life and probably his as well, he still smirks.

"You won't shoot me," the bandit says.

"Won't I?"

"You aren't the type to get blood on your hands."

"Darling, you have no idea what my type is."

The bandit lunges at Monty, cutlass raised over his head.

And then there's a gunshot.

It's somehow the loudest sound I've ever heard, and I flinch, my hands flying up over my face. The bandit flinches too, and I think he must have been hit. Or I must have been. Someone's been shot. I have read in books that men who are shot, fatally or otherwise, sometimes are the last to know it. But I've got no blood on me. The bandit has no blood on him either. We look ourselves up and down, then appraise each other, and seem to realize at the same time that neither of us is dead. Then we both look to Monty, who, in turn, looks down at his gun, puzzled. Then something seems to dawn on him.

"Damn."

Without warning, he shifts his grip from the butt to the barrel, then hurls the heavy pistol at the bandit. It strikes the man in the face, and he staggers, momentarily stunned. I grab his ankle as he takes another wobbly step, and he falls backward, crashing through the window and toppling out onto the street. Tiny pebbles of glass blow back into the room, and I cover my face.

"Good thinking." Monty throws his hand out to me and I let him pull me to my feet. "I'm not sure knocking him in the skull would have done the trick on its own, as I suspect it's rather thick."

"What happened to your gun?" I ask.

"Apparently, when I reloaded, I forgot the main bit." He toes the empty firearm on the floor. "You all right?"

"Yes. I think . . ." I do a quick inventory to be certain I haven't sustained any major injuries. I also check that the spyglass is still in my pocket. "Yes."

"Let's go, then, before he comes around. I've got the

other one locked upstairs, but there's a good chance he's going to jump out the window."

"Where is everyone?" I ask as I follow Monty out the service door behind the bar. "Why didn't anyone come help us?"

"I suspect they all got instructions from the Crown and Cleaver not to interfere. Though I can't say whether that was done via a few coins slipped under the door or delivered at knifepoint. Well. Cutlasspoint."

"They wanted the spyglass."

"Absolutely yes."

"Basira Khan sent them."

"Also absolutely yes. I told you she wasn't finished with it."

So she did want it. She simply must have realized there would be an easier way to get it than slitting my throat on the floor of her bathhouse. Or perhaps she hoped we wouldn't know it was her men who had taken it? The man had had his ink covered. "What does the Crown and Cleaver want with it?"

"Not a clue," Monty says. "But we need to get out of here sooner than planned. Let's hope George's new gentleman friend isn't so handsome he can't be lured from his bed."

13

We spend the rest of the night and most of the next day hidden in the cargo hold of the *Eleftheria*, until George is able to pull off whatever charm, trick, or bribe is required to get permission to leave the harbor. Monty and I don't come up to the deck until Rabat is barely a shadow on the horizon.

The crew is only six men, none of whom speak English, though several know enough French to converse with Monty and me. George translates when he can, though most of the time, when trying to convert their cobbled lingo into coherent sentences, he gives up halfway through with a laugh.

The ship's main mast is carved with the same symbol that was etched into the vessel that took us to Rabat, that snowflake-like rune. Once we're sure we're not being followed and we're on course for Portugal, George finds a bucket of red paint and dips his finger in, then retraces the shape of it.

I watch him for a while, each careful stroke of his fingers through the carved branches of the rune, before I pluck up my courage enough to ask, "What is it?"

George looks up from his work. "It's a stave from Icelandic sailors. The captain before me—Scipio, the man Monty mentioned—he carved it here after we met some Viking lads from up north. I think they were drunk, but he never got more than a few days from port without repainting it." He almost scratches his chin, then remembers at the last second his hands are covered in paint.

"The sailors called it vegvísir."

"And it's meant as protection?" I ask.

George shrugs. "Scipio said it was more of a compass."

"A magic compass?"

"So the story goes."

"If it's a compass, where does it lead?"

"I think that depends on where you're going." He grins at me, impish, and I can't help but grin back. I had tried to maintain some of my dislike for him on account of Monty's adoration, but that grows more and more impossible as I get to know him. With his quick smile and jovial demeanor, it's easy to see why Monty is fond of him. He's the sort of good-natured head boy at school that everyone likes, equally known for organizing holiday programs and looking the other way when he sees classmates out of bed smoking after hours. "Come here."

I hop down from my perch on a barrel of grog and let him take my hand, our palms pressed together. He licks his finger to wet the paint, then draws the same symbol on the back of my hand. The paint is cold, and I can feel the calluses on his palm against the tips of my fingers as he holds me steady. "There." He smacks a wet kiss on the inside of my wrist when he's finished, and I laugh. "Now you've got a charm of your own." A dollop of paint lands on his bare foot, and he scrubs it away against the cuff of his breeches. "With vegvísir, you'll never lose your way, no matter the storms that batter you. Even if the way is not known."

I stare down at my hand, tipping it so the paint doesn't run and disrupt the network of lines opening their fist across my skin. When the sun catches it, it sparkles. "Thank you," I say.

George smiles again. "We can all use a guide sometimes."

"Oy! George!" I hear Monty call across the deck. "Are you tattooing occult symbols on my little brother?"

The first few days of our journey pass without incident, and the crew seems in good spirits. George has plotted a course that veers farther west than one would usually go to sail from Rabat to Portugal, but he says the additional days it tacks on to our journey will guarantee we won't cross any of the Crown and Cleaver's most trafficked routes. Monty and I both help when we can, but George and his men run so smoothly that we're mostly in the way. Monty spends his time napping in the sun and I stare over the rails into the sapphire water that goes on as far as I can see and then farther. I keep thinking of the ships beneath us, wrecks sitting at the bottom of the sea. It starts to feel like stepping on grave after grave, my anxiety mounting with every league that something is following us. Something is coming for us. I can't shake the dread—it's clung to me since we left Rabat. I haven't washed the stave off my hand, but the paint is starting to crack and peel, like my body is rejecting the offer of guidance. Even magic can't help.

Our third day at sea, we wake to a bloodred sky and a sun crowded by storm clouds. By midday, their bellies blush white with lightning. The air begins to feel steamy and oppressive. The fresh coat of paint on vegvísir bubbles.

The storm falls upon us sometime in the night, though it's not the pitching or the bells that wake me. When I sit up in my hammock, it's from a feeling akin to sensing eyes on you in a crowd. For a moment, still groggy from the sharp pivot from sleep into consciousness, I think it must be the remnants of a dream that make the deck around me feel particularly dark and haunted.

Then the ship cants so violently I'm thrown out of my hammock. My hip makes sharp contact with the edge of the stove, and the plate tips with a clang, scattering cold coals. For the first time I hear the bell up on deck tolling relentlessly—a call for all hands. Thunder grumbles like a shaken sheet of tin. There's a lashing sound against the boards above my head, along with the shouts of sailors and heavy footfalls.

Everyone was given a storm station on our first day on the water except me, my seafaring knowledge being so minimal that, in any crisis that could not be rectified with recitations of Pope or the *Iliad*, I would be more hazardous than helpful. When the others ran their storm drills, George told me the best thing I could do were a tempest to rise was stay out of the way. He also assured me that a storm at this latitude, this time of year, in such a short voyage, was as likely as a summer snow. Yet here we are.

I try to clamber back into my hammock, but the canvas is twisted, and I can't stay on my feet long enough to untangle it. It's foolhardy to even try to set it right again, let alone climb back in, curl up, and hope for sleep as the world ends around me. Even if the storm were quiet and still, I would feel myself starting to slip down the embankment and into anxiety, my brain supplying an almost constant list of new catastrophic fates that could befall us. I try to breathe more than a quick gasp but it with the Crown and Cleaver leadership enough for now. I need to do what's best for my men. So it's back to Rabat for us."

I nod, though I hate the idea of traveling without him and the rest of the crew of the *Eleftheria*. "Your handsome boy probably misses you."

He laughs, his head tipped to the sky. "More likely he's forgotten my name."

"I doubt anyone forgets you that easily," I say, surprising myself. I've never been much of a flirt—Louisa and I were both so upfront with our feelings it was never needed.

"Well. You're sweet." George looks down at the ground, hands in his pockets again. "You're not up for a little, you know? Are you?" He grins, nose scrunching. "It doesn't have to mean anything. Only, sometimes it's nice to have a pair of hands that aren't your own when you're so long at sea."

"I'm engaged," I say, then add a clarifier I had never expected to need, "to a woman."

"Ah, that's a shame." He nods, hands still in his pockets. His shoulders are creeping up around his ears. "You're very handsome. Like a prettier version of Monty."

"I'm going to tell him you said that."

He punches my shoulder lightly. "I will cut out your tongue before you have the chance."

"If you left for England today, you'd probably get to

Percy before he could," I say with a laugh.

George grins, but then stops suddenly, his face serious. "Do you know why Monty won't marry him?"

"Well, it's not legal in England if you're two gents."

"I don't think the legality is what's important." His brow furrows. "Monty hasn't been stepping out, has he?"

"On Percy?"

George shrugs. "He doesn't have the best history in that field. Lots of misspent youth, or so I hear." He swats a fly off his ear. "Bother him about it for me, won't you? He and Percy should be married."

I give him a small bow. "It would be my greatest honor to bother Monty on your behalf."

"Ah, you're darling." He leans over and plants a kiss on my cheek. We've reached a fork in the harbor path, one way leading back to the *Eleftheria*. George stops a few steps along it when he realizes I'm not following him. "Coming?"

"I think I'm going to walk for a bit." I try to execute a casual thumb-over-the-shoulder, and almost poke myself in the eye. "Clear my head. A bit. I'll be back for supper."

"Go on, then." George raises his hand in a wave. "Let me know if you change your mind. The offer still stands."

"I promise," I say. "If I find myself in need of a pair of hands not my own, yours will be the first I think of."

He grins at me, walking backward down the path. "You know," he says, "you're more like Monty than you think." Then he turns to the water, and we go our own ways.

Even at midday, the Armas Imperiais is crowded. I pass a bar top that looks sticky from a distance, and follow Saad's directions to the third room, the question of what exactly he meant when he said I would know where to leave him a note again gnawing at me. What if I leave it in the wrong place? What if I don't understand whatever he expected I would? Why do people assume I know more than I do? I'm an idiot about most things.

Then I see it.

One wall is occupied entirely by mounted bottles, each of them containing a ship made in miniature. It's a tiny flotilla behind glass, their yards matchsticks, sails the size of a postage stamp. Beneath each is a small plaque, engraved with the name of the ship and a date. It takes me a moment to realize that they're marking the day the ship went down. Beneath the bottle, each shelf is littered with offerings: flowers turned putrid with age, rosary beads, folded notes, and wrapped pieces of rock-hard candy. Suddenly the weight of the wall feels like it's about to crash over me, the tidal wave that felled these ships. A whole wall of shipwrecks and drowned sailors, bottled up and built into the architecture of this city. We are all so terribly afraid of forgetting.

I follow the dates in descending order and find

it—the *Persephone*. It looks much like the ship Monty and I took to Rabat—three masts, a tiny British flag hanging stiffly from the back, as though it's caught in a perpetual breeze. The rigging lines that run between the yards are as fine as spider silk. There are no offerings for her. Just the plaque, with the name of the ship and the date it went down.

It sank on the summer solstice.

I hadn't remembered that—not sure if I ever knew it to begin with. Her whole life seems pinned to this single day, lurking sly and unseen each year. How many times, as the summer dawned, was my mother's life irrevocably altered?

I ask the bartender for paper and pencil, and, on the back of a receipt for far too much rum left by another patron, I write, *It's in Amsterdam. We'll meet you there*, and leave it wedged under the bottle containing the miniature *Persephone*, hidden like a wreck below the sea.

24

Amsterdam?"

We are on the deck of the *Eleftheria*, the planking slick with the light from a smoldering brazier and the cast-off blaze of the sun setting into the water. Felicity and Monty were playing cards when I returned from the Armas Imperiais, and though I had rehearsed the lie I would tell if asked where I had been the entire walk back, neither asked. Which is really goddamn lucky because I'm not sure I could have delivered it without giving myself away. My back was as wet as if I had dunked myself in the sea.

Now, Felicity and I are sitting on overturned swab buckets, Monty in a chair from the captain's cabin with his bad leg propped up on the rim of one of the hatches. Felicity has her chin balanced on her hand, elbow on her knee, and while I didn't anticipate celebration over the fact that this is, alas, not the place we'll find our answers, her obvious consternation is unexpected.

"Is Amsterdam bad?" I ask.

"Yes, is it?" Monty asks. Felicity's put down her cards, but he's still thumbing through his hand like he's working out his next play. "You lived there, Fel. And Johanna's still there, isn't she? Oh, you'll love Jo," Monty says to me. "She has a tiny house and enormous dogs and no sense of personal space."

"Stop it." Felicity slaps him lightly on his uninjured knee, then says to me, "Johanna's lovely. And she'd put us up."

"So what's the problem?" I ask.

Felicity sits up, shaking out her hands like she's drying them. "Nothing. No problem. What's the man's name we're looking for?"

"Van der Loos."

"How generically Dutch," Monty mutters. "I'm sure there will only be several thousand of them."

"Was there any mention of why he bought the shipwreck claim?" Felicity asks, studying her fingernails.

I shake my head. "The man we spoke to at the harbor suggested maybe he had some stake in the company that owned the ship."

Or maybe he's looking for the same thing we are. Maybe he got there first.

"George has to go back to Rabat," I add.

Felicity and Monty trade glances. "He mentioned that," Monty says, and I try not to linger on the fear of what they were surely saying about me while I was gone.

"But I can get us there," I add. "I have access to Father's bank accounts."

"Oh, brilliant." Monty claps his hands like a man about to feast. "Shall we go by elephant, or hire noblemen to carry us in sedan chairs all the way? Of course we'll pay whatever they ask."

"I thought maybe," I say, "we go overland."

"It would be better if we could keep to one method of transport." Felicity says. "Particularly one that doesn't have to go over bumpy roads. You," she looks to Monty, "are still not as mobile as you seem to think."

"Elephants ride very smoothly, darling," Monty says.

Felicity ignores him. "And if I remember, Spanish roads are so poorly paved that you may be the first man ever to rebreak a bone simply by riding in a carriage."

"What if we go by river?" I ask. "It wouldn't be a direct route, or take us all the way there, but if we can get to the Rhine . . ."

Felicity rubs her temples. "God, that will require so much planning."

"I'll plan it."

"Can we not go by sea?" she asks. She sounds exasperated already. I'm surprised she doesn't suggest we forget the whole thing and make our way back to England instead. "Surely there are ships to Amsterdam—"

"No!" I almost shout it. Monty startles, and one of the cards slips from his hand and flutters to the floor. The queen of hearts. I stare into her black eyes, unable to look at either of them for fear of seeing my strangeness reflected in their concern. "No, sorry, I'd really please prefer if we don't. Sorry, I'm—"

"That's fine," Monty interrupts me.

I wipe my palms on the knees of my trousers. "It is?"

Felicity doesn't look convinced, but Monty leans backward, arms crossed in satisfaction. "Whatever spends as much of your father's money as possible. I'm still in favor of the elephants."

The *Eleftheria* leaves us in Porto, and my father's checkbook gets us to Madrid, then across the Pyrenees, their peaks capped with both snow and wildflowers, to Toulouse. Spring is bursting into summer, and I think of Persephone, the goddess dancing through the seasons with flowers at her feet. The solstice is approaching. One year since my mother died.

From Toulouse, we go to Lyon, then Basel, where we take a passenger liner down the Rhine River. As it's our father footing the bill, whether he likes or knows it, I purchase three first-class cabins, one for each of us on the finest ship available, populated exclusively with tourists traveling the Continent and in possession of enough money to throw at luxury accommodations.

Once we've set sail, I keep to myself in my cabin, desperate to talk to both my siblings but concerned that they'll feel pressured to accept any invitation I offer and not actually want to be with me, which I will then spend the entire time fretting about, and also how much is there really to do on a boat? Whatever limited activities are available, I suspect they're doing them without me. I am also not as steady-stomached as I had hoped I would be. River travel is less choppy than ocean, but the passenger liner is smaller and more prone to being knocked by waves, and I'm so worried about becoming sick that it's hard to eat anything for fear of being ill. The spots from the leeches still dot my arm. I'm not sure the scars will ever fade.

So I spend several days in lonely solitude, not wanting to initiate conversation but also desperate for it, but also certain that once I have it, the only thing I'll want is to be back in my cabin, alone.

My self-imposed exile is broken when Felicity arrives at my door and says, by way of greeting, "Monty's looking for you."

"Is he?" I ask, resisting the urge to check my hair in the glass over the washbasin to be sure it's lying flat. It's only Felicity, and I know she doesn't give a fig what I look like, but I'm still terribly aware of how little regard I've paid my appearance since we boarded. "What for?"

"I don't know. Nothing bad," she adds. I hadn't considered it might be until she warned me it wasn't and now that's all I can think of. They are going to sit me down and have a chat about how they're getting off at the next port and I'll be on my own, or they'll take turns listing everything they don't like about me, or they're angry at me for something I don't know that I've done. Or they're going to tell me they've decided to adopt George as a younger brother in my place and there's only room for one youngest Montague so I'll have to go, and God, what is wrong with me? This goddamn stagnation and loneliness has given me far too much time to think. I'm much better in a crisis, when brooding contemplation isn't an option.

I put on my coat and follow Felicity to the promenade deck, where passengers are allowed to walk or sit and take tea. The weather is warm so the deck is crowded, passengers with binoculars and paper maps marking out the sights along the way. There must have been some message passed around that the countryside we are coming up on is particularly beautiful, for it feels like the entire manifest is squeezed onto the narrow promenade. I nearly turn back to my cabin at the sight of so many people.

But the view is maddeningly gorgeous. Terraced vineyards cling to the lush hillsides, their neat rows interrupted by slate cliffsides crowned with storybook castles. Some are crumbling ruins, but others still fly flags from their highest turret, and the villages that crowd the shore below them are dotted with fishing boats and feather trails of smoke billowing from the rooftops. Steeples rise from between the trees, and in the fields, tiny white sheep dot the grass like snowflakes. The day is warm, and the sun gives the water the bright opacity of blown glass.

We find Monty sitting alone, eyes closed, face turned to the sky. His cheeks have more color than I've seen in them since the storm, though whether that's due to his health or too long in the sun, I'm not sure. The freckles on his forehead have darkened. Felicity touches his shoulder lightly, and he sits up. "Other side," he directs me, tapping his deaf ear, and I change course, pulling one of the deck chairs around so Felicity and I are both facing him.

"Why were you looking for me?" I ask with no prelude.

Monty squints. "What?"

"Felicity said you wanted me for something."

"Did I?" He looks to Felicity, scratching the back of his neck. "What was it again? Mostly I think we wanted to make sure you weren't dead. We haven't seen you in days."

"Oh." I pick at a patch of dry skin along my nail beds. "I've been . . . unwell."

"What sort of unwell?" Felicity asks, and I know she's a doctor, and a sister, and she's trying to be kind, but being asked with that undertone that both of us know means *How insane are you today?* makes me want to curl up in shame.

"Seasick," I say, then amend, "River-sick."

"Would you take something to help?" She pulls on a chain around her neck until a locket appears. The movement pushes back the collar of her dress, and I notice a scar on her shoulder, a small starburst like a bullet hole. "Do you take snuff?"

"Not"—I eye the locket—"medicinally."

Monty laughs when he sees the locket. "Only the finest for our Adrian." He reaches over and pushes my head good-naturedly. "Darling, you're going to be so high."

"Ignore him." Felicity clicks the locket open with her thumb, and rather than a cameo or lock of hair, it's full of a shimmering blue powder. "You can put it on your gums," she says. "Or snort it—that's most effective. It will help settle your stomach—that's all." She tips a fingernail-sized amount onto the back of my hand. I pinch one nostril and breathe deeply with the other pressed over the powder. It hits me straight in the back of the throat and I immediately feel a sneeze coming on. The briny taste makes me gag. Monty hands me a half-finished cup of tea and I choke it down, though it does little to ease the burn.

"What was that?" I ask, my voice hoarse.

Felicity tucks the locket down the front of her shirt again, slipping the chain out of sight. "What do you know about sea monsters?"

I glance at Monty but he raises his hands, removing himself from the conversation. "Is this a trick question?"

"Not entirely." Felicity tugs her neckline back into place, then refastens her scarf. "There is a rare variety of ocean dweller that lives primarily off the Berber coast. The Crown and Cleaver fleet protect them from poachers and hunters who would have them for the restorative properties of their scales."

"Have you cracked it yet?" Monty asks her.

"Not . . . quite." She pushes a strand of hair out of her face before she explains to me, "I've been trying to create a synthetic duplicate of the scales for medicinal purposes."

"Is that what I just took?" I ask. "Your duplicate?"

"Are you testing experimental substances on our little brother?" Monty asks.

"Yes," she replies without clarifying to which of us she's responding. She presses her teeth into her bottom lip, then confesses, "It may not have *much* effect on your seasickness. If I had any of the actual compound with me, I'd give you that—it would do the trick. But there were men I sailed with in the Crown and Cleaver who said it helped their nausea. Speaking of." She turns to

Monty. "Are you sure you won't take anything? It's a tea-spoon of medicinal whiskey, Monty; you'll not fall back into the bottle."

But Monty is shaking his head before she finishes her sentence. "Felicity."

She flaps a hand at him. "I know."

"Please don't ask me again."

"I know, I know. I won't. But I hate that you're mis-erable."

"I'm not miserable." He casts a hand around at the landscape. "How can anyone be miserable amid all this?"

He smiles at me, cheeks dimpling, but I look away. Yes, how *can* I be miserable? How can I be so utterly heartsick in this beautiful place with this family I didn't know I had? What's the matter with my brain that it can't take one nice thing handed to it without dropping it in the mud?

We sit in silence for a few minutes before Felicity stands. "Don't stay in the sun too long. You'll both burn."

"Wait, where are you going?" Monty grabs her wrist, pulling her back though she refuses to sit again. "Stay and talk to us."

"What about?"

"Dunno, but you've been evasive and Adrian's been absent, and it's starting to annoy me. We haven't seen each other in years, Fel. You two"—he waves his free hand between Felicity and me—"have *never* seen each other. And also we just saved you from a fate worse than death! Banishment in a tropical paradise, can you imagine?" When she doesn't move, he prompts, "Come on, Adrian's got a whole list of questions he'll ask you. He wants to know your middle name, and I can't remember it."

Felicity hesitates, struggling to come up with any reason not to. "I have to . . . do . . . a thing."

Monty points to the spot on my other side. "Felicity Ethelburga Montague."

Felicity rolls her eyes. "*That's* not my middle name."

"Sit down and have a nice conversation with your brothers," Monty says. "If you're going to be a shrew, at least have the decency to be it to our faces."

Felicity executes a second eye roll so aggressive it seems to heave through her entire body, then sinks down beside me.

"So when we get to Amsterdam—" I start, but Monty interrupts.

"As the conductor of this conversational orchestra, I'd like to also place a ban on ghost talk right now, thank you very much. No pirates, no ghosts, no spyglasses, no magic. We are going to have a nice family moment, goddammit."

And then none of us says anything. Nice family moments are apparently more difficult to conjure than any of us had anticipated. Along the river's edge, rampart walls jut up like broken teeth, half-collapsed on the crumbling embankment. The castle they border looks as though it's barely clinging to its place on the cliff. One stiff breeze is all it would take to send it plummeting into the river. Maybe it would land on our boat. Maybe not. The idea is surprisingly easy to let go.

"Do you want to start?" Felicity finally says to Monty. "Should we go around the circle and everyone say their favorite thing about you?"

"I wouldn't mind—" Monty says, but I cut in.

"May I ask Felicity about something that is not related to the spyglass but is to Amsterdam?"

"I suppose," Monty says. "Though I should warn you, once Felicity Geraldine Montague—"

"Do you truly not remember it?" Felicity interrupts.

"Hold on, it'll come to me." He presses his fingers to the bridge of his nose. "Mordred. Evangeline. Patience. Kindness—was it meant to be ironic?"

"How did you come to live in Amsterdam?" I ask her. "Did you study there?"

She twists a strand of hair around her fingers, staring out over the rail and across the water. "No, I studied medicine in Algiers, then earned my doctoral degree in Italy. Then spent several years as a ship's surgeon because I couldn't find professional work on the continent." She squints, counting the years backward in her head. "*Then*

I was hired to assist at the Hortus Medicus—the botanical garden in Amsterdam that cultivates medicinal plants from around the world. They're funded by the university, and most of the physicians do at least some of their training there. I started teaching as a substitute when the male professors were traveling or unwell, and eventually they gave me my own classes and let me do my own research."

"Do you speak Dutch?" I ask.

She nods. "And Italian. And Arabic, and some of the Berber dialects, though not fluently."

"And you're a doctor," I say, trying to make it a statement rather than a question though the concept still seems outlandish, not because women don't have the capacity for medical professions, but because I've simply never heard of any reaching such a recognized level of achievement. "A real doctor."

She gives me a half smile. "Improbable as it may seem, I am."

"Felicity Primrose Montague!" I exclaim.

Monty throws back his head and laughs. Felicity rolls her eyes. "Oh good, now there are two of you."

"You're incredible," I say to her.

She looks down at her hands, color rising in her cheeks. "That's very kind, thank you."

"You are!" I say. "You're a doctor! And a professor! At a university!"

"It really is bloody impressive, Fel," Monty adds.

"*And* a pirate!" I say. "You're like an adventure-novel heroine! I wish I could introduce you to my fiancée. She'd go mad over you."

"Is she interested in medicine or piracy?" Felicity asks.

"Neither in particular," I say. "But she's very interested in women who cast off societal expectations and work for change despite the men who endeavor to stand in their way."

"Well then, I think she and I would get on very well." Her mouth twitches, that Montague dimple creasing her cheek. "If we ever get back to London, we'll all have to go out for a drink and I'll chat with your fiancée, and you and Percy can keep Monty from the card tables. It's a two-man operation."

Monty snorts. "One of you between me and the cards, the other between me and the bar."

"Is there a reason you don't drink spirits?" I ask him.

Making him laugh had emboldened me, but then Felicity glances up suddenly, her face drawn, and I worry I've poked a raw wound. Monty ruffles his hair, a gesture I've come to recognize as a nervous habit, but says calmly, "I'm not good at moderation."

"Oh God, me neither," I say before I can stop myself, then add, "Not spirits though, I didn't mean it's the same, sorry." He raises an eyebrow, and I swallow, then correct myself. "Not sorry, I'm not sorry; I misspoke." Though saying *I'm not sorry* sounds so aggressive I almost apologize for that, until I catch Monty's approving nod. "What I meant is that I'm no good at limiting myself either."

Can one grow addicted to worry? At what point does it stop being a way to protect yourself from potential calamity and instead become a crutch to avoid stretching atrophied muscles? I almost ask Felicity if she knows, but then Monty says, "When I was your age, I drank more than I should. More than anyone should. Drank too much and, largely as a result of that, also shagged everyone within reach and lost a lot of money on cards and horses and never slept and made some truly horrifying sartorial choices."

"Why?"

"Because I used to think lavender was a good color for me, Lord knows why." He gives me a half smile, then amends, "Because I was in a lot of pain and I was afraid if I tried to do anything other than smother it, it would kill me."

"Do you mean that literally?" I ask.

"Well." He knits his fingers and presses his closed hands over his heart. "Not literally kill me—I mean, it might have, my liver wasn't going to last much longer. But not . . ." He rubs a hand over the back of his neck, then blows out a short breath. "When I was sixteen, I took a load of arsenic. Well, not a load," he amends.

"Turns out it was only enough to kill a hefty gopher. It did make me well ill, though."

"God, Monty," Felicity says quietly, and I realize this is new information for us both. "When was that?"

"Let's see. I'd just been thrown out of Eton and Father had blacked both my eyes after he caught me with that Quaker girl from Glasgow and I was drinking so much and it was never enough. Oh, don't look at me like that," he says, and Felicity and I both rearrange our faces, though I'm not sure how one is meant to look when a story like this is shared. He mashes the heel of his hand into his cheek, like he's trying to scrub away a stain. "I didn't like who I was, so I thought no one else could possibly like me either. Even Percy—who I was, mind you, bloody obsessed with. He could have told me the sky was green and pigeons shat bubbles and I would have believed it. But him telling me I was worthy of life and love—that was the thing I couldn't make myself believe. And I just wanted to be done with it all." He presses his hands over his eyes, massaging his lids with the pads of his fingers. "Let's talk about something else. I didn't mean to tell you that."

"Does Percy know?" I ask.

"Not about that time specifically, no." He ducks his head, chin to his chest. Felicity reaches out to touch his knee, but he swats her away. "No, don't pity me. I refuse your pity."

"I'm trying to comfort you!" she protests.

"By patting my knee?"

"Maybe!"

"Oh, Fel, you're still so bad at this." She throws up her hands in exasperation, and he smiles fondly at her before turning to me. "It's never gone away. Some days it's so hard to believe anyone wants to be around me, I can't get out of bed. It's so goddamn frustrating to feel as though no matter what you do or how charmed your life is, you'll never be able to shake the shadow. Sometimes the only way I feel I can define myself is by the darkness. I understand what it's like to feel you'll never see the sun again. But you can learn to see in the dark. Or, if not, you trust that night doesn't last forever. Believe me, if I can manage it, anyone can." He swipes a thumb under his nose, then gives me a watery smile. "There are light-soaked days ahead. I promise."

I bite back the urge to say that, if that's the impression he's got of me, he's grossly misread my character. There is no way that, out of the two of us, I possess the stronger will. The stronger anything. There's no test of might in which I won't be found wanting. What if my eyes never adjust, or it only gets darker and darker until the night eats me alive like a swarm of flies, or everyone finds a way to turn their face to the sun but me?

"Someone told me once," Monty continues, "there is life after you survive."

"What does that mean?" I ask.

"It means the feeling that you're not so much living your life as just trying to push through it won't last forever. Someday you'll be able to breathe." He stares over the rail at the banks of the river, where a lush vineyard climbs the slope in military-straight lines. "I don't know what your mind tells you, and I know that no matter what I say you likely won't believe it—can't believe it—but I still want you to hear it." He reaches out and takes my hands, my palms together and his on either side of them. His forehead is nearly touching mine. "You are so young, and you are so brilliant, and you are so good, Adrian. You're so much more of everything than you think you are."

I stare down at our cupped hands. My eyes are welling, and I blink furiously, trying to keep the tears at bay, but one slips down my cheek and falls onto Monty's thumb.

"Oh no, don't cry!" Monty wraps an arm around my shoulder and pulls me against his chest in a fierce, one-armed hug. "That was meant to shore you up! It's a good thing!"

"I'd comfort you as well," Felicity says, "but I've been told I'm rubbish at it."

I laugh wetly. I wipe my eyes with the back of my hand, but the tears go on leaking out of me like I'm a stiff tap. "It's fine," I say, words in total contradiction with my blubbering. "It's fine. You didn't say anything wrong."

"Try not to look so surprised," Monty says to Felicity over the top of my head.

"But I don't think you really know me." I press the heels of my hands against my eyelids so hard that stars pop through the darkness. Enough light to see by. "If you did, you wouldn't think any of that was true."

"If you get to tell me I'm brilliant, we get to tell you the same," Felicity says with a governess's sternness that I find impossibly endearing, scolding deployed for good.

"But I'm not, I'm not . . . *right*." I drag my sleeve over my face. "If I can't get rid of this—if I can't do something about it—"

Felicity interrupts. "But those aren't the same thing, are they? There's a difference between curing an illness and recognizing that some things cannot be cured, but the symptoms can be managed in order to achieve a more comfortable life that is not defined by illness." She pushes a stray hair from her face. It's lost some of its curl away from the tropical climate of the Azores, but the two white stripes at each temple somehow stand out more, like the horns of an owl. "Sorry, that's very medical phraseology."

"You can be medical," I say. It makes me feel less like

a head case and more like an ordinary person with an ordinary thing wrong with them.

The wind tears another strand of her hair free from its arrangement, and Felicity battles with it for a moment before finally shoving the whole mess of it into the neck of her scarf. "For example," she says, her tone like a friendly encyclopedia, and I think what a fantastic physician she must be—confident and thorough and knowledgeable, but not cold. "Percy has epileptic fits."

"Your Percy?" I ask Monty.

He nods, then hesitates. "Well, if George gets to England first, he may not be *my* Percy any longer."

"It's not something he'll likely ever be cured of," Felicity continues, "unless there's some enormous leap forward in medical research in the next few years. However, he's worked with several doctors in London who are informed enough not to write him off as someone who can only be treated by commitment, and who don't think epilepsy is indicative of demonic possession—stop me if any of this isn't true anymore," she says to Monty.

But Monty shakes his head. "No, you've got it in one. Though I don't think we ever got demons as a direct suggestion—masturbation, yes. Though I suppose a lot of people think that's demonic." He ponders this. "Do you think all demons are the same, or are there elite demons whose specialty is inspiring masturbation? Like a concentration in university. Didn't Michelangelo paint masturbating demons in the Sistine Chapel? I seem to recall one of the guidebooks I never read—"

"Monty, focus," Felicity says, and he snaps back from *The Last Judgment*.

"Right, yes. Percy."

"I didn't know he had epilepsy," I say.

"Well, you wouldn't, not by looking at him," Monty replies. "Honestly, you wouldn't even know it by knowing him—lots of our friends aren't aware. It's not his defining feature." A pause, then he adds, "His ass is."

Felicity rolls her eyes. "God, you're wound tight."

"This is the longest we've been apart since I was sixteen!" Monty drags his hands down his face. "I'm going mad for a good pull. Frankly I'd welcome a masturbation demon at this point."

I almost ask Monty why he and Percy aren't married, as he seems faithful to the point of sexual frustration, if only because I promised George I'd bother him, though I'm starting to wonder for myself.

But then he stretches his hands over his head, wincing when his back pops. "Percy sees an acupuncturist at Saint Luke's and a physician who helped him develop a routine for recovery after a fit, so he's down for a day or so after and not a week. They're not treatments he came to overnight, mind you—it took years of trial and error and theories that weren't a lot of fun and them not working and him getting frustrated and angry and losing hope and then getting hopeful again, and then it gets worse and it gets better and you live with it."

I laugh, my tears reappearing suddenly so that it comes out more of a gurgle. "God, is this going to take years?"

"It's going to take your whole life," Felicity says. "But it doesn't have to be the defining element of it. You can find systems to put in place so that even when you're at your worst, there are people around you who know how to help and don't give up on you."

It feels so daunting. I wouldn't know where to start—there are so many things wrong with me, so many cracks in my foundation, that patching one will hardly help with the stability of the whole. One less corner where the cold seeps in doesn't matter when the roof still needs fixing and the doors don't sit right in their frames and why bother with one crack when the whole house is falling down around you? I'll spend my whole life trying to repair myself and still die a broken person. It sounds exhausting.

The only model I have for any of this is my mother, but she wasn't a lunatic. She had something else that manifested as a mania but was due instead to whatever it is that happened when she met the *Flying Dutchman*. Her actions left the seas in disarray. How could her own heart escape unscathed?

Felicity squints at me suddenly. "How are you feeling now?"

"Daunted."

"I meant more your general state of mind. Forgive me for being blunt, but this is the longest I've seen you look either of us in the eye while speaking, and you seem a bit less"—she selects her next word very carefully—"unsettled than usual."

I *feel* less unsettled, I realize. I'm not rattling the bench with my bouncing knee or tearing the seams out of my cuffs to release some of the nervous energy that always lives in my limbs, and though I realize I have been digging my thumbnail hard into my opposite palm, that's small compared to the damage I usually do to my own body. I caught myself apologizing unnecessarily and stopped. I'm always second place in the foot race against my thoughts, but for once, it feels like I've been given a head start.

"Do you feel different?" she asks.

"Not really," I say. "Maybe a bit less seasick. River-sick."

"I need to write something down." Felicity stands, pulling her skirts out from where they've bunched under her. "I'll be right back, I promise, we can finish our nice family moment."

"Felicity Fitzwilliam—" Monty calls after her, and she spins on him.

"For God's sake, it's Josephine Violet. Felicity Josephine Violet Montague. Are you pleased with yourself?"

Monty gives her a cheeky grin, his dimples popping out. "Terribly, thank you." As soon as she's out of earshot, Monty turns back to the riverbank, staring out at the next mountain castle, and says to me, "I truly don't think I knew that."

Amsterdam

25

In Amsterdam, the tulips have died in the window boxes, but the streets are lined with leafy trees, and their reflection in the water mixes with those of the bright-colored row houses, turning the canals into colorful ribbons that snake beneath bridges and along the pavement. Boats bob gently in the current, while gulls circle overhead, chatting loudly among themselves. The canal houses look perfect as gingerbread cookies, their windows frosted by the sun and framed in hard-candy shutters.

Our Dutch hostess—or rather, the woman we are hoping will host us once we show up on her doorstep—is known to everyone but me. And though I had been warned about Johanna Hoffman's friendliness and large dogs, there is no way to be truly prepared for either. When the door to her canal house opens, three dogs that look as though they each weigh more than I do spill out, followed by a plump, bright-faced woman in a pink dress that matches the bows around each dog's neck. When she sees Felicity, she screams. In spite of not having anything in her hands, I swear she somehow still drops a vase. She throws her arms around Felicity, squeezing her so hard she nearly lifts her off the ground. "Felicity Montague, I thought you were dead!"

"Not dead," Felicity says. One of the dogs tries to wedge itself between the two of them, tail wagging so furiously it makes a thumping drumbeat against the door frame. A second snuffles its nose against my palm, trying to flip my hand onto the top of its head in an encouragement to pet.

"It's been years. *Years*, Felicity, I haven't heard from you in *years*." She takes Felicity's face in her hands and presses their foreheads together. "Hardly a word since you left! What on earth are you doing here? I can't believe it!" She releases Felicity just long enough to turn to Monty and throw open her arms to him. "And Harold!"

"Henry," he corrects, the end coming out in a wheeze as she wraps him in a rib-crushing hug. The dog gives up nudging my hand and instead mashes its face into my thigh, leaving a trail of spittle on my trousers.

"Of course, Henry!" She lets go of him, turns to me, and says with just as much enthusiasm, "And I don't know who you are!" And then I too am being hugged. She smells of honey and lavender, which makes the embrace feel like being wrapped in a loaf of warm bread.

"This is Adrian," Felicity says.

"Adrian!" Johanna cries. One of the dogs lets out a long woof in harmony and the others take up the call, an off-key, enthusiastic chorus.

She releases me, then turns to Felicity again, but Felicity holds up a preemptive hand. "All right, that's enough. No more hugs." She brushes an astonishing amount of dog hair off the front of her skirt, then says brusquely, "It's good to see you, Johanna."

In return, Johanna smacks her on the shoulder. "You tell me you're going to Rabat with some scholar and then you never come back and I never hear a single word! Why didn't you write? Come inside, come on, push the dogs out the way, they won't bite."

As we follow her into the hallway and then the parlor, she's speaking so fast I can hardly understand her. "Where are you staying? Wherever it is, cancel it; let me put you up here. Was your luggage sent somewhere? I can have one of my staff collect it. We have plenty of room, and I can make up the parlor for you, Harry—"

"Henry," Monty corrects, then corrects himself. "Monty, Jo, I've told you to call me Monty."

She waves that away. "I know but it always feels so terribly glib! You were nearly a lord! But I'm happy to set you up down here so you needn't navigate the stairs on your leg—gosh, what have you done to it? Your lovely Percy isn't here, is he? Though we'll have to do something so the dogs don't jump on you in the night. They usually sleep with Jan and me, but they get squirrely when we have company. One of Jan's brokers from Antwerp stayed with us last week and he swears he locked the bedroom door, but somehow Seymour still jumped on top of him in the middle of the night. Poor man thought he was being murdered in his bed. Please sit down—the dogs will move if you crowd them."

The dogs have all thrown themselves across various pieces of furniture in the parlor, breathing dramatically. I try to nudge one off the sofa—or at least shift his bottom enough that I can join him—but it's like trying to move a boulder. I perch on the arm instead.

Johanna returns before I realize she left, with a pot of coffee and a plate of ginger biscuits, each stamped with a windmill. "Jan's still at the office, but he'll be so delighted to see you," she says as she sets them down on the table. "Meet you," she adds to me, then "See you," to Monty and Felicity. "Seymour!" She whistles, and the dog on the sofa next to me sits up. A string of drool flies from his lips and adheres itself to the chandelier like an additional crystal. "Down, please," Johanna instructs, and he vacates the sofa with such viscous theatrics that he seems more ointment than dog. "That's Seymour," Johanna says, pointing. "And this is Boleyn, and that big boy under the piano is Cleves. I'd like to have a complete set of six, but Jan has said three is plenty for now."

"Only six?" Monty mumbles, nudging Boleyn with the tip of his cane in an attempt to move her. Instead the dog tips over on her side, paws in the air, shamelessly begging for attention. "Why not a dozen?"

"Oh, wouldn't that be grand?" Johanna sinks onto the bench of the pianoforte. "But six would mean one for each of Henry the VIII's wives. I love a theme." She feeds a biscuit to Cleves and her entire hand disappears beneath his black lips, then emerges covered in a soapy film of drool. "I'm thrilled to bits you're here, but I have a sense this is more than a social call. Particularly since there are two more of you than usually come with Felicity. Oh, how is your darling Percy Newton?"

Monty opens his mouth, just as Seymour puts his head on his knee with a wet suctioning sound. "He's fine," Monty says simply.

Johanna beams. "Oh, that's so good to hear. And you." She turns to me. "You must be Monty's illegitimate son!"

Felicity bursts out laughing. Monty and I both go deeply red. "This is our brother," Monty grumbles, swiping a biscuit off the tray and shoving it whole into his mouth. All three dogs leap to their feet, jockeying for the spot nearest him.

"Your brother?" Johanna peers at me. "Really?"

"He was born after you left," Felicity says.

"Smile," Johanna commands me, and I obey. "Oh yes, I see it now! It's the dimples—dimple. Same as you—oh God, Felicity." She presses her hands to her chest. Her dress is spectacularly low-cut and, though I'm not looking, it's impossible not to notice how perfectly shaped her breasts are. The neckline suggests she knows this too and is deeply proud of it. "It's so good to see you. I've missed you."

Felicity gives Johanna a warm smile that seems both genuine and improbable, considering how opposite they appear to be. "I've missed you too."

"Now tell me why you've actually come." Johanna's eyes flash mischievously, the joy of being visited and the fact that the visit has an ulterior motive not canceling each other out.

Felicity pries her napkin from Boleyn, who picked it up as delicately and stealthily as a dog the size of a small bear can hope to and tried to abscond with it. "Our mother died recently—"

"Oh God, Felicity." I swear Johanna's eyes well up with tears. "I'm so sorry. For all of you." She looks around at Monty and me as well. "I'm so so sorry." She says it with such sincerity that it somehow feels less maudlin than it did all those months in Cheshire of being told the same by a parade of my father's friends.

Felicity continues like Johanna hasn't spoken, and I

have a sense that, if she were to pause each time Johanna became emotional, every conversation would take days. "We recently discovered that she left behind one half of a spyglass that she kept on her person at all times, which we suspect may possess some rather unusual properties."

"Oh, please tell me what these unusual properties are," Johanna says. "May I see it?"

"No," I say too quickly. Monty deals me a curious look, but I suspect I'm twitchy enough that my overzealous response will be written off as yet another personality flaw. I still haven't told either of them about Saad, or our pact. Or that he may be arriving here any day. Or perhaps he outsailed us and has already arrived—we certainly took a long route.

"It belongs to the *Flying Dutchman*," I say.

Johanna gasps. "Good Lord, really?"

"You know it?" I ask.

"I know the lore—about the captain and the bargain and such." She catches sight of our faces. "Do you not?" She pours herself a cup of coffee, then fishes a clump of fur from it with the tip of her pinky. "There are a thousand variations, but I think the common narrative thread is this: In the midst of a storm that was sure to sink them, the young captain of a ship called the *Flying Dutchman* made a deal with the devil. The captain's life would be spared, but he was doomed to sail forever, ferrying the souls of drowned sailors from the land of the living to the dead."

"That's a far more friendly *Dutchman* than we've heard of," Monty replies. "Generally there are more storms and death and shipwrecks and damnation involved."

Johanna picks up another biscuit, and one of the dogs takes it calmly out of her hand without her even offering. "Well, when your job involves death, you're bound to get a bad reputation simply by association. Some people are wary of grave diggers."

"My mother—our mother—was on a ship that was sunk by the *Dutchman* on its way from Barbados to London," I explain. "She was the only survivor."

Johanna looks as though I've just handed her a new puppy. "Did the spyglass come from the shipwreck? Or did she meet the captain of the *Dutchman* on the one day a century he is permitted to make landfall? Perhaps your mother encountered—oh good gracious!" She clasps her hands to her face. "What if your mother is some great lost love of the captain? She slighted him! He's out for revenge! He won't stop until he's wiped out the whole of your family line!"

"Putting that aside," Felicity interrupts, "we have been trying to find any records of the shipwreck, and we have been led to believe they may be here."

Johanna frowns. "In God's name, why?"

"We aren't sure," Felicity replies. "But we were hoping to find the man who purchased them. He lives here."

When she says nothing more, Johanna blinks at her. "So? Tell me everything. Do you know his name? Or where in the city he is or where he works or anything about him?"

Felicity seems suddenly distracted by the stalactite of drool hanging off the chandelier. "Maybe we should wait—" she starts, but I am not about to wait, not for anything, not now that we're here.

"His name is van der Loos," I supply.

"Van der Loos?" Johanna repeats, then looks to Felicity. "The archivist?"

"Do you know him?" I ask.

"I know *a* van der Loos—he works at the university. It must be him. He's why I know the *Dutchman* story, actually. Or all the variations of it. He's a folklorist and has a massive collection relating to Dutch nautical lore." She's still watching my sister. Felicity is still staring at the ceiling. "You know him, don't you, Felicity?"

Felicity reaches for her coffee mug, seems to remember halfway there that it's empty, and lunges instead for a biscuit. "I've met him."

"He's on sabbatical, but he has a lovely boy running his collection at the university," Johanna says to me. "I'm sure he'd show you around and help you find whatever it is you're looking for. Though Felicity might have better connections there than I do. Fel, I swear, wasn't he the one you were talking to about—"

443

Which is when Felicity accidentally overturns the plate of biscuits, and all three dogs lunge to clean up the spill, including Boleyn, who is under the table. She lifts it off the ground, sending the coffeepot flying as well. The clang as it connects with the polished floor sends all three dogs cowering, Cleves straight into Monty's bad leg, and the conversation collapses entirely from there.

26

That night, we meet Johanna's husband, Jan, a tall, stick-thin broker on the Exchange who seems to be known equally for his keen mind for stocks and his enormous mustache. They are a perfectly mismatched pair—her chatty and bursting with energy, him quiet and serious, a man of very few, very carefully chosen words. Physically, she doesn't reach his shoulder, and while he could hide himself behind a flagpole, Johanna is round, like she's made from clouds. They are also clearly and beautifully in love, and seeing them together makes me miss Lou fiercely.

The house is warm, and crowded, and the dogs are so large and present it seems impossible there are only three of them. Johanna makes the parlor into a bedroom for Monty, Felicity shares her bed, and Jan takes the spare, while I'm shuffled to a low cot in the attic. The stairs leading there are so steep it seems impossible for the dogs to navigate, and yet, just like Johanna predicted, as a church clock somewhere down the street tolls two, I hear heavy paws on the stairs, accompanied by very wet, snuffling breaths. Then Cleves slowly hefts himself onto the low cot, as though moving at a glacial pace will render him invisible. The bed ropes whine under his weight, threatening to snap. After a few tottering steps on the uneven mattress, he settles himself directly on top of me, chuffing hotly onto my neck until I make room for his head on the pillow beside mine. He's snoring within moments.

I hardly sleep at all that night, though that can't be blamed entirely on my strange bedfellow. The anticipation of visiting van der Loos's collection the next day builds with every passing hour. I'm so restless that, were I not being held down by this anvil of a dog, I would get up and pace. I keep feeling the need to check the window, though what I expect to find there, I'm not sure. Saad waiting on Johanna's doorstep? Ghostly sails on a distant horizon? Something is nagging at my brain, like a forgotten appointment. I feel like I'm on the cusp of remembering there's somewhere else I have to be. I almost wake Felicity to ask if I can have more of her dragon snuff, but I'd likely wake Johanna as well, and then the dogs, and then the whole house, and I'd have to explain to everyone that I am worried about something but I have no idea what it is. So instead, I lie awake until the sun rises, scratching the skin on my forearm until it bleeds.

I insist we leave for the university as soon as breakfast is finished, though Monty strongly hints that the archive isn't going anywhere and he would have loved a lie-in. Felicity declines the invitation to accompany us with no explanation, so it's Monty and I who go with Johanna. All three dogs come too. They trot along in a pack, unleashed, each with a colorful bow around its neck. It feels a bit like having a royal escort that occasionally stops to piss on curbs.

"I don't know how much you know about Dutch politics," Johanna says brightly, pausing to pry open Boleyn's jaws and extract the rat carcass she found in the gutter and was attempting to hork down before anyone noticed, "but two centuries ago, the government declared the country Protestant and all Catholic worship was made illegal. They either burned all the churches and monasteries or repurposed them. The university bought several, and turned them into professors' offices and archives. That's where van der Loos's collection is housed—just here."

She stops in front of what looks, indeed, like a Catholic chapel, complete with a steeple and rose window and massive oak doors carved with Biblical scenes. The only indication of its modern occupants is the intricate institutional gate on the curb, bearing a phrase I don't remember enough Latin to translate. "I'm going to take the dogs to the Hortus—one of the groundskeepers lets them run on the lawn when there aren't any classes. So I'll leave you here—oh, but we're meeting for supper, aren't we? I gave you directions to the In't Aepjen, didn't I? It's off the Kraans Boom—ask anyone and they can direct you there. Should we say seven? And Cornelius knows you're coming." Johanna nods toward the chapel. "I sent a note yesterday. He's such a sweetheart; you'll adore him." She looks around at her brood, human and canine both, then claps her hands. "All right, good-bye, be good, have fun, don't let the mess put you off. Seymour, don't eat that."

In spite of the presentational archway proclaiming it a hall of scholarship, not theology, there has been little done to make the interior of the chapel look any less like what it was built to be. The gray stone is offset by the enormous domed windows, their scenes obscured by the blazing gold sunlight coursing through them. Colored squares cast by the rose window sparkle across our feet as we walk down the aisle toward what must have once been the altar. Now there's a flimsy-looking partition creating the illusion of an office, albeit with no ceiling and the door half open. I wonder if they merely converted the choir screen for their purposes. The hall is so silent, it feels like we shouldn't be here.

The click of Monty's cane against the stones sets my teeth on edge. Felicity checked his leg the night before and declared it was healing well, though Monty still grimaces with every uneven step.

When we reach the screen, I pause. "Do we just—" I start, raising my hand like I may knock, but before I can, the entire partition is whipped to the side with such force it nearly topples.

Behind the screen is the largest man I've ever seen. He is even taller than I am, which seems physically incompatible with a city as sloped and short as this one, and his shoulders are so broad I suspect he has to turn sideways to go through most doors. His skin is dark umber, and his curly hair is pulled into a severe queue that accentuates the pronounced lines of his face. His cheekbones must blunt razors, they're so sharp.

He greets us with the enthusiasm of meeting royalty, and I wonder if everyone here is so jubilant or if it's just him and Johanna. It's no wonder the two of them get along. "Hullo, hullo, good morning, *Goedemorgen*, hullo!" He kisses us both on the cheek—"Three times, my dear, we kiss three times in Holland," he tells me when I try to break off the unanticipated physical contact after the first *and* second. "You must be the Montagues! Johanna—pardon me, Mrs. Nijhuis—said you'd be coming. It's so lovely to meet you both! And how fares your dear sister?"

"Do you know Felicity?" Monty asks with a frown, but Cornelius has already plowed into the next conversational row.

"Mrs. Nijhuis said you were looking for something in Professor van der Loos's collection—was it a ship's manifest?" He speaks English with a heavy Dutch accent, and a smile so wide it must bend his vowels. He isn't hard to understand, but it takes my mind a moment to adjust, like sitting through the first scene of any play of Shakespeare and despairing over ever understanding the syntax before settling in before the end of the act.

Monty pokes me in the toe with his cane, then inclines his head toward Cornelius, who beams at me. I take a steadying breath, then another when that one fails to do any actual steadying. The spot on my forearm that I rubbed raw the night before is burning. I want to scratch it so badly my fingers twitch. I've just about sufficiently steeled myself when Monty says, "Adrian, you're the only one with the answers here." And I turn red and fall off course.

"It's a ship," I manage to stammer. "He bought a ship—not a . . . a shipwreck. I think it . . . maybe *it's* not here, per se. But he . . . I think he purchased it. The claim. To—it's called the *Persephone*. It wrecked off the coast of Porto, about a decade ago."

Cornelius nods enthusiastically, and I realize he means for me to tell him more. I should have brought notes.

"Uh, there was a court case. I believe. I think. My father mentioned—and we went to Porto and the man at the harbor office told us that the claim had been bought by Professor van der Loos. So. We hoped we might . . . see the things he bought. If we have the right place."

"Oh you certainly do!" Cornelius beams. "I can show you the archive, though in the spirit of full transparency, I must tell you, it's a bit of a mess. Professor van der Loos sends crates and crates and crates back from whatever corner of the world he's visiting and it's so much to sort through, so when I know he won't be back for several years, I tend to let it pile up. He's been gone so long and there's been no word about when he plans to return, so it always feels like the work can be put off another day. It's a terrible habit, I know. Just a moment and I'll fetch the lanterns."

As Cornelius darts behind the screen, I feel Monty press his fingers into my palm. "Breathe," he says quietly. "You're doing fine."

I can't breathe. I still feel as though that goddamn dog is on top of me. Is it possible he did permanent damage to my rib cage? Before I can dwell on that, Cornelius reappears with a tinder box and a lantern for each of us. "We'll want to light them now," he says. "It's very dark down there."

Monty and I look at each other. "Down?" Monty repeats.

"Oh yes," Cornelius replies. "We keep the collection in the crypt."

All the bodies have been moved," Cornelius assures us cheerfully as we descend into the chapel crypt, like that negates the sheer discomfort of being stared at by the carved faces of long-dead bishops on the sarcophagi that populate the floor. They're either too heavy to move or rooted in the earth, so instead, they've become receptacles for the collection itself.

"Excellent," Monty says quietly as we survey the room. "A filing system I understand."

It's true that the mess puts me in mind of nothing so much as the Hoffman office back in London. Amid, atop, and sometimes inside the stone coffins are the contents of entire cargo holds, all of which have clearly spent most of their life underwater. The outsides are oxidized green, frilled with dry seaweed and scabbed with barnacles. There are five figureheads lined up inside one of the vaults, tipped on their backs so it looks as though the women are digging their way out from under the ground, and a folded English flag that appears to be petrified, never to unfurl again. There are passenger trunks and fishing nets and sails hanging from the ceiling, emanating a foul, pickled odor. Then there are busts, paintings, model ships, books, atlases, encyclopedias, journals—some of them pulled from shipwrecks so that their pages have to be cracked apart. And then, seemingly just for the hell of it, one of the sarcophagi is full of seashells, beach glass, stones, dried starfish, and a bottled library of sand in jars, each labeled with a place and a date.

"Is this all of it?" Monty remarks dryly, lifting the lid on one of the trunks with the tip of his cane, then quickly closing it again. It reeks of rotted fish.

"Most of it," Cornelius replies brightly, my brother's acerbity lost on him. He's beaming around at the collection, the proud father of a crypt full of rubbish.

"How does the professor decide what's worth keeping and what's flotsam?" Monty asks. "My untrained eye can hardly tell the difference."

"Ah, well, you see, his concentration is on the nautical folklore of Holland. He has been attempting to map the *Dutchman* around the world, cataloguing every recorded sighting and wreck, and how the story changes from place to place and the variances in its replication. Then he brings it all back here to Amsterdam, and I sort it."

"What will he do after it's sorted?" Monty asks.

"I'm not sure," Cornelius replies. "And I'm not sure he knows either." He ponders this for a moment, then beams again. "The world of academic research is strange!"

"And where in the·world is your professor now?" Monty asks.

"Who knows?" Cornelius replies. "Somewhere in

Africa, the last time I heard from him, but it's been ages. That's the way of these things—feast, then famine. Then more famine, and more famine until it begins to feel Biblical."

"Do you know where we might start?" I cut in. "The shipwreck was off the coast of Portugal, if that helps."

"It absolutely doesn't," Cornelius replies brightly. "Maybe over there?" He swings his lantern toward a corner of the room where atlases are stacked almost to the ceiling. "That odd hat there came from a Spaniard, so perhaps Portugal is nearby. Not much rhyme or reason, I'm afraid. This half here"—he indicates the opposite side of the room—"has all been organized."

The two halves are indistinguishable, but I don't comment.

"Does your professor buy many shipwrecks?" Monty asks.

"Oh, dozens," Cornelius replies, seating himself on one of the sea trunks. Even sitting, his head nearly brushes the low stone ceiling. "Any wreck that carries even a whiff of the *Flying Dutchman* mythology."

"Is that all he studies?"

"His broader field is nautical folklore and superstition, but he has a particular interest in the story of the *Flying Dutchman*. He's descended from the man who painted one of the most famous still lifes in representation of it—done after the death of its captain."

Monty moves to sit on a crate near the foot of the stairs, but reconsiders when the whole thing lists sideways under his weight. "And you're a student of this as well?"

Cornelius nods. "Though I think my specialization will be thirteenth-century Laplandic wind knots."

"I don't know what any of that means," Monty says, and Cornelius lights up like a pyre.

"Oh it's fascinating! Let me explain—so in the thirteenth century—no, best start further back than that." He steeples his hands against his lips in thought. "Would you say you're more familiar with Homer's Aiolos or Hesiod's Uranus?"

"Definitely the anus one," Monty replies.

As Cornelius chatters happily, I drop to my knees and start to sift through the piles, though my work is halfhearted. I'm so overwhelmed it's turned me to stone. I don't know where to start or how to go from there, so I keep reviewing the possibilities in my head while knowing none of them will make even a dent in this mess. Even if van der Loos didn't return for half a century, it seems unlikely this could be sorted before then.

"Adrian." Someone touches my arm lightly, though I startle like I've been slapped. Monty is behind me, his lantern hooked over the top of his cane. "Sorry, I thought you heard me."

"Where's Cornelius?" I ask.

"He went back to his work." Monty leans against the edge of one of the coffins. There's the distinct crunch of sand on stone beneath his boots. "You all right?"

"Course." I flip the top page in front of me. "Why wouldn't I be?"

"You've been going through that stack for half of an hour, and you don't appear to actually be looking at any of them. And you're wheezing. Not a lot—just a little. But a little more than I'd like you to be."

He's right—I can't get enough breath. Every shallow inhale is followed with gasping in attempt to overcompensate, though they too fail to fully inflate my lungs. I try to shuffle the papers into a stack, like the precision of the edges will prove my all-rightness, but most of them are so waterlogged and rippled that they refuse to line up. "I think it's the dust."

"You don't have to do this," Monty says quietly. "Any of this. It doesn't matter that we came all this way, or spent money, or any of it. And . . ." His voice falters, and he clears his throat. "It doesn't matter what she left behind."

"Of course it matters," I reply. "I have to find . . ."

I stop. I haven't told him about my deal with Saad. I haven't told anyone. Somehow I suspect that, if either Monty or Felicity caught wind of our alliance, I would not be gently coaxed into possibly leaving this project behind, but instead dragged by the ear onto the next boat for London.

"I have to find the answer," I say at last. "I have to know what killed her."

I have a sense Monty wants to argue, but he seems to think better of it and instead says, "All right then. Let me help you."

"You can start over there." I gesture vaguely over my shoulder, trying to pretend I have some idea of what I'm doing, though I'm not fooling either of us. Still, Monty pushes himself to his feet, and I turn back to the documents with another halting breath.

The things she left behind have to matter because I'm one of them.

Monty stays in the crypt with me all morning, each of us working silently through different portions of the mess. Every so often, he'll call out about something he found— "Adrian, come look at the tits on this mermaid!"—or the name of a place he's never heard of before. I listen less and less each time. I have seen the words *Flying Dutchman* so many times they start to lose their meaning. I've been chasing a story and now suddenly I'm drowning in it. Though the more accounts I read of other sailors who, like me, saw a misty ship on the horizon in a storm, the less insane I begin to feel, and the more determined to find something here. Some of the transcripts mention a woman aboard the ship, her hair red as a summer sky, raising a spyglass to survey their deck. In other stories, there's no spyglass. Most, there's no woman at all.

But she's here. The *Dutchman* is here, on every page, tucked in every sea chest and sewn into the seams of every molded sail. *You're not insane,* I tell myself over and over with every new stone I turn. *You're not insane you're not alone you're not insane you're not alone.*

But still no mention of the *Persephone*.

"Yoo-hoo!" Cornelius appears at the top of the stairs. He has to bend almost double to squish his enormous frame through the door. No wonder he doesn't want to work down here; he barely fits. "I've made a pot of coffee if either of you would like some."

Monty pushes himself up with a moan, twisting around until his back pops. He touches my head gently as he passes. I look up, and he nods toward the stairs. "Come on, come have some coffee."

"No, I'll stay here."

"You can take a break. Give your eyes a rest. It's so dark, I don't know how you read anything."

I turn back to the book in my lap and flip to the next flapped page. "I want to stay."

A pause, so long I wonder if he somehow left in an

uncharacteristically sneaky fashion, or maybe I just didn't notice. But then he says, "Can I bring some down for you, at least?"

"You can, but I don't want it."

"How long do you intend to stay here?"

I set the book aside and pick up the next one—a heavy atlas with an inscription on the front cover in Dutch. When I open to the frontispiece, there are no words, just a hand-drawn illustration of a charcoal-gray ship, the only color on the page a swatch of flame-red paint. "As long as it takes."

We follow this routine for four days—Monty and I arrive early to the atheneum and I retreat down to the basement for further excavation. I can tell Monty is trying to help, but I don't trust his judgment about what's worth making note of, so I end up going through all his work again, and when he notices this, he retreats. Sometimes I'll throw him a book to look through or a crate to figure out how to open, but mostly I do the work, and he watches. It makes me feel like a child in a nursery, busily stacking blocks with the sincere intention of creating a critical foundation while his nurse watches from the corner, their world in proper scale. Every day, Cornelius makes coffee at two in the afternoon, and, as the old church clock chimes, he folds himself down the stairs to offer us some. Monty always goes. I am pried up from the archives only when Cornelius leaves for the day and has to close the chapel, though I would have asked him to lock me in for the night if I thought Monty would let me get away with it. Afterward, Monty and I meet Johanna and Felicity—usually with dogs but without Jan—for a meal at the In't Aepjen, a sailors' bar that Johanna loves because she knows everyone there.

I find the bar almost unbearable. It's tiny and forever crowded with sailors who smell like it's been years since they crossed paths with a bar of soap. The lacquer on the dark walls is so thick that the candlelight reflects off the wood, making the room look as though it's on fire. Huge casks line the tops of shelves buckling under the weight of more liquor than I've ever seen in one place, bottles of every color and size and shape and with labels in every language. Monkeys run across the rafters, pets brought home from faraway places and then abandoned in port. They stare down at us with bright eyes, occasionally cackling or stealing herring from someone's plate. The dogs wait outside, noses pressed to the glass until it's so fogged they can't see through it, tracking the monkeys' progress with their jowls and barking whenever one of them gets too close to Johanna.

"Today will be the day!" Cornelius says each morning when we arrive. "Today you will have some good luck!" And at the end, "Tomorrow, you will have better luck! Tomorrow you'll find what you need." It feels more buoying in the morning—by the end of the day, I'm covered in dust and smell of seaweed and in no mood for misplaced optimism.

But the fifth day—he isn't wrong.

The first thing I find is a set of books from a Dutch freight company, with a red leather marker stuck in the middle. I open it without much hope and there, in glorious, official documentation, is a catalogue of voyages of the *Flying Dutchman*. The *real* ship, not the story or the ghost, with descriptions of the masts and the names of crew members and freight capacity all spelled out in meticulous detail. The captain's name has been smudged, unreadable, as have the first three entries on the log of its stops.

The final entry, a docking in Iceland, just like Saad predicted.

The date is the summer solstice. One hundred years ago.

And there's nothing after that.

I snap the book shut, heart hammering. It's now. It's this year. The *Dutchman* makes landfall on the summer solstice of this year. Did my mother know? Was that a factor in her death? Did she feel the *Dutchman* coming for her, mark the date in her diary and count down the days to it, or was it lurking unknown on her calendar, not seen but felt, that dread without a source that so often overtakes me rooting itself in her heart?

I have to find Saad. We have to leave now. We're just weeks from the solstice—I don't know if it's even possible to sail to Iceland in that time. And I still don't have the rest of the spyglass.

I start shifting papers, frantic. More manifests, more logs, pages and pages and pages. I have no clue how long I've been at it when I finally—*finally*, impossibly—find a court transcript, all in Portuguese but for the name of the ship—*Persephone*.

"Adrian." I jump, almost knocking over my lamp, and look up. Monty's standing on the bottom of the stairs, the light tumbling from the chapel windows above pinning him in silhouette. "Adrian, are you listening to me?"

I have no idea what he said, but I reply, "Yes, I'm listening."

"Then let's go."

"What? No. It's not time yet."

"Come on, you're done here." He sounds peeved. Or tired. Or both. It had rained on us the whole walk to the chapel, and I could tell his leg was bothering him. He didn't even feel up to taking the stairs down to the crypt, so he's been sitting above with Cornelius all morning, strains of their conversation occasionally wafting down to me.

"What's the matter?" I ask him.

"This is a waste of time," he snaps, raking a hand through his hair. He must have spent all his reserves of tender patience over the last few days, for he sounds like he did that first day we sat down across from each other in a Covent Garden bar: irritated and tense. "There's nothing for you to find."

I flap the book at him. "I've literally just found something."

"Adrian, please." He slumps sideways against the stairway wall, shifting his grip on his cane. I can hear the pain in his voice. "I want to go back to Johanna's."

"So go. I can find my way home alone."

A pause. I flip the book open again, scanning the page frantically. Did I imagine it? Goddamn Monty had come down at exactly the wrong moment.

"We're not going out for supper tonight, all right?" I vaguely hear him say. "Come home when you're finished. Adrian." A pause. "Adrian. Indicate that you—Adrian, do you hear what I'm saying to you?"

I give him a half wave. "Come to Johanna's, I'm listening."

"Could you please . . ." He pinches the bridge of his nose, then shakes his head. "Never mind. Have a wonderful time down here in the dark."

"Why are you being sour?"

The court documents are endless, and all in

463

Portuguese—why hadn't I realized they'd be in Portuguese?

I'm considering running upstairs and asking Cornelius if he reads Portuguese when I find it—the only page I've yet seen in English. A witness statement signed by Caroline Montague.

Breathe, I remind myself, but how can I possibly?

Her handwriting is the neatest I've ever seen it, though the page itself is crinkled with age. I can't remember her hand without a wobble, but here, her penmanship is smooth. Each word is chosen carefully, the sentences constructed with the same precision I remember from the letters she used to send me from the country spas and coastal towns she sometimes visited. That was yet another thing we had in common—we were always better spoken in print.

The Persephone *rolled. That is all I recall.*

We were rescued by another ship that came from the ocean and was unaffected by the storm. We stood on its deck, and the captain inspected us before inviting each passenger to go belowdecks. When she reached me, she asked my name. I found I could not speak, but she told me it was not yet my time. She knew my end and it was not this. When I asked how, she showed me a spyglass with the name of her ship engraved upon the side. She said that, were I to look through it, I would see my own death. She saw it too, and she knew I was not meant to die today. I begged her for a look—would you not want to know? Wouldn't anyone? She would not give it to me and I fought her. I fought her and clung to the spyglass and she pushed me overboard into the water and the spyglass broke.

I was rescued by fishermen and brought to Porto. I have the half of the spyglass I took from her. I recall nothing more.

I do not know whether the bow was cracked intentionally. I do not know anything about the structural integrity of the masts. I do not know if the ballast—

I skim the rest, my eyes glancing across the final paragraphs denying any knowledge of insurance fraud. At the bottom, in a different script, there's a short paragraph with the judge's signature below it. It's all in Portuguese, and I don't recognize any of the words, except one.

Lunática.

On the way home, I stop at the countinghouse where the captains come to pay port taxes and log their ships and wares. Among the vessels listed is the *Dey.* I leave a note with one of the clerks for Saad, telling him I'll be at the In't Aepjen that night at midnight. *I know where the rest of the spyglass is*, I write. *And we're almost out of time.*

As soon as I let myself into Johanna's house, I know something is wrong. All three dogs lie lumped together in the hallway. None of them get up to greet me, even after I shut the front door. They stay in a fluffy puddle, watching me with their eyebrows twitching. The parlor door is closed, and as I bend down to stroke Cleves along the ridge on the top of his head, I hear Monty and Felicity on the other side, shouting at each other.

"—burned every bridge you ever built?" Monty is saying, but Felicity interrupts him.

"Do you know how long I worked without funding? The first classroom I taught in, they put up a screen so the men would not grow distracted looking at me. I was paid half of what my male counterparts were at the university. I should have been promoted long before—my work was twice as good, and I was a better teacher—"

"I don't need your goddamn biography; I know you think you're brilliant—"

"I have seen what the Berbers do with those scales— they save lives. And I cannot duplicate it without money and backing and quite frankly a penis. I proposed to Sim that we might bring him from my university to be the face of our research, and she agreed."

I sit down with the dogs, my knees pulled up to my chest. Boleyn raises her head just enough to put her chin on my foot. The weight is substantial.

"We haven't been able to sail around the Horn for years," Monty says. "Saad's men were targeting our ships and stripping them to the bones. We lost cargo and sailors and vessels, and most of our clients. And investors. We need those shipping routes open to us again. Without that, there's no company left."

"I made a mistake," Felicity says, her voice hoarse. "But I will not apologize for wanting to help people."

"So long as most of those people are you," Monty snaps. "You can talk all you want about healing and medical research and doctor shite, but at your core, you are cunning and ambitious and brutal, and those are brilliant things to be until they almost get you killed and ruin my goddamn livelihood."

"I'm sure she didn't—" Johanna starts, and I realize she's in on this too—hence the pile of dogs, most likely—but Monty cuts her off.

"No, she did. With all due respect, Jo, you stepped back a long time ago, so I'd rather you not weigh in on the subject of who's accountable for the implosion of my life."

"I'm sorry," Felicity says. "You're right. I was ambitious and frustrated and I wasn't thinking. I'm sorry.

Monty, I'm so sorry, if I had known—"

"You had to have known!" He's shouting again. I can hear my father in his voice, walking that same razor's edge between cutting remarks and a cutting blow. My father never hit me. But he hit Monty. I press my face against my knees. "You had to have had a tiny inkling—at least one moment you weren't so goddamn self-obsessed and realized what you did had an effect on someone other than yourself. You're far too smart to be that stupid."

"Don't call me—" Felicity starts but Monty's humorless laugh drowns her out.

"All this, and that's *still* the cruelest thing anyone can call you? Johanna, is there somewhere I can lie down that doesn't involve dogs or stairs or my sister? I'm feeling poorly."

"Oh. Yes of course." There's the scrape of chair legs against the floor. "There's a couch in Jan's study—"

"Brilliant, perfect, thank you."

"Do you want me to show you where—?"

The parlor door bangs open. All three dogs leap up and rush inside, nearly knocking Monty off his feet. He grabs the frame and swears under his breath. It's a moment before he realizes I'm sitting on the floor too. His face is flushed, and his eyes are red. When he sees me, he claps a hand over them. "Jesus Christ, Adrian."

"I found it." I struggle to my feet, pulling my shirt up over the spot I rubbed raw on my collarbone while I read

468

that morning. "I found the—"

He shoves a hand through his hair with such force I'm shocked he doesn't rip it out by the roots. "Sod the couch, I'm going. Where's my coat?"

He starts for the front door, and I am in his way sort of on purpose and sort of just because the hallway is narrow. I step in front of him without thinking, suddenly desperate to show him the page of our mother's testimony tucked in my pocket and for one thing in this moment to be right. "Listen to me. I found—"

But I'm interrupted again when Felicity appears in the parlor doorway behind him. She looks exhausted, but her voice is even, unlike Monty's. She has her hair down, and it hangs almost to her waist in long tangles. The ends have a distinct slope to them, and I remember Monty handing me her surgical scissors and trusting me enough to turn his back and let me cut his hair. "Monty, stop. I'll go."

He's riffling through the overstuffed coatrack, struggling to balance his cane in the crook of his elbow and keep weight off his leg while also searching for his overcoat. "Really?" he snaps over his shoulder at Felicity. "You've ruined everything, do you really want to take the satisfaction of being the one to storm away from me too?"

"Don't speak to her like that," I say, but he rounds on me.

"Stay out of this. You don't get to show up adorable and damaged twenty years later and have everyone fall all over themselves to put your mind at ease. For the love of God, where is my coat?"

"Lower hook nearest the door," Felicity mumbles.

"Finally." Monty shakes his coat free of the rack, nearly pulling the whole thing over, and I can't let him go, not yet. No matter what's happened between them, he has to know. I need him to know, and I need him to stay and tell me why my mother is different from those other sailors who saw the *Dutchman,* why she was labeled a lunatic but none of them were, because it *has* to be the spyglass, this *has* to prove it. I fumble in my pocket, struggling to extricate the folded page of my mother's court testimony. "Monty, wait. Don't go—I found some-thing. I have to show you—"

"For God's sake, Adrian, I don't care! I don't bloody care."

"It doesn't matter if you care, I found—"

And then he puts a hand on my chest and shoves me.

It's not hard. Just enough that I stumble a few steps backward, my elbow knocking a tray of calling cards off the entryway table.

"Henry!" Felicity cries behind me, her voice caught between scolding and shock.

Monty turns sharply from me, face to the door. His shoulders are heaving, and I think for a moment, he won't go. He can't, not after that. Not without another word.

But then he shakes his head, yanks open the front door, and leaves with his coat slung over one arm.

I stare at the spot where he just was, blinking furiously, trying to make sense of what happened. The raw spot on my collarbone is throbbing—he had put his thumb right overtop of it without knowing.

"Adrian, are you all right?" I hear Felicity say behind me.

"I'm fine." I touch the spot on my neck, then turn to her.

She's slumped against the door frame, the back of her fingers pressed to her mouth and her other hand rubbing the burned spot on her forearm. She's red faced but dry eyed, a feat I have never managed to achieve, though she hardly looks able to stand without a prop.

"The reason I know van der Loos," she says, and it takes me a moment to work out what she's saying, and that it's me she's saying it to. She's started in the middle of a thought, like we were midconversation. "Is that I broke my pact with the Crown and Cleaver not to bring any Europeans into their waters. In exchange for access to sunken Dutch freighters, van der Loos agreed to grant me university funding I needed for my research. Sim knew, and she turned a blind eye. Her father did not. When he found out, she lost her inheritance, I was marooned, and our company lost access to all our protected routes in the Atlantic."

"What happened to van der Loos?" I ask quietly.

"He's dead. Shot in a skirmish with the *Dey*."

My stomach drops. "Does anyone—"

"No one knows what happened to him," she says. "No one knew where he was, so no one knows to ask. It's my fault." She pulls her hair over her shoulder, then sighs, a deeper breath than I'm certain I've ever taken. "That's the whole story," she says, and she sounds a thousand years old. "And now everyone knows it."

27

I sup with Jan and Johanna alone that night—Felicity stays in her room, and Monty hasn't reappeared since his storm-out. I sit up with them in the parlor for a while after, Jan reading and Johanna working through a piece on the pianoforte while I sit on the floor and pet the dogs, my knees pulling closer and closer to my chest without me even realizing it. I feel as though I'm shriveling up, like a hermit crab that's lost its shell. Suddenly I long to see the sea. Maybe that's what's pulled me from my bed every night, that urge to check the windows for something I couldn't name.

I go up to bed as usual, wait until I hear Jan and Johanna retire, then come back down again, escaping notice by the dogs only because their snores cover any noise I make.

The In't Aepjen is as crowded at midnight as it was when we came for supper. I'm not sure if I should wait at the bar, or outside, or find a table or order drinks. Maybe Saad is already here and we're sitting on opposite sides of the room wondering where the other is. Maybe he isn't coming. Maybe he didn't get the note. I was certain the *Dey* had been on the harbor log, but perhaps I only saw it because I wanted to. I try to recall the exact shape of the word on the page, but I can't. Or maybe he's changed his mind and absconded with my spyglass after all. I scrape my hands up my arms, trying to look calm and not like I'm wondering how to best navigate the exquisite awkwardness of meeting up with someone in a public place.

"Hey." The bartender raps his knuckles on the bar in front of me. It's the same gent who's been serving us for the past week, his beard trimmed to a stabbing point and white eyebrows that turn up at the ends. He must recognize me, for he asks in accented English, "Did you come to fetch him?"

"What? Fetch who?"

He tips his head down the bar, just as a crash echoes through the room from that direction. Someone shrieks. I glance down, to where a man has pushed over a card table. Dice scatter across the floor, and one of the monkeys darts down from his perch to snatch a gold coin before it rolls beneath the bar. *"Je speelde vals!"* the man is shouting at his opponent, who is still seated at the now-vanished table.

"Come now," his opponent, back to me, says. "It's not cheating just because I win."

"You have cards up your sleeve."

The second man ruffles his hair, considering this. "Yes, I suppose that does make it cheating."

"Oh no," I say aloud without realizing it.

The bartender glares at me. "Tell him to find another place to play. He's putting off my customers."

"Right, of course. I'm so sorry."

The bartender flicks a damp rag in my direction. "He's welcome back when he's sober."

Oh God. I pick my way through the crowd to the circle forming around the overturned table. The irate man—a tan sailor with one eye covered by a patch and skin the texture of tree bark—has Monty by the front of his coat, dragging him out of his chair.

"Come on, stop it, now stop it. You're being dramatic," Monty is saying. "Look at me, I'm crippled."

The man kicks his cane out, and Monty stumbles, nearly knocking his teeth out on the bar.

"Stop!" I manage to grab my brother by the collar and pull him to his feet. "I'll pay for him," I tell the sailor. "Whatever he owes you."

The sailor bares his teeth at me. There aren't many of them, but the menace behind the action is clear. *"Ga weg, kleine muis."*

I swallow. "I don't know what that means."

"Get out of my way." He knocks an empty glass off the bar, the remnants of foam at the bottom spattering Monty and me. "That man's a liar and a cheat."

"I know," I say.

"You should be ashamed of him!"

I shovel a parcel of notes into the man's hands. It's British currency, but far more than they had on the table.

"There. You're settled."

"Deeply ashamed!" the sailor shouts again, grabbing the front of Monty's shirt.

"Fine, I'm deeply ashamed." I manage to push myself in between and drag Monty away. He seizes my arm, his gait unsteady in a way that I am almost sure cannot be blamed solely on the fact that I have his cane hooked around my foot. Warm air off the canals wafts in through the window. It's summer, I realize. I left England in the rainy doldrums of March, and missed the spring blooms. It's odd, to think of a season passing at home without me, the first of my life. I wonder if, back in London, Lou went to Milk Street's May Day celebrations. We have always gone together in Cheshire to watch the Morris dancing and the chimney sweeps' procession, and I'm gripped by a sudden panic that I'm missing my life—my life with her—chasing a story I already know the end to, not to mention a clearly inebriated brother across a crowded barroom.

He's too drunk and I'm too scrawny for me to carry him like this all the way back to Johanna's. I'll be lucky to get him out onto the street. I glance over at the bar to make sure the bartender's attention is elsewhere, then shove Monty down at a table near the door. His knee strikes the edge, and he yips in pain.

I drop into the seat beside his good ear. I should be angry at him. More angry than I am. That spot on my collarbone still stings. "Are you drunk?" I demand.

He puts his head down on the table, nose to the wood. I shudder to think of what's likely rested there before him, and certainly not been wiped up after. "I think so." He sits up again so suddenly he almost smacks me in the face with the back of his head. "Don't go. I need to tell you something."

"I'm not going."

"I have to tell you something."

"All right, tell me."

"It's a secret. Come here, it's secret." He pulls my face very close to his mouth—God, his breath smells flammable—then says at full volume, "Everyone hates me."

"That's not true."

"I know," he moans. "But they should. You should. Percy should."

"What does he—"

"You know when you find a puppy," Monty says, looking into the middle distance with a hand raised like a philosopher. "And the puppy has a really great ass—"

The thought occurs—*Should I just leave him here?*

"But you can't keep him because you know you won't remember to feed him—you hardly cook for yourself, and sometimes all you eat is those really expensive caramels you can't afford but you buy anyway, and those aren't good for puppies." He sucks in a wet breath. "So you try to be mean to him so he'll leave you and go to someone better who will give him flank steaks and blood pudding and"—he wafts his hand through the air, struggling for a word before finally finishing—"other foods for puppies. But he's goddamn stupid and he just keeps following you around and telling you he loves you and he wants to marry you even though you're not a good dog owner, and then you feel like you're cruel for making him think he's happy when he must be an absolutely miserable . . . puppy." He belches, somewhat into his fist, somewhat onto me. "The puppy thing got away from me. It's Percy. The puppy is Percy."

"I worked that out."

"He's got such a great ass."

"You've mentioned."

He lets his head fall forward on his chest. "Everything

is such a bloody mess. The business and money and losing the investors and Percy just keeps goddamn proposing
like he's not going to regret it—I'm saying no for his own
good, you understand that? I'm sending the puppy to a
farm! And then I kept seeing Dick."

And here I had just begun to wonder if he'd notice if
I stopped listening. "Excuse me?"

"Richard Bloody Peele, that bastard."

"Did you . . ." Dear Lord, now here's a question I
hadn't considered I might have to someday ask anyone,
let alone my brother. "Did you shag Richard Peele?"

"Yes." He starts to plummet toward the table again,
then sits up violently. "But a long long time ago. When we
were fifteen or something. Your age. How old are you?
Ten? Forty-five?" He places his hands on the table in
front of him, palms facing each other, then pushes them
together like he's measuring something. "Richard Peele
has got a . . . really tiny penis. Percy doesn't, though."
He starts to expand his hands for reference but I shove
them off the table.

"What happened with Richard Peele?"

"I saw him once—once! At this stupid club. And I
was only there so Percy wouldn't propose to me again."
He opens his hands, waiting for me to applaud his virtue. I don't. "And then he kept showing up everywhere
and buying me drinks and then one night we were at

Jack Dalton's and he showed me his tiny penis."

I deeply regret leading him further down this road.

"But I didn't do anything with it. And now we're going to lose our business and our home and that stupid puppy won't go find someone better for him than me." He leans into me again, another secret. Somehow his breath is even worse. "I've mucked it all up again."

"You haven't mucked anything up," I say.

"I know. It's Felicity's fault."

"We've all made bad choices."

"Especially me. I've never done a goddamn thing right in my whole life." He hiccups. "Couldn't hack it in the peerage. Can't stay sober. Or run a business. Can't tie my shoes. Don't really know what a fraction is and I'm too afraid to ask now. You don't like me." He smashes his face into my shoulder, snuffling around and slobbering nearly as much as Johanna's dogs. "Do you ever want to not be yourself? Just for a night?"

I laugh faintly. "All the bloody time."

"No, no," he sits up. "Don't say it like that. You've got to say, 'Abso-bloody-lutely I do.'"

"Abso-bloody-lutely," I say, my voice breaking into a laugh on the final syllable.

Monty grins. "See? Then it's not tragic—it's just funny."

"It's still quite tragic."

480

"I know. We are so goddamn tragic, aren't we? Bloody operas, we Montagues. At least we're pretty. You know, Goblin—"

"Adrian."

"I wish you were right."

"What about?"

"I wish we were cursed." He stacks his fists upon the table and rests his chin atop them. "Then at least I'd have an excuse."

He's drunk—a command of language is likely one of the first things to go. But a flag goes up inside me, like a warning between ships. Danger ahead. "What do you mean, you wish?" I ask carefully. "We are."

He rolls his neck so that he's facing me. "Come on," he says with a wet giggle. "Surely you must have caught on by now."

"Caught on to what?" I ask.

Monty stares at me, tipping his chin down, like he's trying to work out if I'm having him on. Finally, his mouth quivering with another suppressed laugh, he says, "It's not real."

I can feel it starting. The tremor in my hands. The heat. The fist tightening around my rib cage. *Don't*, I think. *Don't do this. Don't do this now.*

He's drunk. He doesn't mean what he's saying. I haven't shown him the testimony I found, or the logbook.

He didn't read all those accounts and diary entries and letters from all those sailors; he doesn't live inside my goddamn head, because if he did, he'd know this can't be natural. I haven't even given him a chance to explain it, but my thoughts are sliding like snow off a roof and I can't stop the rush. I'm already assuming the worst, and then something worse, then even worse, and then it doesn't feel like an assumption, it feels real, it's real, he doesn't believe me, he's been lying to me this whole time why did we even come here if he didn't—

In spite of the drink, Monty seems to realize he's misstepped. I can feel him struggling to regain his footing as he stammers, "I believe . . . that you believe . . . that our mother believed that she saw the *Flying Dutchman*. And I believe . . . that you believe . . . that she believed . . ." He covers his face with his hands. "God, I'm too drunk for this."

"No, I think this is exactly what I needed." I stand up, my legs smacking the underside of the spindly pub table with such force I almost overturn it.

"Adrian, don't." Monty reaches to stop me, but I yank my arm out of his grip, overbalancing so that I end up half toppling out the door, looking likely more drunk than my brother does as he hobbles to his feet and staggers after me. *If* he's coming after me. Maybe he's not. I don't turn around to see. I don't need to be further disappointed. As I pass the window, one of the monkeys runs along the sill on the other side of the glass, walking his hands along the panes so he leaves tiny smudged prints.

I start toward the harbor, realize that is the wrong direction and turn, then realize there is no wrong direction because I don't have a plan of where to go. I turn again, just as, from the bar door behind me, I hear Monty call, "Adrian, stop. Wait."

I don't. I push my hands into my pockets and dig my fingers into my thighs through the soft linen of my trousers. The smell from a nearby tobacco shop makes me gag, and I walk faster, pressed against the opposite side of the street, the dark bricks grabbing at my shirt.

Suddenly the pavement meets the canal, and I stop. There's a group of sailors standing with a redheaded woman wearing shockingly little on the stoop of one of the inns, spitting peanut shells into the water and cackling, and a beggar with a cat on his shoulder rattling a tin cup. Other than that, the alley is deserted. I turn sharply, head down, forcing myself to ignore whatever is shouted after me by the sailors. There's a bridge just ahead, and I step onto it, just as Monty calls again, "Adrian, please. Stop. I can't chase you."

I can't ignore the pain in his voice. Halfway across the bridge, I turn back to face him. He stops too, at the other end, panting. I wasn't certain if it was the drink or his broken leg keeping him from chasing me, but I realize

483

that he left his cane back at the pub—he's put his full weight on his bad leg to run after me. It would be flattering if I didn't want to shove him in the canal so badly.

"Tell me," I say, furious that my eyes are stinging, furious that my voice sounds so weak, furious that I am the sort of person who could be manipulated this easily for this long and never question it.

He slumps against the rail, head tipped back as he catches his breath. "Come back inside. Or let's go back to Johanna's. Let's talk there."

"No!" The strength of my own voice surprises me. It's almost a shout. I swallow hard. "Why are we here?" I demand. "Why did you let me drag you all over the world looking for something you didn't think existed? Why did you come to Amsterdam with me?"

"Because I wasn't going to leave my daft sister on that island to be killed by pirates, and I couldn't bloody well let you go running off to Portugal on your own." He ruffles a hand through his hair. "None of this went the way I thought it would. I thought we'd go to Morocco and pick up Felicity and then maybe Portugal if you hadn't exhausted yourself, and we could find just enough about the shipwreck to satisfy you, and along the way, you'd realize you had us, and we may be a rubbish family, but we're *your* rubbish family, and you'd be sated."

I laugh without meaning to, and it comes out cold

and disbelieving. "How could you think it would be that easy?"

"Because I wasn't thinking about you, all right?" He presses his fist to his forehead, exhausted by having the truth pried out of him. "Jesus Christ, I wanted it over with. She asked me to make sure you were all right after she died, and I wanted you to be and so I could wash my hands of it and we could go our separate ways. But you weren't, and you aren't, and I couldn't let you go. You had created this whole mystery—"

"What are you talking about?" I interrupt.

"Caroline wrote to me, before she died—"

"About the spyglass."

"No. Yes. Sort of." He hooks his elbows on the rail, trying to take the weight off his bad leg. I can see it shaking under him. "She asked me to look out for you. After she was gone."

I stare at his profile, and he stares at the sky, and there is silence between us for exactly the amount of time it takes for an ax to fall.

"No she didn't."

Monty's head droops forward onto his chest. "Adrian—"

"She couldn't have asked you to look after me," I say, my voice rising over his. "How would she know something was going to happen to her? Why would she have asked you that?"

485

Unless it was the *Dutchman*. Unless it was this cursed spyglass. Unless she could feel the fingers of the sea closing around her neck, unless she knew something was coming for her, that solstice looming, something she couldn't fight—

"Adrian, she killed herself."

He waits for me to say something.

I don't.

He presses his fingers to the bridge of his nose and says, his voice pitched, "I know you know that."

"She didn't." The words crack. My throat has gone bone dry.

"It wasn't supernatural. It wasn't a curse. It wasn't because of the spyglass or this goddamn *Flying Dutchman*." He presses his fist to his forehead. "She just drew a bad hand. She couldn't live with it anymore, and she was alone and she was tired and she killed herself. You have to accept that."

I feel dried out, like I haven't a drop of water left in me. I can't wet my lips enough to speak, or work a sound through my parched throat. I feel brittle as an autumn leaf, one gust all it would take to rip me from the branches. One step enough to crush me against the pavement.

"She wouldn't do that," I finally manage to croak. "She wouldn't do that to me."

"She didn't want to," Monty says. "She tried not to.

But sometimes there comes a day when it's all too much."

"It's not—it can't be that. She didn't do that. She wouldn't—It has to be something else. It's the ship. It's this curse, what about life after survival—"

"Do you want to see it?" He gropes around in his coat pockets, finally coming up with the folded triangle of paper. The letter she sent him that had pulled us into each other's orbits. He holds it out to me, but I don't take it.

"You read it to me," I say. "Back in London. I know what it says."

But Monty shakes his head. I think I might vomit. "Take it." He flaps the paper at me. I can't look. If it's real—if it's there, in her carefully looped *l*'s and spiky *f*'s, capped by her slanted signature, I can't argue anymore. Not with him. Not with myself.

"Please read it," he says again, and I step forward and take the letter.

The penmanship is shaky, the lines spaced out and the ink applied in varying shades, like she wrote it across several weeks at several different desks, adding new lines at sporadic intervals.

Dear Henry,

I was so happy to see you this month past. I am so happy

you found a better life than the one you had with us.

I knew you were unhappy and never did anything. I was unhappy too.

I'm sorry.

I will be dead soon. Once, long ago, I sailed to Barbados. On the return, I came into possession of a cursed spyglass. When I looked through it, I saw my own death. I'm afraid it's coming. And even if it isn't,

I'm tired of waiting.

You do not owe me your forgiveness or any kind of favor, but please,

if you can find it in your heart to do this one last thing for me, please find Adrian once I'm gone.

Don't let him keep the spyglass. He'll never let it go. I never could. I don't want him to lose

Adrian needs someone to live through this

I hope you do it better than I did.

Caroline Montague

She didn't send him looking for the spyglass. She sent him for me. Monty wasn't chasing the same mystery as I was—maybe he didn't even see a mystery at all. He's followed me around the world out of obligation to our dead mother, hoping someday I'll realize the truth on my own, drop the spyglass in the ocean, and he can slip out of my life once again.

"It's not a curse, Adrian," Monty says quietly. "It's not fate or magic or some ghostly encounter she had in the middle of a shipwreck that doomed us all. I know you want something else to believe in, but she had a mind that was always against her, and you have it too. Not because of a curse and not because of any character flaw or defect in your brain or your soul or your heart or whatever you want to call it, but because that's how it is. That's the hand you were dealt. You either have to play it as best you can or . . ." He considers this, swaying for a moment, and I wonder if he's going to fall over and if anyone would judge me for just leaving him there. But then he finishes, "There's no other choice. You live with it. You keep moving. You keep trying."

"You lied to me."

"What was I supposed to do? You think if I'd read you this back in London you would have believed me? You think your mind would have let you believe me? This would have been another clue. More proof of your cause." He drops his chin against his chest, then finishes weakly, "I'm sorry."

I'm shaking my head. "That's wrong. You're wrong."

"Adrian—"

"You're wrong!" I can hardly get words out, my breathing is so stuttered. "I'm not going to spend the rest of my life heaving myself up this goddamn mountain when everyone else gets a flat country road. Something is wrong with me, and I'm either going to fix it or it's going to kill me. It won't go away or heal or get better. I'm either broken or I'm not."

"Adrian." Monty takes a step toward me, holding out a hand, maybe for me, maybe for the letter. I crumple up the letter and throw it on the ground between us.

"I can stop this," I say. "She couldn't, but I will."

I turn, and I run. I follow the canal, past two more bridges and farther than the red-doored church with the walled garden. I start to turn down a cross street, where the whitewashed side of a shop is painted with a ship flying Dutch colors, but my legs are shaking and it's so hard to breathe I'm getting dizzy. I tip sideways into the wall and slide down it. The alley is so narrow I could press my feet flat against the opposite wall if I stretched my legs straight. Above me, the dark outlines of the canal houses loom, the shutters bordering each window so white through the darkness, like bones poking out of a decaying corpse.

I'm not sure I've ever been so angry. Angry at Monty, who lied to me, and Felicity, who broke her promises, and my mother, who left without telling me why or how or being able to see the truth of what was happening to her. Angry at the captain of the *Flying Dutchman*, who dared to touch my family in the first place. Who thought one lousy spyglass was worth exterminating an entire bloodline.

I'm angry at myself, for being this person. For not being strong enough or smart enough or brave enough to just get on with my life. For the way my thoughts become moth-eaten by doubt. For the scars on my body I put there myself. For the feeling of my bones pressing up against my skin. For everything I can't control or change or do a god-damn thing about.

Our family is cursed. We must be. We have to be.

I can't breathe. I can't see straight. My whole body is shaking, and I can't feel my hands. I almost hold them up in front of my face, just to be sure they're still there. *Get a hold of yourself, pull yourself together, stop being this way!* I'm gasping for breath and people are passing me, purposely looking away so they can give themselves an excuse for not stopping to help. My throat is closing. I yank on the collar of my shirt, so hard it rips, but it does nothing. I'm too late. I'm dying. The *Dutchman* got its fingers in already and I'm going to die on a street corner in Amsterdam.

I'm dying. I'm dying. I'm dying. Oh my God, I'm actually dying. I can't breathe. The muscles in my chest are convulsing, trying to loosen enough that I can draw a breath, but it's like trying to pry open a locked castle door with your bare hands. I'm clenching my teeth so hard they squeak, and I can taste blood at the back of my throat.

I realize someone is crouched beside me, and oh my God, it can't be Monty. He can't have followed me that quickly, even with two good legs—he's not sober enough, and my path has been nonsense, impossible to follow in the dark. I don't want it to be Monty, and I don't want it to be a stranger and I don't want it to be anyone. I don't want anyone to ask me what's wrong, what's happening to me, I don't want to attempt to explain it because it doesn't make sense. I'm gagging on my own breath, folded at the waist like I'm praying. I want Louisa. I want my mother. I want her not to have stepped off that cliff, her spyglass and her wedding ring in a box under her bed.

"What's happened?"

It takes a moment for me to recognize the voice.

It's Saad.

Speaking is impossible. I can't even get my muscles in my own control well enough to shake my head. My damaged lungs make this terrible, keening noise when I try to breathe. I sound like a rabbit in a snare, exhausted by its own thrashing. *Put me out of my misery*, I think. That's what we do to animals in pain.

When I don't speak, Saad runs a hand over his shaved head. The gold knobs of his rings glitter in the streetlights. He must think me possessed, or dying, or insane. He might be right on any of those counts. If he had any sense, he'd get up, walk straight back to the harbor, board the *Dey*, and leave me to my insanity.

But instead, he shifts his weight, so he's not crouched but sitting beside me.

"It just has to pass," he says, partly a question, partly an instruction. He reaches into his coat, then takes my hand and presses the spyglass into it. I close my fist around the cracked edge until it cuts me. Saad sits with me and we wait together, beneath the black sky, a painted ship crowning us as the world around me fills with water. "Just let it pass."

I'm not sure how steady I'll be on my feet, but considering the hour and the number of taverns, my wobbling gait doesn't stand out overmuch as Saad and I walk to the harbor. The *Dey* is one of the largest ships moored there, imposing and sturdy among the skeletal fishing boats and schooners. The spikes of cannons and swivel guns poke out from its hull. Even at rest, it's ready for a fight.

As we climb the gangplank, a shadow stretches suddenly in front of us, and when I look up, Sim is standing there, blocking our path. "Adrian?" she calls, pulling back the shade on the brass lantern hanging from the lines. It's hardly more than a flicker, but I feel as though I've stepped from darkness into midday summer sun, and I flinch. "What are you doing here?"

"That's not your concern." Saad tries to push by her, but Sim blocks his path, her small body planted like a boulder. "Adrian," she says again, looking past her brother to where I'm still standing. "Why are you here? Where's Felicity?"

"Adrian is coming with us," Saad says. "That's all you need to know."

She still doesn't move. On deck, several of the crew have stopped their work and are watching, dark shapes against the navy sky.

Saad pushes himself against her, nose to nose, his chest puffed out. "You do as I say," he growls. "When I tell you we have a heading, you set the course. When I tell you Adrian's coming, you don't ask why."

Sim stares at him for a moment, then steps back. I think she's retreating, deferring yet again to her brother, but then she shakes her head and says, "I'm done, Saad."

Saad raises his chin. "What did you say to me?"

"I'm not doing this. I'm not playing along with your whims anymore."

"You were dismissed—" Saad starts, but Sim interrupts him.

"I made a mistake," she says. "I won't deny that. But I am only a liability if I continue to sit by and let you run this fleet into the ground."

"Things will change," Saad says. "Everything will change after this heading. Please, Sim." His voice cracks, and I remember, he's just a boy, and Sim is his sister. He probably grew up idolizing her, watching her study and fight and learn at their father's right hand, never expecting he'd have to take her place. "Trust me," he says, so quiet only she and I can hear. "Please."

"I have trusted you for far too long," she says. "And I trusted our father for far too long before that. You know and I know and all of these men"—she casts a hand behind her at the crew assembled on the deck, none of them even pretending not to listen anymore—"know you should not be at the head of this fleet. I trained and studied and prepared my whole life for a role that was taken from me unfairly because our father was old and out of his mind and hated women. I have watched you make mistake after mistake after mistake and never face consequences, whereas a single wrong decision defined my entire life." She raises her hands and takes another step back from him, onto the deck. "I'm done. I'm not going to let you destroy this fleet because this is my home and my family and I care for every man and woman who sails beneath our banner."

"So this is a mutiny?" Saad demands. He has his arms crossed, hands balled into fists and pressed into his sides.

"Only if you want it to be," Sim says.

Saad glares at her, then stalks to the top of the gangplank to address the men standing behind her. The lamplight polishes his bald head, a sheen of sweat starting to break out along it. "Who agrees with her?" he demands. "Will any of you stand against me on the side of a mutineer?"

There's a pause. The silence pulls as tight as the string of a violin. Then one of the men steps forward. "I am with Sim," he says.

And the first tree falls.

The rest of the crew assemble behind her, shoulder to shoulder.

Sim extends a hand to me, offering a place among them. "Come on, Adrian," she says. "Let's get you home. I'll help you find Felicity."

But I can't. I can't. I still can't breathe and I can't think about that letter and I can't leave Saad—I cannot leave behind the only ally I have left. The only person who believes in the *Flying Dutchman* the way I do. The only other person who needs it to be true.

"I'm going with Saad," I say. Sim gapes at me, and I half expect her to tell me I don't know what I'm saying.

In her defense, my words come out so cluttered and strained and barely understandable that I certainly don't sound as if I do.

"Adrian," she says again, with more emphasis this time, like maybe I just didn't hear her before. "Come on."

"He can choose for himself," Saad says.

Sim snaps her fingers, then points to the ground, like she's calling a dog. "Come here, both of you." She looks meaningfully at her brother. "This isn't your ship anymore, Saad, but you still have a place on it, and in the fleet. I'll take you home."

"I would rather die," Saad spits.

"No you wouldn't," Sim says. "Come on, Saad, it's not too late."

But Saad has already turned his back on her, stomping down the gangplank. "Too late for *you*, Sim," he shouts. "This is treason!"

Sim's shoulders sink, and she looks to me one final time. "Adrian . . ."

But I turn and follow Saad.

28

One of the yawls from the *Dey* is moored in the harbor, having been sent ahead before the warship itself squeezed into port. It has a single mast, with the mainsail low to the deck running parallel to the prow.

It is in this doll-sized boat that Saad and I will sail to Iceland to meet the *Dutchman*.

I fall asleep on the deck soon after we depart, but don't sleep long. When I wake, my whole body aches like I spent the day before scrambling up boulders. My muscles are wobbly, and I still can't draw a proper deep breath. My head is pounding, and the skin of my face feels tight. I stretch my fingers and my jaw, astonished by how much they hurt. The lines of my palm are scabbed with dried blood from where I rubbed the skin off without realizing it.

"Are you all right?"

I sit up. Saad is standing at the helm of the yawl, one arm looped over the wheel like it's an old friend. Amsterdam is behind us, close enough that it's still a soot smudge on the horizon.

"It's this year," I say. I can't remember whether I already told him this. The night before feels like a half-remembered dream. "The *Dutchman* will dock this year," I say again, "on the solstice."

Saad watches me for a moment, then his eyes flick to the edge of the raised skylight set into the deck. I look too, and realize the half of the spyglass is resting there.

"Where's the rest of it?" he asks, his voice suddenly taking on the edge I first heard when he boarded the *Eleftheria*, and I wonder suddenly if he's lured me out to the open sea to murder me and then dump my body.

"It's still with the *Dutchman*—it never left." I retrieve the spyglass, running my fingers along the crack in the side. "I found my mother's court testimony. She tried to look—she wanted to know how she died, if not in that wreck—and she held on to the spyglass as she fell overboard. The spyglass broke, and when she washed up, she still had half of it with her. Without it, the captain doesn't know who is meant to stay and whose time has come, so he takes them all. That's why your seas are in disarray. Without the spyglass, the captain doesn't have a heading."

"So we meet the *Dutchman* in Iceland," Saad says.

"How long will it take us to get there?"

499

"That depends on the winds." He turns his face to the spray off the water. "Ten days, at best."

"And you can crew this by yourself?"

"With your help." He links his hands together and leans forward, staring out at the sea. "You can help, can't you?"

Or are you too insane? feels like the unspoken conclusion to that sentence. I swallow. "If you tell me what needs to be done."

Saad stares forward, his eyes to the sea but his gaze far away. "If I don't go back to my court . . ." He pauses, then corrects himself. "The court. If I go back without a pact with the *Dutchman* . . ." He trails off, and I realize his voice is different. He's dropped the deep affectation he uses around his crew. "I've got nothing to go back to."

"Me neither," I say quietly. A wave catches the side of the boat, spattering the deck with a miasma of water that catches the light and shines in a rainbow.

"I knew Sim would turn on me." He fists his hand around one of the spokes of the helm. "I just never thought she'd have the courage to lead an all-out mutiny."

I'm not sure it counts as a mutiny if the deposed captain is then immediately welcomed back on board, but I don't correct him. "She thinks you'll be a great leader one day," I offer.

He laughs bitterly. "One day. When? When I'm dead and she can select what deeds I'm memorialized by." He presses his forehead to one of the knobs along the helm and says to his feet, "She acts as though she made one mistake that changed her life while I can't stop doing the wrong thing. She's made her share of bad choices. They'll turn on her too— it won't be better with her as commodore."

I don't say anything. I have a sense he doesn't need me to.

When I take a hard-won breath, Saad frowns at me. "Are you ill?"

"Not in a traditional sense." I look down at my hands and realize one of my fingernails is bleeding. I'm not sure whether I broke it on something the night before or I've been unconsciously picking at it while we've been talking.

"Is it the *Dutchman*?"

I wish I could answer with the surety I would have had the week before. Even yesterday would have been different. But Monty had lied to me. My own damn mother had lied to me.

Or maybe they weren't lies. Maybe they didn't know. My memories had reshaped themselves before; maybe my mother's had done the same. She had forgotten what had happened on the deck of the *Dutchman,* but still lived with the memory of it, like an imprint left in the carpet long after the furniture has moved. I can't remember what her letter to Monty said. She had wanted him to find me—to protect me from this curse. She hadn't been begging him to save me from myself, she was hoping he'd fight with me. It was his fault if he didn't realize that.

Instead of answering Saad, I ask, "Do you know any staves?"

Saad frowns, and I can tell he doesn't know what they are, though he's trying to hide that fact. "Those are . . . songs, aren't they?"

"No—they're symbols. Meant for protection. You carve them on your boat and they keep away bad things. George taught me one that works like a compass. It helps guide you even when you don't know where you're going."

"I know where I'm going," he replies indignantly, turning to the helm again.

"That's not the reason you need a stave." I coat my fingers in black from the unlit lantern hanging from the lowest mast and use it to trace the shape of the vegvísir, first on the back of my hand like George did to make sure I remember it before I copy it out on the deck.

When I finish, Saad is watching, his eyes tracing the lines of the stave.

"It's silliness," I say, but Saad turns back to the helm.

"It's not." A pause, then he adds, "Just so long as I don't have to sing."

As we push north, the waters shift to an icy blue-white, the only signs of life the terns that sometimes perch upon the waves, and the massive black backs of whales that crest occasionally, spraying briny mist before diving again. We catch long, thin-nosed fish off the side of the boat and roast them nightly on the deck.

I try not to watch the horizon, but find I can't look anywhere else. I hardly sleep, and when I do, I wake with my ears full of water and a voice in my head calling me, the same one I remember from the storm. Lying in my hammock is uncomfortable or hot or sharp or sometimes all three at once, and my thoughts ricochet like stray bullets. It only takes a night before I give up the sling entirely and instead pass my nights on the deck, sitting quietly while Saad stands at the helm, both of us watching the horizon for ships that aren't there.

I think of my mother with her eye to the captain's spyglass, watching her own death like a scene from a play. Once she knew—once she even had an inkling—its hooks would have been in her. Maybe she did step off that cliff intentionally, but what if it was only to prove the captain wrong or reclaim control of an inevitable end? We all die, but for her, the choice must have been like picking the moment to leap from a runaway carriage. No use staying on board, but no chance of jumping off without pain.

We trade watches, though Saad doesn't sleep much either. I suspect he doesn't trust me to handle the boat on my own, which is well justified. I'd be hopeless in any kind of crisis. Twice I work myself into such a frenzy over invented calamaties that may befall us that I run to the tiny hold and drag him from his hammock, insisting he come on deck with me to prevent some ambiguous bad thing from happening. Both times he does without question. Both times, I find myself able to shake less of the panic. It hangs about like a bad cold.

Our fourth day at sea, Saad comes up from the hold much earlier than the end of my watch, carrying two pewter mugs and a bottle full of amber liquid. "Look what I found." He holds up the bottle, which is unlabeled, but I nod anyway, like I recognize it. He fills both mugs, then hands one to me, and I take it, not entirely sure what's happening until he clinks his against mine. "Cheers. That's what the English say isn't it?"

"Yes. Cheers." We both take a drink, which I regret immediately. The liquor—it's got to be liquor—is warm and has a chewiness that liquid shouldn't have. I swallow hard, trying to suppress a cough. "God, that's awful."

"I know." Saad peers down into his glass. "I think it's supposed to be beer."

"You think?" I repeat. We could have just drunk furniture polish. Based on the taste, I wouldn't have been surprised.

He frowns at the bottle, like a label might appear if he only looks hard enough. "We don't allow hard liquors on the *Dey*."

"Why?"

"I'm Muslim—most of our sailors are. We're not supposed to drink spirits."

"But do you?"

Saad raises his mug for another sip, catches a whiff of the rancid beer, then seems to think better of it. "No. I can't stomach them. If I had my choice, I'd drink sugar cane juice. Don't tell anyone that." He dumps the contents of his mug over the side of the boat. "It's childish."

"Well, you're not exactly . . ." I scratch the back of my neck, something I must have been doing more than I realized, for I find the skin there already raw. "You're not that old yet."

Saad glowers out at the ocean, like age is a personal failing he's been trying to correct. "No one ever misses an opportunity to remind me. 'You're so little!' 'You're such a baby!' 'So much responsibility for someone so young!' It's condescending shite. I'll wager no one told Usama ibn Zayd he was too young to lead an army for the Prophet, and he was only ten and eight when he did." He tosses his empty mug into our swab bucket, and it clangs like a bell. "It's not as though I don't realize it," he mutters. "I know I wasn't the first choice."

"First choice for what?"

"To take over the fleet. Sim was my father's favorite. She always was. But after she and your sister mucked things up, he couldn't make her commodore."

I wedge my finger under a bubble of lacquer on the

rail, sticky and taut. "Is it just the two of you?"

"No, I've got a whole handful of half brothers. They're all older than Sim, even. But they have their own lives. None of them wanted anything to do with the Crown and Cleaver. One of them is married to a Moroccan princess. I'd take that over trying to run a struggling fleet. Maybe there were always problems. It just feels as though I've made everything worse." He scrunches up his nose, then says, "If you tell anyone any of this, I'll kill you."

"Who would I tell?" My already shredded nail cracks again, and I bite the ragged edge. A tiny bead of blood rises up from under it. "If you could see your own death, would you want to?"

"Yes," he says, without hesitation. "Wouldn't anyone? Wouldn't you?"

His certainty disarms me, and maybe he's right. God, wouldn't it be nice? To know that nothing else could touch you. To know what was worth the fear. I wonder again whether, when my mother caught a glimpse through the spyglass before it broke, she saw herself stepping off that cliff in Scotland into the sea. Or maybe it had cracked before she could get a look and that was what had driven her deeper and deeper, that almost knowing. That half an answer always in her pocket.

Or what if she looked through it and saw something else? Was it inevitable if, instead of rolling the loaded dice fate offered you, you simply stood up and walked away from the table?

Saad clasps his hands and leans hard against the rail on his elbows, arching his back. "You'd never have to be afraid again. You'd never hesitate. If you don't fear death, you fear nothing."

I wasn't sure I believed that.

"My father was fearless," he continues. "He never met a foe who didn't blink first. He should have died a thousand times, but nothing could kill him."

"What did?" I ask.

Saad frowns. "He was old. His body stopped working."

It's the kind of thing you tell a child to try and explain death, and he sounds so young when he says it.

"I wish he could see it," he says. "Me, strutting into Rabat after Sim has tried to turn all our men against me with a debt owed me by the *Dutchman*. I wish . . ." He stops and runs a hand over his chin. "I wish I had known the last time I spoke to him that it was the end. I would have asked him so much. Sometimes I don't think I want him back so much as I just want one more day with him to ask him what I'm supposed to do and how I'm supposed to be."

I stare out at the sea, the waves foaming bone white against the black sky.

Maybe it's not my own death I would want to see through the spyglass. Maybe it's everyone else's. The fear of losing someone else the way I lost my mother, sudden and unexpected. Tell me what the last day together will be. Tell me, so I know to write everything down. So I won't spend years at sea without a heading, staring through a spyglass, praying for a shore.

"We only have one chance," Saad says suddenly, "to catch the *Dutchman*. Then . . ." He raises his closed fist and then opens it, like a sudden puff of smoke.

I look down into my mug, consider another drink no matter how foul, but instead, I toss it out to sea. "Better make it count."

Iceland

29

Saad and I arrive in Iceland in the early hours of the morning, though the light is bright as noon. The butter-yellow sky rattles my senses—I can't make myself believe it truly is night, no matter how many times I'm told so. There are three days to the solstice, and this far north, the sun never sets. All the while we'll be here, there will likely be no darkness at all.

We dock in less of a town and more of a bishopric, with several churches and farms, a small main street, and a water mill in the distance. The city is populated mostly by Danes, with some Dutchmen and Germans and a crew of English fishermen drinking and talking loudly at a bar we pass, mixed in with the native Ice-landers.

I've already scraped my palms raw with my fin-gernails, the movement anxious and unconscious, and there's blood beneath my fingernails from it.

It's going to be over soon, I keep telling myself. *There is an end to this. There is an end in sight. The light-soaked days are coming. Just look at all this sun.*

Three days and then . . . what? I wake up a new man, with new habits and new ways of thinking? I return to England and everyone finds me changed and assertive and calm and not strange? I walk straight from the harbor to the House of Lords, where I read my pamphlet myself in a loud, clear voice and do not fear the judgment of my peers? I cannot imagine my life without this constant, battering tide. I've spent my whole life building up fortifications against it, and suddenly I wonder who I'll be without it.

Someone who does not cover himself with leeches. Someone who does not sweat and stammer and struggle to look people in the eyes. Someone who can sit down and eat a meal without his ability to digest it reliant upon his mood. Someone who doesn't look off the edge of a sea cliff and think, *What would happen if I just stepped off?*

It will be quiet, I tell myself. Quiet like a concert hall waiting for the conductor to raise his baton. Not quiet like an empty house, or a dark forest road. Not quiet in a way that feels eerie and vast and alone. When you don't fear yourself so much, I tell myself, you will not fear being alone with yourself.

Our tiny yawl is battered from our journey, and neither of us has enough money or time to pay for repairs or purchase another boat. Instead, we decide to go overland to the bay marked on Saad's father's charts as the last known place from which the *Dutchman* sailed. We sell the boat to a fisherman, and use the money to hire horses. Icelandic steeds, I learn, are singular, in that they are selectively bred so that they maintain short legs, almost pony-sized, but have extraordinary stamina and health. They also have manes of a length and luster that would put society ladies in England to shame.

We set off across the verdant countryside. The coastal trail is buttressed by dark cliffsides, their faces spangled with moss and foliage. Runoff from the glaciers spills from their edges in more waterfalls than I knew could exist in one place, sometimes dozens in a single mile. Their water is fresh and clean, and we stop at the pools that collect beneath them for the horses to drink. The clouds are low over the mountains and the polished peaks glow with the excess daylight.

The countryside is sparsely populated. We pass a few turf houses, which blend into the landscape so well I only notice them because of the sheep grazing nearby. The first night, we stop at one where we are given dark rye bread and thick lamb stew, which we eat crouched outside the barn beneath the sun that never sets. It is impossible to mark any time. The few minutes of darkness each day grow thinner and thinner. It gets harder to breathe, like the sun is sucking up the air around us.

The white cap of the glacier begins to loom over the cliffs, and the air turns colder. As we follow its edge inland, I can see in the distance a vast expanse of something that looks like it can only be the sea. I assume it must be water until, as we draw closer, I realize it's lupine, fields and fields growing hardy and wild, all the way to the horizon. It stretches as far as we can see, and then farther. We sleep among them that last night before we cross the glacier, only a few hours in the bright night, and I wake with my hair full of petals.

When we reach the edge of the glacier, we leave the horses at a farm as collateral for the gear we'll need to cross the ice. We attach spikes to the bottoms of our boots and start the climb, following sleigh tracks the farmer pointed out to us, first up one side, then down toward the lagoon. When I ask him how long it will take to reach the lagoon and he answers with only a vague and unhelpful hand wiggle, I want to grab him and shake him. *Do you not understand how important this is to me?*

The ice climb is brutal. Perhaps it wouldn't have been so difficult if I had slept one full night in the last year, but I'm so tired. My limbs feel gelatinous within an hour from so much scurrying and digging in my heels and trying not to slip to my death.

But I can't stop. If I stop, we'll miss it. We'll run out of time.

It's Saad who finally calls for a rest. He's breathing hard, every gasp misting against the air. I can't make myself sit. I hike ahead while he rests, like the lagoon might be just over the ridge, but the ridge keeps going and going and going and maybe it's the next one. Or the next one. I force myself to come back for him. The sun moves across the sky but the light never changes.

Am I losing my mind? I wonder over and over as I watch the sun set but the light remains unchanged, turning the question over and over until it becomes, *Did I lose it long ago? Am I too far gone to change?*

I feel manic, teetering on the edge of sanity. The urgency chews through me, the need to go, the inability to understand why no one else feels like their brain is on fire. I'm vibrating with it—I want to take off my coat, but I hardly get it to my elbows before Saad asks, "What are you doing? You'll freeze." And though I know he's right, it starts to feel like I've wrapped myself in lead. It's slowing me down. My own body is slowing me down.

I wonder if she knew the date. I wonder if she felt the *Dutchman* coming for her, to claim what was stolen. I wonder if she lived her whole life feeling like she had cheated death once, escaped a shipwreck she was supposed to die in, and if that second life had felt more

515

urgent or less. If borrowed time made life harder or easier to live.

If we miss the solstice, I keep thinking as we hike, the
words in time to the crunch of our spiked shoes. *If we
miss the solstice. If we miss the solstice, if we don't return
the spyglass, if I never know what the captain did to her,
what bad luck or curse or magic fell upon her when she
robbed the ocean's gravedigger.*

I cannot make my brain stop moving. I can't stop my
thoughts, or even redirect them. I can't relax enough to
sleep or eat or do anything but hike and turn over and
over and over in my head all the questions I never asked
her. The things I didn't even know to ask—the things she
didn't tell me.

We hike south until the glacier tapers into clear blue
water studded with pieces of ice that have broken from
its sides and begun to drift out to sea, most of them
small-looking from the distance, though I'm sure they're
larger than the turf farmhouses we passed. Some of the
bergs look like cut diamonds, translucent and distorted,
capturing the light and refracting it back. The surf has
rolled them to a shining luster. Others are opaque, their
frosty edges the pale blue of a robin's egg. A small strip
of black sand beach closes off the bay except for the narrow mouth where it meets the sea.

And upon that narrow bar, a figure sits, their face to
the sea.

I stop, gasping for breath. I close my eyes hard, to be certain I'm not dreaming or delirious or simply seeing what I want to.

But when I open them again, it's all still there.

The *Dutchman* waits just beyond the beach, a ship that, in the overcast shadow of the clouds, seems to have descended from the sky to sit upon the waves. I didn't realize how clearly I remembered it until I see it again. Even in the sunlight, it looks gray and penciled, like it brings storms with it.

Saad stops beside me, leaning backward into the slope of the glacier with the spikes under his boots holding him in place. The fur lining of his hood sticks to his face. I want to grab him and pull him against me, thrust our clasped hands into the air in victory, make him shout with me, *We made it! We found it! We aren't too late!* Why doesn't he look happier?

But then he asks, "How long should we wait?"

The question startles me enough that I tear my eyes away from the ship. "What?"

"Or do you think we missed it?" Each of his quick gasps mists white before his face. "I thought I was keeping good track of the days, but the sunlight ruined my count. I'm not sure if we're too early or too late."

"What are you talking about? It's right there."

"What is?"

"The *Flying Dutchman*—right there, in the bay." He

517

stares into the sun, eyes scrunched against the light, until he raises a mittened hand.

"Can't . . ." I fumble in my jacket for the spyglass. I shed my mittens long ago—having all my fingers bundled together and unable to operate independently yet another source of inexplicable stress. My fingers stick to the metal surface. "Can't you see it?"

Saad is now scanning the horizon wildly, like we're playing a game he's desperate to win. "What is it? What do you see?"

"The ship. The ship, it's right there. And the captain!" I fling a hand toward the black sandbar, but when I look again, it's empty. I scan the horizon frantically, but there's nothing. The charcoal ship is gone. "It was there!" I cry. *Was it?* "It was right there, I saw it! I know I saw it!" *Do you?* "It has to still be there, we just have to find it. We have to get to the beach!"

I kick the back of my boot, struggling to dislodge the spikes from the ice—my muscles are shaking. Saad tries to steady me, but I toss him off. He must think I'm falling—I'm not falling. I'm climbing. I'm climbing down. I have to get to the beach.

"Adrian, stop!" he calls. "There's nothing there."

"There is! There was! I saw it." I swear I catch a glimpse of something on the horizon—clouds or sails or one and the same. I turn so wildly that this time, I do slip. Saad grabs the hood of my coat, so when my feet go out from under me, we both crash to the ice. We're sliding down the embankment, out of control, both of us scrambling for a handhold, but the ice is slick as glass. We hit the lip of the ledge we were standing on and fly off, airborne for a moment before we crash onto the next ledge below us. I land on my back, my thick coat cushioning me though the impact still knocks all the breath from my lungs. Beside me, Saad groans.

I can't breathe. I can't get my breath back. Saad is going to stop me from climbing down any farther. He's going to hold me back, or take the spyglass or tell me I'm insane. He's going to realize he put his faith in a lunatic, and take me away to a madhouse to rave about ghost ships where no one can hear me.

But I have seen the *Dutchman*. I have steered too close to the dark rocks.

I have not come this far to only come this far.

I scoot along the shelf until I can see over the side and down the next patch of the glacier. The slope is gentler, and instead of a fall, I slide on my back like a seal. I can feel pieces of ice slip down the back of my coat and into my boots. The terrain turns jagged as the glacier slopes into the bay, and I hit several more of the hard ledges of ice like the one Saad and I fell from. I feel bounced around like a coin in a pocket, but I'm ready to slide all the way to the sea if that's what it takes. I'll put my boots on that black sand and the captain will be there. I'm so sure of it.

I reach another shelf, this one the widest yet and with the steepest drop-off, and I'm forced to stop my descent. The ice here has flattened into a glassy blue sheet before the sharp slope into the bay, and I'm stuck, unsure what to do. The ice face below me is too slick to climb. I'd need spikes and ropes—or maybe I don't. Maybe I can do it alone. I'm not cold—I could take off my shoes and my coat and the pads of my fingers and toes would stick to the ice. I could scale it like a monkey.

"Adrian!" I hear Saad shout, and I glance backward. He's followed me in a controlled slide, the edge of his ice hook dug into the glacier. That's what I need—that pickax. I could climb down the cliff if I had it. I look down to the lagoon again and realize the figure on the beach is back. I watch as they stand, brushing their hands off on their trousers, then retrieve their hat from the sand and cover their long, red hair. It feels like someone put a lid over the sun. The sky darkens for the first time in days.

"Wait!" I try to shout it, but I can't get enough breath in my lungs for the sound to carry down to them.

"Adrian, stop!" Saad is above me, his shoes dug into the slope. He's jammed his ice hook deep into the hard-packed snow to hold him in place. A shower of ice and pebbles breaks off beneath his heel and spatters the ledge I'm on like rain. "What are you doing?"

"It's there!" I point wildly to the horizon. "The *Flying Dutchman* is right there."

Saad adjusts his grip on the ice hook. "Give me your hand. I'll pull you up."

He throws out a hand to me, but I lurch away from him, almost stepping off the edge of the shelf.

Saad gasps. "Stop, you're going to fall."

"I'm going to die!" I shout back at him. "Unless I get to that ship."

"No one's dying—come on, Adrian, give me your hand."

Before I can move, there's a low crack somewhere deep in the ice, like the warning before an avalanche. Saad and I both freeze.

There's a moment of cold silence. Then a chattering sound, as white veins appear beneath me in the clear ice.

"Adrian, grab my hand!" Saad shouts, and I look up at him. My spiked heel bites the ground. There's another low crack, then the ice beneath me collapses.

30

I have no sense of how far I fall—it seems both an instant, and long enough for my brain to realize this is too far to survive.

Then I hit the water.

It's shockingly cold, though not deep. I'm disoriented for a moment until I feel my feet against the bottom. I push upward, my muscles already starting to stagnate from the cold. My clothes are weighing me down—I fish the spyglass from the pocket of my coat, then manage to wiggle out of it and let it sink. The lift I feel toward the surface without the added weight is immediate, and I kick off my boots too. By the time I'm free, there's no breath left in me, and even if there were, I couldn't make my lungs work; they're too shriveled from the cold.

My head breaks the surface and I gasp, half blind from the water and the sudden light, coughing and not shivering so much as shuddering. I cannot stop shaking enough to swim or even float. I drop under the water twice more without meaning to, simply because my limbs are too clenched by the cold to do anything helpful. I'm wheezing but getting no air, my body convulsing from the cold. My vision is beginning to spot.

You have to stay calm, I tell myself. *You have to focus. You will not die here.*

I close my eyes, thinking only of my breath, and for once, try to thank my lungs for what a goddamn fantastic job they're doing, like that will encourage them to keep it up.

I open my eyes. A stream of light tumbles down from the hole I fell through. I can hear Saad shouting above me, though he's too far to help. I can't even make out what he's saying. I want to call back so he knows I'm alive, but I don't have enough breath. Ice is all around me, glassy and crystal blue like the center of a flame. I've fallen through the top of some sort of cave in the glacier, carved out by the warmer water from the sea flooding the bay, and now I'm trapped here, floating in cobalt water, surrounded by glassy sapphire ice.

It would be so goddamn beautiful if it weren't trying to kill me.

In the refracted light filtering in through the ice, I can make out a small bar of black sand ahead of me and I force my body to swim toward it, pushing myself through the freezing water until I'm close enough to drag myself up onto it. It's less relief than I had hoped it would be. I may be out of the water, but I'm still soaking wet, my muscles convulsing with cold. I lie on my back, clutching the spyglass in both hands against my stomach, trying to stop my shivering and think about anything other than how cold I am.

Think about the *Dutchman*. Think about the figure on the beach. Think about being free. The curse choking my bloodline like weeds dies here. I can breathe. I can live. I scrub a hand over my eyes, not sure if I'm crying or if it's the water. My shirt squelches against my skin and I tip my head back, staring up at the jagged cave ceiling and thinking of my mother.

I have to find a way out of here. There has to be a way.

The current has pushed me toward this sandy strip of detritus. Water would be flowing into this cave, not out of it—I can tell by the direction of the rippled patterns in the ice. Which means I have to swim against the current. Just the thought makes me want to give up. I want to stay here. I want to sleep. For the first time in weeks, I feel as though, were I to lie still here, I would drift off.

I force myself to sit up. There's no point waiting for my breath to even out or my limbs to warm. I have to go now.

I lower myself back into the freezing water and strike

out, pushing against the waves in a clumsy stroke. My muscles have stopped shaking, which I know in some instinctive part of my brain is worse than the trembling, and even as I paddle forward, I know I won't make it very far. I've already spent too long in this cold. My lungs are burning. Fog is starting to gather at the corners of my vision, and I think of Persephone running through a field of red ranunculus, smoke rising from beneath each footfall, hell always on her heels.

Breathe, Adrian.

I struggle forward, clutching the spyglass. The black sand slope reappears along the ice walls at random intervals, and I crawl along it when I can, though it quickly becomes more exhausting to pull myself out of the water again and again than to stay in it. I swim through the ice cave, wondering if I'm simply climbing farther into the glacier, but I can feel an inexplicable pull. I can still see the faint outline of the stave drawn on my hand, not entirely washed away. *Even when the way is not known.*

And then I see the light.

Relief floods me, loosening the grip of the cold enough that I actually swim forward for the first time rather than the pathetic combination of bobbing and paddling I have been barely managing. A wave strikes me, shoving me under, but when my head breaks the surface, there's sun on my face. There is sky above me—wide, brilliant sky—and light so bright and thick I feel as though I could drink it.

But then I realize—I am not on the lagoon beach as I expected, but have been spat out into the open ocean. The bar of sand separating the bay from the sea is far behind me, and when I turn in the water, searching the shores for a figure, there's no one there. The captain is gone. I manage to hook myself on one of the chunks of ice that has flowed off the glacier, this one smaller than the elephantine bergs in the lagoon, and scan the horizon, searching for sails. For anything.

But there's nothing. Just sea and sea and goddamn empty sea and that golden, sunless sky.

I'm too late.

All this way, and all this time, and all my mother's goddamn life, every second she lost a prisoner of this curse and this ship and her own mind. Fearful of what would happen if she could not see the ship she was sure was hunting her, fearful of what would happen on the day she did see it. Afraid of the choice she had made, and the choice she hadn't, and obsessed with wondering if she should have done it differently. I understand it all, in a way I never have before. My whole life and hers unfurl side by side like manuscripts. Scribbled runes translated into a language I understand when held up against hers.

It isn't the cold or the water or the sheer exhaustion

that leaves me sagging, barely able to hold myself above the surface. It's the weight of the whole goddamn world. It's how hard it is to get out of bed. To believe people who say they love me. To believe my ideas have value or that I am capable of speaking them. The certainty that I'm silly and odd and wrong, a body and soul incorrectly assembled with all the right pieces in the wrong places. The urge to scratch myself until I tear away my skin, to bleed myself dry and starve myself and look away, to say the cruelest things possible to myself before anyone else has a chance, to keep saying them until they're all I can hear. All the simple things that seem as easy as breathing for everyone else.

It's so hard to breathe.

And then I see it, butting up against the horizon. The sky turns pink and gold behind the sails.

The *Flying Dutchman* glides forward, eerily fast and the color of a storm cloud, as though no matter how close it draws, it will never be more than a silhouette. From the prow of the ship, the painted masthead stares down at me, a woman with flowers in her hair and one hand to her heart. A ripe pomegranate bursts between her fingers, the juice dribbling down her like blood.

A line drops from the side of the boat. The captain swings down, hand over hand until she stops just above the waves. She's wearing a tricornered hat and a heavy sea coat, her boots pulled up to her knees over her breeches. She braces herself with her feet planted flat against the side of the ship, the bristly rope knotted around her wrist. I could not have conjured her face before this moment, but when I see her again, it's like I've always known her. Her hair the color of a sunset, her eyes dark and her mouth set. She looks like a woman who has fought wars. Who has lost them.

This is the woman I saw at the prow, the night of the storm aboard the *Eleftheria*. The one who called me to her deck in a voice that rang through my heart.

I manage to drag my hand from the water and hold out the spyglass to her. She takes it, and when her fingers close, I feel like I'm being lifted. Like she could pull me aboard her ship as though I weighed nothing. My head rises high enough that I stop swallowing seawater, and I take a deep, clear breath.

Adrian.

I let go of the spyglass, and the iceberg bucks, throwing me off. My head slips under the waves, and I fight toward the light again. I can't feel my limbs and my heart is beating too slowly.

When my head breaks the surface, she's still there. She reaches into her coat and pulls out the other half of the spyglass. I watch her long fingers as she tightens the fastening between the two pieces, then unfolds the lenses. The cracks along her piece and mine align perfectly, and I can see the words spelled out there. *The Flying Dutchman.*

"Help me," I gasp, reaching out to her.

She stares at me, then raises the spyglass. My vision blurs. I'm not sure if she speaks aloud or if the words are only in my head.

Is that what you want?

I want to sleep, I think. I want to stop struggling and give in. I want to let the water take me and never have to be in my own company again. I want to stop dragging myself around, stop feeling the weight of every thought like they're stones pulling me farther and farther under, the seafloor and surface both out of sight. I want to stop feeling weak just because some days, I can hardly carry my heavy heart.

You can.

But more than that, I want to see the stars. I want to eat syllabub and rye bread and drink black tea with three lumps of sugar for my breakfast. I want to feel grass on my bare feet, and wear a red suit and high heels and dance until I'm breathless and hot. I want to kiss Louisa on our wedding day. I want to ride along the banks of the River Dee with her and share a bottle of wine and buy her libraries of books. I want us to make a life together, to fill our home with ideas and curiosities brought back from our travels and off-key singing, to challenge each other and speak our minds and put my lips to her palm when we disagree. I want to scatter handfuls of wildflower seeds over the manor gardens that have wilted since my mother died, watch them bloom, chaotic, and sparkle with fire-flies on heady summer nights. I want to stand up to my father. I want to stand up in the House of Lords and speak my mind. I want to take the raw ore I have been given and forge it into a blade. I want to be brave enough to think I can do any of that. To believe that it is a life I deserve.

I want to belong to myself. I want to stop feeling worthless and pointless and hopeless and less, less, less than everyone else around me. I want to live, not just survive, and fill myself up with all the people who have loved me into this moment and this man. I want to believe I am good and kind and clever and worthy with as much conviction as I have believed the opposites. I want to stop picking at life like it's a meal I don't want to eat, because *I want to.* I want to taste it all. I want life to be a feast, even if I have to eat it raw and bloody and burned some days. I will pick bones from my teeth. I will let the juice drip down my chin.

The captain holds out a hand to me. Her fingers are long and her skin white, wrinkled faintly like someone who has spent too long soaking in a hot bath.

What do you want, Adrian?

I want to sleep, I think as the sea rocks me, my name on its breath and my body suspended in its gentle embrace.

But what I say is, "I want to wake up."

"So wake up," she replies.

I come to vomiting mouthfuls of seawater and unsure how I am still alive. *If* I am still alive. My chest feels caved in, as though someone has been dropping stones upon it, one relentless boulder after another.

The vomiting turns to coughing, expelling more water from my lungs. I open my eyes, but the sun is so bright I close them again. Someone drags me onto my side and I spit up another impossible amount of water. My throat burns and I'm so cold, the coldest I've ever been. When I finally manage to open my eyes, my lashes are crusted with ice. Everything around me feels slow and distorted, like I'm looking at the world from beneath the rippled ice of the glacier cave.

I'm on a ship—the *Dutchman*. No. Not the *Dutchman*, because Sim is standing over me, sopping wet, water cascading off her shirt and her scarf plastered to her face like it's her skin. Sim, somehow, here, and surely I'm hallucinating. Or I'm dead. And Sim is also dead.

But Felicity is here too, throwing a blanket over Sim's shoulders and rubbing her arms and saying something I can't hear because there's still too much water in my ears.

I'm not on the *Dutchman*. I'm on the *Dey*, and Monty is on his knees beside me. He thumps me on the back and I cough again, this time managing to suck in a breath through the water in my lungs.

"Adrian? Adrian?" Monty has my face in his hands. "You're all right," he says, though I'm not sure if it's for his benefit or mine. "We've got you, you're safe, you're all right. It's going to be all right."

I'm shivering so hard I can feel my teeth clack together, and he throws his coat over my shoulders, tugging it around me hard enough that I feel a sharp bite of pain in my rib cage and I'm still here.

Monty pulls me up until I'm sitting, trying to pull my arms through the sleeves of his coat but then suddenly, he's pressing me to his chest, his embrace fierce and his body warm against mine.

"Did you see her?" I whisper.

He doesn't answer, just holds me tighter.

And in that moment, I feel wide awake.

31

Later, once we're back on land, the story is pieced together for me like a quilt assembled square by square.

Sim took the *Dey*, and Monty and Felicity, in pursuit of Saad and me to Iceland. They found the fisherman we had sold our yawl to, and followed our path by sea down the coast.

It was Monty who spotted me in the water, floating on that iceberg I do not remember pulling myself onto. It was an impossible thing, that they came near enough to me, and that he spotted me at all among the diamond chunks of glacier floating out to sea. Almost like a compass pointed him straight there.

When they pulled me from the water, my skin was mottled blue and white, and I was barely breathing. The water was so cold it should have stopped my heart. I was wrapped in every fur on the ship, and tucked in bundles

533

of hot coal wrapped in oiled paper between the layers. It seems miraculous I wasn't accidentally burned alive in the process of trying to get me warm again.

Everyone on board denies seeing another ship anywhere near the *Dey*. But my spyglass is gone.

Between retellings of this miraculous rescue, first from Sim, then Monty, then Monty and Felicity at the same time, I dip in and out of sleep. I wake first on the deck of the *Dey*, then in a hammock belowdecks, then a camp on the beach. Once I wake with Saad beside me, his eyes closed and his breathing heavy and even.

Once I'm able to stay awake for longer than a few minutes at a time, our camp moves off the ice and into a green glen with a hot spring that Felicity makes me soak in until I sweat. The places my skin was blue blister, then turn black, and days after, the feeling still hasn't entirely returned to my hands or feet. I grow drowsy and stiff again. Then and only then does Felicity propose drastic action.

I lose two fingers from my left hand and three toes, in what Felicity deems the easiest amputation she's ever done, as I have almost no feeling in the dead tissue nor any blood flowing there. My right hand—the one I drew the stave upon—is untouched by the cold, and the lampblack lines of vegvísir have sealed into my skin like a tattoo. I'm not sure it will ever wash away.

Felicity also stitches the few cuts on my face from the

fall, though the only one likely to scar travels down from my hairline and bisects my eyebrow, which Monty tells me is very handsome placement.

"If I had planned this a bit better," he says, tapping the scarred side of his face, "I would have had him shoot me through the eyebrow instead."

"Yes, that would have gone well," Felicity remarks dryly.

We are at the hot spring, Monty and I both submerged to our necks as the water steams against the cold air. Felicity has her skirt pulled up and her feet in the water. In the nearby glen, I can hear the sounds of the crew packing up their camp. The Crown and Cleaver is returning to warmer waters, Sim in command.

"When I lost my ear," Monty tells me, tipping his head backward so the warm water soaks the back of his head, "people gave me loads of stuff. I was sitting at a coffeehouse once and a man dropped a farthing into my coffee because he thought I was a beggar."

I think he's trying to make me feel better, though there's nothing to soothe. While I would have preferred to leave Iceland with all my fingers, I am, for the first time in a long while, simply happy I'm alive. Felicity's prescription of warm water and her duplicate of the scale powder have loosened my chest so I can almost breathe deeply enough to feel sated.

Felicity pulls one leg out of the water, then mops

sweat from her forehead with her sleeve. She picked up an English newspaper somewhere in Amsterdam, and she has it propped up against a stone, reading selections to us at random. "Weavers are rioting in London demanding fair pay," she says as she licks her finger and turns the page. "The Royal Society is hearing papers read on artificial magnets. Like that will ever have any practical use, but go on, that seems like an excellent use of your time and resources." She flicks the paper onto the grass, then lies backward beside it, staring up at the sky with one foot trailing in the water. The steam from the hot spring fogs her spectacles.

Monty grabs her foot beneath the water and tries to pull her in, but she yanks out of his grip and sits up, her skirt pulling tight as she crosses her legs beneath it. "If you try that again, I swear I'll drown you."

"You could still go with them," Monty says, nodding toward the camp, but Felicity shakes her head.

"Can you imagine? They'd never let me past Gibraltar."

"Adrian and I would protect you," Monty says. "We're very tough. We have a whole fifteen fingers and three ears between us."

"Eighteen," I correct him.

Monty frowns. "What did I say?"

"As fearsome as you may be," Felicity says, "you're both overdue in England. I'm sure you're missed dearly."

She flicks a handful of water from the surface at me. "Oh, stop looking at me like I'm a lost kitten."

"You're lonely," I say, but she shakes her head.

"I'm not, actually. I'm just a bit adrift right now. It happens to us all sometimes. Nothing to do when the tide comes in but wait for it to turn."

"Or swim," Monty mutters, fiddling with the curls at the back of his head. They're starting to get long again.

"Before I make any long-term plans, I need to go back to Amsterdam and set things right with the university about Professor van der Loos." She studies her nails. "See if he had a family I can contact. Do what I can."

"Then back to your research?" I ask.

She shrugs. "I don't know if any of it's worth pursuing. Maybe I couldn't get funding because I'm a woman, but maybe my ideas simply aren't good enough."

"That's not true. What about your scale powder?" I ask.

Felicity frowns. "What about it? It doesn't do anything."

"It did for me. It might not be the panacea for all ails that you hoped for, or an exact duplicate of the dragon scales, but maybe it could help me. And maybe other people as well. I've been thinking . . ." I swallow, take a hard, heavy breath, then start again. "Someday—not today, or not soon, I mean, obviously—but maybe once

I've had a few years in the House and I feel a bit, you know, better about it all, I think I might try to campaign for reform in the mental institutions in England."

"That would be brilliant," Monty says.

"And you could help," I say to Felicity, then add to Monty, "I mean, you also could."

He raises his hands. "No no, it's fine. I know my strengths lie elsewhere."

"What about the company?" Felicity asks.

"If Sim can convince the governors to reinstate her, she'll open the shipping routes to us again," Monty says. "Though it'll be a son of a bitch to pay off the debt we're in, and I'm not sure there's a creditor in London we don't already owe."

"I could give you a loan," I say. "Or give me stock. Let me be an investor."

"You can't run a shipping company," Felicity says. "You're about to become a Peer of the Realm."

"Then you keep running it," I say to Monty.

He splashes a handful of water over his neck. It's unclear whether the strawberry-red patches there are burns from the sun or he's simply spent too long in the water and is starting to cook. "I think that's behind me. Percy and I need a new start." He stares up at the sky, scratching his chin idlly. "Mostly me. It's always me."

"Don't say that," Felicity says.

"You could find a job in London," I tell him. "You've been running a shipping company for the last fifteen years, for God's sake, someone will hire you for . . . something."

"Especially if that shipping company doesn't shutter in financial ruin," Felicity adds.

"Maybe." Monty says. "Or maybe it's time for change." He stares out at the bright sky over the treetops for a moment. "George could run it," he says suddenly. "He's losing his mind digging up shipwrecks for Saad. Why don't we give him a majority share? And he's in good standing with the Crown and Cleaver, so Sim wouldn't have to fight as hard to get permission for him to sail. Adrian can loan him the money if he doesn't have it now, and George can pay him back once he gets things running again. And you know he will." He pushes my head affectionately. "That way your quiet life in a quiet town with your quiet books won't be disrupted by investing in a dying company linked to a notorious pirate fleet."

"I don't think the two are mutually exclusive," I say.

"And books can be loud, if you know how to listen to them," Felicity pipes up.

"Books," Monty says, "are only loud if you slam them aggressively to make a point."

Felicity hauls herself up from the edge of the hot spring. "Come on." She wipes her feet on the ground, leaving them covered in stray blades of grass that look like embroidery. "We should see the *Dey* off."

"We'll be along shortly," Monty says. "I have not yet sweated out every pore of my body." Felicity rolls her eyes, but sets off alone toward the trees. I start to climb out and follow her, but Monty puts a hand on my arm. "Give her a moment. She won't admit it, but she's going to want time alone with Sim." I sink down on the edge of the hot spring, my feet still submerged. My skin is sticky, and the cool grass is a welcome relief from the heat.

Monty cups a handful of water between his hands and splashes it across his face. "Ready to go home?" he asks me.

I stare up at the white sky of the endless summer. "I'm ready to see Louisa," I say. "And sleep in my own bed."

"Not quite the enthusiastic yes I expected. Did you think you'd come this far?"

"I hoped I'd be farther."

"What—the North Pole?"

"Not literally." I weave my hand through the grass. "What if nothing's different?" I say quietly.

Monty looks up at me, one hand raised to shield his face from the sun. "What do you mean?"

"What if I go back and it's just as hard and frightening and overwhelming as it was before, and I'm just as frozen and afraid?" I pull up a handful of grass and

540

toss it into the wind. "I didn't fix anything. I didn't fix myself."

"Who says you needed fixing?"

"I don't want it to be the same," I say. "But I don't know how it won't be."

"It won't be the same because you're not the same," he says. "That's the most important thing. You know yourself better now—accepting that person comes later. But you've come so goddamn far. Believe me. Coming from an impartial observer."

"You're hardly impartial."

"I know; I really wanted you to be a dick." He stretches his arms out across the lip of the hot spring and lets his legs float. "I'm sorry for what I said to you in Amsterdam. And that I hit you."

"You didn't hit me."

He laughs hollowly. "As good as."

"You're not like Father," I say quietly.

"Dunno. We all start somewhere, don't we? The first time he laid hands on me wasn't the worst. You have to work your way to cracked ribs and black eyes." He swipes his thumb under his nose. "What I should have said—what I was far too drunk to say—is that I didn't come to find you because I was worried you'd be like your father. Either that, or he'd have ruined your life the way he did mine and I would have to face knowing that I had left you with that. Better to just avoid it all. But I swear to God, Adrian, I have thought of you for years." He looks up at me. The sun on his face makes his skin look like glass. "There wasn't a day I didn't wonder who you were."

Disappointed? I want to say. But I stop myself. "I hope I've lived up to years of expectation."

"Oh, far exceeded," he replies. "You may be the best of all of us."

I look out across the mossy landscape. The gray clouds make the sky feel low to the earth. The distant emerald peaks are spotted with misty columns where other hot springs bubble against the cold.

Perhaps my mother was cursed by a ghost ship, and died trying to escape it. Perhaps she'll sail the sea forever. Perhaps I'll see her again someday.

Or perhaps her mind was treacherous, her thoughts unquiet; all the voices that whispered horrid things to her and kept her isolated and exhausted simply became too much to bear. Perhaps she was haunted. Perhaps we all are, our souls crumbling houses where unquiet spirits walk the halls. Some of us have manors with rooms and rooms for them to wander and pace, while others crowd a single hallway. Some fear the demons, and some learn to live with them.

Perhaps the ghosts are what we come for.

"Here." I take Monty by the wrist, then press the back of our hands together. The charcoal lines I traced absently over vegvísir at breakfast this morning transfer to his skin. "It's a stave," I say. "George taught it to me."

"What does it mean?"

"It's a compass," I say. "He said it shows you the way, even when there doesn't seem to be one."

Monty holds up his hand to the sunlight filtering in through the heavy clouds. "Helpful," he says after a moment of consideration. "And far less painful than the last time I let someone draw something on my skin." He gives me that sideways grin, the one that both makes him look younger, and emphasizes the pleasant lines starting to form around the corners of his eyes. I imagine it's that smile that made them. "You don't think—"

"Don't say it," I say.

"You don't think"—he pushes overtop of me, careening out of the water to clap a playful hand to my mouth before I can ruin his joke—"you'd be willing to put this on my ass, would you?"

Sussex

One Year Later

32

The cottage is small, too far from the sea to hear the waves but high enough on the hillside that, on clear days, the white cliffs smile from the horizon. In late August, the meadow that abuts the garden is blooming with wildflowers, their colors still riotous even though they're starting to smell fermented. An assortment of chairs has been collected from the house, along with several items that are not meant to be seating but are being used as such anyway, and set up before the copse that forms a natural archway leading into the forest beyond, the branches interwoven for so long that they have grown together. Even the trees do not know each other apart any longer.

The crowd is almost as sparse as the chairs, not because of poor attendance but rather a scarcity of invitations. Everyone who was asked found a way to make it. We always do.

I watch the guests spread their picnic blankets across the lawn from the back window of the parlor, the curtains twitched just far enough apart for me to peer through. Any wider and Monty shrieks at me to close them. He seems unclear whether the superstition is that it's bad luck for him to be seen by anyone, or just Percy, but he's accounting for both, just in case.

When I turn to him, he's sitting on one of the many trunks scattered throughout the house containing his and Percy's belongings. In spite of having spent the summer here, they never truly unpacked—Monty seems to feel obliged to remind us constantly they're only tenants; they can't afford to buy the cottage, as much as they'd like to. There were no dishes in the cupboard the first time Lou and I came to stay and, in frustration, Louisa started unpacking the china for them midway through making supper, and refused to stop until she had at least unwrapped all the cutlery so there would be a goddamn spoon by the stove when she reached for it. Monty was hungry enough that he took over for her, and by the time the meal was ready, the cupboards were less bare than they had been.

"Your brother struggles with the concept of permanence," Percy said quietly to me as we washed dishes together that night.

"Some people don't like to be tied down," I replied.

"Oh no, he definitely enjoys that." I almost dropped

the dish I was holding. It took Percy a moment to realize what he'd said, and he buckled at the waist with laughter. "That came out entirely wrong."

I had already gone red. "I should hope so."

"What are you laughing about?" Monty called from the parlor where he and Louisa were engaged in the fifth game of a ferocious backgammon tournament that would span the summer.

"Nothing," I said at the same time Percy called, "You."

"Well, stop it, you're distracting me."

"They're not distracting you, you're just losing," I heard Louisa say as Percy and I returned to the basin.

Percy smudged the corner of his eye with his wrist, still chuckling. "What I meant," he said, "is that Monty *wants* to put down roots. The trick is convincing him that other people want to plant their garden beside his."

Now, sitting on the same trunk upon which he was repeatedly trounced at backgammon by Louisa, Monty is strangling the top of his cane, his fingers working on the polished handle with such vigor he seems likely to tarnish it. "This is daft," he says for the fifteenth time today. "I don't know why we're doing this. Why did I agree to this? Why did you let me agree to do this?" As I have attempted to answer this question every previous time he's asked it only to be met with further protestations, I decide to take it as rhetorical.

I part the curtains again, doing a quick tally of the assembly. "I think everyone's here." I turn back to Monty. "Are you nervous?"

"No." He scoffs too enthusiastically and accidentally spits. "Why? Should I be? Are *you*?"

"I'm not the one getting married."

"Yes, well, you will be! Soon." He points his cane at me, but when I don't react further than folding my arms, he drops it and resumes rubbing the handle. "We're not doing the aisle thing, are we?"

"You mean walking down it?" I ask.

"Yes, because I didn't ask anyone to escort me. Or give me away." He scratches the back of his neck. "That's a thing I was supposed to do, isn't it?"

"No one is walking you down the aisle," I say. "There isn't even an aisle."

He looks alarmed. "Why not?"

"Because you've only got about three chairs."

"God." He presses his face into the crook of his elbow. "Why is Percy marrying me? I've only got three chairs. One ear. One leg."

"You have two legs."

It has taken almost the full time we have known each other—nearly a year and a half now—for me to train my nerves to recognize that when Monty is theatrically worked up about something, that's usually a sign

550

that I needn't be. "When he stops complaining," Felicity advised me, "that's when you should be concerned."

Monty brushes something invisible off the lapel of his coat, then brushes it again, more vigorously. "Do I look all right? I mean, I know it's not ideal. There's a hole under the arm I didn't have time to fix and also I don't think it was worth fixing because I really don't care and all this is daft theater and I don't know why I agreed to it."

"You look fine," I tell him. "You look like yourself."

"Yes, that's the problem." His shoulders slump, and he ruffles his hair. That familiar, nervous gesture. "Me being myself is exactly why we haven't done this until now."

Before I can reply, Felicity appears in the door to the parlor, carrying mismatched wine glasses with the stems wedged between her fingers. "Everyone's arrived, if you're ready," she says, looking from me to Monty. She gives him a quick up-and-down and frowns. "Is that what you're wearing?"

Monty throws up his hands. "I'm going to change."

"Into what?" I mutter. In spite of how vigorously he claims none of this matters, he pulled out every stitch of clothing he owns last night and tried them all on in a variety of combinations before deciding this was the only thing he owned that was appropriate for a wedding.

"Where's Percy?" Monty pushes himself to his feet, wincing when he puts too much weight on his bad leg. In spite of Felicity's best efforts, the break never healed right, and most days he walks with a cane. The spate of summer storms that has sat stubbornly over Sussex for the past week has exacerbated his pain—and my anxiety that it would rain today. There's not room in the house for everyone, no matter how small the crowd is, and any venue outside their own yard would have called the constabulatory. I resist the urge to check out the window once more to make sure storm clouds haven't suddenly blown in from nowhere.

"I think he's with George," Felicity replies. "Why, do you need him?"

"God, no," Monty says. "Isn't it bad luck to see the bride before the wedding? Wait—am I the bride or the groom?"

"You're both the grooms," Felicity says. "And that's a silly superstition. It doesn't mean anything."

As if on cue, Percy appears behind her in the doorway, his dark suit freshly pressed and noticeably free of holes. "Are you ready?"

Felicity shrieks and throws her arms up in front of him. The wine glasses she's holding tinkle against each other like wind chimes. "What are you doing? It's bad luck for you to see each other!"

"Aren't you looking forward to when we get to do

this for you?" Monty asks, poking me in the ribs as he passes. "Let him in, Felicity. Who believes in silly superstition, anyway?"

Felicity shuffles to the side and Percy enters. He's got something cupped between his hands, so delicately I think for a moment it must be a baby bird nestled there. "I have something for you," he says to Monty. "It may fall apart the moment you put it on. And you don't have to. But I made it anyway. Nervous hands." He smiles sheepishly, then opens his cupped palms to reveal a garland woven from meadow flowers.

Percy holds it out, but Monty doesn't take it. He stares at the plait of tiny blossoms like he doesn't know what they are.

"It's a flower crown," Percy prompts. "I made it for you. I've got one too."

Still, Monty says nothing. Just goes on staring at the small piece of their meadow Percy has presented, rampion and ragwort and pimpernel gathered just for him.

The silence is uncharacteristic. Percy's forehead crinkles. "You don't have to wear it," he says, just as Monty bursts into tears.

"He loves it," Felicity says. "Now let's get a move on."

There isn't an aisle, and they don't walk down it. Instead, they're suddenly there, silhouetted by the arched trees with the sun behind them. The assembled crowd falls silent. There are maybe twenty-five people in total, a few of whom I know, most I don't.

"Do you think we could get away with something this intimate?" Louisa says to me as I flop down beside her on the blanket she's spread for us.

"Only if you consider upward of five hundred guests intimate."

She wrinkles her nose. "We're still six months away, and I already want to scream at anyone who asks me my feelings about lilies."

I kiss her on the nose, and she rests her head on my shoulder. Her hair is wrapped around her head in two soft plaits, and in her plain cotton dress and crowned in the golden light of the evening, she looks like a painting of a summer deity. Persephone in her mother's garden, with the sun on her shoulders. I place my hand upon my knee, palm up, and she weaves our fingers together.

There seems to be some debate at the altar as to how this is meant to start. George, in a clean shirt and English breeches, though still stubbornly barefoot, is consulting the back of an envelope onto which he has presumably scribbled notes on officiating. "Dearly departed. Oh. No, wait that's the . . ." He glances at Felicity in the front, who gives him the tiniest shake of the head. He tries again. "Dearly beloved."

"That's the one," Louisa says under her breath, and I bite back a laugh.

"Dearly beloved," George starts again, after an approving nod from Felicity. "We are gathered here today in the sight of God—oh shit, that part doesn't really apply." He consults his envelope again, then asks the crowd. "Does anyone have a pencil?"

Again, he catches Felicity's eye, and she gives him a gesture that clearly says *move on*.

"Right. So. Not God. Sort of God—I don't think he'd have anything against this, to be honest. But we're here." He looks up again from his notes, and seems to see Monty and Percy for the first time. His shoulders relax, and his face breaks into a smile so big his eyes crinkle, like there are no two people on earth he loves more. "To join these two in matrimony. And we don't give a damn if it's holy or not."

"Please don't be crass at my wedding," Monty says. His dark hair is studded with splashes of color from the wildflower garland. A single stem of yarrow has come free and is dangling down over his ear.

"In lieu of scripture," George says, as though he wasn't interrupted, "Monty has requested I read an erotic poem."

The assembly laughs and Monty goes fantastically red. He glares at George, mouth puckered mostly to keep himself from smiling. Percy has to turn away to conceal his laughter.

"Will you write me erotic poetry for our wedding night?" Louisa asks, biting my earlobe.

"If I haven't any other deadlines to occupy me."

She kisses my neck. "Just because you're a famous political writer now—"

"Not famous."

"Doesn't mean you get to neglect my needs."

"Your need for bawdy limericks written in your honor?"

She turns forward again, nose in the air. "Precisely."

At the altar, the wedding party seems to have recovered their composure—Monty's face is slightly less red, and George clears his throat, shaking out his sleeves. "All right, next. Next, you will both read the vows you wrote."

"What?" Monty looks from George to Percy. "No, we don't . . . no. Wait. We said we weren't doing those! You"—he points an accusatory finger at Percy—"said I didn't have to write anything, I just had to show up! Did you write something? Oh my God!" He shrieks as Percy reaches into the pocket of his jacket and pulls out a folded piece of paper. "You bastard, you *wrote* something?"

"I didn't want you to stress over it," Percy says.

"Son of a bitch."

"I thought you'd prefer to come up with something on the spot."

"Goddammit, Percy, I'm going to murder you."

"See, that's perfect."

Percy starts to unfold the paper, but Monty grabs it, crumpling it between their hands. "No no, you don't get to read your thoughtful shite first! I'll look like even more of an idiot."

"All right, you go first, then."

Monty takes a deep breath, then another, at a loss for words for perhaps the first time in his life. "What do I have to say?" he asks, looking to George, who shrugs, then back to Percy.

"You don't have to say anything," Percy replies.

"Well, yes, I know that, but then I look like an insensitive twat who didn't write his own wedding vows, though in my defense," and here he addresses the crowd, "he told me we weren't doing these."

Percy unfolds Monty's fist from around the crumpled vows, then takes his hand. "Just tell me you love me," he says. "That's more than enough."

There's a shared supper after the ceremony, which I excuse myself from and instead spend some time alone in the upstairs guestroom of the cottage. I take a pinch of the snuff—Felicity's newest formulation, and though she has yet to make a judgment on its effectiveness, I swear it helps—and lie on the bed, breathing deeply and repeating to myself, *Everyone here is kind and talking with them cannot hurt you,* followed by *but it's still all right you're nervous; it doesn't have to make sense or be talked down by rational thinking.* It's a difficult balancing act. Harder to make myself believe it.

When I return to the yard, my brain feels less fuzzy. With supper finished, the wedding has become a proper party. Candles have been lit in the trees and ribbons strung between the branches. A pair of musicians Percy knows from his days of playing in quartets has started a lively jig, and, at the table, George is dividing champagne among mismatched glasses. I look around for Lou, wondering whether she already has a drink for me or I should take one, when someone touches my arm lightly. "Excuse me."

I turn. A man who looks about my brother's age is standing at my elbow, handsome in a bookish way, with spectacles framing startlingly blue eyes. He smiles, suddenly bashful, and ducks his head. "I'm sorry to bother you, but . . . are you Adrian Montague?"

I fight to corral my thoughts, like a sheepdog trying to manage a flock, keeping strays from wandering down fatalistic paths. "Yes. Do we know each other?"

"No—but I've read all your political pamphlets."

"Oh God, have you?" I feel myself blush. I'm still growing accustomed to the fact that they are now published, and distributed, under my name. *He's not going to start arguing with you,* I tell myself. *And he's not going to correct your spelling.*

The gentleman flushes too, though his seems to be more in delight than embarrassment. "Yes! I happened to be visiting the House of Lords last year when Edward Davies read your piece on workhouse reform, and it moved me to tears. I've read everything you've written since."

Don't apologize. Don't point out your flaws. Just say— "Thank you."

God, it takes so much effort. But I do it.

"It's such a relief to know there are men like you in the House of Lords," he says.

"I'm not in the House yet," I reply, though he waves that triviality away.

In the year since our return from abroad, my father's health has deteriorated, and at the beginning of the summer, he surrendered his seat in Parliament to me, that long-ago drafted writ of acceleration finally signed by all parties, including me. I haven't sat a session yet— the next one doesn't begin until November. My father is staying in Cheshire, and Lou and I have taken up residence in the London townhouse. If my father knows we are living in unwedded sin, he's chosen not to mention it, same as he has chosen to never mention Edward's now-infamous reading of my pamphlet in the House of Lords, during which one of the Tory leaders actually swooned. It will have to be made official eventually, and there have already been rumblings about the new young Whigs, with their unwed partners and short queues. Father wants it to be a grand affair, a wedding befitting his only son. And I suppose Lou and I will go along with it, though, as I watched Monty and Percy exchange rings, I thought maybe I would steal her away for our own private celebration before the big to-do.

"When Mr. Davies first read your name," the spectacled gentleman says, "I remember thinking, now that young man can't possibly be from the same Montague family I know. And yet here you stand!" He reaches out, and I take his hand and let him shake it vigorously. He has a sincere enthusiasm that I suspect is not reserved simply for politics, but could be just as easily ignited by a well-buttered crumpet, though that doesn't make it matter less. I have been compared to far worse than a buttered crumpet by the London political rags. Louisa and Edward have forbidden me from reading any critiques of my pamphlets, but I have anyway. It's difficult not to take every criticism as an arrow, no matter who lobs it. A column in the *Spectator* printed side by side with my latest work even called attention to my overuse of the phrase *simply put*, which sent me to bed, despondent, for days, vowing I'd never write anything again. But then I got up. And I did. And I am. And when I asked Edward if it ever got easier to have such things written about you, he laughed and replied, "No, but eventually you learn to trust your opinion of yourself more than other people's."

The gentleman gives my hand one last shake in both of his. "Should you ever find yourself in Vienna, please call upon me. I'm serving there as a diplomat."

"Did you come all the way here just for this wedding?" I ask.

"Of course," he says, surprised by my surprise. "I wouldn't miss it." On the other side of the meadow, the two string musicians each begin playing different songs, stop, and laugh at their error. The man's eyes dart over my shoulder, and he holds up a finger of *one moment* to someone before turning back to me. "I shan't take up any more of your time. Thank you for letting me fawn. Good luck in Parliament this fall. I will be cheering for you from the Continent."

"Thank you. Oh." He stops when I call him back. "I didn't catch your name."

"Westfall. Sinjon Westfall. Monty and I went to Eton together many years ago." He smiles fondly to where Monty and Percy are standing together in the middle of the dance floor that's also a meadow, up to their knees in wildflowers and their eyes only for each other. "It's good to see your brother married at last," Westfall says.

"I suspect he's received fewer congratulations and more sentiments of *about bloody time*." He reaches across the table and retrieves two glasses of champagne. "For my friend," he says, indicating the second, then corrects himself. "Husband." He smiles. "Force of habit. A pleasure to meet you, Adrian."

I stand alone at the table for a while, watching the soft shadows cast by the party waft between the sunset and the candlelight, edged in golden sprays of pollen kicked up from the wildflowers. The height difference between Monty and Percy is even more comical when they dance together. Monty still has the remains of the flower crown in his hair, though most of the stems have fallen away, leaving only petals. That unruly spot in the back I cut for him on the porch of Felicity's house in the Azores has gotten too long again.

When the song ends, Monty spots me and comes over. He still limps when he walks—I do sometimes as well. It took a few months to grow accustomed to balancing without my missing toes, but my own stride has evened out. It's only noticeable when someone comments on my fingers and Louisa says with great pride, "He's missing toes as well!"

Monty retrieves his cane from where it's leaning against the end of the table. He slings his arm around my neck, seems to realize how much it requires him to stretch upward, and immediately reconsiders. "Glad you came down. Where's Felicity?"

"With Lou, I think."

"Good Lord, Percy's got George and Felicity's got Louisa. We are both at risk of losing our beloveds to someone younger and fitter than we are." He isn't entirely wrong—I think Felicity sees more of Louisa than I do lately, and Lou has started taking her recommendations for books over mine, which, I told her, was grounds for ending our engagement. Lou has even started wearing the same style of heavy locket as Felicity does, packed with blue powder, should I ever need it unexpectedly.

"Louisa's older than I am," I tell him. "And Percy's your husband now."

"Husband." He scratches his chin. "I think I prefer consort."

"I'm sure he'll love that."

"Come on." He plucks the champagne glass out of my hand and sets it on the table. "Let's go steal Felicity away."

Louisa and Felicity are sitting on the picnic blanket with their heads together. A plate of food Lou put aside for me rests between them, notable pinches missing from the bread. I suspect they will be talking, as they almost always are, about books or politics or the opera, but as we draw close, I hear Felicity say, "I think you have more to work with than I do. God, your breasts really do look fabulous."

Monty pulls up short, his neck coloring. "Are we interrupting something?"

"Just talking about breasts." Louisa puffs out her chest proudly and gives a little shimmy. Felicity laughs. "Monty, this champagne is terrible."

"Yes, well." He picks a wilted head of clover from his hair and wipes it on my shoulder. "I'm not wasting a good vintage on you lot."

"Might I remind you," Felicity says, "that we lot are all here in celebration of your love."

"I know," Monty says. "A love that makes you all believe in love—you're welcome, by the by."

"Have you come to sit with me finally?" Lou asks, holding out a hand to me. "I thought I'd never get you back from Mr. Westfall. He was asking about you before you came down—did he have you inscribe his arm? He was furious he didn't have a pamphlet for you to sign."

"I'm afraid I'm next on Adrian's dance card," Monty says, clapping a hand to my chest before I can reply. "And Felicity as well. Come on, this is my favorite song."

"What is it?" she asks as he offers his hand and pulls her to her feet.

"Not a clue. Apologies, Miss Davies," he says, "but the Montagues must dance."

"Are you drunk?" Felicity asks as Monty leads us out

into the meadow, each of us holding on to some part of the other so it's more of a collective stagger.

"Absolutely not," Monty replies. "I have been sober for three whole months."

"Well done," Felicity says.

Monty dips his chin. "Wish it was longer but I had a bit of a rough go when we first got here. All this country stillness can really jangle a man's nerves—"

"I mean it," Felicity interrupts. "Really, Monty. Well done."

Monty nods, then takes a wobbly breath. "I have something to tell you both."

"You're having a baby," I say with as much serious-ness as I can muster.

"That explains why he finally agreed to be married," Felicity says. "What's the word for that again?"

"Coercion?"

Monty flaps a hand at us. "Stop it, both of you. I actually have something to say." We both give him our full attention, and he immediately blushes and looks at the ground. "So. There is a publisher in London that has agreed to pay me a tiny bit of money in advance to write a serialized adventure story for their magazine."

"Monty!" I cry at the same time Felicity screams in delight. Several people look our way, particularly when I nearly lift him off the ground with my embrace.

"All right, stop it. I've not discovered a cure for cholera."

"You didn't tell me you had submitted it!" I say.

"Yes, well, I didn't want to have to say anything if they rejected it. And now I've got to write the bloody thing so this could still all go to hell rather quickly."

"How much are they paying you?" Felicity asks.

Monty's mouth turns up, both dimples appearing suddenly. "Enough that we're buying the house."

"For God's sake, how long have you kept this from us?" Felicity looks as though she can't decide whether she's furious or delighted.

"Only about a week," he says. "I'd like it to be known, I agreed to this wedding nonsense before, so rest assured Percy isn't marrying me for my money." He catches my eye. "Thank you for the help. And I'll have to tell Louisa the same."

"You're going to have to learn how to spell," I say with a laugh.

"Sod spelling; I'm worried about finishing the god-damn thing."

"It's a serial; you never have to finish." I butt my head against his. A gently insistent ram. "Well done, Monty."

"Seconded," Felicity adds, and I feel her squeeze my shoulder. "Well done."

Monty smiles for a moment, then plants his face in my shoulder. "Stop it, I'm going to cry again. Let's dance."

It's not much of a dance, as there are three of us, and none are very good at it. Instead, we just put our arms around each other and sway to the music.

"I want to tell you both," Monty says, his face still against my shoulder. On my other side, Felicity raises our linked hands and twirls under them. "Only because I'm feeling sentimental and silly and I've cried a lot today. And this may be the one and only time you hear these words from my lips, so listen carefully."

"Oh God, steel yourself," Felicity mutters.

"I love you both very much. And I'm glad you're here with me." He looks straight at me when he says it. One of the petals from his flower crown tumbles free and lands on my jacket. "I'm glad we're all here."

"That's very nice," Felicity says, patting him on the side of the head like he's a dog. "May I go now?"

"You're such a shrew." Monty hooks an arm around her neck, pulling her against him and planting a kiss on her cheek. She shrieks in surprise, nearly toppling them both in her attempt to get away. He grabs me for balance, and it feels like being children with them in a way I never was. Barefoot in an English field, reckless and young, tumbling into each other with the wild abandon of those who have never known themselves apart and have no reason to doubt that the others will always be there, holding on to them and holding them up when they can't stand any longer.

I close my eyes. Turn my face to the light-soaked sky.

And take a breath.

Dear Mum,

I know you'll never read this, but I'd like to write it anyway. Perhaps I'll leave it in a tree or tear it into pieces and let the wind scatter it or I'll burn it beneath the full moon on the beach and the smoke will turn red as blood. Was I always this whimsical? I feel as though I hardly remember myself as I was when you were here. How strange it is that there are versions of myself you'll never know—though there's still so much I don't know about you. I suppose it's only fair.

I'm not sure what sort of omnipotence death grants you, so forgive me if I repeat what you already know, but I wanted to catch you up on the family. Monty and Percy have officially taken ownership of the cottage in Sussex. Percy is teaching violin lessons to children in their village, and Monty has re-signed for a second adventure serial. It's with a dreadful publication—too rubbish even to wrap fish in—but there seems to be some money in it. Lou and I visit often. Marital bliss suits them both.

Felicity has gone back to Amsterdam to petition for reinstatement at the university. Before she left, she and I made plans that, once Edward's reform bill passes and I am established in the

House, she will return to London and we will begin working together on a bill for the reformation of the ~~mentally unfit hysterical melancholic.~~

God, I hate every word there is for it. Can we not simply be people, each of us with cogs in our brains that turn slightly differently, and some that need oiling and alignment and upkeep more than others?

Louisa and I will be married in a month— maybe sooner if she makes good on her oath to stuff me in a trunk and ship me to Gretna Green. We're neither of us very good at the business of planning a wedding, but I'd like to do a proper job of it. We're lucky we can, and I want the whole world to know I love her. Parliament is draining, which feels a strange thing to say, as mostly I do nothing but sit and listen. You wouldn't think it would so thoroughly exhaust me. We hoped Edward's workhouse reform bill would be passed by now, but it's been held up and is in revision. I don't know if it will get through. Edward says it doesn't matter if it does—what matters is that it gets people to think. It makes them consider their own position in life, and how they might use it to help others. That's all it comes down to—helping each other.

I would not say I'm well, but I would say

I'm better, which feels more important. I have a piece being printed in the Times *next month that Louisa is editing for me across the table at this very moment, and its writing has consumed me in a way that has left no room for self-doubt or the feeling I'm a fraud, though now that it's finished, I'm sure I'll have plenty of time to ruminate on its flaws. But I try not to let the fear of those flaws keep me from writing at all. Lou and I spend many of our evenings with Edward and Imogene. We talk about politics, and Edward has introduced me to some of his friends who have ideas about the future of our country that thrill me. I love the work I'm doing. I'm excited about the future. That hasn't happened in a while. Certainly not since you died. These days, the prospect of continuing to live is not so daunting.*

I write all this knowing today is a good day. I got out of bed without difficulty. I washed and dressed and did not think how stupid I look in my clothes, or apologize to Lou for something I said that upset her, though I don't know what that thing is. I took the medicine Felicity left me without feeling the shame of needing it at all, or the despair that it will never be enough and I'll never be cured of this mind I was born with. I didn't think of it as something I need to be cured of.

I know it will not always be like this. There will be days it is loud, and others it is heavy. For every summer solstice, there is darkness on the other side of the world. There will be days that staying alive will be an all-consuming challenge, and accepting love an act of tremendous courage. Asking for help even more so. Days of loneliness and doubt will compound and maybe there will be whole months when I cannot see the sky, and all the perspective I have now is lost in the crush. There will be peaks and dales. Rivers and roads. But I will do my best to keep walking out of the darkness. I will let it all happen to me, beauty and terror and love and hate and ugliness and anger and fear. I know that no feeling is final, and that fear only wins when I stop fighting. I will push through it all, and see you on the other side. I'll see myself on the other side.

Until then, I will do my best to keep breathing.

Yours,
Adrian Montague

Author's Note

Here we are! The final author's note of the series! Surreal, unexpected, and bittersweet all at once. More on the Montague books later—for now, join me as, one final time, we break down the real history behind the things I made up.

Ghost Ships

The myth of the *Flying Dutchman* is one of thousands of stories of ghost ships from around the world. This particular version likely originated in the seventeenth century, during the Dutch Golden Age, though the oldest written records date to the late eighteenth century. Since then, the *Flying Dutchman* has been a touchstone of Western mythos. It has inspired poetry, opera, theater, and film, been retold by auteurs from Samuel Taylor Coleridge to Rod Serling, and challenged some of our greatest modern heroes, including Scrooge McDuck, Scooby-Doo, Xena: Warrior Princess, Jack Sparrow, and SpongeBob SquarePants, none of which are references I expected would make it into this series for any reason.

While sightings of the *Dutchman* can most likely be attributed to an optical illusion called a *fata morgana*, sightings of a ghost ship were reported into the twentieth century. The myth varies with the telling, though the common thread is that the *Flying Dutchman* is a ship cursed to sail the seas forever, and that a sighting of it portends doom. In some stories, it is a vessel for ferrying those who die at sea to the afterlife, while in others it's a siren that lures other ships to wreck. I poached several elements of several iterations for the version of it that appears in this book.

Mental Illness

In depicting Adrian's mental illness, I focused my research on generalized anxiety disorder with some obsessive-compulsive tendencies. I drew upon my own experiences with these illnesses and their symptoms (symptoms that, ironically, resulted in the release of this book being delayed several times). Everyone's experience with mental illness is different, even within the same diagnostic category. This book is not meant to be a universal portrayal of generalized anxiety disorder or OCD, merely one experience with it.

While we have records of patients being treated for anxiety and depression that date back to ancient Egypt, anxiety was not considered an official medical condition until 1980, and prior to the 1950s, only two books had been written on the subject, one by Freud and one by Kierkegaard. A variety of names were used to describe the disease, including hysteria, nerves, hypochondria, neurasthenia, mania, vapors, deliria, and melancholia (which can refer to symptoms of both anxiety and depression), though anxiety was often considered a symptom of another disease rather than something to be treated on its own. Treatment options were limited, and varied from self-medication with drugs and alcohol to involuntary commitment to asylums. Statistics about anxiety in both the past and the present are difficult to locate due to the elusive nature of its diagnosis.

My aim with this book was to depict mental illness in a historical context, and acknowledge that conditions like anxiety, depression, OCD, PTSD, and so many more are not inventions of the twenty-first century, but rather have always been part of the human experience.

If you or someone you know is struggling with mental illness or suicidal thoughts, you are not alone. There is help, and there is always, always hope.

National Suicide Prevention Lifeline:
1-800-273-8255
Chat online at www.suicidepreventionlifeline.org

Crisis Text Line:
Text HOME to 741741 (24/7)

A Note on Locations

The Republic of Salé was a real pirate city on the opposite side of the river from Rabat, Morocco. Though the official republic only lasted from 1624 to 1688, pirate activity continued, and it was a haven for corsairs for several centuries. Ten percent of what the pirates looted was paid to the sultan. Though only briefly mentioned in this book, one of the main sources of income for these pirates was the slave trade. Enslavement of captured sailors from all countries was common. Piracy—it wasn't pretty!

Contrary to what I thought before starting the research for this book, Iceland is not a discovery of twenty-first-century tourism! Like many other islands in the North Atlantic, Iceland was a dependency of Denmark–Norway in the eighteenth century, when it had a population of just over fifty thousand people. That number fluctuated over the century due to an influx of European sailors, explorers, fishers, and traders, as well as the disease they brought with them, and a volcanic eruption and the famine that followed it.

Magic has always been a very real and present part of Icelandic culture, and still is today. Much like Europe and America, Iceland had its own period of witch burning, in which almost two hundred people were charged with practicing sorcery and twenty were put to death. The galdrastafirs, or staves, in this book, are all real. Staves are used for a variety of purposes, from protection to preventing fox bite to navigation to keeping your sheep docile. They first appeared in the late Middle Ages, but the most well-known date from the eighteenth century, when they were recorded in magical textbooks called grimoires.

I learned about staves while visiting Iceland several years before *The Gentleman's Guide to Vice and Virtue* was released. I was months from seeing a therapist for the first time and being given a diagnosis and medication to help treat my own mental illness. At the time, all I knew was that I had spent months in an unending cloud of sadness and worry that had left me feeling like barely a person. I struggled to write. I struggled to look people in the eyes. I struggled to breathe. I struggled and struggled and struggled without ever thinking myself sick enough to need help, or considering that a future without anxiety was possible.

In a gift shop in Reykjavík, I purchased a vegvísir, the stave Adrian is given in the book, which is meant to give the bearer direction. I still carry it with me almost every day. Shortly after the trip, I started writing *The Gentleman's Guide to Vice and Virtue*, the book that brought me back to life. So ending here, with three books and an Icelandic stave I hoped would give me direction, feels satisfyingly symmetrical in a way real life almost never is.

A Final Word on the Montagues

The Montague Siblings was never meant to be a series.

It was hardly meant to be a book. For me, all three volumes represent finding joy and pride in pieces of my own identity that did not always inspire such feelings. I have always found strength and confidence in my sense of self by finding stories of people like me in history, and in those stories, the affirmation that we have always existed. More than existed, and more than survived in spite of their identity. They have flourished, and found ways to make happy, fulfilling lives without compromising who they were, in spite of society at large not always accepting or understanding. These books are tributes to the campy adventure stories I have always loved and the people I did not see populating them. I am so grateful they have found a home with so many readers, and so grateful you loved them enough to follow me all the way here to literally the last pages of the last book.

Acknowledgments

There are too many people to thank for their involvement in the Montague Siblings series, but I will attempt to shout out a few of the leading players, with my trademark anxiety that I am forgetting someone:

The Home Team

Claudia Gabel; Katherine Tegen; Suzanne Murphy; Rebecca Aronson; Louisa Currigan; Stephanie Guerdan; Nellie Kurtzman; Sabrina Abballe; Bess Braswell; Michael D'Angelo; Audrey Diestelkamp; Ebony LaDelle; Alanna Whitman; Jennifer Corcoran; Aubrey Churchward; Rosanne Romanello; Kathleen Carter; Barbara Fitzsimmons; David Curtis; Amy Ryan; Andrea Pappenheimer; Heather Doss; Jessie Elliot; Kathleen Faber; Deborah Murphy; Fran Olson; Kerry Moynagh; Jennifer Wygand; Susan Yeager; Josh Weiss; Bethany Reis; Shona McCarthy; Mark Rifkin; Janet Fletcher; Maya Myers; Jill Amack; the entirety of team Epic Reads; Rebecca Podos; Tayrn Fagerness; Lucy Cleveland; Laurie Liss; Chris Licata; Jiah Shin; Beth Ives, Caitlin Garing, and the HarperAudio crew; Christian Coulson; Moira Quirk; Greg Berlanti; Michael McGrath; Matthew Barry; Gaby Salpeter; the American Bookseller's Association, NEIBA, and independent bookstores across the country, in particular Porter Square Books, Trident Booksellers and Cafe, and the King's English Bookshop; ALA and the Stonewall Book Award Committee of 2017; the Audie Awards; and Korrina Ede and her team at OwlCrate.

The Overseas Crew
Leonel Teti; Georgina Dristos; Luke Ortega and the Bolivian Embassy; Amelia Lush and the Sydney Writers' Festival; Georgia Williams and HarperCollins Australia; and the many teams of people who worked on the many foreign editions of these books whose names I don't know and whose language I don't speak but for whom my gratitude is endless.

The Emotional Support Humans
Highlights Foundation Retreat and Matt de la Peña; the SPA Day organizers (Christa Desir, Adam Gidwitz, Alex London, Terra Elan McVoy, Cristin Terrill); Emily Martin; Mickey George; Zach Grigg; Briana Clarke; Becky Albertalli; Mindy McGinnis; Lindsay Eager; Kendall Kulper; Jason June; Brittany Cavallaro; Destiny Soria; Kiersten White; Claire Legrand; Alison Cherry; and Melissa Lee.

My unbelievably delightful parents, Billy and Toot, my sister, MT, and Q, who arrived the same day the *Gent's Guide* paperbacks did.

And, because I don't want to leave you with any questions—no, I don't know who the cover models are, and no, you can't have their phone numbers.

Go on a hilarious and heartwarming romp through 18th-century Europe!

More from Mackenzi Lee!